Alec left without another word. Though it was freezing cold, Sam walked outside onto the landing, watching him go again, feeling much different than she had the first time. His pace quick, he jogged down the steps. He looked up only once, after he was behind the wheel. With a quick flash of that sexy smile, he started the car and took off.

Once he was gone, she quickly went back inside. She had been standing out there under the bright security lights, fully visible from the dark street below. It had been a disconcerting feeling, almost like being exposed, as if anyone could have been watching her from the shadows.

She laughed at her own vivid imagination and shrugged off the odd thought. After all, it was late; every window around here was darkened, not a soul out in this bitter weather. And she wasn't exactly the most exciting personality in Baltimore.

Who would possibly want to watch her?

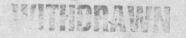

ALSO BY LESLIE PARRISH

Fade to Black

Pitch Black

A BLACK CATs NOVEL

Leslie Parrish

A SIGNET ECLIPSE BOOK

SIGNET ECLIPSE
Published by New American Library, a division of
Penguin Group (USA) Inc., 375 Hudson Street,
New York, New York 10014, USA
Penguin Group (Canada), 90 Eglinton Avenue East, Suite 700, Toronto,
Ontario M4P 2Y3, Canada (a division of Pearson Penguin Canada Inc.)
Penguin Books Ltd., 80 Strand, London WC2R 0RL, England
Penguin Ireland, 25 St. Stephen's Green, Dublin 2,
Ireland (a division of Penguin Books Ltd.)
Penguin Group (Australia), 250 Camberwell Road, Camberwell, Victoria 3124,
Australia (a division of Pearson Australia Group Pty. Ltd.)
Penguin Books India Pvt. Ltd., 11 Community Centre, Panchsheel Park,
New Delhi - 110 017, India
Penguin Group (NZ), 67 Apollo Drive, Rosedale, North Shore 0632,
New Zealand (a division of Pearson New Zealand Ltd.)
Penguin Books (South Africa) (Pty.) Ltd., 24 Sturdee Avenue,
Rosebank, Johannesburg 2196, South Africa

Penguin Books Ltd., Registered Offices:
80 Strand, London WC2R 0RL, England

First published by Signet Eclipse, an imprint of New American Library,
a division of Penguin Group (USA) Inc.

First Printing, August 2009
10 9 8 7 6 5 4 3 2 1

To Lauren.
You wanted me to make you a villain. . . .
Will a dedication do instead?
I love you, sweetheart.

Acknowledgments

Bruce—thanks so much for being my beta reader, my sounding board, and a fantastic husband. None of this would be possible without you.

To Janelle Denison, Julie E. Leto, and Carly Phillips—the constant messages of support, griping, friendship, kvetching, laughter, and companionship are some of the best parts of my day. Thank you for stepping outside your own reading boundaries to help me with this project.

Sincere thanks also to Leo A. Notenboom (www.ask-leo.com) for the technical advice and consultation. All the computer expertise is his . . . any errors are entirely my own.

Prologue

Hello. I am the former finance minister for a once great nation. I am writing to you about an issue of utmost urgency.

Recent upheavals in my country make it impossible for me to retrieve monies hidden by my government. I write to you begging for assistance. I am needing a partner to help me retrieve the monies. I can trace the funds but must work through a third party for my own safety and the safety of my family.

In exchange for your help you will be paid half of what is recovered, or ten million dollars. Please respond to me to arrange the transfer of money.

Your Friend,
Dr. Malik Waffi

"I still can't believe you fell for this bullshit."

Ignoring his passenger, Jason Todd clenched the steering wheel of his father's Buick, which he fought to keep on the dark, slippery road. His heart pounded furiously as he strained to see through the snow-streaked windshield. His short, jerky breaths punctuated his excitement.

"We coulda been at a party," Ryan added from the other side of the car, where he'd been hunched since they'd left home an hour ago. "Instead we're in a blizzard, about to get scammed."

"Nobody forced you to come along."

"Shut up, loser. You know I wouldn't have let you go alone."

No, he wouldn't have. They'd been best friends since first grade, and Jason didn't know whether he'd have had the stones to go through with this if Ryan didn't have his back.

"This snow sucks. I can't see shit." Ryan used a grimy Taco Bell napkin to try to clear away some steam from the windshield.

The light snow that had begun falling at sunset had spat down relentlessly for the past hour. The tires fought for every bit of traction they could get. The highway from Wilmington had been fine, but these back roads were untouched. Winter might have started late, with temperatures near fifty at Christmas a couple of weeks ago, but now that it had arrived, it was kicking ass and taking names.

"When's the last time your dad changed the wiper blades?"

"It's not like I could ask him, since he's in Florida." And by the time Jason's parents got back from vacation, he planned to be driving his own car. A nice one, not this crapmobile.

"You know this is all bogus, right? Internet Scam 101."

Man, the guy just wouldn't give up. "You saw the check."

Ryan nodded. He'd been as shocked as Jason when a check for a cool grand had arrived in Jason's mail, a down payment, according to this Waffi guy. "Yeah, yeah, the money," Ryan conceded. "But I still say the check could bounce."

"It's certified. They don't bounce."

"They do if they're fake," Ryan muttered, holding on to his skepticism harder than he'd held on to his belief in Santa Claus.

"It's not fake. Come on, dude, admit you were wrong. Nobody would part with a thousand bucks as part of an e-mail scam. Not even your cyber fantasy woman could deny that."

Ryan's lopsided grin made him look even younger than his sixteen years. "Bite me. You know she's a babe. You're just jealous because she never sent you a personalized e-mail."

Jason was happy to have been e-mailed by someone who wanted to make him a millionaire. But he had to admit, judging by the picture on her Web site, Sam the Spaminator was way hot.

"We shoulda waited for her to write me back," Ryan added. "I know she'll say this is all bogus. She's written about this exact scam."

"The mo-ney," Jason replied in a singsong voice.

The check in his pocket was all the proof Jason needed that this was legit. Waffi had sent it, no strings attached, saying he wanted to prove he was on the up-and-up. Jason could have cashed it and walked away. That alone proved this wasn't a scam. But by bringing it to meet the doctor in person tonight, he'd get to exchange it for another one containing a whole lot more zeroes. By tomorrow, he'd be so rich he could do anything he wanted.

Picturing it, he almost missed the gravel road Dr. Waffi had told him to look for. Nearly obscured by tangled brush, it would have been hard to spot even in good weather. He swerved onto it, maintaining control as the car fishtailed.

He hadn't gone fifty feet when Ryan yelled, "Watch out!"

Suddenly spying the huge truck parked across the entire lane, Jason jerked the wheel hard. They went into a skid, the car spinning wildly as it careened toward the trees. Gravel and snow spewed into the air, the clack of sharp limbs hitting the roof sounding like knives on bone. Ryan flew out of his seat, smashing against Jason, who was punched against the driver's-side window so hard he heard his cheekbone crunch.

As the Buick finally came to a halt a few yards above a slope dropping into a frozen pond, Jason felt sticky moisture dripping down his forehead. His face throbbed; salty fluid saturated his lips. His eyelids were heavy, his vision blurring. But right before he blacked out, he saw a dark shape approaching the car. Someone was out there. "S'okay, man," he mumbled. "Help's here."

They were the last words he managed before darkness washed over him.

And they were the first he thought of when he came to. *Help's here.*

He'd been unconscious for a few minutes. Or a few hours. As he moved from oblivion to awareness, Jason couldn't be sure. He knew only one thing: He was cold. Whatever warmth the car's heater had provided was gone. Sharp pricks of frigid air thrust like needles into his face and body. Trying to force the murky clouds from his brain, he struggled to remember what had happened and where he was.

It didn't take long. They'd crashed. Violently.

But help is here. Right?

"Don't try to move, Jason."

The voice was strong and even, yet not comforting. It held a note of iron firmness that would stand for no disobedience.

It also wasn't the only sound. From nearby, he heard

a loud creak, like a giant rocking chair set in motion. "Who . . ."

"Quiet."

He wondered whether he was in a hospital, being tended to by a stern doctor. If so, maybe his parents were there. They'd be mad at him for crashing, but so relieved he was all right, they'd let it go. And Jason would tell them he was sorry. So sorry.

Though the fantasy enticed him, he didn't open his eyes. Partly because he was in so much pain. And partly because he already knew his parents were not there. That was a kid's dream. The nearly adult Jason knew he wasn't in a hospital. Not only was it dark; it was still snowing. The tiny drops of moisture landing on his skin and turning instantly to ice confirmed it. Plus, his lips were bloody. And every inch of him hurt.

"Jason, you were told to come alone."

"Who's there?" he whispered.

Bright light suddenly flashed, cutting through the pitch-black night. It drove like a spike through the fine skin of his eyelids and into his pupils. Jason turned away, instinctively trying to escape. His head, however, was the only part of his body he could move. Forcing himself to go slowly, he shifted his eyes down, then began to lift his lids, letting the light in bit by bit.

Definitely outside. His chest was bare. The skin he could see through the crystallized snow had turned gray with cold, possibly even frostbitten. His legs, too, shone gray in the snow-whitened moonlight. And oddly, he was sitting upright in a chair.

"Jason?" More stern now.

He didn't look up, stalling as he tried to get his brain working. Icy snow, tinged pink with blood, covered his bare thighs. Seeing a solid strip of silver running across them, and across his middle, he realized why he couldn't move. *Duct tape. What the fuck?*

"What's happening? Where's Ryan?"

"He's right behind you."

He jerked his head back. It banged against something with a thunk, garnering a moan in response. Ryan was alive, for now. Attached to him somehow, their backs touching.

His eyes shifted frantically and he squinted against the brutal light. *Headlights*. "What's going on?" Another crack sounded nearby. His panic rose. Something in his brain told him he knew the sound and understood its meaning.

"You were told to come alone." The tone remained harsh, yet patient, as if he were some kid whose lesson had to be repeated.

He suddenly had a suspicion. "Dr. Waffi?"

"Ahh, it learns. Now, what have I been saying?"

"I was told to come alone," he admitted.

"You disobeyed. I would think you were being willful, but knowing what I do about you, I'll assume it was pure stupidity."

Tears oozed out of Jason's eyes, sliding an inch or so down each cheek before freezing hard. "Please let me go."

"Go where? To do what?"

"To go home to my parents." Oh, did he wish they hadn't gone away and he hadn't answered that e-mail.

"Your parents should never have given you life."

Jason started crying like a baby. How could this be happening? He was only seventeen. He'd barely lived. He'd never even banged a girl, despite what he said in the locker room.

"Who is the other one? Is he as stupid as you?"

"Ryan." Hearing a groan, Jason regretted all the shit he'd ever gotten his best friend into. "He knew this was a scam."

"So, he's no fool. But he has poor taste in friends." The man's coldness was underscored by one of those maddening cracking noises. It was longer. Louder. "He'll pay for that now."

"Are you crazy?" Jason screamed. "Let us go!"

Another crack. Jason could now feel something crackling beneath his frozen feet. The hard ground felt uneven, rock hard, yet still unstable. *So very cold.*

Terrified, Jason suddenly realized what the sounds were. And what was about to happen. He jerked, fighting the tape, knowing he should remain still. "No, don't do this!"

He finally stared directly at the light—high beams from his dad's banged-up Buick. Facing him, it sat at the top of a small slope a few yards away. As he watched, a dark, shadowy figure, faintly visible in the snowy night, walked up the slope toward it.

For one brief moment, the figure passed in front of the headlights, casting a shadow so long it seemed to stretch for miles, enveloping Jason in its blackness. Then it moved on until reaching the open car door.

Jason knew what the man was going to do even before he bent into the car and flipped off the lights. The sudden darkness was almost as blinding, the terror infinitely more extreme. Because he didn't have to see the car being shifted into neutral or hear the emergency brake being released to know exactly what was happening. "God, no, please."

The vehicle began to roll down the slope, drawing irrevocably closer to the icy pond on which Jason and Ryan were trapped. "Why are you doing this?" he yelled, straining against the tape even as the front tires reached the frozen shoreline.

Behind him, he felt movement. Ryan was coming to.

"Good-bye, Jason," the voice called. "The world will be better off without you. Shame about your friend. You really should have come alone."

The shadowy figure moved, disappearing into the swirling snow. A moment later, an engine rumbled, then slowly faded away. He barely heard it as the car eased closer, sliding across the snow-slicked ice. Adding weight . . . so much weight.

Crack.

How deep is the water? How thick could the ice be?

Will we freeze or will we drown?

"Jase?"

"Ryan, I'm sorry I got you into this," he sobbed.

Ryan's head moved, his frozen hair scraping Jason's spine. "S'okay. Sidekick's always got the hero's back."

"Sorry!" Jason cried, trying not to move yet desperate to break away. But before he could do a thing, even say good-bye to his best friend, another crack came and the ice gave way beneath them. Freezing liquid rushed over his feet and ankles, bringing them back to life to experience the agony.

They plunged down until blackness covered their heads and ice seared his lungs. And as the water turned the world above him into an icy grave, Jason could think only of his parents.

God, how he wished he'd gone with them to Florida.

Chapter 1

Nine Days Later

From the outside, the Hoover Building looked like every other D.C. government facility built in the sixties. Square and boxy, with limestone-tinged concrete walls, it lacked the crisp, white grandeur of the monuments farther down on Pennsylvania Avenue or ringing the Mall.

In fact, to Alec Lambert's slightly jaded eyes, it looked a little like a prison.

Considering his feelings more resembled a convict's than a special agent's on this cold winter morning, that wasn't inappropriate. Because walking through the doors of FBI headquarters for the first day of his new assignment felt like the start of a sentence for a heinous crime.

Yeah. A heinous crime: trusting the wrong woman. And getting shot for the privilege.

It had been a hard lesson, but he'd definitely learned it. Because his error in judgment had not only landed him in the hospital with a couple of bullet holes in him; it had come at a much higher cost.

Another agent's life.

The incident in Atlanta had wounded him physically and crushed him emotionally. It had destroyed his chance to nail the serial-killing bastard he'd obsessed about catching for the last three years, because it had also cost him his position in the Behavioral Analysis Unit. And it had cost him a friend, Dave Ferguson, whom he'd known since his academy days.

That was what kept him up nights.

He could have been tossed out of the FBI altogether. Maybe the higher-ups had figured it would be better to keep him close, saturated in the memories so he could torture himself over it even more. Round-the-clock atonement.

Which was, perhaps, why he'd so desperately wanted his job back.

"Last chance. Don't blow it," he kept reminding himself as he worked his way through security, finally arriving on the fourth floor. It was time to report to his new boss, the guy who'd saved his ass from having to work as a department store security guard. Wyatt Blackstone.

"Special Agent Alec Lambert," he said when he reached the outer office of the FBI's newest Cyber Action Team, or CAT, as someone with no imagination had started calling them. After a widely publicized case last summer, the media had taken things a step further, picked up on an in-house nickname, and started calling Blackstone's team the Black CATs. *Wonderful.*

The receptionist, a dour middle-aged woman with graying brown hair and drawn-on eyebrows, studied his ID. "You're expected."

Rising from behind her government-issue metal desk, she gestured for him to follow. Alec did, keeping pace as she led him down a narrow hallway. Lined with groaning bookshelves and dented file cabinets, the dimly lit corridor also boasted a few framed black-and-whites of the Hoover glory days. They were smeared with dust, some lopsided. Everything combined to provide a dull backdrop that was probably invisible to the people who worked in this place from day to day. But to newcomers, it was like stepping into a time machine and coming out in 1970.

Each staccato click of the woman's heels on the dingy tile floor stabbed into Alec's brain, an audible emphasis of his change in status. No longer a hotshot agent with the Behavioral Analysis Unit, about which TV shows and movies were made, he was the black sheep now. Far from being a respected, experienced criminal investigative analyst, he was a newcomer to an already established team, the members of which had to have heard everything about him.

Well, everything except the truth.

Forcing himself to focus, he noted the small, cluttered offices they passed. Each office had another of those old metal desks buried under stacks of files and paperwork. But they also had state-of-the-art computer equipment. Way better than the POS laptop he'd been using for the past few years at the BAU.

That was probably a perk of being a part of the Cyber Division. They might be stuck in offices that hadn't been renovated since the Carter administration, but the Black CATs got good computer equipment. Even if they were new and on probation. Kind of like him.

"You'll be in there," the receptionist said, not even slowing her stride as she pointed into a shadowy, empty office. Or closet. He couldn't be sure which.

"Great," he muttered.

She must have heard the tone in his voice. "We hear they're going to move us to better quarters if things pan out."

Alec had been briefed by Wyatt Blackstone during his interview down at Quantico. He was well aware that Blackstone's team's future, like Alec's, was up in the air. Apparently the supervisory special agent had pissed off the wrong people, though Alec didn't know the details.

"How's that looking so far?" he asked.

She gave him a tight, impersonal smile. "We manage to keep busy."

He'd like to know how. This particular CAT was unlike any other in the agency, and it focused on a new type of Internet-related crime. Rather than ferreting out weak, pimple-faced college students who liked to unleash viruses into the world's computers, or perverts who exchanged vile pictures of little kids in pedophile chat rooms, this team investigated murder. Internet-related killings.

It sounded very limited. Besides, most of the cases would probably involve interaction with the BAU and ViCAP—the Violent Criminal Apprehension Program— some members of which were notoriously territorial with their files. As he had been mere months ago.

He'd been driven and focused, working seventy-hour weeks and not often accused of playing nice with others. While doing his own job to the best of his ability—and the detriment of his personal life, as most women he'd dated could attest—he'd sought to learn everything he could about profiling. The next coveted supervisory special agent position to become available should have had his name written all over it.

Until Atlanta. The screwup, the shootings. After that, the only thing his name had ended up on were a slew of hospital reports and disciplinary actions. And a Dear John e-mail from his girlfriend, who'd decided the glamour of dating an FBI agent faded when bullets started flying.

Alec's chance to become a senior profiler in the BAU was over. That didn't mean he wouldn't be using his profiling skills, however. Because he suspected they were the reason he'd been plucked from the verge of termination and thrown into the Black CATs' den. Blackstone had enough computer geeks, it seemed. He needed a behavioral analyst, his own unofficial pet profiler. And Alec had fit the bill, even if he was an outcast.

He wasn't complaining. It sure beat civilian life or

practicing law with the degree he'd obtained a month before applying to the bureau.

"Excuse me, sir?" The receptionist knocked on a partially closed door. "Special Agent Lambert is here."

Alec entered, realizing Blackstone's entire team was present, which explained the empty offices he'd passed. Judging by the frowns on their faces, the meeting was an intense one.

Lucky for them, he'd provided a distraction. Which wasn't so lucky for him. Because as soon as the receptionist nodded and bowed out, every voice silenced, every head turned, and the six people sitting around the table focused their attention solely on Alec.

He maintained his stiff, aloof stance, offering a brief nod to one agent he recognized from the publicity on last summer's Reaper case. Then he focused on the team leader, who was rounding the table, his hand extended. "Glad to see you, Lambert. Your timing is appropriate, given the topic of this morning's briefing," the man said, his voice smooth and solid.

That smoothness had impressed Alec during his interview. Blackstone seemed very calm, even tempered, and eminently professional.

Alec shook the extended hand. "This morning's briefing?"

"We'll get to that. First, introductions."

Gesturing toward the conference table, which dominated the small room, he pointed to each team member, introducing them in rapid succession. Alec put the names together with the faces as Blackstone ran down their backgrounds.

"Dean Taggert," Blackstone said, gesturing toward the agent Alec had recognized as the one who'd helped bring down the Reaper. He remembered the man's history—a hard-nosed former street cop, he'd recently been in ViCAP working the most violent of crimes. Had a temper. Tough and intuitive.

"Brandon Cole."

A punked-out blond who would never have gotten away with the hairstyle in any other bureau office. Young and good-looking, he should have been wearing a neon sign over his head proclaiming, I'M A REBEL WITH A BRAIN AND DON'T YOU FORGET IT. Alec wasn't surprised to hear he'd been a hacker as a teenager, which probably hadn't been more than a half dozen years ago.

"Lily Fletcher."

A pale-haired, fair-skinned programmer who'd been lured over from cyber crimes. He'd heard of her, too. Something about a tragedy in her family, though he couldn't remember the details. She was probably in her late twenties, and appeared quiet, serene. He'd lay money she didn't have field experience, but the intensity in her eyes said she was devoted.

"Kyle Mulrooney."

A stout, middle-aged bureau man all the way. From the side-parted, slicked-down hair to the loose-fitting suit and the too-narrow tie, this guy had probably been on the job for a few decades. He was old-school and probably as tough as a week-old steak.

"Jackie Stokes."

Also from cyber crimes. The attractive African-American looked tougher, more street-smart than the blonde. Probably in her early forties, maybe ten years his senior, she'd been with the bureau for fifteen years. She'd also been one of the first people Blackstone had brought in. The man apparently wanted agents who were experienced but open to new things.

Like him.

He would bet Jackie Stokes hadn't landed on the team because it was Blackstone or the unemployment line, however.

"Please take a seat, Alec. We were just getting started." Blackstone returned to his position at the head of the table and tapped on the keys of a laptop. Behind him, on a portable screen, two yearbook-type pictures appeared.

"Those are the boys?" Lily Fletcher asked, shaking her head slightly, her mouth pulled down at the corners. The blonde wore her emotions on her face. Not a good trait to have when working violent crimes.

"Yes," Blackstone replied.

Like everyone else, Alec stared at the bright, smiling faces of the all-American teenagers enlarged on the screen before him. Their ordinary appearances gave not the slightest indication of whether they were victims or suspects. Knowing from experience they could be either, Alec waited for a hint.

"Poor kids," Fletcher murmured.

Victims. Though of what, he did not yet know.

Blackstone swiveled in his chair to stare up at the screen with the rest of them. "Jason Todd, age seventeen. Ryan Smith, sixteen, both from Wilmington, Delaware."

The picture changed, a collage of images appearing. Mostly joint photos of the two boys, side by side, mugging for the camera. In a few, the bigger boy, blond-haired Jason Todd, had his skinny friend in a mock choke hold and was noogeying him on the head.

Alec began analyzing the details, seeing a picture of the boys' relationship. Jason was undoubtedly the ringleader, Ryan the follower. *Did the loyal friend follow his buddy into danger this time?*

"High school juniors, good students, lacrosse players, best friends from childhood." Blackstone ticked off the details in that smooth, calm manner, betraying no emotion. "They disappeared nine days ago."

Knowing better than to ask Blackstone to back the meeting up and go over familiar ground just for him, since he'd always been annoyed by latecomers himself, Alec figured he'd do what he always did and leap into the action. It was time to dive into the deep end rather than safely tread water on the sidelines.

He'd been treading on the sidelines for months, trying to recapture his health, his job, his life, maybe even his sanity. *Play it safe, go slowly, be careful*—they were words of advice he'd heard from everyone, including his doctor, his bureau-ordered therapist, and his friends. But he'd realized something: The longer he played it safe, the lower his self-confidence went. For someone used to accomplishing anything he set out to do, self-doubt was simply unacceptable. Period.

Clearing his throat, he asked the obvious. "Kidnapping?"

It was a reasonable assumption. The FBI would have been brought in by the locals. Blackstone's team could have been made a part of the investigation because the ransom demand had come in electronically. Of course, Blackstone's involvement probably meant the boys were already dead. Damn shame.

Blackstone shook his head. Then he tapped his keyboard again, not elaborating. The man apparently thought Alec knew enough to keep up. Meaning the team hadn't heard much more than the basics—like that the two kids pictured on the screen were dead.

The next set of images confirmed it.

"Jesus," Taggert muttered.

Everyone at the table stared, taking in the awful visual.

The two boys had been turned into a single crystallized statue. Their bodies were upright, back-to-back, one sitting, tied or taped to a chair, the other on his knees. They appeared to be naked, their skin a uniform bluish white from their foreheads to their feet. Judging by the grainy outdoor backdrop—a slushy shoreline dotted with spiky trees and dead brush—the victims had been pulled out of a lake. A pretty fucking cold one.

And judging by the openmouthed expressions of horror frozen on their faces, they'd been thrown into it alive.

Blackstone confirmed as much, his tone matter-of-fact. "I don't have copies of the reports yet, but the coroner says drowning is the cause of death."

Exposure had obviously come in a close second. Alec honestly couldn't decide which was worse.

"A farmer spotted the submerged car in a pond on his property two days ago, during a warm spell that melted off some of the ice. The bodies were pulled up yesterday."

"Were they held elsewhere, then brought to the lake to be killed?" asked Stokes. The frown on her brow and the tightness of her lips indicated she wasn't quite as dispassionate about what they were seeing as her boss.

"Judging by the evidence gathered so far, we believe the boys were killed the night they disappeared. We know they were lured to this particular spot. I think it's safe to assume they were not brought here by someone else but arrived of their own volition."

The program continued to flash thorough, detailed images, which everyone silently studied, looking down occasionally to take notes.

Alec never looked down. He kept his attention focused on the photos, waiting for something about them to click with him. He'd spent three years as a profile coordinator in the Richmond field office before transferring up to Quantico last year. And one thing he'd learned was that every murder scene had a story to tell. Once he'd spotted the right opening into that story, it often unfolded in his head with remarkable clarity.

In this one, it was the victims' vehicle. It had been photographed as it was being removed from the lake, as well as once it was onshore. There was something about it, something unexpected.

"I'd say we're looking at a single unsub, acting on his own," Alec murmured, realizing what had been bothering him.

Six pairs of eyes shifted in his direction.

"Quite a leap, don't you think, based on nothing but

some crime scene photos?" Stokes said, one brow raised in skepticism.

"They were lured to the scene and killed almost right away."

"So?"

"So the unsub wasn't sure he could overpower and manage a pair of strong, lacrosse-playing teenage boys for any length of time."

"We think he was expecting only one of the boys to be there, and the other might have been an unexpected complication," Blackstone said. "But please continue, Alec. Jason Todd was, indeed, a big, strong young man, so your reasoning could still be correct."

More certain now, Alec said, "That makes it even more likely. Our suspect caused an accident to surprise or incapacitate his intended victim, Jason, again suggesting he wasn't sure he could handle a single boy for long, and he didn't have assistance."

"An accident?" Stokes wasn't giving up. "How do you figure? You can see in the pictures of the car there was no air bag deployment. For all we know, the kids parked, got out, and walked into someone with a gun and he pushed the car in the lake."

Alec shook his head. "Look at the damage. The car impacted something on the side." He narrowed his eyes, studying the picture harder. "That's a Riviera. They stopped making them in, oh, 1999, I think. No side air bags."

"Now he's a car expert?" the woman mumbled.

Alec ignored her, figuring he was getting a little new-kid treatment. "The suspect could have blocked the road, forcing the driver to swerve to avoid the obstacle. From there, the car probably spun sideways into one of those trees near the shoreline."

"Maybe our suspect didn't have anything to do with the crash," offered Mulrooney. He leaned back in his chair and smirked. "Coulda stumbled across it, pretended to be a bystander, then whammo."

"Whammo? You're saying some random psychopath stumbled across two helpless, injured crash victims and murdered them because he didn't have anything better to do that night?" Taggert shot back. He rolled his eyes in irritation. "Who are we looking for here, Freddy Krueger? That shit only happens in teenage slasher movies and Girl Scouts campfire stories."

Mulrooney chuckled, which was when Alec pegged their relationship. The older agent was blustery and obviously liked to taunt bears. The bear, in this case, being Dean Taggert.

"If we could continue," Blackstone interjected smoothly. Everyone quieted down, if not convinced of Alec's assertion, at least no longer arguing about it. One thing Alec noted: Nobody questioned whether his point made a damn bit of difference. Because they all knew it did. Knowing whether they were dealing with one unsub or multiple ones could mean the difference between a weeklong investigation and a six-month-long one.

Surprisingly, it was the single-suspect situation that could drag things out. Accomplices tended to talk to somebody, so pairs or groups were usually easier to catch.

"I believe Special Agent Lambert could be correct," the team leader said. "Judging by some residual paint discovered on a tree near the water, the car might have crashed into it."

Though not surprised, Alec was relieved his instincts hadn't dulled with the months of inactivity. He also couldn't help wondering why Blackstone had let him theorize if he knew all along the car had crashed. But hell, the guy was whispered to be almost supernaturally perceptive. Maybe he just knew Alec needed to start believing he was any damn good at this job anymore.

"And yes, we are looking at one suspect, and he typically acts alone."

The tension in the room rose, everyone realizing Blackstone had more to tell them.

"This is somebody we know?" asked Brandon Cole, who'd been silent until this point.

Nodding, Blackstone clicked a few keys again, changing the image on the screen to an enlarged shot of a single-spaced page of text. An e-mail. Alec read it quickly, wondering what some Internet scam that had landed in his in-box a hundred times had to do with their case.

Confirming everyone had finished, Blackstone typed again and the image flashed forward. Several e-mails appeared now, many of them signed, "Jason." And a few, "Your friend, Dr. Waffi." The doctor reminded his friend to come alone to their meeting.

Hence the unexpected complication—Ryan Smith.

It was the "your friend, Dr. Waffi" that got Alec's instincts sizzling. He shifted in his chair, leaning forward to drop his forearms onto the surface of the broad, pitted oak table gouged with the shadows of decades' worth of handwritten notes. He tried to catch the random thoughts winging through his head but was unable to do it right away.

"These e-mails were retrieved from Jason Todd's computer during the days before the bodies were discovered. The local police had at first assumed they were dealing with a pair of teen runaways, which is why the media hasn't been all over this."

Two kidnapped teen boys would have made national news. Two runaways not even a blip on the radar.

"Once Jason's parents discovered these messages, the police began to take things more seriously. You can follow the e-mails sequentially and see he was taken in by a get-rich-quick scheme."

It appeared Jason Todd truly believed some foreign

diplomat was going to give him millions of dollars to help him get to hidden bank accounts. God, it was hard to believe anyone, even a teenager, would fall for one of the oldest scams on the Net.

"So the e-mails are directly tied to the murders," Lily said. "Which is why we're in?"

Blackstone nodded. "Yes. They were used to lure Jason Todd and his friend Ryan Smith to their deaths. Exactly the kind of thing we're supposed to be involved with. I've already been in touch with the local authorities, who would be grateful for the help." Casting a level stare in Alec's direction, he added, "These aren't his first victims. I believe the same unsub lured a young woman to her death using an online help-wanted ad five weeks ago."

Talk about a bombshell. The entire team, who obviously hadn't known, reacted to the news, spewing questions and speculation.

"We aren't officially part of that investigation yet," Wyatt explained. "Though I've talked to the lead detectives. I had a suspicion and have been watching it." Those intense eyes gleamed. "Let's just say the murders of Jason and Ryan have increased my suspicions."

Everyone continued talking. Everyone except Alec, who still felt his boss's attention solely on him. Those quick, random thoughts continued to click away in his head, connecting the pieces, adding one more.

It had been five weeks ago, before Alec was even medically cleared to go back to the job, when Blackstone had approached him to come work with his team.

Blackstone held one hand up, silencing the voices. "The national media hasn't gotten hold of the discovery of the bodies yet, but the story did hit the Wilmington press yesterday evening. Last night another e-mail came into Jason's account. Obviously the person writing it knew it would be intercepted, because it was addressed to Jason's parents. And to the FBI."

The whirring of the computer the only sound in the room, the picture changed again. The message on the screen was simple. *Such a stupid boy. You are quite welcome for the service I provided in giving him the chance to prove his worth. Unfortunately for him, he failed. Which, I must say, is perhaps not so unfortunate for the rest of us trapped in a world populated by utter fools. Signed, Your Friend.*

And suddenly Alec got it. Why Blackstone had come to him, had plucked him up from certain termination and given him a place on his team. Why he hadn't been kicked on his ass out of the bureau.

Why he was so badly needed.

"Son of a bitch," he whispered, every cell in his body going on high alert.

Blackstone had suspected whom he was dealing with at the time of the help-wanted murder and had started working to get Alec on board. Now, on his very first day, the man's intuition had paid off.

Alec's heart raced; his pulse surged. Adrenaline coursed through him, as it always did when the chase was on. "It's him."

Blackstone nodded once, but Alec didn't need the confirmation. He'd recognize the tone, the arrogance in the final e-mail, absolutely anywhere. The "your friend" signoff had been used in a note in one of the earlier murders for which Alec suspected this unsub had been responsible. It was only because he'd been focused on the bogus "Dr. Waffi" name that he hadn't realized it before.

He should have figured it out sooner for other reasons. The unusual crime scene was a dead giveaway, as was the intentional psychological torment of the victims. Jason and Ryan had been put on the ice conscious and aware, intentionally left to spend their last moments in utter terror, wondering when it would break beneath them.

The teens had been lured into a trap that had been well thought out and beyond cruel. Murdered without their killer ever lifting his own violent hand against them. That alone revealed a wealth of information about the psyche of the suspect they were dealing with. Oh, yes. It all fit.

"Who?" Stokes sounded annoyed at being out of the loop. "What's he talking about?"

Still not quite believing that he was going to get another crack at the criminal who'd haunted his most vivid nightmares, Alec sprawled back in his chair.

"Well?" Taggert asked. Appearing equally agitated that the newcomer was the only other person in the know, he glanced back and forth between his boss and Alec.

"Alec?" Blackstone said.

Not even quite believing he was about to say it, Alec smiled—a determined, dangerous smile holding absolutely no humor.

"We're going after the Professor."

InXile: Can u talk?

Wndygrl1: Yes. I was hoping youd b online. I'm lvng for work.

InXile: Wish I could visit you. But hav 2 b careful. Being watched.

Wndygrl1: You must go to the police! They can protect you.

InXile: Police in my own country couldn't protect me.

Wndygrl1: It is so unfair that you had to leave your homeland. Can I help somehow?

InXile: Being my friend is huge help.

Wndygrl1: I want to do more. What else can I do?

InXile: Cannot trust online conversation. Traceable.

Wndygrl1: What are you saying?

InXile: If we could meet . . .

InXile: Friend?

InXile: R U there?

InXile: Never mind. Is a lot to ask, helping a stranger.

Wndygrl1: No! I feel like I've known you all my life, but we haven't met in person.

InXile: Of course. You think I am thief wanting your money?

Wndygrl1: Of course not!!!!

InXile: Good. I would never ask for money. I have much of my own. Just cannot go out to spend it for fear of reprisals.

Wndygrl1: How sad!

InXile: If only I could see you and shower you with gifts.

Wndygrl1: You don't have to buy me a thing.

InXile: Someday I will take you on a shopping spree. For now, though, we could meet somewhere safe, where I won't be followed.

Wndygrl1: Well ...

InXile: What?

Wndygrl1: It's just ... they say you shouldn't meet someone you met online face-to-face.

InXile: They?

Wndygrl1: You know. Experts.

InXile: Right. You are wise. Don't trust strangers. I am sorry to bother you.

Wndygrl1: Don't go! You aren't bothering me.

InXile: I have offended, though?

Wndygrl1: Not at all. I'm so sorry. You've never done anything to offend or bother me.

Wndygrl1: Sometimes I feel like you're the only person who really knows me.

InXile: I am glad. So our friendship will stay as it is. Through computers and wires. You are my only ray of sunshine in these dark days.

Wndygrl1: You say such lovely things.

Wndygrl1: Maybe we could work something out.

InXile: No. Out of question. I don't want u 2 feel uncomfortable.

Wndygrl1: I don't.

InXile: So we think about it for now. Is that . . . how do you say it, okeydokey?

Wndygrl1: lol! Yes, we'll think about it. That would absolutely be okeydokey.

Chapter 2

"So tell me again everything you know about this Professor guy. All the stuff you told us yesterday in the briefing and anything else you *didn't*."

Alec glanced over at Jackie Stokes, his new partner. For the past thirty minutes, since they'd left the office, he'd tried to keep his eyes down, focusing on the case file in his lap. Studying ugly crime scene photos was somehow easier than watching her weave the dark sedan through the afternoon D.C. traffic, narrowly missing other cars. And pedestrians. And a poodle whose owner had snatched it from certain death-by-government-vehicle.

Alec hoped she hadn't seen him surreptitiously double-check his seat belt. He'd recently finished rehabbing his arm and shoulder after the shooting, and he didn't particularly care to break any limbs, or his neck, in a car crash. "You planning to drive for NASCAR or something?" he muttered under his breath.

She pretended not to hear. "Why have I never heard of him?"

"He's kept a pretty low profile."

"A low-profile serial killer, huh?"

If there was such a thing.

"He's been picky and methodical. Six kills in three years."

"Including these latest two, plus the woman from the help-wanted ad?"

"Make that nine. He's obviously accelerating."

Maybe because he'd realized how easy it was to lure his victims via the Internet.

"Nine," Jackie murmured, shaking her head.

Those nine lives had certainly meant a lot to the victims and their loved ones. But when compared to a Dahmer, a Bundy, or a Gacy, the number wasn't too shocking. The crimes, however, had been. The Professor was one sick, malicious fuck.

"Nine murders but he's the invisible man?"

"He's never gone to the press, never tried for infamy. He simply does his thing, taunts the bureau occasionally, always in his condescending, arrogant way, and moves on. Sometimes he goes more than a year between victims, sometimes a few weeks."

"Any particular location?"

"All in the mid-Atlantic region."

"Sex of the victims?"

"Varies." Before she could ask, he added, "And yes, that is unusual. We've got a lot on him, but we haven't been able to determine a specific victim profile because the guy's pretty indiscriminate in who he kills. Varying ages, races, sexes, economic backgrounds. He's an equal opportunity bastard."

"Why do they call him the Professor?"

Sensing Stokes wasn't going to ease up on the questions until she'd gotten all the answers she wanted, Alec closed the file. Just his luck to draw the inquisitive talker for a partner.

Alec didn't want conversation. He wanted to think, to go deep into unexplored fields of possibility in his mind, where every bit of information he had ever learned about the Professor had been taking root and sprouting.

To get back inside the unsub's head again, as he'd been trying so hard to do before getting sidelined by that damned woman and those twice-damned bullets.

"Lambert?" Stokes prodded. "The nickname?"

He sighed. "One of the first investigators started calling him that after a character on that old show *Gilligan's Island* because of the intricate scenarios this guy uses to kill his victims. He specializes in setting people up to kill themselves while making sure they can't possibly escape."

"Like the boys."

"Exactly. He didn't hold them underwater to drown them; he put them on the ice and let it happen. One victim was decapitated in his own garage. The one Wyatt told us about, with the woman responding to the online job listing. You heard what he did to her."

"Yeah. Sick. And he'd never used the Internet to lure his victims before?"

Alec shook his head. "Never. It is impressive if your boss really did figure out who he was dealing with last month. I was . . ." He had been about to say he was on medical leave, but didn't want to open that issue up for questioning yet. "I wasn't in the office at the time, but if the BAU had known there was another Professor case, I would have heard about it."

Oh, would he ever.

"*Our* boss," Stokes explained, "is better than anybody I've ever worked with. Or anybody you've ever worked with." There was no slavish vehemence in her voice, no defensiveness. Just pure confidence. "So this change in his MO, using the Internet—does it mean anything?"

"I'm sure it means something," he admitted. "Any change in the pattern can leave him vulnerable to mistakes he'd been careful not to make in the past."

The timing of that change had been fortuitous. The killer had begun using the Web to lure his victims around the same time Alec had been on the verge of disciplinary action, possibly even of losing his job. Considering Alec knew more about the Professor than anyone else in the bureau, landing on Blackstone's team had seemed a stroke of luck. Bullet holes in his body notwithstanding. But he already knew it was not luck at all. Wyatt Blackstone had known whom he was up against before anyone else had figured it out and had moved Alec into place like a chess master positioning his knight.

That fascinated him, and Alec took no offense at the manipulation. He wanted to stay in the FBI. He wanted to nail the Professor. So, if anything, his respect for his new boss had gone up a notch once he'd figured everything out.

"Think he doesn't want to get his hands dirty? Or doesn't think he's really a killer if he doesn't pull a trigger or plunge a knife?"

Alec considered it. He had been considering it for a long time. He slowly shook his head. "I don't think so. Deep down, my gut tells me he's trying to prove how much smarter he is than anyone else. That it's easy for him to kill because he's so brilliant, and each kill is an in-your-face taunt to prove it."

"Yeah, real smart to commit murder." Stokes frowned. "I don't remember the Professor in *Gilligan's Island* inventing wild scenarios. Maybe you guys should have called him MacGyver."

"I didn't call him anything," Alec pointed out. "Besides, there was another reason for the name. He typically writes to the family after the crime. The messages are condescending and arrogant. Very literate. All on the same stationery, which was expensive but not easy to trace."

Until he'd suddenly switched to e-mails.

"What else do you know about him?"

Having memorized the profile, since he'd contributed to it when he'd first been brought in after the Richmond killing, Alec quickly rattled off the details. "He's highly organized. Above-average intelligence. Probably not involved in a relationship right now, but he might have been in the past. Likely a professional, an engineer, maybe a lawyer or a doctor."

Stokes snorted. "Right. White male, in his thirties, and his mama didn't love him? I asked what you *know* about him."

He glanced at her through half-lowered lashes. "I take it you don't think highly of profiling?"

Stokes shrugged. "I think profilers are a lot like those crime-solving psychics. They always look back and focus on the stuff they got right, like, 'The missing person will be found near water,' and they claim victory when the vic shows up a block from a fire hydrant."

Alec chuckled despite himself. Stokes obviously had attitude. Her own personality, rather than any rumors she might have heard about him, had likely been behind her posturing when they'd first met at yesterday's meeting. He relaxed in his seat, beginning to suspect he could actually like her, if only she'd stop talking so much. And perhaps not kill him in a car crash.

"Give me numbers and calculations over guesses and hypotheses any day."

Her opinion wasn't unique. Lots of people both in the bureau and out of it cast a skeptical eye at some of the work done by the BAU. Usually it was because they got caught up in the thriller novels and the serial-killer movies that romanticized the job of profiler until it became unrealistic. As if they were the crime-solving psychics she spoke of so disdainfully.

"Human beings often behave in patterns, like computer programs," he replied. "Profilers keep track of the patterns and use them to their advantage. No magic. No psychic powers. It's almost mathematical, really. Statistics and probability."

"And a bunch of psychobabble. But math and computers I get." The other agent's frown eased. "Meaning

I should be the one to talk to this Dalton woman. Her being into computers, too."

They'd just exited the city and were on the beltway heading toward Baltimore to interview one Samantha Dalton. During yesterday's examination of a computer belonging to one of the victims, the IT specialists had found communication between Ms. Dalton and Ryan Smith. They'd e-mailed within hours of the boy's death, and he and Stokes had been assigned to go interview the woman, some computer expert.

Stokes's presence made sense, with her cyber crimes background. Alec's? Not so much. He'd have been of more use going up to Wilmington and walking the crime scene. But toeing the line was what he was all about these days. Even though his tongue had nearly bled when he'd bitten on it to keep from arguing the issue with his new boss. He didn't figure it would be a good thing to get fired his second day on the job.

"Why don't we play it by ear?" The frown snapped back into place.

"I mean," he calmly explained as he reopened the file and glanced at it, "let's meet her before deciding how to proceed."

"I bet with your looks you like playing good cop for the ladies." If words could actually sneer, those would have.

Alec didn't look up. His hand remained flat on the autopsy report in his lap. The only sign that her jab had hit home was a slight tightening in his fingers, the tips of which turned white. "Do you have a problem working with me?"

"Let's say pretty boys in expensive suits make me itchy."

Pretty boy. He'd been called worse. Rich dude. Hotshot. Maverick.

Thrill-seeking bastard. That had been the one his ex-girlfriend had thrown at him when he'd refused her demands to quit the bureau in the days following the shooting.

Whatever. As long as Stokes wasn't talking about Atlanta, and he suspected she was not, his new partner could think whatever the hell she wanted.

"Well, drivers who can't keep all four tires on the road make me itchy, too." He grabbed the dashboard as Stokes zipped around a tractor trailer doing seventy on the bumper-to-bumper beltway. "How about whoever lives for the rest of this ride gets to decide how to conduct the interview?"

For the first time since he'd set eyes on her, Stokes cracked a real smile. "Snarky, huh? Maybe you're not just a pretty boy after all." She put the pedal down, sending them hurtling off the 295 exit ramp at near warp speed. "I guess I'll give you more than the week I predicted you'd last."

"You keep driving like this," Alec mumbled, taking no offense, "and I'll be lucky to make it through the day."

With a pencil stuck behind her ear, reading glasses perched on the tip of her nose, and her fingers flying across her keyboard so fast they barely connected with the letters, the last thing Samantha Dalton wanted to do was answer her front door, on which someone had just knocked. She'd finally hit her stride. The flicker of an idea had met the tinder of her own creativity and burst into an inferno of words that had to erupt out of her or be lost forever. Overblown imagery, but, as usual when she was on a deadline, she'd take whatever she could get if it kept her glued to her chair.

Knock-knock. Harder now.

She continued to ignore the interruption, riding the wave of energy she always relied upon when working on the columns and articles she wrote for her site, samthespaminator.com. Especially ones like this, her weekly Sam's Rant, which would go live on her blog late tomorrow night. The Wednesday-night rant, her most popular feature, was also the toughest for her to write. Getting things off her chest while maintaining her professional credibility had become a weekly balancing act. She chose every word carefully, despite the title of the column, never truly ranting. Though, right now, she wanted to because of the annoying knocking.

Having become a hermit since her divorce—at least, so her mother called her—she'd become adept at ignoring the odd salesman or nosy neighbor who dared to disregard the warning on her front door. But as the knocking continued, her eye started to twitch. Her voice low, she mumbled, "Can't you read?"

She'd put the Do Not Disturb sign outside at noon, feeling optimistic that she'd spend the whole afternoon actually writing. Maybe even do something as adventurous as get dressed in real clothes.

It hadn't happened. Instead, she'd surfed the day away, still wearing the sweats she'd donned after her shower. The Web had sucked up hours of her life, as it so often did lately.

Somehow, since the moment a judge with emotionless eyes had signed the piece of paper ending the four-year roller-coaster ride of her marriage, she hadn't felt like Miss Get Up and Go. These days, Miss Got Up, Went, and Got Her Ass Handed Back to Her was content to stay right where she was.

Fortunately, the day hadn't been totally wasted. She had found inspiration for tomorrow night's column. But while researching, she'd also cruised blogs, played a few—okay, ten—hands of Spider Solitaire, and stumbled across stories here and tidbits there that grabbed her attention.

Still, she'd finally gotten down to business and the piece was coming along nicely. At least, it had been until the arrival of the person at the door, whose voice brought her irritation level up a notch.

"Ma'am, please answer the door."

Fat chance. She still had to do updates for her weekly top-ten SPIT—aka Sam's SPam hIT—list. There was research to be done on a new phishing scheme targeting Facebook users. She had an interview to do for a tech blog. And she had about three dozen e-mails to answer. Not much time for chitchat. Not much time for life, even.

Yet she'd surfed away many of her working hours.

"Loser," she muttered.

"Miss Dalton? We need to talk to you," the voice said.

If she had a real office, rather than working out of the living room of her Baltimore apartment, she might have been able to continue ignoring the intrusion. But as it was, she had no escape. So Sam saved her file, then trudged to the door.

Glancing through a part in the drapes and seeing a man wearing a suit, she figured she was in for some soul saving or a high-end sales pitch. Or both. "What is it?" she snapped, yanking the door open.

The man had his hand raised, ready to knock again, and her first impression was that he had big hands. Big fists. Strong-looking fingers. Her second was that if door-to-door salesmen now looked like this, lots more women would be lining up to buy vacuum cleaners and magazine subscriptions. Female shoppers all over the world were probably clamoring for deliveries.

Not her, though. She wasn't buying. Especially not from men who looked like him.

"I'm sorry to disturb you," the man said. "It really is important."

The face was handsome—square jawed, strong featured, with heavily lashed eyes and sculpted cheekbones. Handsome enough to put Sam's guard up. She didn't trust handsome men, not after Samuel Dalton Jr. Her ex had been movie-star gorgeous.

Sam and Sam. God, why hadn't someone slapped her when she'd accepted his proposal?

As he stepped closer, Sam had to tilt her head back. He was tall, easily topping her five-eight by several inches. Broad shoulders seemed to fill all the empty space between one side of the doorframe and the other. His light brown hair was slightly windblown and his pale green eyes held a friendly gleam. The friendliness didn't extend to his nicely shaped lips, however. No smile widened them. His expression remained polite but entirely neutral.

Absolutely the only thing that said he wasn't one hundred percent professional was the way his stare lingered for half a beat too long on her mouth. Which instantly made her want to lick her lips, even while she mentally cursed herself for the reaction.

"You are Miss Dalton? Samantha Dalton?"

"Mrs. Dalton," she clarified, strictly from habit. Technically, she was no longer a Mrs. Dalton, not since her Mr. Dalton had found a Miss Slut-face to shack up with instead. *Sam and Ashley. So much better.* But she'd found the moniker useful in dealing with the occasional cyber stalker, and it fell off her lips as a matter of course these days.

"You are the Sam Dalton from the Sam the Spaminator Web site?"

Still feeling awkward about answering the door in sweats and slippers, she nodded hard. Her glasses slipped past the tip of her nose as she did so. Sam caught them as they bounced off, smudging the lenses with her tight fingers.

Reminding herself that she didn't care what the hot guy with the sexy jaw and rock-hard body thought of her looks, she asked, "Do you need me to sign for something?"

He waved the leather wallet he'd been holding, which she hadn't even noticed. It contained a badge. Sam immediately tensed.

"I'm Special Agent Lambert of the FBI. This is Special Agent Stokes. May we come in?"

She hadn't even seen the woman. Sam nodded at her, saw the same emotionless expression, then let herself process the situation.

It didn't take long. "Did you say FBI?" she snapped.

"Yes. We'd like to talk to you."

God, not again. "Look, I tell people how to avoid scams; I'm not running one myself." She thrust a frustrated hand through her hair, her fingers tangling in the loose ponytail, knocking several long, blond strands down around her face. "I'm not a hacker and my site and book are not secret instruction manuals for criminals looking for new ways to steal people's money."

She'd heard it all since she'd started her blog, and since she'd published her book, *Don't Get Tangled in the Web.* Some legal types seemed to think she was helping the criminals more than hurting them. "Don't you cyber crimes geeks have enough to do without harassing me?"

The man's shoulders unstiffened a fraction, but his partner didn't look at all amused.

"You're not in any trouble, ma'am," he said. "We're actually here to ask for your assistance. We're researching a crime, and have reason to think you were in contact with one of the people involved. We're hoping you can help us figure out what happened."

She hesitated. Sam didn't like people invading her space, especially people who called her *ma'am.* When she wanted contact with the outside world, she sought it out herself. Sometimes. She did not invite it in when it showed up unannounced at her door, nor did she generally accept unwanted invitations.

Especially from men. And there had been a few— including some from her own divorce attorney, who had made it clear that whenever she was ready to get back into the dating game, he wanted to be first in line.

Sure. Like any woman wanted to go out with the man who'd seen her at the lowest point in her life. Who'd heard every ugly, vicious word her ex-husband had said about her.

She had to hand it to him, though: Rick Young, the attorney in question, hadn't given up, even though she'd kept saying no.

"Ma'am?"

Sam sighed, already knowing this agent would not take no for an answer. Stepping back, she gestured the pair in. "Fine." She'd give them five minutes; then it was back to her column. And maybe an ice cream dinner break courtesy of Ben & Jerry—who had, until this very minute, been the only males inside her apartment in months.

But before they'd taken a half dozen steps inside, the female agent glanced out Sam's living room window, peering at the street one story below. "Oh, no, he is *not*!"

Realizing what was happening, Sam suppressed a smile. Seemed the local police hadn't gotten the memo that they should ignore illegally parked, unmarked cars driven by FBI agents.

"Go," the male agent said. He spoke to his partner's retreating back. She had already stalked out the door, obviously planning to talk her way out of a ticket.

"Yeah, good luck with that one," Sam muttered, having had more than a few herself. She didn't think God himself could talk his way out of a parking ticket once Baltimore's finest had him in his sights. Cal Ripken, maybe. But nobody else.

"I take it you've got some firsthand experience?" the agent said.

"You have no idea. I'm on a first-name basis with the local beat cop. He waves at me and smiles as he tickets me when I forget to move my car on trash days."

A twinkle of amusement flashed in his green eyes. The stranger suddenly looked less intimidating and more appealing than before. Younger than she'd first thought, too—he was probably only around thirty, close to her age.

Well, the age she would be for another few days. Then she moved beyond the actual three-zero and proceeded directly into her thirties. *Do not pass go; do not try to pretend you're just a day or two beyond twenty-nine.*

"Almost makes me wish I could watch. I don't think she'll like being told no." His mouth relaxed into a slow smile, a friendly one that invited her to reciprocate.

Though her heart skipped a single beat in her chest and her pulse did a little flip, Sam's lips remained tight by sheer force of will. The way she had been feeling about men these days, she wished he'd paste a frown on his mouth. She couldn't handle an attraction to anyone right now. She'd been burned so badly her hair probably still smelled smoky.

"What is it I can do for you, Agent Lambert?" she asked, her tone curt.

He took her cue, his form stiffening again under his perfectly tailored suit, which looked more appropriate for a Wall Street executive than an FBI agent. "I'd like to show you some correspondence."

He glanced around the room, seeking a place to sit. Her sofa, a flowery monstrosity her mother had insisted on giving her when Sam had moved out of her ex's house, was covered with files and industry magazines. Well, mostly industry magazines. There were a few issues of *People* and *Entertainment Weekly* thrown in there, too. Not to mention a small pile of unfolded, clean laundry, freshly dumped from the dryer.

Two empty Diet Coke cans stood in the middle of their own permanent rings on the coffee table. A crumpled Snickers wrapper protruded from the opening of one can, looking like a castaway's note stuck into a poor man's substitute for a bottle, and on the TV, DVD sleeves for *The Notebook* and *Beaches* taunted her about her sadly sappy Netflix movie list.

Her picture should be on Wikipedia as an illustration of a pathetic thirtysomething divorcée.

If not for her desk, she'd probably look like a slovenly hausfrau. Oh, the desk was a wreck, too, but at least it looked as though it was used. Very used. On it were three mountains of paper, in varying heights—one critical, one urgent, and one just important. The just-important one was about one-quarter the size of the others. There was no pile called Take Your Time.

Clearing her throat, she headed toward the kitchen. "Let's talk in here. I could do with some coffee. You?"

"Sure, thanks." He followed her, remaining silent while she put the pot on.

Joining him at her small table, Sam tried to force herself to relax. After all, she used to like law enforcement types. Her late father had been a state trooper, and the closest thing she had to a father these days was her dad's old partner, who was now a judge. It was only recently, since her work had been targeted by some supposed experts who wanted to kick the amateur off their playing field, that she'd begun to question the intelligence of those in any legal profession.

The parking tickets didn't help, either.

"What's this all about?"

He opened a folder, spreading what looked like e-mail printouts on her kitchen table. "Did you write these?"

Sam glanced at the pages, seeing her e-mail address on the top of them. "I exchange e-mails with people all the time," she murmured doubtfully. "This looks like a typical response to someone asking for Web advice."

Lifting one of the pages, Sam quickly read the original message, and her own response. A smile suddenly widened her lips. "Oh, yeah, I know this kid—what a sweetheart. He's written to me several times. He even got his parents to bring him to a signing I did last summer."

"A signing for your Internet scam book?"

She leveled a steady gaze at the man. "My book on how to avoid Internet scams."

"That's what I meant."

Sure it was.

"How long have you been corresponding with him?"

"Probably about a year." Suddenly remembering what Special Agent Lambert had said when he'd first arrived, Sam met his stare directly. "Wait, you said crime. Is he all right? Nothing's happened to him, has it?"

Alec noticed right away that Samantha Dalton's immediate response was to assume young Ryan Smith was a victim, and she sounded worried. Considering she'd met him only once and had a strictly e-mail relationship with the boy, he filed the detail away, because it said a lot about her. So did her clothes. Her apartment. Her job. Her lifestyle.

But, Jesus, none of that meshed with the visual picture of the woman who'd opened the door to him ten minutes ago.

He'd been prepared for a vigilante computer nerd. Not the brown-eyed, golden-haired beauty with lush lips and a fragile throat. He'd seen fewer curves on a figure eight, despite the shapeless, washed-out sweats she had on. Though she wore no makeup and her hair was a mess, she'd been striking enough to suck every thought out of his head for a long, breathless moment.

Yet she lived as if she'd never had a date and didn't much care. Which didn't jibe with that Mrs. Dalton thing she'd carefully pointed out. Or the bare ring finger on her left hand.

Yeah, he'd looked.

All in all, the woman presented an interesting puzzle, one his brain was already trying to take apart and fit back together.

"Agent Lambert?"

"When is the last time you heard from him?"

She met his stare, and he could see the silent debate

going on behind those dark eyes. He'd seen it before. Everyone in law enforcement had. Sometimes wanting to know the truth was outweighed by the desire to put off unhappy news for a while. When she shifted her gaze, choosing to delay the inevitable, Alec added another piece to the puzzle: She'd known loss.

She tapped the tip of her index finger on the top page. "This message. About a week and a half ago."

Alec had memorized the victim's final e-mail to Sam the Spaminator. "He asked about an e-mail offer a friend of his received?"

"Typical Nigerian four-one-nine scam. I wrote back and sent him links to tons of articles about it, including recent ones I'd written."

The thing had landed in his own in-box dozens of times, so he knew exactly what she meant, but he let her expound.

"It's amazing how many people still fall for this scheme. Losses in the hundreds of millions, all because Joe Naive thinks he's going to get rich if he just puts out a little more money for bribes or taxes or legal fees or security. Until the money's all gone and the 'finance minister' or 'bank manager' or 'estate executor' is gone with it."

Her tone had gone from conversational to hard, verging on bitter. The tautness in her form told him even more about her—like exposing fraud online might be a personal crusade, rather than a professional one. She was emotionally affected by the issue, not a bit detached.

He had a feeling she was going to take Ryan Smith's murder very hard.

"Did he forward you the actual e-mail?"

She shook her head, pushing back a few long strands of silky hair, which had escaped the ponytail. "No. He told me about it and I responded." A tiny furrow appeared on her brow, and she added, "Oh, I just remembered: He also asked about certified checks. Whether the scheme ever included them."

Alec leaned forward, leafing quickly through the copies of the e-mails. "Where?"

Frowning in concentration, she said, "It was ... Wait, actually I think it was in an instant message."

That surprised him. "Strangers can IM you?"

"He was a bright kid with a lot of potential, so when he figured out my ID, I was impressed enough to chat with him on occasion."

The investigative team already had Ryan Smith's computer and would find the history, but going to the source was quicker. "Can you tell me what you remember?"

As she closed her eyes to concentrate, Alec couldn't help noticing the long sweep of the woman's lashes brushing against her high cheekbones. He shifted in his chair, uncomfortably aware of his attraction to her. To a potential witness. Which was not only a no-no, but in his case, possibly a career killer.

Not that attraction had been the problem in Atlanta. Sympathy and misplaced trust had been his downfall there. But the lesson was the same: No mixing it up with witnesses. Emotionally or physically.

"I'd responded to his e-mail"—she glanced at the printed version, checking the time—"at around five. I told him it was a scam and I was shocked he didn't know about it." She nibbled her bottom lip. "I told him he wasn't much of a fan if he hadn't noticed I'd written a whole chapter about it in my book. Then I suggested he print out the articles I linked to, roll them up, and smack his buddy in the head with them for even considering going along."

She managed a weak smile. Alec couldn't bring himself to return it. Judging by what he knew of the boys, he suspected there was nothing Ryan wouldn't have done to try to stop his friend. Yet, in the end, he'd gone with him to his death.

Tragic. So damned tragic.

"And the instant messages?"

"I had run down to the corner market, and didn't log off. When I came back, I saw he had IM'd me a couple of times."

"What did he say?"

"He was asking if any of these scams ever included getting a certified check, and if those checks could bounce. Which, of course, they can, if they're faked. It's happening all the time, especially to people who sell stuff on Craigslist and Internet auction sites. Or those who respond to ads for 'mystery shoppers' or work-at-home opportunities."

Alec made a note to look into the certified-check angle. There'd been no mention of it in the crime scene report, or in any of the interviews with Jason's or Ryan's parents. He also wanted to know more about those work-at-home ads she'd mentioned, given the other murder five weeks ago.

"I tried to respond, but he was offline by then. It was the night of the big snowstorm, and my Internet connection went out, and I forgot about it."

The night of the snowstorm. The night the boys had disappeared. Would they have gone through with the meeting, driven to their deaths, if the scam expert Ryan so trusted had personally warned him of the danger? From what the computer guys could tell, Ryan had not opened Samantha's return e-mail. It had been hung up in one of those cyberspace black holes and hadn't shown up in his e-mail account until the next morning.

But the IMs . . . If Samantha Dalton had been sitting at her desk to receive them and respond right away, how different might things be today?

She was definitely going to take the news of Ryan Smith's murder very hard.

And though she was a perfect stranger, Alec already dreaded having to tell her.

They'd discovered the bodies right on schedule.

He'd been watching for the story on the news, knowing that as the weather warmed back up to above-normal temperatures, the chances of the car being spotted in the thawing pond would improve. And that once the car was found, the water would be searched for its occupants.

He laughed softly, wondering how the state police divers had enjoyed dipping beneath the frigid surface.

How had the boys looked after their winter dip? Had their toes snapped off like the tips of delicate icicles? Had their eyes become glittering glass marbles? Was the skin as fine as porcelain or veined like marble? Did their hair float about their heads before freezing, forming beautiful, crystallized halos of white?

He would have enjoyed seeing them. Two fools frozen in a pose of eternal stupidity.

"Not two fools," he reminded himself. "Not the second boy."

No, Jason's unfortunate friend had exhibited a modicum of intelligence. But not enough to keep him from riding along to a cold and dark final destination.

"Ahh, well." He shrugged off the unease. Because misplaced loyalty was nearly as damning as outright stupidity. The world had no place for it.

He studied the article on his computer screen for a moment longer, looking for nuances in the tone or quotes from the investigators that might hint at whether they had determined his involvement. The moment the FBI became part of the investigation, he'd know for sure, but there was no mention of that particular entity.

Not yet, anyway. But there would be. His last taunting message to the boys' parents, sent after he'd seen the story on the Wilmington news station's Web site, had ensured it.

Having studied every word of the article, and being unable to contact his latest project, the dull and unimaginative Wndygrl1, from here at work, he skipped over to another familiar site. The newest weekly "rant" column wouldn't go up until late tomorrow night, and he would be alert and awake, hungering for her words, her thoughts, the entrée into her beautiful mind.

Until then, he couldn't resist reading over the entry from last Wednesday night. And the one from the week before. And the week before that. All the way back to the article warning about so-called finance ministers offering to make people rich.

He *tsk*ed. "They really should listen to you, darling."

He'd certainly paid close attention. Close enough to know how to word his lure and cast his reel. He'd hooked quite a few prospects, but only one, young Mr. Todd, had followed the bait all the way into the net.

"Youngsters. Can't teach them anything."

Ahh, well. If the fools were incapable of appreciating the advice to be gained and the lessons to be learned on this, his favorite Web site, he himself was not. After all, how better to test the intelligence of his prey than by seducing them with a promise that could be easily disproved with a few flicks of the fingers on a keyboard?

Those too gullible to spend two minutes searching for the information that could save their lives didn't deserve to live.

As he gathered his things to leave for the day, he smiled in anticipation of tomorrow night's column. The "deposed royalty" dating scheme was progressing nicely, but should be coming to its inevitable conclusion soon.

After that it was anyone's guess. He mightn't find anything to amuse him for weeks, perhaps months. Or he could receive inspiration for his next project tomorrow at midnight. Not knowing simply heightened the excitement.

Carefully choosing his destination to ensure safe distance from his real life, so he could cast his lures and toy with his online friend, Wendy, he drove into the cold winter evening. Though the car radio remained off, his fingers tapped on the steering wheel in time to an internal melody. It was classical and refined, nothing like the filth the people around him every day chose to listen to. The kind of music a woman with a brain would appreciate. Too bad he knew so few.

Except her. A woman both smart and beautiful, she had become his muse, providing inspiration, quietly whispering suggestions through her articles.

She was a kindred spirit, an inquisitive mind in a lovely physical package.

He found himself thinking about her often. Dwelling in the memory of the softness of her skin when they touched. The slenderness of her hand in his own. The sheen of her hair. The lyrical sound of her voice.

He knew everything about her—where she lived, whom she socialized with. Knew she was often alone, intelligent enough to know she needed no company. Oh, yes, he knew it all. He would, in fact, call himself her number-one fan. A devotee.

She had but one fault: her girlish desire to do good. But she could be cured of that, reformed. He knew a bit about curing the soul without crushing the spirit. He didn't want to crush her; he wanted to free her. Release her from all the societal constraints that said she had to be nice, had to be good, had to help those who were too stupid to help themselves.

He would mold her until they became a perfect pair, an ideal couple.

It would happen. Someday he'd teach her. With his help, she would escape from her bonds and she would realize, as he already had, that she was his. The one woman he had ever really wanted.

Samantha Dalton belonged to him.

Chapter 3

In the five months since members of her own team had stopped the monster known as the Reaper from murdering an innocent child, IT specialist Lily Fletcher's nightmares had grown more violent. More extreme. Much more disturbing.

The Reaper, Seth Covey, had added a new dimension to the horror taking place in her head every night as she slept, but he wasn't entirely responsible. She had been tormented long before that case, the first she'd worked after joining Blackstone's team.

Lily's dreams had grown dark on the night she'd caught a fleeting glimpse of her nephew's face through the window of a stranger's van as it disappeared down the street.

They'd become bloody on the night his body was discovered.

And vicious when her sister, her only other living relative, had killed herself rather than live with the loss of her little boy.

There was no befriending the dead. No whispers of love and sorrow could make their bodies any less brutalized, their expressions any less terrified. No matter how many happy memories she focused on, or smiling pictures she cherished, at night, her loved ones always appeared the same. Ravaged victims who lived in her subconscious, emerging the moment she fell into a restless sleep.

Now the horrific crimes Covey had committed played out in her head too. She'd seen them firsthand, witnessed the atrocities he'd recorded and uploaded to the Internet for the viewing pleasure of his sick, deviant friends at a sick, deviant Web site.

The site was gone now. And so was Covey, dead by his own hand. Yet she still saw him night after night. Just a young punk, barely more than a kid himself, but so filled with hatred and rage he'd become a monster in human skin.

Sometimes his face replaced the one of the bastard who'd killed Zachary. Or she beheld her nephew in place of the little boy who'd been saved. Saving Zach was a common theme. She always came so close, only to be devastated all over again when she failed.

Those dreams broke her heart.

They said you could withstand anything if you prayed enough, hoped enough, loved enough. But Lily no longer believed it. Prayer, hope, and love could never bring Zach or Laura back. Nor could they give her the kind of peace she longed for during the sweat-filled nights when she twisted and writhed in her bed, running, chasing, trying to stop the insane sequence of events before it started.

She never could. She never would. The result would always be a dead child in her arms and her sister's thin, wasted body in a bathtub full of reddish water, blood still slowly trickling from her slashed wrists.

"Stop," she told herself. She needed to get her mind off last night's torment and back into the here and now. There were other things to worry about. Namely, the one thing she had left to live for. Because, even though she'd realized love, prayer, and hope weren't enough to ease the pain, with the help of a pretty good therapist, she'd found other things that were.

A thirst for justice. The need to stop any other family from going through what hers had. Stopping one monster from luring another boy like Zach into his van.

Those things helped. They were enough to live for. Enough for her to get up every morning and put on her clothes and walk through yet another lonely day.

The job was enough.

"Did you say something?"

Lily shook her head, flushing as she realized she'd lapsed into such dark musings right in the middle of a case. She and Brandon—the coworker and office mate who had also become a friend—were at the computer forensics lab. Hoping Jason Todd's hard drive might hold a clue to the identity of his killer, they were watching while a computer forensics expert ran it through ACES, the Automated Computer Examination System.

"Sorry. Guess I was muttering to myself."

"Okay, but make sure nobody answers. You know the bureau frowns on agents who hear voices in their heads," he said with a grin.

She managed a weak smile. "Deal."

Usually Brandon could tease her out of her darkest moods. There was something irresistibly charming about his big green eyes and spiky bleached-blond hair. He looked more like an underwear model than an FBI cyber nerd, and she suspected, judging by some of his hacker knowledge, that he'd had a little larceny in his soul as a teenager.

Today, though, she could find nothing to smile about. Her heart was heavy, filled with sadness for the families of Jason Todd and Ryan Smith. She was also a bit uncomfortable being here. Though she trusted Brandon, she didn't want to have to answer his inevitable questions if they ran into any of the forensics guys she'd been working with on another case.

He said you could work on it.

Months ago, Wyatt Blackstone had told her she could offer assistance in the investigation into Satan's Playground, the now defunct Internet world where the Reaper had aired his videos. There he had hooked up with a perverted client with the handle Lovesprettyboys who had paid to have a young boy raped and murdered for his viewing pleasure. That was the boy they'd saved. The boy who sometimes wore Zach's face.

But while he hadn't forbidden her to assist, Blackstone hadn't been enthusiastic about it, either. He'd insisted that it not interfere with her current job. So she'd done it quietly. She'd offered after-hours assistance to the child-protection CAT trying to track down Lovesprettyboys and others like him.

She had no choice. Because since the moment she'd first seen the pedophile's vicious avatar having his fun in the cyber world, she had known he had to be stopped before he could move his crimes to the real one. If he hadn't already.

"You know this is probably a waste of time," she said to Brandon as she glanced at her watch, wondering how much longer they would have to be here.

"I know. Unless this guy is some kind of idiot, he didn't write from an IP address that might actually lead back to him."

Judging from what she'd learned about their unsub in the past thirty-six hours, he most definitely wasn't an idiot. He'd never be careless enough to use an easily traceable computer.

"Okay, I've isolated all the individual e-mails between Jason and this Dr. Waffi," said the specialist, Parker, who sat before a state-of-the-art terminal. "They came from three areas: Philadelphia, Wilmington, and Trenton. I've been able to determine via some hidden software coding that they all came from the same computer. But the IP addresses come from a half dozen different servers, one of which, I can already tell you, is from a fast-food restaurant chain offering free wifi."

"Playing terrorize-the-teen while scarfing a burger," Brandon said. "Nice."

Lily sighed. "So he packed up his laptop, cruised around to find hot spots in a tristate area, jumped online, and then moved on before writing again."

"Looks like it," Parker said. "As for the original message opening contact with Jason Todd, it looks like he used a 'bot net. Probably generated thousands of these 'former finance minister' letters, spammed them all over the place, and Jason was gullible enough to respond."

Gullible enough. Or just a kid dreaming big.

The specialist continued going over his findings. As they'd supposed, the Professor hadn't been stupid. He certainly wouldn't have written from his home or work computer, and he would never have paid for Internet service at a café or a hotel, where there would be some record of his presence. Not when it was so easy to cruise around and steal access from any unsecured system. Sure, if they ever found a suspect, they would be able to link his computer to all the messages. But first they needed to find him.

Smothering her disappointment, Lily listened to the report, even while wishing Parker would hurry. When she spied a familiar face, she knew the wishes hadn't helped. *Damn*.

"Hey, Fletcher, back so soon?"

Cursing her luck, she offered a brisk nod to the agent—Anspaugh—who was heading up the very investigation she'd been helping on.

"Caught another case," she explained, hoping Brandon was paying careful attention to their own tech, and not her conversation.

"Is it a big one?"

She wasn't sure how much Blackstone had shared beyond the walls of the Black CATs' den. The BAU had to know they'd gotten a lead on the Professor, but that might be as far as it had gone. "Possibly."

Anspaugh smirked, reminding her of how little she liked the man. He had a big bully's personality and a big bully's body, and, unfortunately, a big bully's tiny brain to go with the package.

She liked him even less when he added, "So, did Blackstone manage to find another Reaper to justify his team's existence?"

It wasn't the first time Lily had heard snide comments from others in the bureau. Wyatt had burned bridges and made enemies by blowing the whistle on some of his colleagues. The evidence tampering and manipulation had run deep, from the forensics lab all the way up to the deputy director's office, and a whole lot of heads had rolled. The friends of those heads placed the blame squarely on Blackstone, who'd done nothing more than the right thing.

"Why do you ask? Hoping to nose in the way you did the last time, with Satan's Playground?" The retort didn't come from Lily, but from Brandon, who had obviously been listening. *Double damn.*

"Cole," Anspaugh said with a brief nod.

"I'm not sure you guys have thanked us enough for handing that case to you on a platter."

Anspaugh's body stiffened; he hadn't liked taking somebody else's leftovers, especially since the cyber playground had been belly-up before he'd gotten hold of the case. "Good thing you didn't keep it yourselves. You mighta cost another teenager her head."

Direct hit. Brandon's eyes narrowed behind his wire-framed glasses. Lily instinctively put a hand on his arm, though she felt the sting of the accusation, too. Because it was true. They hadn't found the Reaper in time to save the last young woman who'd crossed his path. Her body had been found in the Pennsylvania woods a few days after her kidnapping.

"We were just leaving," she said.

"Yeah, right. Let's hit it, Tiger Lily," Brandon muttered, snapping his gum as if he were trying to save his own tongue from being bitten off.

Anspaugh, pleased with himself for inspiring a reaction, turned his attention back to her. "You should stick around. We're getting somewhere. It's been a long trail, but we're close to isolating Lovesprettyboys. We know his general vicinity; now we're zoning in on his real identity."

Lily had longed for that day for months. But now, she had another case to work. Her team needed her, and she wouldn't have the time to help anyone else until the Professor was captured. "Keep me posted, okay? I'd like to hear how it pans out."

His Cro-Magnon brow furrowed in confusion. Lily didn't wait for him to ask why she was acting as if she had only an impartial interest. Her hand still gripping Brandon's arm, she tugged him toward the exit, not releasing him until they'd left the room.

"Asshole," Brandon snapped.

"Yes."

"Acting like Wyatt should hide and pretend he's not even around anymore."

"That's exactly what some people want."

Wyatt Blackstone had gone from rising superstar to ostracized outcast. After he'd blown the whistle and received public commendations, he had quietly been shoved into the Cyber Division. Handed a Cyber Action Team nobody thought would succeed, he'd been expected to keep his mouth shut and put in his time for the next twenty years until his retirement, never to be heard from again.

Fortunately her new boss wasn't wired that way. He was given a job to do, and by God, he was going to do it.

"He should have gotten recognition after the Reaper

case. Not to mention support and resources for the team." Brandon sounded as frustrated as Lily felt when the subject came up.

He was absolutely right. But it hadn't happened. Oh, they'd gotten credit for solving it, but the investigation hadn't been deemed entirely successful. The team had known someone was going to be killed and had known how it would happen, yet they still hadn't been able to prevent it. Plus, once they had identified him, the perpetrator had leaped out of the hands of justice by leaping into his own noose.

"So what's with you and Anspaugh?" Brandon asked as they walked down the corridor. "You cheating on me? Messing around with somebody else's hard drive?"

She laughed softly. Brandon was hot, but he was also young, probably no more than twenty-five or -six. Not to mention a player. Their relationship was strictly platonic, meaning she could appreciate his hotness without actually being burned and enjoy his playfulness without being played.

"Seriously. What's up?"

"I've been lending a hand now and then on the Loves-prettyboys investigation."

His trendy glasses couldn't conceal the sympathetic look in his eyes. Brandon knew Lily's story; everyone on the team did, except the new guy, Lambert. "I see."

Immediately defensive, she explained, "I asked Wyatt if I could work it on my own time before we caught the Reaper."

She should have known Brandon wouldn't leave it alone. One brow arched in frank disbelief. "And he said yes?"

Catching her bottom lip between her teeth, she hesitated before replying, "Yes. He did."

He pressed harder. "Recently? Even after the site went dark and the investigation turned to the users of it, not the owners?"

She didn't answer. Here was where it got particularly sticky.

"I get it. And begging forgiveness is easier than asking permission?"

"Something like that." She didn't ask Brandon to cover for her. She wasn't totally sure she'd done anything wrong, but just in case, she wasn't about to drag him into it with her.

"Okay. I guess you know what you're doing. Please, though, don't let it get to you." His handsome face growing more serious, he added, "If it starts to get in your head, promise me you'll walk away."

A laugh, small and bitter, escaped her mouth. "Oh, my friend, you don't even want to know the kinds of things that go on in my head."

She began walking again, telling him without words the subject was closed. Though Lily appreciated his warning, and knew it came from a good place, she was far beyond being warned. He hadn't worn her shoes, lived what she'd lived. Few people had or ever would in their lifetime.

I'm doing okay. As long as I have the job, I'm fine.

Yeah. The job. It kept her moving forward, one foot at a time, one case at a time, one scumbag at a time.

There would be more than that someday. There had to be. They said after every nightmare came another dawn, and Lily Fletcher believed it.

She had to. Because God help her if it wasn't true.

Sixteen and dead.

Sixteen and murdered.

Sam couldn't speak for a moment after the FBI special agent in her kitchen broke the news. In fact, she couldn't quite breathe. Or hear. Or think.

Rising from her chair, she walked as if in a daze to the sink. She leaned over it, turned on the faucet, and splashed cold water on her face, needing to clear her

head and get a grip on her emotions. Sam kept her back
to the man whose professional expression had not entirely hidden his sympathy. He knew she had barely
known Ryan Smith. Yet he also knew she was devastated by his death. Which said either that the man had
very good intuition, or that Sam was very bad at disguis-
ing her feelings.

"Are you all right?" he asked from behind her.

Sam nodded, saying nothing as she grabbed a paper
towel and dried her face. The cold water had snapped
her out of her moment of shock, though she didn't turn
around right away. She wanted a little more time, a second or two to pretend she had merely imagined a nice
young kid she knew had been murdered.

Then she remembered something. "Wilmington." She
spun around. "I saw a story blurb online about missing
Delaware teens found in a frozen pond."

He nodded once, confirming the suspicion.

She shuddered. What a horrible way to die. "How can
you be so sure he didn't fall through the ice? How do
you know he was murdered?"

"Trust me."

Two words she never wanted to hear coming out of a
man's mouth again. "I don't even know you."

"I mean, trust me when I say there is no way it was an
accident." His jaw flexing, he bit out a reluctant explanation. "They were bound."

She closed her eyes briefly as her stomach churned
and her throat tightened.

"They," she mumbled, acknowledging the rest of
it. "Were they random victims? Or was the other boy
someone Ryan knew?"

"His best friend."

Two teenage boys. This was more awful by the moment. "His friend—not the friend he was writing to ask
me about? Not the one who was being taken in by an
e-mail scheme?"

Agent Lambert nodded, his sympathy still evident. And suddenly she realized why he was here. Why he was asking these questions. Why he had come to her. It was more than the fact that they'd exchanged a few e-mails. Much more.

"My God. Were they killed by whoever was trying to scam him?"

He didn't answer her question, countering with several of his own. "Is there anything else you can remember about your interactions with Ryan Smith? Did he mention even in passing where he might be headed that night or who he was meeting?"

"That night?" she asked, gulping as she realized the hits hadn't stopped coming. "The night he IM'd me?"

"Yes."

She shuffled to her chair and sank onto it. Like most people, Sam read the news; she was aware awful things happened to people every single day. She'd been touched by tragedy herself, with the accidental death of her father when she'd been only eleven.

But these were just kids. Nice, friendly kids whose only crimes had been gullibility and loyalty. Kids who'd ended up on the bottom of a frozen lake, never to go to their senior prom or set off for college or meet the right girl and get married. All that possibility—gone.

And if she hadn't gone out for a loaf of bread, a gallon of milk, and some damned ice cream, and had been home to answer Ryan Smith's instant message, they might be alive today.

"There's nothing you could have done," Lambert said. He moved behind her, but she didn't turn around, not even when he dropped a hand onto her shoulder and gently squeezed.

It was the first intimate touch she had received from a man in almost a year.

Even Uncle Nate—her late father's partner in the force, whom her mother leaned on for everything except romance—did nothing more than shake her hand when they saw each other. As if he recognized the mental barricade she had erected between herself and any man.

This man hadn't seen that barricade. And Sam found herself going very still, trying to decide how she felt about it.

When she'd pictured being touched again by a male of the species, she'd had typical divorcée daydreams. Running into her ex and his skank-ho with Josh Duhamel on one arm and Johnny Depp on the other. That would be good. Not this. Not comfort from a complete stranger.

But then, never in her darkest dreams had she envisioned getting caught up in a double murder investigation, or that her heart would feel on the verge of breaking over a sweet teenager she barely knew.

"You can't blame yourself," the agent said, his hand still heavy and warm on her shoulder. "The scam was convincing. I think the other boy would have gone no matter what you said, and Ryan would have tagged along with him. They had that kind of friendship."

She nodded, appreciating the words, knowing they could be true. She had Tricia, her own through-thick-or-thin friend, and they would do anything for each other. So maybe her being home and trying to talk Ryan out of going with his buddy by IM wouldn't have changed a thing.

But maybe it would have.

"You okay?"

Sam tore her thoughts off the dark imaginings of the boys' final moments and became more aware of the pressure of his strong hand on her shoulder. It didn't feel threatening or inappropriate. This man was a stranger, however. Besides, she had spent the last several months telling herself she would never lean on another man again.

Still, the small bit of human connection felt nice. Very nice.

Before she could say a word, a sharp knock intruded from the front of the apartment. It was repeated a split second later, the impatience of the person audible in the hard punctuation of knuckle on wood.

Agent Lambert stepped away. Looking up, Sam saw a quick frown cross his face and knew he regretted stepping out of professional bounds, even if only for a moment. Sam couldn't bring herself to regret it, though. The quieting touch had existed long enough for her to swallow down her emotions and stop herself from bursting into tears at the utter senselessness of Ryan Smith's murder.

"I'm sure that's my partner."

"I would bet she's going to be in a bad mood," Sam said, glad for the distraction. "No way did she get off without a ticket."

"We're law enforcement on official business. He might have made her jump through a hoop or two, but there's no way she got cited."

Maybe. But those hoops had probably reached his not-petite partner's chin.

Leaving the kitchen, she went to the door and opened it. The attractive female FBI agent wore a scowl and her lips were thin. "Special Agent Jackie Stokes," she said, sticking out her hand. "Sorry for the disruption."

Sam shook it, liking the other woman's strong grip, not to mention the look of intelligence in her brown eyes. Sam suspected the gruff Agent Stokes was an excellent foil for her too-handsome-for-his-own-good partner. Stokes could undoubtedly intimidate a suspect with her clipped tone and hard stare. Just by virtue of his looks, Lambert could probably say *please* and have any woman ready to spill her guts about anything he asked.

Except her. She was immune to anything resembling charm. She'd had an inoculation the size of a two-liter bottle of Coke injected into her veins courtesy of her ex-husband. Masculine charm was no threat to her at all.

But niceness, like the comforting drop of a hand on a shoulder? Well, with too much of that she could be in trouble.

"I've filled Mrs. Dalton in on our investigation," Agent Lambert said. He'd followed Sam into the living room, which seemed to shrink around the three of them.

Sam had liked the confined space after her divorce, liked having almost no cleaning to do, no monstrous, five-thousand-square-foot house to take care of anymore. That, however, was before she'd realized she'd be entertaining FBI agents in her dinky city apartment.

"Coffee?" she asked Agent Stokes, who had removed her long overcoat and shivered lightly. The woman nodded once.

Going to pour her a cup, Sam half listened from the kitchen as the male FBI agent filled his colleague in on what he'd learned since his arrival. Special Agent Stokes appeared as interested in the bogus-check angle as he had been, and even more in the instant messages.

Sam's fingers tightened on the stoneware mug when she thought of Ryan's desperate IMs that had gone unread. But she forced the emotion away, knowing there was no time to deal with it now. Later, when she was alone, she'd let herself dwell on the regret. On the guilt. Now, though, she needed to try to gain momentary absolution from the guilt in any way she could—starting by doing anything possible to help solve the boys' murder.

By the time Sam returned, holding the steaming cup, the two agents were seated on her sofa, poring over an open folder and flipping through pages made yellow with sticky notes and file tabs. In their excitement, they'd shoved her clean laundry out of the way. It sat on the cushion beside Alec Lambert.

Perfect. Considering there was a plain, serviceable white bra sticking out of the pile, she couldn't say that made her day. And she didn't even want to think about whether either agent had read the front of the pink nightshirt that read, GRADUATE OF THE SCHOOL OF ALL MEN SUCK, a divorce gift from Tricia.

So stop living like a slob. She would. Starting the minute these two left. Which, judging by their intense conversation, they didn't seem in any hurry to do.

"If Jason deposited the check, we'll be able to find who sent it to him," Stokes was saying, animated and visibly energized by the idea.

Sam grunted, and both pairs of eyes shifted in her direction.

Feeling intrusive, even though they'd made themselves at home on her couch and her laundry, she murmured, "The check would be fake. Fake name, fake account, coming from nowhere, going nowhere." When they merely stared, she added, "I guess it's possible he left a fingerprint; you guys would know more about that than I would. But from the sound of it, this killer's not stupid, so I can't picture him being so careless."

"He's not," Agent Lambert muttered, sounding frustrated.

Almost wishing she'd kept her mouth shut, Sam quickly said, "Look, forget it; go after the check angle. I could be wrong; maybe he's not as good at check fraud as most of these lowlifes are."

"It's that common?" Lambert asked, though, as a cyber crimes expert, he should know.

Sam laughed bitterly. "You wouldn't believe how common. I could paper my ex's house with the fake certified checks passed via Craigslist sales alone. There are warnings everywhere on the site, but people still fall for the 'My secretary sent you a check for a thousand dollars more than the asking price by mistake. Please cash it and wire me back the difference' line."

"Sure." Stokes appeared familiar with the scheme. "Then they cash it, send back the money, the check bounces, and the bank comes after them to repay it."

"Exactly. If there was a good way to stop the fraud

and trace the criminals who perpetrate it, you FBI types would be all over it already and would have a way to catch this murderer."

The two FBI types exchanged a quick look, obviously hearing her icy tone. Sam couldn't help it. The FBI had never been her biggest fan, even though they were on the same side, and, frankly, the feeling was mutual. They'd been no help to her family three years ago, when everything had gone so wrong.

Maybe she should thank them, though. If not for the callousness of the agents she'd gone to for help when her grandmother had been taken in by some ruthless Internet con men, Sam might not ever have launched her new career. She might not have become an Internet vigilante, the author of a best-selling book. And might not have been able to afford to tell Samuel to shove his alimony money the same place he'd shoved his broken marriage vows.

Not that she wouldn't happily trade it all to have her grandmother alive and well today.

"So how would you suggest the authorities handle it?" Special Agent Lambert asked, sounding more interested than sarcastic.

"Education," she replied. "And I am not all about lots of government intrusion, but subjecting the online auction and classified sites to some kind of vetting and oversight would be a good thing, rather than leaving them completely unregulated, free to be filled with thieves and, obviously, murderers."

She sounded bitter because she was. Even three years after her grandmother's death, her anger toward the con artists who'd contributed to it still sometimes threatened to choke her.

Agent Stokes frowned. "I've been working in the Cyber Division for years. You want to talk about education? I can't tell you how often we get the word out. And there are big warning notices on these sites you mentioned. Only a fool would overlook them."

Wrong thing to say. Sam's spine went pole straight. "Or a lonely, trusting old person who has never dealt with the kind of high-tech deceit these bastards practice." Realizing her personal feelings were coloring her comments, she quickly got back to the topic at hand, the reason they were here. Not her own history. "Or a bright teenager who thinks he's too smart to ever be taken and has in his hand what looks like an incredibly real check with a lot of zeroes."

The other woman nodded once, acknowledging the point.

Before Sam could say another word, the phone on her desk rang. She didn't answer, not only not in the mood to talk to anyone, but unwilling to delay or inconvenience the agents who were trying to do their job. The sooner they left, the better. She wanted to be alone—needed to be alone to wrap her mind around the sad news Agent Lambert had brought her.

They both watched her expectantly, and when they realized she was ignoring the call, nodded in appreciation. Unfortunately, though, her answering machine wasn't muted. So all three of them were able to hear Tricia Scott, her best friend since middle school, whose volume control had two settings: loud and earsplitting. "Girl, pick up! I know you're there; don't be all cyber silent on me."

Oh, hell.

"I've got to talk to you. I met a guy last night, and he has a friend who is so hot he'll make you want to—"

She lunged for the phone, yanking it to her ear. "I'm here, but I can't talk."

"You don't need to talk; just listen. We're goin' out Friday night, and I won't take no for an answer. 'Cause if you don't get out and start getting a little, your girl parts are gonna dry up and fall off from lack of use."

Across from her, Agent Stokes snorted, then bent over her coffee cup, her shoulders shaking. Her partner had lifted one brow, a small smile playing on those sexy lips.

Which was when she realized her answering machine was still recording, amplifying every word her friend had said.

"Oh, my God. Tricia, the answering machine is broadcasting everything you say, and I am *not* alone." She hung up without another word, jerking her chin in the air, silently daring either of the two agents to so much as let their eyes twinkle. She had to hand it to them: They both managed to pretend they hadn't heard a thing. Which gave her the strength to open her mouth to proceed as if nothing had happened.

Then her answering machine beeped loudly, indicating she had a message. And the female agent chuckled.

Sam closed her eyes, not knowing whether to laugh, cry, or get up and leave the room. Her emotions were a wreck; she felt like a Ping-Pong ball, bouncing from sadness to embarrassment, mourning to humiliation. She didn't know how much more she could take before either bursting into tears or punching something.

Agent Lambert seemed to realize it. He somehow managed to go right back to what they had been talking about, not giving the phone call another moment's attention. "You mentioned online classified sites," he said, fixing those green eyes firmly on her face. "How often do you hear about crimes that don't involve a certified check or money wiring, but physical assaults?"

Sam took a deep, even breath, following his lead and forgetting the call. Sitting at her desk, she replied, "All the time. People show up to look at a couch advertised online and find themselves the victim of strong-armed robbery. Or they're trying to sell their gas-guzzling SUV and are carjacked. I hear from victims every single day." She clicked her keyboard, quickly bringing up her own Web site. "I did a feature post on that issue six weeks ago, with tips on how to avoid being victimized. Starting with *never* going alone to see someone you've only met online. Whether it's for a sale, a job interview, a dating service . . ."

Dating service. Her mother's latest brilliant idea. God, if she went through with it, Sam was going to tie up the fifty-going-on-fifteen-year-old woman and lock her in the basement. The idea had upset her so much, Sam had done a rant about the dangers two weeks ago. Uncle Nate had even tried talking to Mom. He'd been a cop many years ago, and now as a judge he saw some awful stuff on a daily basis. But he'd had no more luck than Sam. Her mother simply had no yellow warning light in her brain; she was all green, all the time.

Kind of like Tricia.

"Job interview?" Agent Lambert said, exchanging a meaningful look with his partner.

Sam nodded. "Sure. There was a case about a month and a half ago of a woman killed when she responded to an online help-wanted listing."

As if thinking in tandem, knowing they had gotten as much as they could out of her, the two agents rose. "We know," Lambert said.

She sensed they knew a lot. A whole lot. But she wasn't exactly in a position to ask them to share. And honestly, she didn't want them to. Realizing she'd had a brush with one murder victim, however slightly, was going to keep her up tonight. She didn't want to picture all the other ugly things these agents had to deal with.

"Here's my card," Agent Lambert said. Before he passed it to her, he grabbed an expensive-looking pen from his inside jacket pocket and scratched through the phone number, scrawling another. "This is my cell number. If you think of anything else regarding your interactions with Ryan Smith, please let us know."

Agent Stokes blew out a huffy breath and tugged her own business card out of her pocket. "Here. The office number. Call either of us if you come up with anything else."

Realizing Lambert had given her his personal number, Sam swallowed quickly. What was she supposed to make of that?

"I was recently reassigned and haven't had time to get new business cards printed up," he said, as if reading her thoughts and sending a gentle message of clarification.

His partner was less gentle. "Yeah, and he hasn't even had time to memorize his new work number yet."

Okay, clarified. Sam mentally kicked herself for the moment of wondering. Why should it matter, anyway? Even if the good-looking agent had wanted her to get in touch with him for private reasons, Sam wouldn't necessarily do it.

Not interested. Nice touch or not.

Especially not since he'd just heard her best friend talking about her drying-up girl parts.

Agent Stokes tugged on her coat, nodded at Sam, and said, "Thanks for the coffee," before heading out the front door.

Lambert began to follow, then paused to extend his hand. As Sam took it, she noted the sympathy still evident in his eyes. "I know you're blaming yourself, and it won't do any good to tell you not to. Logically, you're smart enough to know there's nothing you could have done. Emotionally, though, you're not ready to believe it."

Sam nodded once, wondering if she was usually so easy to read or if it was just this particular FBI agent's forte.

"Remember, the man who did this is good at what he does, and his victims usually want to believe the line he's selling them. I think you could have stood in the driveway and tried to physically block the other boy's car, and he would have driven around you, his buddy Ryan Smith riding shotgun the way he had throughout their lives."

Then, with a final encouraging nod, he walked out the door, letting Sam return to her solitary night. And her work.

The work, however, didn't come easily. Sitting at her desk, she kept going over everything she'd been told, picturing those poor boys. Wondering yet again why people put themselves in such dangerous situations.

"Mom," she whispered. Would her crazy, irresponsible mother really go through with her Internet dating idea? Hard to believe, but yes, Sam knew damn well she would.

Knowing she'd never be able to focus until she tried to do something, she grabbed her iPhone, wanting to talk to Uncle Nate about it. Since she never knew what his court schedule was like, she didn't try just voice dialing. Besides, the middle-aged man liked to try out every new high-tech toy he could find, and texting had become his new "thing."

Her thumbs clicking on the keypad, she typed, *U there?*

His response came less than sixty seconds later: *Sure, kiddo. Whasup?*

Any luck w/ Mom re e-dating craziness?

Talked 2 her again. Doubt she lstnd.

Sam gritted her teeth. *Maybe we shld lock hr up & thro away key.*

Better u thn me.

Yeah, her mother definitely had a mind of her own. *Wl u keep tryng pls?*

U got it! TTYL.

He even had the lingo down. Cute.

But her smile quickly faded. Yes, she had backup to help deal with her mother's situation. If only she'd been able to do something about Ryan Smith's.

Swiveling her chair, she faced her monitor again, pulling up the column she'd been writing before the FBI agents had arrived and blown a sad hole in her safe, normal day. Glancing it over, she realized it just wasn't good enough. Though she hadn't known him well, she owed Ryan something, if only a few words warning others against sharing his fate.

Sam certainly wasn't stupid enough to reveal any information about an ongoing criminal investigation. Still, part of her needed to vent, to release some of the anguish and rage she'd felt since learning Ryan had been murdered. So when she put her hands on her keyboard, she did not add to those six hundred words she'd written before Alec Lambert had walked through her front door. She instead opened a blank document.

And ranted.

Chapter 4

Wendy Cramer had a secret. A delicious, wonderful secret.

She was in love.

She had never experienced that emotion before. Not really. She couldn't call the feelings she had for the newscaster on channel nine love. After all, she knew him only from the TV; she'd never really spoken to him, even though he spoke to her every night at five and eleven.

This was different. This was real. And not only was she in love, but she had the feeling he loved her, too.

Most miraculous of all, he was a duke or a lord. Maybe even a prince. He hadn't said.

Bona fide royalty.

Rafe hadn't wanted to admit it at first, so she knew he wasn't making things up. She'd been the one who'd focused on his screen name, who'd read between the lines of his comments in the chat room where they'd met. Only after they'd e-mailed several times had he told her the truth about himself, so used to being betrayed he hadn't trusted her immediately.

"I can be trusted," she whispered as she lay in her narrow bed Wednesday morning. The luxury of sleeping in on a workday had come at a perfect time, since she'd had the most wonderful dreams and would have hated for them to end with the shrill shriek of an alarm. She'd taken the next three days off from her job as an answering service operator, and was free to drift in and out between those sweet dreams and sweeter reality. Thoughts of Rafe had filled her mind, swelling her imagination since their last conversation late the night before.

She flung back the covers, not trying to hide her giggles. Her roommate, Sarah, had left two hours ago and couldn't overhear. Good thing, since Sarah was already suspicious, asking why Wendy was online all the time and whom she was instant messaging with. Her friend found it odd that Wendy had requested the rest of the week off, using valuable vacation time so soon after the holidays.

She trusted her friend, really. But even somebody as nice as Sarah could accidentally let something slip, exposing the prince—or duke or whatever—to danger. So it was best to do as he asked, keeping their online relationship a secret from everyone for the time being.

But not for much longer. Soon there would be no reason for the secrecy. They would be together, a normal couple. She had to get over her shyness and her silly fears and do what her heart had been telling her to do. There was one step to take before they could move on with what she knew would be the most important relationship of her life.

She had to meet him face-to-face.

As she looked at her reflection in the mirror, she wondered if he would notice the few strands of gray in her dark brown hair or the tiny lines at the corners of her eyes. She hadn't lied about her age when she'd first begun to chat with InXile in a chat room a few weeks ago. She really was in her mid-thirties, as long as you considered thirty-eight to be the end of the mids.

Besides, he clearly didn't care about things like age or looks or the fact that she was a small-town girl at heart, still half-scared of her own shadow even after ten years of living in Baltimore.

He was patient, kind, and warm. Everything she'd ever dreamed of. The perfect man. Hers for the taking. She just had to step out there and take him.

"Soon," she told her reflection. This vacation time had been about getting herself ready, mentally and physically. Starting with a visit to the beauty salon for a color job. Maybe even some highlights. Then a trip to the mall for some new clothes.

She had to look perfect. Even if the world could never know her love was a prince, deep down, Wendy wanted to look good enough to be his princess.

And once she was ready, she'd take a deep breath and set up a meeting with her destiny.

Last night, after completing his long second day on his new job, Alec should have gone home, had a beer, thought about how much he missed the dog he no longer had, thanks to the girlfriend he no longer had—whom he did not miss—then grabbed a bite and read over his case files.

He hadn't. Instead, he'd had something else to focus on, something to read other than dry reports and files.

Her book. Samantha Dalton's.

"Damn, she's good," he told himself as he flipped through its pages again in his office Wednesday morning. The first time, he had read it in one long sitting. Today, he'd gone over it again more slowly, making notes and jotting questions.

Alec had come from the BAU, not the Cyber Division. But he had still always considered himself pretty savvy when it came to making sure no scumbag online con artist absconded with his social security number or hacked into his bank accounts.

After reading Sam the Spaminator's book, however, he had begun to realize he knew almost nothing about the subject she was so passionate about. Phishing, sure, he'd heard of it. But SMiShing? Pharming? Spoofing? Ponzi? Keylogging? Matrix schemes? Pump-and-dumps? The list was never-ending. And even though he didn't see himself ever getting caught up in one, it was all too easy to see John Q. Public clicking on the wrong link and inadvertently offering some thug the keys to his entire financial life.

She was good. The book was well written and informative. But it also had a snappy, ironic zing to it, at odds with the morose woman he'd met.

She interested him, the puzzle of her life confusing. Her looks had been obvious, her personality not so much. Her loud friend had made it sound as though she was single, yet Sam had insisted on being called Mrs. Unless she had just moved in, he couldn't imagine a recent breakup, because there'd been no sign of a man in her shoebox-size apartment crammed with feminine furniture and feminine laundry.

God help him for his moment of insanity when he realized he was sitting on a pair of her skimpy cotton underwear.

"Forget her," he told himself as he sipped his coffee—his third cup of the morning.

But he wouldn't forget her writing. Her book had exposed the possibilities. If the Professor really was luring his victims using the latest Internet scams, there was almost no limit to what he could do. And given the statistics Samantha Dalton quoted, there was an untold number of people who fell for these things every single day.

Would all of them drive to meet a stranger in the middle of a blizzard? Probably not. But it didn't take all. It took only one. Or two, as poor Jason Todd and Ryan Smith could attest.

Why did they do it?

Not just Jason and Ryan, but all of the Professor's victims. Though he wasn't a doctor, his dual major in criminal justice and psychology, and his background in profiling, had him very curious. What had made them trust a stranger they'd met only on the Internet? And how did the unsub know who would respond to which lure? Both of those things could be very important to figuring out the identity of the killer.

In her book, Sam had mentioned interviewing a number of victims of cyber crime, as well as perpetrators. Which meant she was a step up on him in understanding the motivations of these people. Which meant she could be a big help.

Knowing it might not do any good, he still found Sam Dalton's phone number in his notes and punched it in.

She answered on the third ring, mumbling a distracted, "Hello?"

"Mrs. Dalton? This is Special Agent Alec Lambert. Do you have a moment?"

"Sure, what can I do for you?" she said, clearing her throat. Her voice sounded husky, with an I-just-woke-up note of sexiness that his whole body responded to.

"Did I wake you?" he asked, wishing he'd kept his mouth shut rather than admit he'd been thinking about her in her bed.

"Yeah, pathetic, I know. I'm a night owl. If you'd called at three a.m., you would have heard me chipper and perky." She sighed. "Well, maybe not chipper. And definitely not perky. Haven't had that word used in a description of me in a long time."

Perky wasn't nearly a good enough word to describe her. Sexy. Wounded. Intriguing. Any of those would be much better, not that he was about to say so.

"How can I help you?" she asked with an audible yawn.

He forced away thoughts of everything but the case. "I've been reading your book."

"You and every other cyber crimes nerd who wants to shut me down."

He couldn't contain a low chuckle. "Actually, it's just the opposite. I'm hoping you can help me."

He quickly explained what he was looking for, still not sure she could assist him, but unable to regret making the call. That one dig, which sounded so much like the woman who'd written the entertaining book he'd read, made it entirely worthwhile.

"So you're basically asking what kind of person allows himself to be victimized in this way. Didn't we talk about this yesterday?"

"I mean beyond the non-cyber-savvy, vulnerable elderly or the teenager who wants to get rich quick. I'm looking for the psychological slant, of both the victims and the perpetrators."

She didn't respond at first. Through the phone, he heard her moving around. A quick visual of her in that nightshirt shot through his mind, but he shut it down.

"I think with the victims, it's an it-won't-happen-to-me philosophy," she finally said. "People always truly believe good things can happen to them—like winning a lottery jackpot despite having a better chance of contracting Ebola. Conversely, the bad things are always reserved for someone else."

True.

"So despite the warnings all over the news, they are still convinced they are much too savvy to be taken in by a fake Rolex hawked by a guy on the corner. . . ."

"Or a check-kiting scam for something they sold on eBay," he said.

"Exactly. It's the innate desire of people to believe they're smart that gets them every time. At least, that's what Flynt says."

"Who?"

"James Tucker Flynt."

"The name sounds familiar." He tried to place the memory.

"It should. Your agency busted him several years ago.

He did five years in federal prison; now he's locked up on state convictions in Maryland. He was a pioneer in the Internet fraud movement." Her voice dripped disgust. "One of the founding fathers, you might say."

He thought about it. "I think I remember that case."

"He'd be so pleased," she said. "He's charming, in an aw-shucks way. You can almost see how people fell for his shtick. And the ego is something to behold."

"You *know* him?"

"I interviewed him, and his attorney, when I was writing my book. Who better to reveal how these scams work and what the dangers are than someone who invented and ran them, and the man who defended him?"

"He actually talked to you about his crimes?"

"Yes. Like I said, ego. Plus I guess he doesn't get many visitors; the warden said Flynt has turned down other journalists, but he heard I was young and attractive, so he accepted." She sighed audibly. "I think he likes me a little too much. I get letters from him just about every week."

"You actually went to a maximum-security prison to talk to this man," he said, dumbfounded by the idea.

"Medium-security."

Semantics.

He stood and stared at the stained wall of his office, the phone held tightly in his grip. Something inside him rebelled at the very thought of the beautiful, intelligent woman walking into a prison to talk to a scumbag like Flynt. But he kept his reaction to himself. "And the letters? What do they say?"

"I have no idea. I stopped opening them. In fact, just a few days ago I decided to try to get the message across to him, so I put them all in a large envelope and mailed it to the warden with 'refused by addressee' written on the outside."

Okay, so she was handling the situation with the same common sense he'd seen in her book. Still, the idea that she'd gone there, started a relationship with a scummy criminal, bothered him. A lot. "Are you telling me your book was worth exposing yourself to someone like that?"

"I didn't *expose* myself," she snapped. "But yes, the project meant a great deal to me. I have a background as a journalist, and I'm used to doing whatever it takes to get the story."

Knowing he had offended her, he muttered, "I see."

God, he had blown this. He had let his completely unexpected reaction to her mold his responses to things that were none of his business. "I'm sorry for disturbing you. Thanks for your help."

"You're welcome, Agent Lambert. Good luck to you." Her voice no longer sounded sleepy and sexy, but decidedly cool.

Yeah, he'd definitely blown it.

She didn't ask him to call back if he needed more assistance, didn't hint in any way that she was bothered they would likely never speak again. Which should be a very good thing. But somehow, as he ended the call and hung up, Alec couldn't help wondering if he'd just missed out on something pretty fantastic.

After a brief, restless night, and an annoying morning phone conversation with a sexy FBI agent who had passed judgment on the choices she'd made regarding her book, Sam really wasn't in the mood for company. Especially not male company. Still, when someone knocked on her door at around noon, her first thought was of Agent Lambert, and her pulse doubled its speed.

Her second thought was that she hadn't put the Do Not Disturb sign up. So she might instead be getting a visit from her nosy, chatty neighbor, whose "Bal'mer" accent was so thick Sam sometimes didn't even understand what the woman was saying.

Feeling kind of like the guy who'd opened the door

not knowing whether he would see the lady or the tiger, she turned the knob. And found herself face-to-face with option three. The lawyer.

"Rick?" she murmured, both surprised and wary.

"Hello, Mrs. Dalton," he said, stepping closer to the doorjamb, shivering a little as he tried to avoid the bitter January wind.

Let him in, her polite mother's voice whispered in her head.

But she couldn't do it. She just couldn't.

Most women would probably like having two different, very good-looking men show up on her doorstep two days in a row. But not Sam. No matter how much she respected Rick Young, who'd done a great job handling her divorce, she could never get past the thought of him being privy to all the painful, ugly details of the final days of her marriage.

Sure, he was nice, and successful, and he obviously liked her. But this man had read the awful things her ex had said about her. He'd seen the disgusting pictures—vivid proof of her husband's infidelity. He'd heard her break down and weep during mediation. He'd witnessed her at her very lowest point.

Some chapters of her life just needed to remain closed, including that one. So there was no way she could ever be comfortable getting too friendly with this man, no matter how attractive he was, with his handsome face, sandy blond hair, and solid, strong body.

"I would have called, but I was driving by here on my way out to take a deposition." He lifted a gloved hand, extending a large manila envelope. "My assistant reminded me of this a few days ago. It's about to expire. I wasn't sure if you were ready to take it."

She eyed the envelope, feeling as if she were face-to-face with a poisonous snake. Because she had no doubt about what it contained. "I told you I didn't want it."

"I know. I just wasn't sure if you'd change your mind.

You are entitled to this money under the terms of the divorce. Actually, you were entitled to a lot more, and you could have gotten it if you'd demanded it."

She didn't want her ex-husband's payoff money any more now than she had a year ago, when their divorce had been finalized. Frankly, she hadn't expected Rick to hold on to the certified check that had shown up a few weeks after the final decree came through.

"I haven't changed my mind."

"I understand. Still, you do need to be the one to do something with it."

She contemplated tearing the entire envelope in half, check included. But she suddenly hesitated, realizing that while she didn't want any money from the Dalton family, others might.

"Wait." Grabbing a pen from a table by the door, she yanked the envelope from him, tore it open, and scribbled on the back of the check, not even glancing at the numbers on the front. "There. Will you make sure the Red Cross gets it?"

A small, admiring smile widened his mouth and he nodded once. "Yes, I will." He took the check from her and tucked it back in the envelope. Then, his voice lowering a little, he murmured, "Are you doing well?"

"Fine," she replied, steeling herself for what she knew was coming next. God, she didn't want to come right out and tell the man why she wasn't interested.

"I was wondering, now that it's been a year, if perhaps we might—"

Suddenly her phone rang, and she was literally saved by the bell. Sam eyed it, then offered him an apologetic shrug. "Sorry, I'm expecting an important call. Thanks so much for stopping by—I hope that money does some good for people who need it." Meaning it, she added, "It's nice to have it over with once and for all."

"Mrs. Dalton ... Samantha," he said, glancing back and forth between her and the phone, speaking quickly and obviously uncomfortable at being rushed, "would you like to go to dinner with me?"

There was no easy way out of this. No simple explanation. So she had to provide a simple answer without even trying to explain. Her tone as gentle as her expression, she murmured, "I don't think so. But thank you very much."

Rick stared, and she hoped he saw the finality in her face. Eventually he replied, "You're welcome."

Without giving him a chance to say more, Sam reached for the phone. She waved good-bye to Young as she picked it up without even glancing at the caller ID.

Noting the lawyer's broad shoulders were perhaps a bit slumped as he walked away, she felt her heart twist. Maybe she'd been a little abrupt, but getting the message across that she wasn't interested was like pulling off a bandage: best done quickly.

The phone tucked into the curve of her neck, she shut and locked the door as she mumbled, "Hello?"

"Mrs. Dalton? This is Martin Connolly."

She hesitated, not placing the name.

He cleared his throat, then, with a note of irritation in his voice, added, "I'm the warden at the Maryland House of Corrections. You visited here?"

"Of course," she said, suddenly remembering the warden, whom she had met when she'd gone to interview Jimmy Flynt for her book. The older man had been a bit pompous, a bureaucrat through and through. Flynt's defense attorney, Dale Carter, had told her Connolly had completely turned the previously troubled facility around during his tenure.

"I'm calling about your package."

She sank into a chair, realizing he meant Jimmy's letters. "Yes?"

"I assume you intentionally returned them? That they weren't delivered to an incorrect address?"

"That's right. I'm sorry, I should have written to explain. Frankly, I wanted them out of here."

"Very well. Before I destroy them, though, I wished to assure you that no mail ever leaves this facility without thorough screening. If you were concerned you might read something inappropriate, you needn't have been."

"That wasn't it. I just needed to cut the connection. I don't want to encourage Mr. Flynt into thinking we have any sort of personal relationship."

"Wise," he said. "He's not the kind of man you want for your friend or your enemy. I think you're right in ending any contact." He hesitated for a moment, as if debating whether to continue, then added, "Mr. Flynt may seem harmless, friendly, and cooperative now that he's safely locked away. But I fear he does still have substantial reach. The man has contacts, friends on the outside who might do favors for him."

She tensed. "Favors? Should I be concerned?"

Another hesitation, as if he wanted to warn her but didn't quite know what he was warning her against; then he said, "No, no. I'm sure there's nothing to worry about. I just wanted to reiterate that I think you've done the right thing. I'll destroy the letters and make sure no more are forwarded." Another brief delay; then he mumbled, "Though perhaps it's wise not to let Jimmy know that."

His audible concern did little to make her feel better.

Sam thanked him, hung up, then sat down to absorb all that had happened in one short morning.

She'd had a terse final conversation with an FBI agent she couldn't stop thinking about.

She'd refused the attention of a successful, handsome attorney.

She'd given away a small fortune.

She'd been warned that a convicted felon who seemed to have a thing for her might be keeping tabs on her from his prison cell.

All before one o'clock.

Well, there was one silver lining. All those little issues had now been dealt with, and she shouldn't have to worry about a single one of them ever again. Which was fine by her.

Mostly fine.

Because, if she was completely honest with herself, knowing she had shared her final conversation with Special Agent Alec Lambert wasn't fine with Sam at all.

As Lily Fletcher walked through the parking garage Wednesday evening, finally having let Brandon convince her to go home after another long day, she saw a large form lurking in the shadows. She instinctively tightened her hand around her key ring, then laughed at herself. She was at the FBI headquarters building, for God's sake, and she was armed. Why on earth was she reacting like a woman leaving a twenty-four-hour Wal-Mart, who needed to defend herself with a sharp jab of a key?

She hesitated when she realized the person standing by her car was Special Agent Tom Anspaugh. Something big must have happened for him to stake out her vehicle.

"Hello, Anspaugh," she said as she reached him.

"Where have you been? I've been calling."

"I know." Anspaugh had tried to reach her in her office hours ago. She'd been away from her desk. He'd also tried her on her cell. Seeing his name on the caller ID, she'd ignored it.

She had promised Wyatt she would not allow her real job to come second to any side investigations. She meant to keep her word. Besides, there was no way she would bring Brandon any further into the situation. His knowledge that she was proceeding without technically having their boss's permission was bad enough.

Anspaugh, on the other hand, didn't seem to give a damn whether Wyatt approved of what she was up to or not. In fact, she suspected he'd like nothing better than to think Lily was less than loyal, or that her work on the other CAT could inconvenience Blackstone's team.

"I've been very busy; we're working on a case," she explained out of courtesy, not about to let him put her on the defensive. "That came first."

"Oh, right, hunting up phantom killers who attack through the Internet. Is Dr. Horrible sending electric shocks via DSL to strike down anyone who touches his keyboard?"

Jerk. "What is it you want?" she asked. "Has something happened?"

"Yeah. And I want you . . . in on it."

She had the feeling the hesitation between his words had been intentional. Anspaugh had never made a move on her, but she'd seen the way his stare sometimes lingered, noticed how frequently he found an excuse to touch her. Like now, as he moved a bit closer.

She intentionally stepped around him. Even if she weren't a block of solid ice beneath her warm skin, with no interest in being close to anyone ever again, she would have recoiled from that particular touch. Anspaugh might be good-looking in a big-jock-football-player way, but she truly couldn't stand his type.

"Lil?"

God, she hated that nickname. "What happened?"

"You know we were finally able to sift through the history of Satan's Playground and isolate a general geographic area of Lovesprettyboys."

Her stomach knotted, as it always did when she thought of him. "You said as much earlier."

"He's somewhere near Richmond, which is where we've focused our investigation. We've been monitoring message boards, chat rooms, anything that would draw residents in a hundred-mile radius, particularly kids."

"And he showed up?"

"We think so."

"My God," she whispered.

He stiffened. "You sure you're okay talking about this? I mean, with everything else?"

He hadn't been part of the team that had investigated her nephew's case, but he knew about it. Few people working crimes against children didn't. It wasn't every day that kind of tragedy touched one of the bureau's own.

"I'm fine. Tell me what happened."

"One we were watching was a Web site with a bunch of message boards for kids involved in a community program in Williamsburg. Sports, after-school activities, stuff like that."

Classic pedophile territory. She sucked in a breath of freezing air, then, shivering, tugged her coat tighter.

"We're not certain. But there have been a few comments this one supposed kid has made that sound like some things our perp said in the transcripts from Satan's Playground. He didn't use the same handle, of course; he's been posting as Peter Pan."

The boy who never grew up, who wanted only to be with his lost boys. Sick bastard.

"That's not an ID a child would choose." The Peter Pan fantasy was one grown men enjoyed. Certainly not seven-year-olds who were much more into superheroes like Spider-Man or the Dark Knight.

"No, I guess not," Anspaugh said. "We can't know for sure this is the same guy, but there doesn't seem to be much doubt he's a pedophile. So either way, we want him."

"How can I help?"

He smiled down at her, as if she'd offered to do him a personal favor. In truth, she would find it hard to turn on a light if he asked her for personal reasons.

"We've had no luck drawing him out. One of my agents has been posting as an eight-year-old boy, but he can't get anything started with this prick."

"He's going to be incredibly careful, of course," she said. "He would never engage with someone who sought him out. Every pedophile in the country knows those sites are monitored."

"We haven't directly engaged him," he said, an edge of irritation in his voice. He wasn't the type who enjoyed being questioned or corrected.

She ignored him. "So we'd need to come up with a reason for him to seek us out. Something to draw his attention to us, over all the other kids using the site." Many of whom were probably perverts trolling for victims themselves. At least, so thought the pessimist in her.

"Yeah, my thoughts exactly. Which brings me to my point."

"What?"

"I checked out the Peter Pan story, read the book looking for an opening."

Probably the first book he had cracked open since his last college English class.

"Yesterday, when I heard Cole call you Tiger Lily, it all sorta clicked."

She immediately followed. "That name might interest him enough to say hello. As long as we're not too obvious about casting the bait. For instance, if I post on a board he has never commented on as Peter Pan, he might not immediately suspect a setup."

"Right."

The idea wasn't a bad one. No, she still didn't see a real seven- or eight-year-old boy wanting other "big" kids to think he was into Peter Pan. However, girls might still enjoy picturing themselves as fairies like Tinker Bell, or Indian princesses like Tiger Lily.

"Wait," she said, suddenly realizing what she had overlooked. "Lovesprettyboys is into boys. Most sexual abusers are pretty discriminating in their predilections."

"I know." Anspaugh fidgeted. "But it might work anyway, if he's just trying to get in with any kid right now, hoping it'll lead to the right type."

She wondered if he truly believed his own spiel. Or if he had already decided this Peter Pan was not Lovesprettyboys, but wanted Lily's help and figured she'd offer it more readily if she had a personal stake in the case.

Believing he had to manipulate her into wanting to catch a scum who preyed on children, boys or girls, said a lot more about Anspaugh than it did about her. None of it good.

Still, she would help, no question about it. If by chance this Peter Pan was the same monster she'd become obsessed with finding five months ago, when she'd first entered Satan's Playground, all the better.

"If he responds to Tiger Lily and shows serious interest in her, we'll know we're dealing with someone else," she murmured, rubbing her temple as she thought it out. "If, on the other hand, he responds and shows interest in the younger brother Tiger Lily complains about . . ."

Anspaugh barked an approving laugh. "I like the way you think, Fletcher. What a waste, you working for Blackstone."

Her tone frigid, she bit out, "Another crack about Wyatt Blackstone and you can find somebody else to help you. Got it?"

He fell silent, visibly shocked by her words and the way she'd said them.

She couldn't believe the man hadn't noticed her loyalty to her boss by now. Wyatt had given her the opportunity to do something she truly needed to do—help solve violent crimes—in the one way she was skilled to do it: via her computer expertise. Nobody else would have given her the chance, especially not fresh off her family tragedy.

She owed him. She respected him. Furthermore, she liked him. He might leave her tongue-tied half the time, and he might intimidate her with those intense good looks, but she couldn't deny she enjoyed being around him. She almost felt safe with Wyatt. At least, as safe as she ever felt these days.

"I had a couple of friends, good agents, who got caught up in his shit."

"If they were good agents, they wouldn't have been tampering with evidence."

His scowl said she'd scored a hit. She hadn't intended to. She merely wanted him to stop blaming the one person who'd had the guts to do something about the lawlessness he'd seen inside the bureau and place the blame where it belonged: on the lawbreakers.

"You don't know that—"

She cut him off. "I don't want to hear about it, okay? It's not my fight, and it's not yours either. Just so we understand each other." Giving him a pointed stare, she added, "It's been a long day and I want to go home. Are we finished?"

With a tight frown, he got out of her way. "Call me tomorrow," he said, before she could get in, "so we can set this up."

Lily nodded. Then, without another word, she slipped into the driver's seat and shut the door. Not even waiting for the engine to warm up, as she always did, she backed up and drove away, leaving him standing there, watching her as she departed.

Chapter 5

Ever since he'd spoken with Sam Dalton on the phone yesterday morning, Alec had struggled to keep the woman off his mind. Not too hard during the day, when the investigation had been first and foremost.

Nighttime was a different story.

Sleep had proved difficult, and he'd found himself replaying their conversation, wishing he'd been less belligerent. It bothered him that she'd formed an opinion of him as some kind of overbearing he-man because he'd instinctively rebelled against the idea of her being ogled by a sleaze like Flynt. Bothered him so much he barely slept, shutting his eyes only at around four a.m., which caused him to oversleep Thursday.

Fortunately, he lived in a condo in northern Virginia and had commuted down to Quantico when he was with the BAU, so he had been well positioned for the transfer into the city. The drive was shorter in mileage now. Still, the traffic lengthened it to twice what it should be, and there was no way he was going to be on time.

It was a typical morning, roads choked with cars whose bumpers all but kissed. The bridges groaned under the weight of stopped vehicles. Idle drivers familiar with the city's history had uncomfortable flashbacks of the Air

Florida plane hitting the one at Fourteenth Street on a cold day like this. Thick clouds of steam rose from the grates above the Metro, and every few minutes a stream of humanity emerged from the top of the stairs at each station, surging out into the workday. Quite a change from the warm, Southern city where he'd grown up and had been expected to stay.

Frankly, even with the scars from the bullets, he wouldn't change a thing. The idea of showing up every morning for the past ten years at the firm his grandfather had started and his father now ran made him queasy. Handling divorces for socialites who lunched with his mother wasn't his idea of a good job. Another reason to be grateful to Wyatt Blackstone.

Arriving at the Black CATs' suite, he entered his own dingy office and flipped on the light. It flickered overhead, providing just enough weak illumination to showcase the cracks in the floor, the flecks of mildew on the walls, and the water stain on the ceiling.

And yet Alec found himself smiling. It wasn't the slick, glossy office he'd had at the BAU. But it also came without the formality, weight, and competitiveness of that division. He'd been with Blackstone's CAT for only a few days, yet he'd already noted the intense loyalty of the people who worked for the man and the cohesiveness of the unit.

As soon as he set his leather briefcase on the battered desk he'd been assigned, his new partner entered the office. "You're late. I was beginning to wonder if you were coming back."

"Was there any doubt?"

"There was some question about whether you'd show up at all on Tuesday, after you got a taste of what you were in for on your first day. It's lightened up every day since." She glanced at the clock. "But when we hit eight ten without seeing your pretty face, I had to wonder."

Jackie's curiosity had been restrained for most of

the week. Obviously her restraint had run out. "Why wouldn't I come back?"

"Kind of slumming, aren't you? I mean, you being a BAU hotshot and all."

"If you know anything about me, you know I wore out my welcome with the BAU."

"Yeah, got your ass shot last summer, right when we needed your help nailing that psycho Reaper."

Alec frowned, not liking the reminder. Not merely about the shooting—hell, the scars and occasional twinge of pain wouldn't let him forget it. But he didn't like to think he might have been in any way responsible for delaying the capture of the murderer, Seth Covey, who'd killed several innocent victims for the viewing pleasure of a bunch of sickos on an Internet site called Satan's Playground.

As if seeing the self-recrimination he couldn't hide, Jackie grudgingly admitted, "Worked out okay, though. Taggert and the local sheriff were able to save the last victim; no others were killed between when you got shot and Covey offed himself."

Funny, being consoled by the hard-ass FBI agent, who wore her attitude on her face. Then again, she'd mentioned having a couple of kids. Apparently that maternal instinct extended to her colleagues. If it existed. Which, considering his own mother, who put the frigid in the term *ice queen*, he couldn't confirm or deny.

"I was poking around online as soon as I got in, checking into some stuff. I found something you ought to see."

"Oh?"

Jackie handed him a sheet of paper, a screen shot from an Internet page. Glancing at it, he recognized the name of the site immediately. He flinched, wondering if she somehow knew he'd spent the past two nights thinking about Samantha Dalton.

"I wanted to go back and read the post she mentioned

to us the other day, about responding to online classified listings. But this new one popped up right away. It's her latest piece, went live last night. I think we touched a nerve with our online vigilante."

Alec scanned the headline and the opening of what looked like a blog post. "Oh, no."

"Yeah."

"Tell me she didn't reveal anything important."

"Nothing about the case, or us going to see her. It's a generic rant expounding on the physical dangers of using the Internet, that you risk not only your identity but actually your life. A plea to people to wise up and see the craziness of interacting with someone they met online."

He nodded, glad he hadn't misread Mrs. Dalton completely. She hadn't looked like the type who would go back on her word, but she'd flat out stated she was a journalist at heart.

"Go ahead and read it for yourself," Jackie said.

Leaning on the edge of his desk, he did. As his new partner claimed, it was pretty general. But there was an unmistakable undertone, a righteous anger underscoring her words. Maybe because he'd read her book, and had met her, he was able to filter what she said through an internal voice that sounded a lot like Sam Dalton's.

And what he heard told a story.

He'd known she was wounded by the news of Ryan Smith's death. This, however, went deeper. She was angry. Personally angry. Her emotion shone through every line, and he suddenly wondered whether there was more to that anger than her tenuous connection to a murder victim.

What had happened in her life to make her choose to do what she did? Her book had come out almost a year ago, but, according to her bio, she had been running her site for three. Without compensation, he suspected, since she described herself as a former journalist who had decided to begin her own grassroots campaign.

The journalism part he'd confirmed. Last night's quick Google search had turned up her byline, under a hyphenated name, on some articles four or five years back. It had also turned up in a few society articles, but he hadn't read them. That felt too personal for professional research.

But no Internet search was going to tell him why she'd quit her job. Why she'd started writing a free blog when she could never have anticipated it going viral and landing her a book deal and a spot on the best-seller list.

So what had set her off? Call it curiosity, or the profiler's need to understand what made people tick, but he found himself wanting to know why she stayed in her tiny apartment living on Diet Coke and candy bars. Why she hid behind that Mrs. when she'd later mentioned having an ex. Why she worked in her pajamas, refused to answer her door, and interacted with the living mainly via cyber communication. Why she'd made it her mission to save people from their own mistakes.

"Now," Jackie said, seeing he had finished reading, "take a look at this."

He hadn't even realized she'd been holding another sheet of paper.

"These are comments posted last night after her blog went up."

There were a lot, and they'd begun shortly after midnight. Apparently avid fans waited for her weekly article and pounced right on it as soon as it went live.

The first several were "attagirl" posts from people who were probably her regulars. Then he got to the sixth one, posted at twelve forty a.m. He read it, and then read it again, this time aloud. " 'My dear Samantha, you must know some people simply deserve what they get. What folly it would be to try to save everyone. Why do you even want to try?' "

The post was signed *Darwin*.

His senses started to tingle, the way they had when he'd read the e-mails Monday in the conference room. The wording was formal, ostentatious. The message cold and reprehensible.

"Condescending," he murmured.

"Arrogant and literate," Jackie said. "Like someone out to prove how much smarter he is than everyone else."

It took a second; then he remembered what he'd said about the Professor in the car the other day, using exactly those words. "You really think he's posting on a public message board?" he asked, trying to wrap his mind around the possibility.

"You're the expert. Would the Professor do it?"

Alec considered it. Just because the killer had never reached out to the press didn't mean he lacked the narcissistic need to be recognized. Many serial killers had done the same, wanting to evade capture, yet also, somehow, wanting their work to be acknowledged. Admired, even. And interacting with someone who worked to educate people about the very scams he was using to lure his victims—well, it made sense, in a twisted way.

"Yes," he finally replied, frowning as the implications washed over him. "I think he might. We've already noticed other graphic changes in the past few months. He's accelerating, less downtime between kills. He's changed his MO in how he lures his victims. Why not reach out and try to engage someone in cyberspace? Someone who's familiar with the kinds of things he's doing, perhaps even someone he wants to educate?"

Not just someone, though. Samantha Dalton. They were talking about the woman he'd been thinking about nonstop since he'd met her.

"It's thin," he said, shaking his head, torn between the thrill of a lead and his concern over a woman he barely knew.

"Supermodel thin. But keep reading. He posted two more times before six a.m. Got wordier each time, pompous blowhard," Jackie said, pointing to comments farther down the page. "I didn't even begin to suspect until I read his third message. I guess you saw it quicker because you know him better."

Alec read the second comment, left about an hour after the first. A little stronger in the wording, every bit as blasé about his fellow man as the first. Then he read the third. In an instant, he zoned in on exactly what Jackie was talking about. "Damn."

"Yeah."

They were definitely onto something. It seemed crazy that this guy could end up in their lap within a couple of days of their meeting with Sam. Then again, their visit to the woman had provided the catalyst for her blog post—which had apparently stirred the Professor enough to draw him out of hiding. Circular motion.

Alec quickly zoomed through the rest of the pages, looking for any response from Samantha, but saw none. It was perhaps because of her lack of response that this Darwin kept coming back. He seemed to want to know she'd read his words. Validation, almost, of his ideas. But she hadn't given it to him. Most likely, she'd been in bed asleep.

This morning, though, she would sign on and almost certainly give him what he was asking for. Acknowledgment. Considering how upset she'd been by Ryan's murder, especially judging by the rant she'd written, that acknowledgment would probably be very strongly worded. And could really tick off the man she was addressing.

If this Darwin was the Professor, he'd be the last person anybody should ever tick off.

"We need to talk to her before she posts anything back to him." He heard the urgency in his own voice and wondered whether Jackie did, too.

Jackie nodded. "No kidding. I've already tried calling but got no answer, e-mailed but got no response. So I guess we're taking another road trip." She reached into her pocket, pulled out her car keys, and gave him an evil smile. "I'll drive."

"I'm glad I didn't have breakfast," he muttered as he followed her out into the corridor. But instead of heading for the exit, he glanced toward a partially open door. "Fletcher and Cole's office, right? And they're the computer geniuses on the team?"

She realized where he was headed. "I wonder if they can track him from these posts."

"I'm not the cyber crimes nerd," he said, hiding a slight smile as he remembered Sam Dalton's words. "Can they?"

She nodded once. "It's possible."

"So let's bring in the rest of the team and go at this together," he said, the entire concept tasting strange, since he was used to a more cutthroat environment. Strange, but good.

Cole and Fletcher, however, weren't in their office. A quick visit to Blackstone's told them why. "They left a few minutes ago, going to see what kind of computer forensics they can get from the local PD investigating the help-wanted murder." Wyatt handed back the screenshot printouts. "But you can start working on the IP, can't you, Jackie?"

"Yeah. But we still need to get to Mrs. Dalton and make sure she doesn't respond to him."

"At least, not until we decide how we want her to respond," Alec interjected.

Wyatt stared at him, nodding once to indicate his thoughts had gone in the same direction. "Very well, then. Jackie stays here and works on identifying where those posts came from. Alec, you'll have to go up to Baltimore and convince Mrs. Dalton to remain silent for the time being. We'll keep trying to reach her on the phone to make sure she stays offline."

Ordinarily, it would have been a simple task. Alec, though, found his stomach rolling at the thought of it. Not that he couldn't control his libido, or keep himself from revealing the attraction he'd felt for her from the minute she'd opened the door Tuesday afternoon. He just wondered whether he'd be able to resist trying to get into her head a little. Searching to find the caustic woman whose words he'd read, figuring out more about what made her tick and why she'd chosen the path she was on. Filling in the profile.

And, yeah, concealing that attraction.

Throughout her marriage, Sam had become accustomed to getting up early. Not by choice—she wasn't what anybody would call a morning person.

She had always done her best thinking and her best work in the silence of the night, preferring the thick, heavy darkness of a sleeping world to the bright, loud one awash with daylight. She'd made friends with the shadows and the soothing voices of the smooth-toned, late-night radio deejays, had become accustomed to eating cereal at one a.m.

Her ex, however, had liked to get up with the dawn. When she'd moved into his house, she'd been expected to conform to his routine. Alarm at six a.m. Then a workout, which he'd harass her into doing with him, even though she'd rather go through an IRS audit than exercise. But she'd been eager to please, still shocked such a rich, handsome man had wanted her. Had pursued her. Had married her.

Then he would dress in a beautifully tailored suit and set off for another beautiful day of screwing people over in the beautiful land of get-rich-quick corporate America. *Beautiful.*

Since the divorce, she hadn't set her alarm. Not once.

She could therefore muster no surprise when she opened one bleary eye and saw the numbers nine-five-zero shining in neon green from her bedside clock. Late for most people, especially on a weekday. Not for her.

The only question was, why had she awakened at all? She'd shut down her computer right after putting the final touches on her Sam's Rant column at midnight. Not tired enough for bed, she had turned off all the lights and curled up on her couch in the living room, wishing she could turn her brain off, too.

Impossible. Instead, she spent a few hours mentally rewriting history, imagining she'd been home to receive Ryan Smith's IMs that snowy night.

It had been after three before she'd finally moved into her bedroom and fallen into her bed. Yet sleep had still proved elusive after those wide-awake dreams, and she'd last looked at the clock at four thirty.

Then she heard the knocking and realized what had awakened her. "Wonderful," she muttered. Visitors Tuesday. A tense early-morning call from Alec Wednesday, followed by a visit from her lawyer. Now this.

It couldn't be her mother. She never came over without calling first, ever hopeful that one day Sam would find somebody and there might be an embarrassing situation to walk in on. Tricia would be at the realty office where she worked. Sam had a smile-and-nod relationship with most of her neighbors, which was how she liked it. Rick Young had to have gotten the message that she wouldn't go out with him. And the rest of her more casual friends had given up trying to draw her out, figuring she'd leave her postdivorce hibernation when she was ready.

The knocking continued. Her teeth grinding together so hard her jaw hurt, she got up and stalked out of the bedroom, not even stopping for a robe, a hair check, or a swish of mouthwash.

All of which she regretted when she flung the door

open and saw Special Agent Alec Lambert standing on the other side of it.

"Shit," she snapped, unable to help it.

His lips quirked. Sam almost slammed the door again. As if realizing it, Lambert moved closer, blocking the jamb with his body like some determined kid peddling magazine subscriptions. "I need to talk to you."

"Ever heard of making an appointment?" She squirmed, bunching the front of her nightshirt in her fists, knowing there was no chance he hadn't read the man-bashing sentiment this time.

"Ever heard of answering your phone?" he countered. Without waiting for an invitation, he stepped around her into the living room. "We've been calling all morning."

Sam cast a quick, guilty look toward the telephone. Last night, after Tricia's third or fourth call demanding info on who had been in her apartment Tuesday, she had turned the ringer off. "Sorry."

She didn't mention she'd just gotten up and might not have answered anyway. The bare feet and nightshirt, not to mention the rat's nest disguised as her hair, made that eminently clear.

"What do you want? What's so important to have you at my door at this ungodly hour?"

He managed to avoid rolling his eyes. "I know you're a night owl and this is the crack of dawn for you. But it is important. Why don't you get cleaned up and dressed? I can wait a few minutes." His mouth tightened. "As long as you still haven't gone online this morning."

Her curiosity rising, she shook her head. "I haven't."

"Good. Now go; I'll be right here."

Sam sidestepped toward her bedroom, not turning her back on him. Letting the FBI agent fully appreciate the angry-divorcée message on her nightie seemed preferable to flashing her underwear as she departed. Hopefully he had been focused on the saucy words, not on the fact that she was nearly naked beneath the shirt. She'd opened the door to a bitterly cold morning and had almost certainly greeted him with high beams fully lit.

Once in the privacy of her bathroom, Sam multitasked, raking a comb through her hair with one hand while she brutally brushed her teeth with the other. Afterward, she quickly rummaged through her drawers and pulled out a pair of old, premarried khakis that still fit. Considering she'd gained back the fifteen pounds she'd lost on the good-wife-diet-and-exercise program, she didn't have many other options, unless she wanted to again entertain an FBI agent in her sweats.

When she returned to her living room, she found he'd made himself at home on the couch, which no longer held the mountain of laundry. She hadn't exactly gone on a cleaning binge, but she'd picked up at least a little.

"What's this about?" Sitting down at her desk, she flipped the power button on the surge protector behind her CPU. "You mentioned my being online?"

"You haven't been since last night?" he confirmed again.

She shook her head.

"I read your weekly rant."

She stiffened, though she had done nothing wrong. She hadn't hinted about knowing a murder victim, or about being contacted by the FBI. She'd merely called the criminals who preyed on people online the scumbags they were. "And?"

"It was good."

Though she hadn't been looking for his approval, only his acknowledgment that she had kept her word to stay quiet about the FBI's visit, she still liked the compliment.

"It was also pretty passionate," he added.

"Who wouldn't be passionate after hearing about the murders of two teenage boys?"

"You might be surprised."

That said a lot about the human race that she didn't want to contemplate. "So what's the problem? I kept my word; there's nothing in it about Ryan or the investigation. Or you."

Especially you. She'd made a concerted effort to think of anything but Lambert. Especially after he'd called yesterday, all big, bad, protective FBI agent criticizing choices she'd made when writing her book. Screw him. He knew nothing about what drove her. Few did.

Actually, maybe he'd done her a favor with the disapproving reaction. It had made it easier to pretend she hadn't felt a spark of interest in the man. To suppose she'd simply imagined how his hand had felt on her shoulder.

Instead of answering, he reached into his leather attaché and pulled out a few sheets of paper. When he handed them to her, she realized what they were and frowned in bewilderment. "I know what I wrote."

"Look at the second page. The comments."

She did, quickly scanning them from the top down.

"Regulars?" he asked.

"Most."

"What about number six?"

She read it. "Darwin? Doesn't ring any bells, beyond the obvious reference."

"So he's not a frequent visitor?"

"Not under this name." Frowning, she read the words again. "And I don't usually have visitors who are quite so . . ."

"Condescending?"

"I was going to say hateful. I guess you were right about being surprised by people's reactions." She shook her head in disgust. "This guy doesn't sound at all bothered by the idea of victims walking right into the hands of psychopaths who want to do them harm."

"We don't think he is."

The words were low, measured, his tone even. Sam's

gaze flew up as she realized he was telling her something big. Very big.

She forced herself to remain calm, despite a sudden rising dismay. "Are you saying what I think you're saying?"

He didn't reply, waiting for her to lay it out there.

"Do you think this Darwin could be the person who killed the boys?"

He leaned forward, dropping his elbows onto his knees. "Read his other comments."

She immediately obeyed, noting they were again signed Darwin, though he'd apparently been so riled up he'd mistyped his own name once. "Darwen?"

Alec pointed to the paragraph below. Sam studied the words, gasping as their implication sank in. Then, needing to be sure, she read them again, out loud this time.

" 'What would you have us do, Samantha? Should we who have a brain cell in our heads lie in front of the cars of those so foolish they willingly drive into peril? Do we save the reckless ones from the mishaps that so rightfully remove them from our world? Stop the imbecilic female from falling into the machine, or the greedy youth from drowning or freezing to death?' "

Her voice trailed off in shock as the reality of it hit her. Swallowing hard, she let the pages flutter from her hand to the floor, as if she'd been touched by something toxic.

Maybe she had.

"Coincidence?" she asked, trying to convince herself more than him. "He could have chosen those words because he saw the story about the boys on the news."

"The woman killed after answering the online help-wanted ad five weeks ago was tricked into falling into an industrial hopper." The details in the case file had been horrific, and he did not elaborate.

She couldn't manage more than a whisper. "That case was also in the news. I saw it."

"The specific details weren't." Some things were too gruesome even for the evening news.

He fell silent, waiting for her to accept it. Something she truly didn't want to do. But finally, seeing the certainty in his stare, she knew she had to believe it, to swallow down the truth like bitter medicine and move on.

"A psychotic killer is trying to contact me."

Lambert nodded. "I think so."

Her head spinning, she sagged back in her chair. God, no wonder he had been so anxious to reach her. What if she'd gotten back online this morning—or if she'd checked the site one more time before going to sleep last night? In the state she'd been in, she would have given Darwin a piece of her mind.

Which could have angered him so much he might have wanted to rip the rest of her to pieces, too.

She shuddered. "Thank God I didn't respond."

For the first time since he'd arrived, the agent's stare didn't quite meet her own. He glanced down at his hands, folded together and dangling between his knees. "Yes. Thank God."

She hesitated; then understanding washed over her. She finally got the whole picture. What he'd come for, what he wanted from her, why he looked both excited and disturbed. Why he couldn't meet her eye right now.

Excited because he had a lead in his case. Disturbed and unable to look her in the eye because . . . "Wait. You *want* there to be a response."

He nodded.

Speaking in a voice that had suddenly lost most of its volume, she continued. "You want to use my Web site to strike up a conversation with a murderer?"

"No, Mrs. Dalton." He didn't offend her intelligence by even trying to soften it. "I want *you* to use your Web site to strike up a conversation with a murderer."

InXile: R u still there?
InXile: My friend?
Wndygrl1: Im here. This is so sudden. Tonight?

InXile: Must be tonight. Sorry. Has to be nine o'clock.

Wndygrl1: That's very late.

InXile: You get in trouble to stay out late?

Wndygrl1: lol! Just wondering if I dare.

InXile: Dare to come to me?

Wndygrl1: Dare to start this new life.

InXile: U know how I feel.

Wndygrl1: I didn't expect it to happen so soon. Tho I have been thinking about it. I was just about to go shop for something pretty to wear.

InXile: I am sure you make anything pretty.

Wndygrl1: You say such nice things, Rafe. But this is so sudden. You made no mention of having to go away when we talked last night.

InXile: I know. Things go so quickly. I would love 2 give u all the time in the world to get ready. But my time runs out. If not tonight I don't know when. Could be months.

Wndygrl1: Oh, dear . . . you will be gone that long?

InXile: Yes. My life is so different from yours. So much difficulties. I wish only to see you, to romance you, one time before I go, so you might wait for me to come back.

Wndygrl1: I'll wait!!!!!!

InXile: My sweet. Can I convince you? A public meeting . . . ?

Wndygrl1: We would meet in a public place?

InXile: I promise, I will take you somewhere with no walls, no doors, where you can be seen at any time.

Wndygrl1: That sounds safe.

InXile: And maybe tempting?

Wndygrl1: Yes.

InXile: Yes, I have tempted you?

Wndygrl1: I meant *yes*. I'll come tonight.

Chapter 6

"You know, Agent Lambert, if you're going to use me as bait to catch a serial killer, you might as well call me Sam."

Alec managed to keep his eyes on the road and not look over at his passenger, whose mood had vacillated from shock to horror to acceptance in the hour since he'd shown up at her door. They'd left her apartment, heading back to headquarters. Not his first choice, but she had given him no other options. "It's Alec. And we're not using you as bait."

She blew out a disbelieving breath. "Oh, right. Uh, what should we call me? An appetizer? First course?"

He glanced over, gauging how serious she was. If she was having second thoughts, no way would he force her. "Nobody said you had to do this. Do you want me to turn around?"

She huffed a little and crossed her arms over her chest, running her hands up and down her arms to ward off the morning chill. He reached out and jacked up the slow-to-warm heater in the government-issue sedan. Focusing on the road and the city traffic, he ordered himself not to notice the way her soft sweater hugged her body with every move, or the visible puffs of air emerging from her full lips each time she exhaled.

In close confines, the sexual attraction he'd been telling himself did not exist had become an elephant sitting in the backseat. A whole herd of elephants. Because even when snappish and frightened, the woman was still attractive enough to make his heart skip a beat when he looked at her.

"Of course I'm doing it," she finally said with a sigh, after he'd almost forgotten his own question. "But you'd better drive faster. I usually post by noon. Twelve thirty at the latest. Won't your guy think it's strange if I don't?"

"Yes." His foot pressed the gas pedal harder. "We want to stick as close to your normal routine as we possibly can."

"I know." Staring at the dashboard as if it held answers to some deep question, she added in a low voice, "Just how deep am I about to dive into the psychotic end of the gene pool, Alec?"

A frown tugged at his mouth at the hint of nervousness in her voice. "Deep. But not for long and not into shark-infested waters."

"Yeah, right." She turned in her seat to face him. "If I were a character in a book or on an episode of *Criminal Minds*, I'm sure I'd be feisty, brave, and raring to go. But to tell you the truth, I'm scared spitless."

He dropped a hand on hers and squeezed. Her slender fingers were ice-cold. Rubbing them lightly, he shared the warmth of his skin, though he knew some of Sam's coldness probably came from the fear that had her in its grip.

He liked her more for the admission. For the fear. It showed she had common sense, was intelligent enough to know what she was letting herself in for. But he didn't want it overwhelming her. "Nothing's going to happen to you, Sam. The unsub has no idea you're working with us, or that we're watching."

"Unsub?"

"Unknown subject. He'd have no reason to target you at all."

"Unless I piss him off."

"You won't," he insisted. "All you have to do is act interested in what he has to say. We want him to keep coming back to your site. If he thinks you're listening, he might do it, if only to try to prove he's smarter than you. If we're lucky, since he doesn't know we've pegged him as our guy, he'll post from work or from his house and then we'll have him."

It made sense; the plan was a good one. Still, Alec hated the thought of this woman exchanging even written words with a man who had killed so many.

"Thank you," she murmured. It wasn't until he felt her fingers tighten that he realized she was thanking him for warming her hand.

He pulled away, reaching for the controls to turn up the heat another notch. Though, honestly, he felt like opening a window and getting a solid faceful of cold air so he'd stop noticing things like the way she said his name. Not to mention how smooth her skin was or the way her hair smelled sweet, like something tropical, in the close confines of the car.

Wrapping both hands on the wheel, he shifted in his seat and put up a mental wall. A big one covered with Do Not Climb signs. *No climbing on the witness, jackass.*

His annoyance at his own reaction to her made him reach for something to keep that wall in place despite her warmth and her smell and the hitch in her voice when she'd asked how deep she was getting. "I still can't believe you didn't trust me with your CPU," he snapped.

"Huh?"

He hadn't wanted to drag her to D.C., and had tried to get her to let him take it. They needed to go through her old cache of e-mails, to see if the Professor had ever reached out to her before, perhaps under a different name. Figuring she could use a laptop to post to her message board from home, he'd planned to tell her what to say by phone.

But she wouldn't let her damned computer out of her sight. "If you had let me take it, you wouldn't be sitting here freezing your fingers off in a government car with a heater that blows cold air. Don't you own gloves?"

"You know how socks disappear in the dryer when you're doing laundry?"

Startled by the subject change, he nodded.

"Well, gloves disappear from my coat pockets. One at a time. I'm the black hole of death for winter gloves. I have a dozen of them, none that match."

It was almost cute that she was being intentionally flip, wanting to avoid the real issue. But considering she was already too damn beautiful, he didn't need her to be cute as well. "Which wouldn't matter if you'd just let me take the computer."

"We talked about this at my apartment. . . ."

"Our techs know what they're doing. They could have examined it and gotten it back to you within twenty-four hours."

"Big Brother equipped? No way. Besides, how am I supposed to work?"

He ignored the spying accusation. "You have to have a laptop. A backup computer."

"In an apartment too small to do jumping jacks in? Why would I need one?"

"Well, with what you do . . ."

"I had a laptop," she admitted grudgingly. "It had a run-in with a golf club."

Startled, he glanced at her. "Excuse me?"

"Watch the road. I locked down the hard drive so it might survive a fender-bender. But I'm not sure *I* would if it comes flying into the back of my head."

He hid his amusement. And the indignation over the insult to his driving. "Golf club?"

"Long story."

Damn, she was stubborn. "No backup, huh? What do you do if it breaks down?"

"I have a local computer repair shop on speed dial, and the owner makes house calls. That thing is all I've got, and my life is in it. So forget about taking it out of my sight."

Her words sounded a little too vehement. He suspected they were true, especially judging by what he'd seen of Sam Dalton's life.

What the hell was he thinking, dragging this woman, who lived like a self-protective hermit, into the middle of a serial-murder investigation? "Look," he said, realizing there was another option. Maybe not the best one, given how smart the Professor was, but it was at least a possibility. "You can still get out of this altogether. Take a vacation. You give us your passwords, fly to the Caribbean for a week or two, and we'll take it from there." They could study her wording, make the messages sound like they were coming from Sam the Spaminator.

"Sorry, no way." She glanced out the window, not meeting his gaze, and her voice lowered. "I've had a man speak for me. I won't let it happen again."

He suddenly suspected she was talking about her ex-husband. Though he sympathized, sensing the divorce had been a bad one, he couldn't let it go, really liking the idea of getting her out of town altogether. "So what if you're sitting there typing? We're going to be telling you what to say, aren't we?"

"Maybe. But I still maintain some kind of control. I have a say, a choice."

Again, that hint of emotion told him he had hit a nerve. Unable to help it, he murmured, "And it wasn't always that way?"

She eyed him warily, but finally admitted, "No, it wasn't."

His curiosity got the better of him. "So why the Mrs.?"

"What?"

He'd done it now; there was no backing out. "When we met yesterday, why did you insist I call you Mrs. Dalton? You mentioned an ex. So did your loud friend who called."

She groaned audibly.

"Sorry," he said, remembering exactly what else her loud friend had said. "Forget I said anything."

"Will you forget you heard it?"

"Done. But back to the point: Your ex-Mr. doesn't sound like much of a prize."

"Shh. Nobody's told him that yet," she said, rubbing a hand over her eyes.

"How long?"

"A year."

"Married a year, or divorced a year?"

"Married four, divorced one. I guess I haven't gotten used to being a Ms. or a Miss. Besides, though I'm not what anybody would consider a celebrity, I am in the public eye. I'd rather people not know my marital status or anything personal about me, which is why I try to keep any of that stuff off my Web site or my bio."

He didn't tell her how easily he could have found out her personal info if he'd been ass enough to do more than professional research on her.

"I know, I know," she said, as if reading his thoughts. "I'm not a teacher who doesn't understand the subject matter. Someone who wants to know all there is to know about me could probably find it. I put up the basic walls, but there's still a trail out there for anybody who cares to look." She glanced out the window again. "Including my divorce decree."

Her tone ended that line of conversation, and Alec respected her wishes. Driving in silence, he maneuvered through the late-morning traffic. They'd finally exited the downtown area and had a clear shot to the highway.

Baltimore and D.C. weren't separated by much land, but when you factored in all the cars, they might as well have been on different continents.

"So where's your partner?" she eventually asked.

"Back at the office working on the IP addresses from Darwin's comments."

"If it were that easy, you would have caught him after he killed that help-wanted victim he pushed into the machine, wouldn't you?"

The victim hadn't been pushed, though he didn't correct Sam, not wanting to speak of it. Because that poor woman had been led like a mouse through a maze, drugged, deafened by loud machinery, blinded by darkness and what must have been extreme terror. And in her panic to escape the person who had locked her in the manufacturing warehouse where she was found, she'd stepped through a gate the Professor had left open and had fallen right into an enormous industrial hopper.

He couldn't imagine an uglier death.

"No, it probably won't be easy. But there's a slim chance. He couldn't possibly suspect we'd be reading your site first thing this morning, or that we'd recognize his posts so quickly. He might not have been as careful as he is when corresponding with his victims, whose communications will, he knows, be carefully examined."

She tilted her head back against the headrest. "I still can't believe Ryan was killed. Lured by a scam I warned about on my site a dozen times."

"Well, like you said yesterday, most people think those warnings and cautionary tales are meant for others. They know the danger, but proceed right into it, figuring they're the exception; they can't possibly be gullible enough to be a victim."

"I know. Which, Jimmy says, is what makes his job so easy."

"Who?" he asked, surprised. Was she involved with someone? He wouldn't have guessed it, based on how she lived, but it made sense given her obvious attractiveness.

He tried to ignore the sudden rolling in his stomach at the thought.

"James—Jimmy—Flynt. The con man I told you about on the phone." Sounding almost bitter, she added, "I think he was amused by my sad efforts to save his future victims. The man has no conscience, despite lots of efforts to prove otherwise."

Alec shifted uncomfortably in his seat, not wanting to overreact the way he had the previous morning, even though he didn't like hearing Sam call the scumbag by such a chummy first name. He also was loath to point out the obvious. Though she hadn't connected it, her observation about Flynt sounded a lot like the current situation. The Professor might very well be feeling the same way: amused by Sam's efforts to save his victims from their fate. It was one explanation for his reaching out to her on her blog.

His own personal amusement.

He only hoped that amusement led the unsub to make a mistake. They needed only one break, one moment of carelessness. Then, with any luck, they'd nail the bastard.

Alec had called ahead to get things rolling, so, to Sam's surprise, she wasn't put through the Spanish Inquisition to get into the Hoover Building. Could have been because Agent Lambert's boss, a handsome fortyish man introduced as Supervisory Special Agent Blackstone, was waiting for them when they arrived. With quiet determination, he pushed the guards to get her through as quickly as possible, something she doubted they often did for civilians.

As she rode in the elevator with Alec and his boss, she couldn't help comparing them. Alec's brown hair was lighter, with golden streaks, and his eyes a soft, glittering green. A few lines beside them said he was capable of laughter. She'd gotten a glimpse or two of his smile and suspected the full throttle would be devastating.

Blackstone was as dark as his name. Inky black hair that contrasted starkly with eyes a deep shade of blue. A hair taller, but leaner. And while he was cordial to the point of formality, nothing about him hinted at a jolly side.

Alec was sexy in a playful way, his boss in a brainy one. Any way you looked at it, they were both attractive as hell, and she had never felt more aware of how those fifteen pounds filled out her old khakis and tight sweater. Nor of the fact that she hadn't even had time to put a drop of makeup on.

No more sleeping in for you.

"We appreciate your assistance, Mrs. Dalton," Blackstone said. "I hope we haven't inconvenienced you too much."

"Ms. Dalton," she murmured, though she cursed the impulse after the words had left her mouth. Especially when she sensed Alec Lambert's shoulders move, as if he had silently chuckled. "I'm willing to do whatever I can to help."

"Except let your CPU out of your sight."

She cast a quick glare to the right, seeing no expression on Lambert's face, though he'd obviously murmured the jab. She said nothing. Considering he was the one stuck carrying the big box containing the computer all the way from the car, she didn't figure she had the right.

"Alec, you should know I have calls in to the Behavioral Analysis Unit," Blackstone said.

She didn't have to glance over at his face to see this news didn't please Alec Lambert. She saw the way his big hands tightened on the box, clenching it so hard his fingers left indentations in the cardboard.

"You know we have to bring them up to speed on this case."

"Of course." His bland tone revealed nothing. "What was the response?"

"They haven't returned my calls." Sam would have thought that a bad thing, but the impassive expression on Blackstone's face hinted it wasn't. In fact, she would swear his mouth was curved up the tiniest bit at the corners as he added, "It certainly isn't our responsibility to make them respond to their messages."

Alec's fingers loosened. "Nope. It sure isn't."

Interesting exchange. It seemed neither man wanted the help of this other unit, which she found surprising. Then again, the big brick wall she'd run up against when she'd tried to interact with the FBI in the past told her they weren't always as interested in solving crimes as they were in making themselves look good.

She didn't know his boss, but nothing about Alec's behavior thus far said he was that type. Still, something was making these two professional-looking men sound like a couple of kids who didn't want Dad to find out they'd been messing around with his tools in the garage.

None of your business.

Even if it were, she might feel comfortable enough with Alec to ask him about it, but his boss intimidated her. She'd never seen a more intense, professional-looking man in law enforcement, and she wasn't about to accuse him of playing childish king-of-the-mountain turf games.

When they reached the correct floor and the door swished open, Blackstone extended an arm to hold it out of the way, gesturing her out first. She stepped onto a carpeted floor, in a hallway lined with large-windowed offices and computer labs. On the other side of those windows, agents buzzed about and studied images projected from various computers onto large overhead screens. It was pretty much as she'd always imagined the Cyber Division would look, at least from what she'd seen on TV and in the movies.

But they didn't turn into one of those slick, glossy rooms. They kept walking, turning down corridors until she began to feel a little lost, and the ambience became decidedly less techno-chic. The carpet disappeared; so did the glass-walled suites. Greasy dust on a few of the doors hinted they hadn't been opened in a couple of years, as if this part of the building had been abandoned.

Not entirely, though. They finally reached their destination, and it took willpower not to gawk at how antiquated and dingy the offices assigned to Supervisory Special Agent Blackstone and his team were.

"Lily and Brandon are back and are assisting Jackie with last night's messages," he said to Alec as they entered. "Dean and Kyle drove up to Wilmington this morning to meet with the detectives investigating the double murder there and talk to the ME about the autopsies. They should be back soon."

Double murder. Autopsies.

Ryan and his friend. God.

Nodding to a receptionist who offered Sam a cursory smile, Blackstone entered what appeared to be a conference room. Considering dusty boxes stood in lopsided columns from floor to ceiling in all four corners, she doubted it had been one for long.

"That for me?" a man asked, nodding toward the CPU Alec held in his arms. He was young, with spiked blond hair. His bright yellow dress shirt and trendy, pinstriped trousers weren't what she'd expected to see in this particular government office, and his smile was infectious. "Brandon Cole," he said as he moved past her to take the computer from Alec. "I'll treat her like a baby, okay?"

Whether she liked it or not, her link with the outside world did have to leave her sight, at least for a while. Knowing she couldn't be petty enough to deny law enforcement any chance at finding clues to catch the boys' murderer, she nodded. "Okay. Here are my passwords."

She handed him the notes she'd jotted down during the drive from Baltimore. Then, frowning, she added, "No reading e-mails from anybody named Tricia, aka Delish-trish. I'll vouch for her."

Her friend was occasionally overdescriptive when talking about her dates. She seemed to think if Sam read about somebody else occasionally getting laid, she might be more apt to want to do it herself. Sam always hit delete after the first paragraph.

"You got it," the young man said before he left the room, taking with him her most prized possession—including the bulk of her already contracted second book. Talk about redundant backups: She hadn't gone with Alec today until she'd burned it to CD and a portable hard drive.

"Delishtrish who leaves loud messages?" Alec asked as he pulled a chair out and beckoned for her to take a seat. A glint of humor appeared in his eyes again, and for a moment, she thought he was laughing at her.

Then she felt the quick, reassuring brush of his hand on her shoulder and realized his light teasing and humor were his way of trying to keep her calm and comfortable. The realization was as nice as it was unexpected. "My best friend. She's a pain in the butt, but she's loyal."

Swallowing, she quietly added, "Thank you."

"Don't mention it." Glancing at the antique industrial round clock on the wall, he frowned, the hint of warmth evaporating. "We're running out of time."

Almost twelve thirty. He was right.

"You ready?"

She nodded. "As I'll ever be."

Alec bent and reached around her, his strong arm brushing hers, pushing an open laptop in front of her. "Why don't you log in so you'll be set to go once we decide exactly what you're going to say." As she did so, he addressed the others in the room—two women who also sat at the conference table. "Anything?"

His partner, Stokes, offered Sam a curt nod of hello. "Our boy did some driving last night. His posts came from three different servers. We've isolated them, so we know one was from a hotel offering free wifi, one from a small-time auto repair shop without a firewall." Not quite meeting Sam's eye, as if she realized how it would affect her, she admitted, "Which was on Reisterstown Road, near Druid Hill Park."

Close. Very close to where she lived. God, she had never thought about how close her hometown was to Delaware—where the boys had been killed. Or that the monster they were chasing could actually operate right in this area.

Alec obviously thought the same thing. She saw his sudden tension and the scowl on his handsome face.

Sam closed her eyes for a moment, forcing herself to take a deep, calming breath. She lived in a large metropolitan area with an untold number of servers. Of course someone wanting to disguise his location from the FBI would be drawn to a big city. He'd headed south, that was all, and Baltimore was the first big city south of Wilmington.

Besides, almost nobody knew her real address, including many of her old friends. Her Web site was registered through a hosting service, she used a PO box for almost all her correspondence, and she had an unlisted, unpublished number.

Coincidence.

Still, knowing the killer had ended up so physically close when he had responded to her blog—on top of the fact that he visited her site at all—didn't exactly make her day.

"And the other location?" Blackstone asked.

"A residential neighborhood near BWI, probably some Joe Blow with an unsecured Linksys router."

BWI Airport. South of the city. Even farther from Wilmington. *So he circled the entire beltway and then drove back to Delaware, damn it.*

Sounding hopeful, Alec asked, "Was it the first one? Did he post from home, then think better of it and go out to find a more secure location?"

Sam was less hopeful. Because she did not want to think this bastard might live so close.

Agent Stokes shook her head. "Uh-uh. The third. A brand new ISP was assigned within minutes of his post."

Sam, who had been listening quietly, talking only in her head, couldn't help muttering, "You guys are good, taking it all the way to street level so soon."

Jackie Stokes shrugged. "We've got access most people don't. Amazing how quickly a federal warrant goes through when bodies start to fall."

"No doubt."

"All right, give me some good news," said Blackstone.

"Well, the good news is, if we ever *do* have a suspect, we'll be able to prove all this through his laptop's history. Without one, we're shooting in the dark."

Wyatt's eyes narrowed. "Tell me one of those connections was in the vicinity of a surveillance camera."

The other woman, a pretty blonde who had been busily typing on her keyboard, lifted her head. "Already on it, sir. The residential area, no go, but it's possible he was seen by a late-night dog walker or nosy neighbor."

Blackstone nodded. "Note the area, please."

"Already sent the information to your BlackBerry, sir."

He sighed, saying, "We really don't need the sirs in this office, Lily."

The woman stammered an apology, which her boss waved off. "Continue," he said.

"The hotel is part of a budget chain. They might offer free wifi, but they don't put any money into security. It is across the street from a bank ATM, though. Depending on where he parked, it could have caught something." The blonde, Lily, didn't sound hopeful. "And the Baltimore auto repair shop he used to send the middle post is located near an intersection with a red-light cam. I've already contacted the locals to get the ID of the specific camera, and can pull it up for examination."

"Excellent." Blackstone turned his attention back to Alec and Sam. "But obviously it's not enough. So we're going to have to proceed with the backup plan. Are you certain you're willing to do this?"

Sam nodded. "But we need to get going."

"Alec, this is your show. I assume you know the best way to deal with the psyche of this unsub, so why don't you write out the initial response."

"All right." Alec turned to face her. "If you had gotten up this morning and read these messages, how would you have dealt with them? Would you address the first comments first, or skip right to the ones that . . ."

"Made my blood boil?"

"Exactly."

She thought about it. "I always give a nod to my regulars before diving into any debates."

He sat beside her and pulled a pen from the inside pocket of his suit jacket. "Okay, you go ahead and respond to those and I'll write down what to say to the Professor."

She lifted a brow. "He's a professor?"

"It's not important. For all intents and purposes, you know him as Darwin."

"Got it."

Seeing the way her own fingers shook as she touched them to the unfamiliar keys, Sam closed her eyes for one moment, trying to hear her own normal, daily voice, wondering if her fear sounded as loud when she spoke as it did inside her head.

Doesn't matter as long as it doesn't come through in the writing.

Swallowing down the nervousness, she began to type. She addressed the first few messages in one bunch, since they were all agreements with her column. A couple of other visitors had related their own horror stories, which she tackled next. She didn't have to feign the sadness she felt for the man whose teenage daughter had run away with an abusive rapist she'd met on MySpace, or the man whose wife had been robbed and beaten when she'd met with someone she thought was selling a dining room set.

She gave a shout-out to those who begged her not to feed the troll—Darwin. Then she was finished. There was nothing to do but find something to say to the man who thought people should be allowed to be slaughtered without anyone else's interference. "Okay," she whispered.

"Alec?" Blackstone said. He had been watching from the end of the conference table, sitting quietly, one leg crossed over the other, his hands, fingers entwined, resting casually on his lap. She sensed the man saw quite a lot with that dark, intense stare, but neither his pose nor his expression revealed his thoughts.

"Got it," Alec said. He cleared his throat, glancing at Sam as if to ask her one more time if she really wanted to do this. When she nodded slightly, he lifted his notebook and read aloud the words he'd written.

She listened, thought about them, then said, "Okay, if I had decided not to blast him off the Internet, that sounds like something I might say. Might need to tweak a word or two."

He pushed the paper over. "Fine."

She took it, but didn't write, waiting for a final go-ahead from the guy in charge. When Blackstone nodded once, she jotted her changes on the page, her small, neat print nearly lost in Alec's bold, spiky handwriting.

There was a metaphor in there somewhere. She knew it. Something about her small, neat life being sucked into his big, bold one.

God, she hoped she wasn't making a mistake.

"Go ahead, Sam."

She began to type.

Dear Darwin . . .

Chapter 7

You're a first-timer, aren't you? Welcome, glad to have you. Can't say I agree with your theory, but it's a free country, right? I understand it can be frustrating that some people don't learn from their mistakes. But do you really think the answer is to do nothing at all? Pretty harsh view, isn't it?

Interesting comments, hope you stick around!

In his quiet office, behind a closed door, Darwin leaned back in his chair and stared at Samantha's words. They were, he had to admit, more than he'd hoped for. He'd read them several times since they'd shown up an hour ago, searching for more—hidden messages, private meanings. Something to indicate she knew how important this interaction was.

Hope you stick around.

That said it all, didn't it? Of course she knew.

"You never disappoint me," he told the screen, his gaze shifting between it and her photo on the inside back cover of her book. Her beautiful face, the intelligence shining from her eyes—they weren't a disguise for a woman with no substance. She might be naive, and foolishly kind, but she was open-minded and smart.

Smart enough to recognize a kindred spirit, even if, on the surface, their views seemed quite different.

"You had me worried for a while," he admitted. "Keeping me waiting as you did."

That worry had made him refresh the computer page every minute or two throughout the morning. A man not used to feeling impatient over anything, he had found the reaction disconcerting and had to leave the office for a while because he could not focus.

The delayed response had not angered him; he could never be angry at someone who took the time to evaluate all options before speaking or acting. But he couldn't deny a moment of worry when he'd thought he was being intentionally ignored.

He would not tolerate being ignored.

Finally, she had spoken, and the weight of wondering had been lifted. It just remained to decide how—and when—to respond.

When a knock sounded, he minimized the screen. "Yes?"

His office door swung open and one of his employees entered, a subservient, wishing-to-please expression on his face. "Got a minute?"

He nodded. "Of course, Steve; you know my door is always open."

Even though it almost never was. Not in the literal sense, anyway. But Steve wasn't wired to think so literally. Not stupid at all, oh, no—the man was cunning. Above all, he was loyal. And these days, loyalty outweighed everything else. "What can I do for you?"

"I want to thank you for the overtime hours. I know you pulled some strings to get them for me."

A simple phone call, nothing more, and it had earned him one more layer of gratitude from someone who might be of use someday. "It's nothing."

"Well, it's something to me. The extra money's great with the baby coming. So thanks again."

Offering a slight smile, he murmured, "You are quite deserving. It's nice to have people we can count on around here."

"You can count on me!" Vehemence laced his voice, and an almost slavish devotion was visible in the younger man's eyes. "And on everyone who works here."

They might not be quite as supportive if they realized how thoroughly he disliked most of them. But he kept his opinions well hidden. He was as good an actor as he was a . . .

"Killer morning, huh?"

Appropriate terminology. Though considering he had never really killed anyone, merely set their inevitable deaths in motion, he wouldn't bestow such a stark title upon himself. Nor was he an executioner, for the same reason. Or even a punisher—he didn't choose to punish his victims, or to change them.

He simply wanted them gone.

"Did your meeting go okay?" Steve asked.

Knowing the man referred to the fictional meeting he had used to explain his sudden departure this morning, Darwin nodded. "Yes, indeed. Things are looking much better now."

Much better.

"Glad to hear it. Well, guess I'll get back to work."

"Fine, fine." Wanting to free up his schedule, to pre-pare for the evening he had planned, he added, "I do have another appointment this afternoon. It will require me to leave a few hours early today. Far too much run-ning around, I'm afraid."

"That's why they pay you the big bucks!" Steve-the-sycophant said with a grin. "Have a good one, and stay warm. It's cold out there."

Master of the obvious.

Nodding pleasantly, he watched the subordinate leave, shutting the door firmly behind him, then brought up the Web site again. "I didn't mean to ignore you, my dear," he whispered. "Though you gave me a fright thinking you were ignoring me."

Her lack of response to his comments had bothered him less during the night than it had this morning. But still, it had bothered him. Enough that, after he had posted his first two comments and seen no reply, he'd driven to her home. Seeing her car parked in one of the spots in front of her building and noting the absence of any sign of life behind the pitch-black windows of her apartment, he'd assumed she was asleep. A normal assumption, given the late hour, though he knew Samantha to be a night owl, often staying up until three a.m.

Not last night, though. She must have exhausted herself working up her useless cautionary piece for people who would never learn from it.

She had not been ignoring him at all. Samantha had simply not been awake to read his messages and realize he'd opened the most important line of communication of her entire life.

How wonderful it had been to sit outside in the night, studying her bedroom window. It hadn't been the first time, though he wasn't foolish enough to become a frequent visitor to this neighborhood. He satisfied his craving once a week at most.

On one occasion last summer, he had seen her moving behind the gently billowing sheers as she prepared for sleep behind an open window. He'd held his breath as her silhouette was spotlighted by the bedroom lamp before she'd flicked it off. And had continued to hold it when she moved even closer to the window to turn on the small night-light plugged in directly beneath it.

How nice that he no longer had to wonder what that night-light looked like. It was colorful, stained-glass, delicate. Closing his eyes, he could see it, as well as the pretty jewelry box on her dresser and the framed sunflower print on the wall. He remembered the softness of her bed, the shape of each pillow.

His familiarity with everything in her apartment added depth and texture to his nighttime visions as he sat outside and pictured what she was doing.

Fortunately, she had gone to spend the night Christmas Eve at her mother's home. Because Darwin had then been able to spend his Christmas Eve indulging in a thorough overnight exploration of Samantha's.

He had often pictured her in bed, her golden hair against the cream-colored linens, her face softly lit by the glow from the night-light. Imagining climbing inside, surprising her awake, he hadn't known which he would want to do first: converse with her about philosophy or fuck her until she sobbed.

His body had stirred at the possibility. He had never been a man overpowered by physical needs or messy lusts. But with her, it was different. He wanted her mind, wanted to bend it, even to the point of breaking, if he had to, until her thoughts matched his own.

He also, however, wanted her body. Wanted to bend it to the point of breaking as well, if only he could satisfy the unrelenting craving he'd felt for her for so long.

"Soon," he whispered, still smiling. "Now that we've begun I will most definitely be 'sticking around.' "

Closer than she'd ever imagined. He'd already begun inserting himself in her life in ways she could not even comprehend. Preparing for the inevitable, when he'd have to strip away the dregs who kept her down: her friends, her family, all who prevented her from reaching her fullest potential.

"Not much longer," he reminded himself, frustrated that he could not reply to her, not yet, anyway. Certainly not from here.

But perhaps it was fortunate after all. She'd kept him waiting; now he'd give her a taste of the same frustration. Let her think about Darwin, grow more interested in him. Until she was almost aching with curiosity by the time he came back around.

"Perfect," he mused, liking the visual.

It wasn't as if he had nothing else to do today. Already nearly two—he had preparations to make. Though he had originally intended to dangle his little telephone operator friend for another week or so, he had decided to free himself of that encumbrance. Wendy Cramer was a distraction. Furthermore, she was a loose end.

Not for much longer. The plan for her disposal was in place. While off-site this morning, he had contacted her and set it in motion. Once that was done, he could clear his mind and give all of himself to Samantha. He would be free to reach out to her, to put her out of the torment she would be feeling after a full day of his silence. And he would be so close when he did it.

How fortuitous for him that both women lived in the same city. He could kill two birds with one stone.

Well, literally speaking, only one bird would die tonight.

A bird. He chuckled under his breath at his own wit. Because how his little Wendy was going to fly. She just didn't know it yet.

Anticipation lifting his spirits, he quickly tidied his desk, removing every item, every bit of paper, until it was entirely bare, as he liked it. His step held a jaunty bounce as he walked to the closet to retrieve his coat, and he couldn't recall a time when he'd felt more certain about what he was doing.

It was all coming together. Things were truly starting to happen. Tonight, he would reach out to Samantha Dalton again, and continue with his two-part plan.

Teach her. Then take her.

Nothing.

An entire day in a cramped, musty conference room with visible dust motes filling every breath of air, and they had heard absolutely nothing from the unsub they were trying to engage.

What a complete waste of time.

Alec did his best to hide his frustration and his impatience. Samantha had done everything she'd been asked to do and had cooperated fully. The last thing he wanted was for her to think the failure of their plan was in any way her fault. This had been his idea, and the responsibility belonged squarely on his shoulders.

"He posted late last night," she said, hiding a yawn that punctuated her weariness. They had sent out for lunch, and taken only brief breaks from chairs about as comfortable as park benches. "Maybe he's a shift worker; he might not even be home from work yet."

That was a possible explanation, and one he'd already thought of. But it didn't offer much solace. "Trust me, from what we know about him, he doesn't sound like a blue-collar shift worker pulling the noon-to-eight. I believe he's a professional, an executive even. Someone used to power and being in charge. Someone who enjoys controlling other people and has gone from managing their jobs to managing their deaths."

She blinked, thinking about it, then said, "Don't give up; it's still possible. Okay, so he's a nine-to-fiver, a professional. But if he's an executive, he works late. And if he's a commuter and there's an accident, he could still be sitting on a highway with all the other poor slobs running the rat race." A slight hint of irony in her voice, she added, "Or maybe he's home playing perfect husband to an unsuspecting wife, waiting for her to get busy doing something else so he can sneak out and do his nasty laptop business."

The comment interested him, given everything else he knew about her, especially the golf club–versus-laptop incident she'd mentioned earlier. In other circumstances, he might have asked her about it.

Besides which, she was right. Something like that could have prevented the Professor from returning. Maybe his damn laptop was broken, too.

There were, however, a few other, less comforting possibilities. For instance, maybe Darwin wasn't the Professor after all.

He is. Alec truly believed it.

Still, maybe their unsub wasn't interested enough to come back and hadn't even realized she'd responded. His posting could have been a one-time thing, a break from the boredom of not killing anyone last night.

At least, they hoped he hadn't killed anyone last night.

There was also a chance he was suspicious about something in Sam's responses. So far, she had addressed him twice. They had come up with a reason for her to bring him into the conversation again at around five o'clock, after several hours had gone by without any acknowledgment about the first posting. It hadn't been hard. Her regular visitors had had a lot to say about Darwin's comments. Not to mention the lack of heat in Sam's response.

Hell. Maybe they'd misfired. They'd wanted him to engage in a debate with someone who disagreed with him, without enraging him toward Sam. Who, as she'd admitted, wouldn't be too hard to find if he got angry enough to look.

Maybe they'd used the wrong tactic. Perhaps she should have come out guns and sarcasm blazing. The unsub might have been angry, but he also might have been less suspicious.

And if he had, indeed, blown up, they could have arranged for her protection.

If only he'd had more time to think it all through this morning. *Damn it.*

Six months ago, he wouldn't be questioning his decision. He'd trusted his instincts, had never taken a step he hadn't deep down thought was the right one. Never looking back, always confident enough to go with his gut.

No more. It seemed as though a lot of that confidence had been blown away along with chunks of his skin and chips of his bones last August.

"You know, I'd like to think everybody in the world reads my blog the minute they get up in the morning," she said. "But maybe he just isn't a fan."

"Whether he's a fan or not, he started something last night. Narcissists like this one don't like being ignored; they like to hear themselves talk. They also like to spread their message. For him to engage you like he did, to address you personally, to try to interest you in his cause . . . it meant something." He stared into his nearly empty coffee cup. "I had honestly pictured him sitting up all night, writing again and again out of frustration that you hadn't responded. I never expected him to start this and then walk away."

The Professor always finished what he started. He never walked away without leaving a dead body behind him. "I felt sure we would hear from him."

"I know. So did I." As if she'd realized he was beating himself up, she added, "So did everyone, your boss included."

He thought about going down the hall to talk to Wyatt about it. The supervisory special agent was in his office, working late doing the BS paperwork people in his position always seemed to have to do. But he didn't want to leave Sam, in case they got lucky.

He trusted her, knew she was smart and incredibly quick to learn. She was also exhausted, and so tense he could see the clench of the muscles in her neck. If she got a sudden, unexpected message from the Professor, pure impulse and excitement could lead her to whip off a reply before she thought better of it. Not likely, but it was possible.

No, he couldn't leave her, not for a long, private discussion with Wyatt about what he might have done wrong.

Trust your instincts; this will work. Give it time.

Time. More time. It was down to just the two of them, and time was all they had left in the quiet offices of the nearly empty building.

Stokes had headed home to see her kids, though she remained on call. Lily had departed at the same time, mumbling something about an evening appointment. Taggert and Mulrooney had gone to canvass the residential neighborhood the unsub had posted from last night, trying to find anyone who had seen a stranger, or his vehicle. They'd both since headed home, also keeping their cell phones by their sides at all times. Brandon was around, but in the lab, working on Sam's hard drive.

He was once again alone with the woman who'd seriously messed with his head since the minute he'd met her. Lucky him.

"Are you one of those profiler guys like in the movies or on TV?"

"No."

"You sounded like one when you described this suspect."

Not wanting to go there, but figuring he owed her some kind of explanation, he admitted, "There's no such thing as a 'profiler' in the bureau. Some agents profile, but it's not a job title. And yes, to answer your question, I have experience with it. Now I'm with the Cyber Division."

Sam absently reached for the keyboard, refreshed the page, looked for any new postings, then breathed a disappointed sigh. "Agent Stokes said you were new; that's why you didn't have the right business card or know the office number."

He managed a weak smile. "Monday was my first day."

"Wow, talk about walking into the fire."

"No kidding. Though I've already walked in the fire with this guy. We've been after him for a while."

"I hope it will be all over soon."

"So do I, Sam."

Rising from her chair, as if she couldn't stand being in it any longer, she began to pace the room, visibly impatient and probably bored. "Were you with the Behavioral Analysis Unit?"

Wishing he'd never answered her original question about profiling, he nodded once, hoping his expression would forestall any further inquiries.

He should have known better.

"Why'd you leave?"

Because I was practically invited to get the hell out.

"Wyatt offered me a job. I took it."

She had circled the table once, paused to glance at the laptop screen, then walked around again. "Did you leave on bad terms?"

"Do you always ask such intrusive questions?"

Shrugging, she replied, "Do you always answer questions with questions?"

"Look who's talking."

Her soft laughter gave him the first real flush of pleasure he'd had in hours. He liked this woman's laugh. Liked its huskiness and the way it brightened her eyes.

"I was a journalist, remember," she explained after she had circumnavigated the table once more. She seemed to have gotten her wanderlust out of her system, because she sank into her chair again. "I couldn't help noticing your reaction when your boss mentioned the BAU."

"They're going to want in on this the moment they realize the suspect we're chasing is the same one they've been after for a couple of years. At least, we think he is."

"Isn't that a good thing?"

Of course it was. It just wasn't going to be a comfortable thing, not for any of them. Him, because seeing his former colleagues again wasn't going to be the highlight of his millennium. Wyatt because, judging by the way they were stonewalling him—and had been since last summer's Reaper case—somebody in the BAU had it in for the man.

"It'll be fine," he replied, wondering if he sounded as unconvinced as he felt. "We're all on the same team."

"Okay," she said, dropping the subject, as he had hoped she would.

Silence descended between them, though it wasn't an uncomfortable one. It was broken every minute or so, when Sam would refresh the screen, emit a sigh, then perhaps tap a response to another of her visitors. Somehow, during the long day, they'd fallen into sync with each other. A snap of tension might still exist beneath the surface, but they'd maintained complete focus on the job for hours.

Alec had long since given up on the jacket and tie and had loosened the top buttons of his dress shirt. After five, he didn't give a damn where they were. A fourteen-hour day entitled him to an unbuttoned collar.

As for Sam, she'd held up beautifully, as patient and thorough as a professional. Her response had exceeded anything he'd have expected from a civilian who hadn't even known this monster existed until yesterday. Though she didn't try to pretend her fear had left her entirely, she'd grown at least a little more relaxed during the day, both when the room had been filled with agents, and now, when they were alone. As if she'd accepted the fact that they—that he—would not let anything happen to her.

While calm, though, she was visibly fatigued. Dark smudges had appeared beneath her eyes, and she stretched occasionally, as if to relieve cramped muscles.

"Need some more coffee?" he asked.

She shook her head. "Despite how exhausted I am, I'm also wired. I'll be awake all night as it is. How do you handle this kind of tension all the time?"

"Scotch and video games."

One fine brow arched, and a soft trill of surprised laughter emerged from her pretty mouth. "Excuse me?"

"What can I say? Beating the hell out of little cyber dudes on the Wii helps my mood tremendously at the end of a crappy day." His words brought another tiny laugh and a smile that stayed on her lips.

"Okay. Scotch and video games. Can't say I have any scotch, but I can twist the top off the bottle of Jose Cuervo Tricia gave me for Christmas."

"Tequila instead of a sweater or one of those plastic bags full of flour and chocolate chips that you're supposed to use to make your own damn cookies? Maybe you should forgive her phone manners."

She laughed again, and this time a gorgeous dimple, which she probably hated, if she was like most women, appeared in her cheek. Obviously she had gotten over the embarrassing answering machine incident. "Like I said, a pain in the butt. But she's also the best friend I've ever had." Clearing her throat, she softly added, "She's the one who got me, the, uh, nightshirt I was wearing this morning."

He'd noticed the nightshirt. Actually he'd noticed what she had on under the nightshirt. Especially the absolutely nothing she had on under the nightshirt.

"It probably seemed a bit angry."

Actually, it had seemed sexy as hell to him. But he'd go with angry if it made her feel better. "I think divorce is a pretty angry subject."

"You?"

He shook his head. "Never married." Something made him add, "I did go through a breakup last summer. We had dated for over a year."

"Rough," she murmured. "Do you miss her?"

"I miss my dog."

Her jaw dropped. "She took your dog?"

"Yeah. I was ..." He thought about how to explain

without really explaining. "I couldn't take care of him for a while. She had given him to me in the first place, and she loved him. So she got him from my place and took him to hers, temporarily, then refused to give him back."

"What a bitch."

Her anger on his behalf both amused and warmed him. "Nah, he was male."

She rolled her eyes. "That was so not funny."

"What can I say? Considering my ass is falling asleep after being in this chair all day, I guess I'm not at my wittiest."

He wasn't exaggerating. Having given up on finding any comfortable position, he was now sprawled back in one of the uncomfortable seats, arms linked across his chest and legs extended, crossed at the ankle.

She shifted in her own chair, obviously feeling the same way. Like the tenacious woman she was, she got right back to the subject. "How could your girlfriend do such a thing?"

"She thought he would be better off with her."

Another eye roll. "Lame excuse."

"Actually, it wasn't. At the time, she was probably right, which is why I didn't fight her on it. I was away from home for quite a while."

"Yeah, but stealing your dog—that's cold."

As cold as whacking up your laptop with a golf club? The question almost emerged, but he swallowed it down. Along with the curiosity that had been nagging at him today as he'd pictured the possible reasons for the incident, and the identity of the person holding the club.

"Anyway, once I got back, I wasn't capable of running with him or taking care of him the way I once did."

"Why not?"

He hesitated, wishing he'd cut the story short. He should have thought about how inquisitive she was and expected her to quickly stop focusing on the dog and zone in on the backstory. "I had been pretty badly injured."

She cast a quick, instinctive glance over him, from his head down the length of his body, as if she might spot some sign of what had happened to him.

Then she looked again. Nothing quick about it this time.

Her attention shifted. The perusal became about something other than casual conversation. Almost feeling the heat of her stare sliding all over him, he knew what she was seeing. With his clothes rumpled and his jaw lightly grizzled, he probably didn't much resemble the guy who'd shown up at her door Tuesday.

She didn't seem to mind. In fact, her expression implied the opposite.

Her lashes slowly lowered in almost sultry fashion, until she was watching him from behind half-closed lids. Those expressive eyes darkened; the lush lips parted. A soft, nearly inaudible sigh flowed across them, and a flush crawled up her cheeks.

No. She no longer looked afraid. She looked hungry.

He was being visually devoured by a beautiful, sensual woman who'd been wearing a shield of angry armor toward men since her divorce and had suddenly remembered she once had a sex drive.

His heart picked up its pace, and he felt the blood in his veins heat to near boiling. He hadn't bargained for this. Being physically attracted to her was one thing. He could handle that. At least, he thought he could, despite knowing, after spending a whole day with her, how much he could like this woman.

Just now, though, realizing she was attracted to him, too, things had gone from intense to almost dangerous.

Dangerous for him because, with his track record, getting tangled up with a witness was about the dumbest career move he could make. Dangerous for her because . . . well, because Alec's head wasn't in the game right now.

He was still too screwed up from what had happened to even think about involving somebody else in his battle with his own demons.

Easy to remember earlier, when she'd been afraid, on edge, and uncertain. Now that she'd segued into aware, sultry, and sensual, he could get into serious trouble.

When she realized he'd seen her response, Sam caught the corner of her bottom lip between her teeth. The room, old and poorly ventilated with one small heating vent, usually felt chilly. It suddenly got warmer, the walls almost seeming to shrink around them, making the cramped space even more intimate.

"Sorry," she whispered.

He didn't know if her apology was for the intrusive questions or the deliberate, provocative stare. Good manners said she should owe him one for being nosy. But his own need to keep thinking of her as just a witness meant it had better be the look. That dangerous, oh-it's-bad-but-it's-still-so-good look.

"It's okay."

Though she was visibly embarrassed, Sam didn't turn away. She made no effort to avert her eyes or change the subject. She watched him closely, waiting for him to speak. The woman wanted either a left turn into the tale of his injury, or a right one into something a whole lot more dangerous: an acknowledgment that he'd seen, that he understood. That he'd responded.

When he didn't humor her, didn't take the conversation one way or another, she finally blew out an impatient sigh. "Well?"

"Well what?"

"Well, how were you hurt?"

She'd gone left. And he was suddenly so relieved, he spat out the truth. "Shot."

Her gasp could have been heard outside. "You were *shot*? Like, with a gun?"

"No *like* about it." Reading her dismay in the quiver

of her mouth, he shrugged in unconcern. "It was five months ago; I'm fine."

Sam obviously wasn't so sure. She reached out and put a hand on his arm, touching him so lightly, so fleetingly, he wondered afterward if he had imagined it. "I'm sorry."

"Wasn't anything I ever want to repeat, but I survived it."

"Who shot you?"

The question he most didn't want to answer. Because being shot by a psychopath or a bank robber, an abusive dirtbag, any of those would have been okay to talk about. Heroic maybe. At least something he could wrap his mind around.

He still hadn't wrapped his mind around what had really happened that hot summer day.

He intentionally averted his gaze, staring past her. "It's a long story."

She refreshed the screen, sighing when it came back unchanged. "It's not like I'm going anywhere."

As if having time to kill meant he should spill his guts about something he hadn't even discussed with his parents, with his ex, with anybody except an FBI shrink and the big shots at his disciplinary hearing. Oh, and Wyatt. Who'd probably been the most understanding of all of them.

Offering her the bare bones, he said, "I got too close to a witness. Got involved, let down my guard. And paid a very serious price for it." He fell silent, his entire body stiffening in discomfort, physically telling her to step back from her line of questioning.

"Okay, sure. You don't know me; it was rude to ask. I apologize."

"Don't. I opened the door." And promptly closed it.

"Tell me one thing."

He tensed.

"The person who did it, was he caught? Prosecuted?"

Alec waited for a long moment before lifting his eyes to meet her inquisitive stare. Finally he answered, "She's incarcerated, awaiting trial down in Georgia."

Sam processed the sex of his assailant with a quick flare of the eyes and a brief clench of her mouth. Otherwise, she didn't react in any way. But he could almost see the churning of those wheels in her brain and knew exactly where that imagination—and bruised-divorcée spirit—had taken her. Hearing a woman had tried to murder him, his admission that he'd gotten too close to a witness . . . well, she had undoubtedly painted quite a picture in her mind with that small palette of colors. She wouldn't be the first.

He almost spat out the truth, not wanting those kinds of speculations influencing her opinion of him. The idea that she thought he was that kind of agent, that kind of *man*, ripped at his guts. But he kept his mouth shut. His lapse in judgment—not seeing the kindly looking mother of the killer he'd been after for the dangerous, murderous bitch she was—had been the greatest mistake of his life.

Jesus, I'm sorry, Ferguson. Sorrier than I can ever say.

His sympathy toward a frightened mom, who seemed to want her son captured so no one else would get hurt, had led him to believe her when she'd said she had no idea where their suspect was. Not to mention neglect to check her for weapons of her own.

She'd been lying. And when they'd moved to stop her son from escaping through a back window, she'd opened fire.

He had learned his lesson about letting his guard down around witnesses. Learned it the hard way. Judging by how Sam had devoured him with her eyes five minutes ago, it was on the verge of happening again.

So Alec remained silent.

Sam looked way from him and leaned forward in her chair. Dropping her elbows onto the table, she lowered her face onto her hands, cupping her forehead and rubbing at her temples with her thumbs, visibly exhausted and disheartened.

"Okay, this isn't getting us anywhere," he said, making a sudden decision. "It doesn't mean we're giving up. Our guy could just be cautious, suspicious about being directly engaged. He might have only the dead of night to ride around and do his thing, and nobody expects you to sit here until three a.m."

She lifted her head, appearing hopeful. "You think he might still show up?"

"It's possible. We've had a long day. Let's go check in with Brandon, see if he's finished with your hard drive, and work on getting you home sometime before tomorrow."

"You'll take me home?" she asked, her brow rising in surprise. "Really? I can go?"

In those moments when Sam had created scenarios in her mind about his shooting, probably deciding he was at the very least unprofessional, or worse, a womanizer, he suspected she'd built a mental wall of her own. One that reminded her she was a graduate of the School of All Men Suck, if he remembered her nightshirt correctly. Now, though, the wall was down and she sounded relieved and appreciative.

"Yeah. I'll get you home." He rose from the chair, touching the back of hers to pull it out so she could stand, too. "Swear to me you won't do anything if he responds tonight. No more angry blog entries, no acknowledgment whatsoever without my go-ahead."

"I won't."

"I've got to have your promise on this," he said, knowing he sounded fierce, but needing to make sure she knew how serious he was. He stepped closer, blocking her exit, crowding her against the table. The subtle intimidation was intentional, meant to ensure her cooperation.

It also, he suddenly realized, probably revealed his

frustration that she'd so quickly assumed the worst about him. And the second he acknowledged that about himself, he stepped back and thrust a hand through his hair. "Sorry."

"You have my word," she said, not moving, though he'd cleared the path to the door. "No matter what happens tonight, I won't do a thing without talking to you first."

Chapter 8

Wendy Cramer did not own a car.

She didn't like driving in the city and lived within a few blocks of the answering service office where she worked, so there had never been a need for her own vehicle. But tonight, as she rode toward the man of her dreams, she couldn't help thinking it wasn't much of a way to enter her new life. Stepping off a smelly city bus coated with dirt and road salt would almost ruin all the efforts she'd gone through to prepare for this eventual night.

"Not eventual anymore," she whispered, still shocked her love had begged her to meet him tonight. "It's finally here."

He had to go away, he'd said, and wanted to make sure she'd be waiting for him. He must know there was no chance she wouldn't; she had made her devotion clear. As had he.

She'd had to wonder if the impassioned invitation had been about something else. Perhaps a way to get her to come to him so he could make love to her before he went away?

She quivered at the thought. Her body, untouched by any man for so many years, ached, and she allowed im-

ages of the passionate kisses he would offer her to fill
her mind. She felt like one of the heroines of the romance books she received in the mail every month.

Lost in the fantasy, Wendy almost missed her stop.
She noticed the sign as the driver was about to pull away
from her final destination. Leaping to her feet, she cried,
"Wait!"

The others on the uncrowded bus watched her progress down the center aisle. With her newly colored and
freshly cut hair, more makeup than she ever wore, and a
new dress, she didn't mind the stares. She needed to get
used to them, didn't she? If—*when*—Rafe was restored
to his position, whatever that was, she would probably
be in the public eye. Doing charitable works and what-
not, like Princess Di, who had been her favorite royal.

Getting off at the stop, she watched the bus chug
away with a belch of inky black smoke that snaked into
the cold air before dissipating. When alone, she quickly
looked around. She had never come to this part of the
city at night. On the south side of the harbor, this was an
industrial zone, crowded with shipping companies and
docks servicing the big freighters. Nothing at all like the
trendy Harbor Place side, which she could see across the
water. Lights from the stores and restaurants brightened
the sky. A whole world of people likely bustled about
inside.

Unlike here, where she was completely alone, not another soul in sight.

Trepidation crawled through her. Where was Rafe?
Surely he wouldn't leave her alone in such a deserted
place, at the mercy of anyone who happened by? He was
too gentlemanly.

She glanced at her watch. Eight fifty-five. *You're a few
minutes early. Don't panic.* But something made her pull
her cell phone out of her purse and keep it in her hand.

As the minutes ticked by, her nervousness rose. She
noted the hiding places around each corner and the way

the long shadows of the monstrously tall buildings darkened the moon-brightened landscape. The ships docked nearby appeared almost ghostly. The current slapped wetly against them, sounding like the *thwack* of an angry hand against flesh.

"Where are you?" she whispered.

Suddenly, the phone rang, the name Smith appearing on the caller ID. Hoping he was using a false identity, she answered, "Rafe?"

"Darling, I'm so sorry I've kept you waiting."

His voice. At last. So warm and deep and masculine. She wanted to cry from relief, not only because he hadn't stood her up, but also because he was *real*. Though she had never permitted herself to dwell on it, the awful possibility that someone had been playing a cruel joke on her had flashed through her mind once or twice.

It wasn't true. Her faith hadn't been misplaced.

"Where are you? I'm afraid. I've been out here all alone."

"I know, I know."

She sniffed, then frowned. "What do you mean? How could you know?"

"I'm so sorry. I saw you arrive. I wanted everything to be perfect, so I didn't come down right away."

Down?

"I kept you waiting; how rude of me, not thinking of your discomfort."

Not understanding, she asked, "Where are you?"

"Step out of the shelter and look up."

Still confused, she did as he asked, not sure what she was looking for. The high-rises around her were closed and deserted. But a few random lights piercing the darkness hinted at late-working employees. Was he among them?

"Turn and walk to the north side of the awning. See the building directly in front of you?"

The building directly in front of her wasn't a building at all. It was a construction site. A midrise only half completed, it stood skeletal against the night sky—bare, raw, and imposing, a shell made of metal beams, wood planking, and rough cement.

Then she saw it: a glimmer of illumination on the highest level. She tilted her head all the way back, narrowing her eyes, craning for a better look. As the light moved, she tried to make out the shape of the person holding it. It was, however, far too high, and too dark. "Oh, Rafe, is that you all the way up there?"

"It is, Wendy. I'm watching you with a pair of binoculars."

She bit her lip in sheer nervousness. He had gotten a good look at her before she'd even known he was there.

"This is my surprise."

"But you're trespassing!"

"No, this is *my* building, condominiums and office suites, an investment to keep me in comfort for many years. And here on the top floor will be my penthouse, my home."

Oh, goodness. She had known he had wealth, but she had thought most of it was hidden for his protection. "Has something happened? Can you come out of hiding?"

"Yes, how quick you are. All is well and the world is perfect, especially from up here. Will you forgive my deception for saying I was going away? I wanted you to come, right away, to share this night with me. But I didn't want to spoil the surprise."

Surprise. She almost gasped, understanding washing over her. Was he saying he wanted to show her his under-construction home because he wanted her to share it? Good Lord, had she come here tonight for a marriage proposal?

"Be careful, but do hurry. Cross the street; go through the gate, which is open. Proceed to the elevator on the east side of the building. You won't miss it—I've left a light on for you."

She hesitated, the hint of nervousness returning. She had no fear of Rafe; the man loved her. But she had to admit the prospect of going up into the dizzying heights of that frail-looking, half-built structure frightened her. "Is it safe?"

"Oh, sweet, of course it is safe. I wouldn't put you in danger. I would come down to meet you but I am not quite ready; I want everything just right. But I'll be there to carry you over the threshold when you arrive at the top."

Carry her over the threshold. She felt like swooning.

Despite the cold night breeze blowing across her body and chilling her hose-covered legs, she felt his warmth as he added, "I have something very special for you."

A ring? Her whole body tingled with excitement. "All right. I'm on my way."

"I—and your future—await."

The connection ended, and she hugged the phone to her chest, so grateful, so filled with anticipation she could hardly stand it. Tonight would bring everything she'd ever dreamed of. Her perfect future with her perfect man.

Tugging her coat tightly around her as protection from the wind, which had picked up and whipped over the choppy water, she hurried across the street. The light of the bus shelter didn't extend far, and his from above certainly didn't either, but she easily found the gate. As he'd promised, it was unlocked. Beyond it, safety reflectors shone a path through the construction zone.

Entering, she got only a few steps before a shrill noise assaulted her ears, the screech making her jerk to a halt. She remained still for a moment, her heart thudding against her ribs. But she quickly realized it was the winter wind, gustily whistling into the openings of the structure, rushing through to burst forth from the other side. *Stop jumping at shadows.*

She laughed at herself. The noise had been startling, even eerie. But certainly not supernatural, and nothing to be frightened of. Though she did wish the air had remained calm. As strong as the gusts were down here, they had to be much worse high above.

"He wouldn't bring you up there if they were," she whispered.

She proceeded carefully, alone and nearly blind in a world of bare steel and hard concrete. Nails strewn on the ground, sharp scraps of metal with jagged edges, piles of debris and broken drywall, heavy equipment to maneuver past. She walked a gauntlet of construction material, constantly reminding herself the price was worth it for the payoff coming after it.

When she saw the cagelike elevator, she picked up her pace, the glow from within beckoning like a lighthouse from a rocky shore. She breathed a deep sigh of relief the moment she stepped inside, even though it was one of those open-construction types, like none she'd ever ridden in before, not exactly the picture of safety.

And then she laughed. "You charmer." Because the light he'd mentioned was provided by two tall candles in glass holders. Despite the wind drifting through the grating and making the flames dance, they remained lit, casting soft illumination and banishing the shadows. *What a romantic gesture.*

It wasn't the only one. Wendy stared down at the floor, watching thin streams of red wax drip down the candles to land on the bouquet of red roses lying at their base. No one had ever given her roses.

"You're wonderful," she whispered. And when she saw the fluffy stuffed teddy bear beside the flowers, tears of joy spilled onto her cheeks.

She wanted to hurry, but wasn't entirely sure how to operate the elevator. Fortunately, he seemed to have anticipated that. Taped to the handle was a handwritten note with instructions. At the bottom of it, in a postscript, he had written, *Please enjoy a glass of champagne before you begin this journey up to my world. I already have one and will be drinking to you the moment I hear the elevator start to ascend. We will toast to our lives together on your arrival.*

Had there ever been a more romantic man?

Wendy quickly looked around. She hadn't even noticed the open champagne bottle, wrapped in a towel, standing in an ice bucket. It had been nearly hidden by the flowers, which had taken up all her attention. Behind it was a tapered glass.

Though not much of a drinker, she wouldn't refuse the offer. Not only so she could toast to him, but also because she needed to calm her nerves. So she poured. And she sipped. She had never liked champagne, and she liked this dry, bitter stuff even less. Still, she drank again, swallowing until she'd downed the glass, feeling the bubbles tickle her nose and the effervescent alcohol hit her stomach.

Feeling fortified, she closed the grated door with a clang of metal, screwed her courage tight, and followed Rafe's operating instructions. Nothing happened at first; then the steel enclosure finally creaked to life. With a grinding of gears, the elevator began to move.

Funny, the world already seemed to be lighter, somehow. As she slowly began to rise, she began to feel light, weightless. As if she were floating. Which was as it should be. She was being released from the darkness of her dreary, average life. Unencumbered, free.

Up she went. Higher. Toward the heavens. And toward her destiny.

Almost as if she were flying.

His little bird was unconscious before she reached the fifteenth floor.

Wanting to ensure Wendy Cramer's arrival would go exactly the way he'd planned it, Darwin had watched her every move from the nanny-cam teddy bear he'd left for her. So he witnessed the precise moment of the woman's collapse. *Perfect timing.*

So far, she had not disappointed him, reacting exactly as he'd expected her to. From her accepting his urgent invitation, to her nervousness building as he kept her waiting, to her downing a glass of champagne to combat her fear, everything had gone as planned.

"You are so shockingly predictable," he said when the elevator finally came to a stop on his level. She might have thought she'd started its ascent, using his directions, but she hadn't. Wanting to delay her after she'd consumed the champagne, to give the ketamine a few extra moments to do its job, he had lied in the note, and used the landing call station on this level to get the elevator moving. "You had so many chances to avoid this fate and squandered them all."

She could have refused to come, of course. Only an utter fool would believe the nonsense he'd been spoon-feeding her for weeks. A member of an anonymous royal family in hiding? A prince falling passionately in love with a timid operator he'd never even seen? God, it was a wonder the idiotic woman had survived to adulthood.

"How foolish you were to not even question the name on the phone." He'd intentionally called her with that telephone, for a number of reasons. Not least of which was to give her another chance to defy his opinion of her, develop some modicum of good sense, and back away.

She'd blazed forward instead. Despite the name. Despite the sound of his voice—not an accented word. Right past a sign identifying the under-construction building as the new headquarters for a major local shipping company.

No penthouse. No condos. No royal investment.

"And any teenage girl knows better than to drink from an unattended bottle someone else opened. You stupid, awful woman. Didn't you notice the taste?"

She moaned. Though he had allowed adequate time, he moved quickly. The drug was very fast-acting, but he hadn't wanted her out for long. And despite the bitter taste, he hadn't been sure the twit would drink only one glass, so he couldn't lace the champagne too heavily.

Good thing he had expected her to fib about her weight. He'd dosed her for a woman twenty pounds heavier than she portrayed herself to be. By his calculations, one glass would keep her down for about an hour.

One hour should suffice for what he had to do. Ten or fifteen minutes at most here, leaving plenty of time to get out of the area. He would take up his position at the vantage point he'd selected earlier, a perfect spot to watch what happened.

"I kept my promise, didn't I?" he told her as he dragged her outside. "No walls, no doors. You can be seen by anyone looking in the right direction, as long as they're at the appropriate height."

He was counting on it.

As he had told her on the phone, he had been busy preparing for her arrival. He had severed the security netting and covered the safety lights. The tape was brand-new, the knife sharpened. He had only to get her ready and depart.

The steely blade of the knife glittered in the darkness. Cutting off her clothes, he took care not to let it nick her plump flesh, not wanting to hurt her.

He didn't want to do anything to her. He just wanted her to stop polluting his world with her presence. Having no godlike delusions, he couldn't make the choice between life or death. He could only put her in the position of having to do it herself. She could adapt, or she could die.

So far, she was on a direct course for death. But she might surprise him yet.

Once he'd stripped her bare, he rolled her onto her

stomach. Grabbing the duct tape with one gloved hand, he wrapped it around her wrists, securing them together behind her back. More tape for her eyes—he wound it around her head several times, so it stuck to itself, to her hair, to her skin.

She moaned again. "Shh, my dear," he murmured, not worried. She might be fighting to regain consciousness, but there was only so much a body could do against an unfamiliar narcotic.

The wind howled wildly through the top floor of the building, which swayed a little under its power. He couldn't have chosen more perfect weather. The shriek the air made as it rushed past the metal frame was reminiscent of a woman's scream. It would disconcert her— terrify her even more.

"I do wish I could stay and say hello to you in person, after all this time. But it wouldn't be prudent to wait until things are over to take my leave." He stared down at her naked body, pale and helpless in the moonlight, wondering why he felt no pity. Why he never felt pity, never experienced remorse or concern for a single one of them. His victims. His sheep.

He'd been born without the gene, he supposed.

"I'm not merciless," he told her. "You have a chance. Don't lose your head; use your brain for once and you might survive this. Embarrassed in the light of day when you're found by the construction crew, but otherwise safe and sound."

As long as she didn't lose her head.

With a smile and a softly blown kiss, he took his leave of her. He tucked the tape and the knife into his knapsack, along with the minilaptop into which he had plugged the nanny-cam receiver, and entered the elevator. During its long descent, he removed everything—the note, the bear, the roses, and the candles. He even looked for clumps of wax or a random flower petal. Though he had no confidence in the FBI agents who pursued him, there was no point in making things easy for them. The phone had been clue enough.

Reaching the ground floor, he watched for any sign of life, then quickly strode across the deserted street. He glanced at his watch—another forty minutes, at least, before she awoke.

He had parked down a side alley, a few blocks away, and, once inside his vehicle, made his way out of the area. Careful to stay away from intersections with cameras that might record his passing, he took backstreets, avoiding streetlights in favor of stop signs.

Everything went perfectly. At ten twenty, he entered the upscale hotel on the opposite side of the harbor. He'd checked in earlier, booking a room on the twenty-fifth floor, facing the water, due south. Once in his room, he didn't turn on the light, moving across the darkness to the window. He had already set up the telescope, training it on his point of interest. Within seconds, he was looking into the top floor of the site he'd left a short time ago.

From here, he had an excellent vantage point of the perimeter along the north- and east-facing sides. The west portion of the building, which fronted the street and was out of his line of sight, was blocked by a temporary wall, nowhere for her to go.

No temporary wall guarded the remaining three sides of the structure, though, not since he'd cut away the safety netting. His only real worry was that she would move toward the southern edge. He couldn't see it at all. What a disappointment that would be, to have set up something so entertaining and then miss the show.

And there would be a show. He had told her she could avoid it. He knew she wouldn't.

A glance at his watch confirmed that it had been more than an hour since she'd drunk the champagne. "Come on, wake up now; I have other things to do." Namely, drive to an area not far from here, where the woman he was truly interested in awaited his response. The moment this was over, he intended to pack up his things, slip quietly from the hotel, and head to Samantha's.

How delicious to write to her while parked outside of her building.

He could make it even more delicious by using some of the knowledge he had gained while visiting her apartment. But that might be too much for now. He didn't want to frighten her; he merely wanted to intrigue her. As she intrigued him.

Unlike Miss Wendy Cramer.

Suddenly a movement. A shape in the darkness. *Awake at last.*

"Yes, yes, you're confused, aren't you? Not sure if you're even conscious, or you're having a nightmare. Lost in blackness."

A long minute passed. She was trying to get her head to stop spinning, still under the effects of the drug. Shocked, terrified.

Not a dream. Cold. What's happened? Rafe, where are you?

He practically heard her every thought.

Where am I? So dark! Why can't I see?

Realization sinking in.

My hands! Oh, God, what have you done? Why are you doing this?

A flash of white. Her naked body, struggling to her knees, then managing to stand. Her balance uncertain, she staggered forward.

She stood no more than five feet from the edge of the building.

"Careful, now. Don't panic."

But she did. Of course she did. *Fool.*

She could have sat back down, remained in place. Felt her way an inch at a time, making sure there was floor beneath her before moving at all. Waited for rescue. Used her fucking brain.

Instead, the stupid bitch let her terror overwhelm her.

Blind and bound, only her feet moving, she spun in a frenzied circle. She staggered drunkenly, somehow oblivious to the clues to where she was. The cold cement floor. The wind blowing wildly across her body. Perhaps even the softly audible lap of the water far below. Christ, it was as if she'd forgotten where she had been headed before she'd blacked out.

Then, of course, a step too far. She reached the eastern edge, so close to falling he would swear her toes had actually hit empty air.

And she knew it.

Surprisingly, she had some fight in her. Wendy Cramer pulled back just in time, spinning away from the drop-off. Sheer terror and the fight-or-flight instinct sent her running in the opposite direction, away from the danger. Unfortunately for her, she couldn't really determine the opposite direction, being blind, bound, and drugged like that.

She ran right off the north side of the building.

Interesting. She obviously hadn't anticipated it. There had been no jerk back, no attempt to avoid the fall. The panicked woman had truly thought she was running on solid surface up until the very second that surface disappeared beneath her feet.

Darwin *tsk*ed, having been proved right yet again. Had there ever been any doubt?

Watching her descent, he wondered what she was thinking. That she would fall forever? No, several long seconds at most. But what lovely seconds, and how he enjoyed them.

His Wendy had done exactly what he'd thought she would do. His little bird had flown. Oh, how she'd flown.

True to his word, Alec was on track to get her home before tomorrow. Barely. They turned onto Sam's street with about five minutes to spare.

The ride from D.C. had been a mostly silent one. Alec appeared frustrated by the wasted day and their failure to engage his suspect, his pose reflecting his irritation. The sexy, smiling, maybe-verging-on-flirtatious man had been replaced by this scowling, hard-edged agent, who looked ready to pick a fight with anyone who crossed his path. Including her.

It wasn't merely frustration over the case; something else had happened. His mood had gone dark back there in the conference room, right around the time he told her he'd been shot.

Maybe he had cued in to her reaction. Because while Sam's first thought had been genuine concern for his well-being, she had also been taken aback to learn he was shot by a woman. Given the way he refused to discuss it, and had averted his eyes during that refusal, her curiosity had grown. Sam had some experience with men who averted their eyes when they were trying to hide something involving a woman, or when they were ashamed. Her ex had often done the former, though he'd rarely felt the latter.

She just hadn't expected it of Alec.

She shouldn't think of him in those terms, or in any personal terms. Simply because they worked well together and she enjoyed talking to him—both the serious issues and the unexpected lighter moments—didn't mean she had the right to be disappointed in him. Disappointment indicated far too much emotional involvement. She had no stake in what Alec did.

But she couldn't deny she'd felt let down, wondering if he was the type to get himself into trouble with women. Considering one had shot him, she had to think that'd be a big ten-four.

"Almost there," he said, breaking the heavy, thought-filled silence. "I'm sure you're ready to be home."

"Sure."

She had the feeling he intended to escort her to her

door, say good-bye, and never see her again, unless the psychopath he sought reached out to her once more. Which should have been a relief, given how annoyed she'd been by his intrusion into her life a few short days ago.

It wasn't.

What was she supposed to do, forget about this Darwin, this Professor? Act like his world had never brushed against her own and the FBI had never whisked her away to help them? Go back to her regularly scheduled life?

As if.

She was in this. Moreover, she wanted to be in this. She had reached out to the FBI once before, when she realized how deeply in trouble her grandmother had gotten, only to be left feeling abandoned and helpless. Now she was no longer helpless. She had played a part today.

How could she give up just because their first efforts to engage the killer had failed?

There was more to it, however.

Sam wasn't ready to go into her apartment and watch Alec Lambert drive away, never to see him again. Something inside her had awakened during their long, quiet hours together in the conference room. A bit of her spirit, perhaps.

Even more surprising, so had her long-dormant libido. One intense, steady look at him, with all the caution lights in her brain turned off, all the hurt pride and rejected-woman anger shoved aside, had forced her to acknowledge the truth.

The man was sex on a stick, to put it in Tricia terms. A pure confection of masculine heat, all hard-bodied and hot enough to burn anyone who got too close.

In that moment, she'd wanted him. Not only mentally acknowledging how good-looking he was, or how much she liked the feel of his hand on her shoulder. She had wanted him sexually, with the kind of intensity she didn't know she was even capable of experiencing anymore. The desire had dimmed somewhat with his admission about being shot by a woman, and her suspicions of why, but it hadn't gone away completely.

Throughout the car ride home, despite the tension, the awareness had slowly rebuilt. She'd felt the warmth of his body, heard his slow exhalations. She had watched the way his eyes narrowed and his jaw clenched when he was deep in thought. Noted the muscular build of his shoulders and arms beneath his shirt, and the solidness of his chest. Inhaled the spicy, masculine scent of his skin.

Yes, her libido had definitely woken back up, with a vengeance. Shooting or no shooting, it was screaming at her to do something before he walked back out of her life.

But could she, really? Could she do what her friends and her mother had been telling her to do for months? Take a chance, let a man make her laugh again? Let a man into her bed again? Into her life?

Uh-uh. No way. Women shoot this guy. He's trouble.

She knew she should listen to the little voice in her head. She also knew she probably wouldn't. Because she wasn't talking about falling in love with him, or letting her emotions get tangled up in it. Would some physical connection—before her girl parts dried up and fell off, as Tricia so eloquently put it—really be so bad?

Not as long as she remembered it was purely physical.

Unfortunately, she had no idea about how to make something happen. She had been out of the romance game so long she didn't even know if he was at all interested in her; though she'd seen a few long glances that made her suspect he had at least noticed she was female.

They were within a block of her place now. Alec was

probably already picturing waving good-bye and going home to his glass of scotch and a boxing match with a cyber character. He would put her out of this investigation as quickly as he'd brought her into it.

"You know, you ought to talk to Jimmy," she suddenly said.

"What?"

She shifted in the seat, staring at him, watching the way the dashboard lights sent soft beams of illumination over him. That handsome face was even more attractive with the addition of a slight five-o'clock shadow. "Jimmy Flynt. The con man I told you about."

He glanced over, appearing puzzled, not noticing the light change from red to green.

"Why should I talk to him?"

"If this unsub of yours is using e-mail scams to lure his victims, Jimmy's the man you should see. I know a few, but he could write an encyclopedia." There was more to it, though. "Besides, you said you wanted to try to get into this killer's head. I suspect Jimmy and this Darwin have a lot of the same views. Flynt really looked down on the people he stole from, almost like they had been asking for it. Which sounds like your guy, doesn't it?"

"I suppose."

"So maybe if you need to try to get inside this killer's head, to profile him, talking to someone who thinks the same way and did the same sort of thing—though not so violently, of course—wouldn't be a bad idea. It beats just waiting around for another body to turn up."

As soon as the words had left her mouth, she realized she'd put that badly, as if she'd been criticizing the job he and his colleagues had done so far. She hadn't been; nor would she. Today, sitting with them all, watching them come together as a team to work on this case, Sam had gained a whole new respect for the FBI.

"You might be right," he said with a hint of reluctance.

She let out the breath she didn't know she'd been holding, glad she hadn't offended him. Even gladder that he seemed to be considering her suggestion. Because he hadn't yet realized he wouldn't be able to pull it off without her help.

He nodded slowly, still thinking about it. Finally noticing the light, he touched the gas pedal, and within seconds they arrived at her building. Alec pulled into a parking space outside, lucky to get one—the street was crowded, cars lined down each side. As he cut the engine, he muttered, "That's actually a good idea."

"Good. Let me know when you want to set it up."

Startled, he raised a brow.

"He hates the FBI for bringing him down." She wasn't exaggerating. "But he likes me. A lot." Also not an exaggeration. "I told you about his letters."

Alec dropped his gaze, as if not wanting to reveal the anger she suspected he felt. "Does he e-mail you?"

"Of course not. He'll never be allowed to go near the Internet again. They were handwritten letters."

Though she wouldn't see any ever again. She'd made sure of that. Thank goodness the warden had had the foresight to decide not to tell Jimmy she didn't want to receive them anymore. He might not feel as friendly toward her.

It wasn't that she didn't appreciate the inmate talking to her, helping her with the book. But that in no way meant she had any liking for him. Though Flynt had been incarcerated by the time her grandmother had even learned how to use the computer Sam had given her, he was just like the men who'd stolen everything the elderly woman had. She detested him, as she detested all who preyed on the weak and vulnerable.

That didn't mean she wouldn't use him, or help the FBI use him, if it meant stopping a monster. "I can call his attorney or the prison directly. The sooner, the better, I'd imagine."

"Forget it. You've been dragged far enough into this."

"I volunteered."

"It's not happening, Sam."

"I am telling you, Flynt will not give you the time of day," she insisted. "He might not even talk to me if you're in the room, but I'm about the only shot you've got with him."

His lips compressed tightly, as if he'd said all he was going to say. But he didn't open the door and usher her out to silently announce his decision was final. Instead, he stayed in his seat, rubbing at his eyes with his thumb and index finger. Obviously thinking.

Reconsidering? Sam remained quiet, waiting for him to realize her idea was a good one. He was a smart man; he'd see the sense in it.

She couldn't stay entirely still for long, however. The bitterly cold night had been held at bay, though not defeated, by the weak heater. Now, with the engine turned off, the frigid air began to sift through the closed windows. She could already see her breath in front of her face, and the tip of her nose felt like an ice cube. Shivering, she wrapped her coat more tightly around herself, crossing her arms and tucking her hands beneath them for warmth.

He noticed. Without a word, Alec restarted the car, another sign he wasn't going to just shove her out and ignore her offer.

To her surprise, though, he went a step further. Reaching into the backseat, he grabbed his overcoat. He had thrown it there when they had gotten in, obviously having a little lava in his blood. Without a word, he tugged it up front, reached into the pockets, and pulled out a pair of leather gloves. Not even looking over, he tossed them onto her lap, still silent, still considering.

Sam couldn't have spoken either, even if she wanted to. Her breath had lodged in her throat. She was so taken aback, she didn't know how to react. Staring at the gloves, she studied them mutely, not even aware moisture had risen in her eyes until she felt a tear on her cheek.

In the entire four years she had been married, her ex had never done something as thoughtful as worrying about whether her hands were cold. One of their first fights, in fact, had started because she'd pulled a pair of his cashmere socks on her cold feet one morning when she couldn't find her slippers.

Simple courtesy had been beyond Samuel Dalton Jr., who'd been raised with such a big silver spoon in his mouth he hadn't even needed the bowl.

To Alec Lambert, the thoughtful gesture had been second nature. And it touched her the way Samuel's diamonds and huge bouquets of roses never had. She'd known this man for only a couple of days, but already she had begun to wonder if his entry into her life was going to leave her changed forever.

Maybe. If only by making her hold out for a man who gave a damn if her hands were cold. Or her feet.

He finally broke the silence. "It's a bad idea."

Still touched by the simple kindness, she didn't respond.

"You should forget all about this day."

"How am I supposed to do that?" She slid her hands into the gloves, her gaze locked on them, fearful her eyes might still be glassy. "For all we know, your suspect posted a response to me in the hour we've been on the road."

"Hell," he muttered, as if he had been hoping she could go back inside her apartment and be free of the whole situation. She suspected part of him wouldn't mind that, even though the other part, the professional FBI agent, had to be anxious for Darwin to crawl out of the woodwork.

He rubbed at his eyes, then asked, "You have an iPhone, don't you?"

"Yes."

"Faster than waiting to hook your system back up."

That was true. It was also true, however, that Alec seemed to want to avoid going inside.

Retrieving the phone, she got online and checked her own blog. Tension rolled off him, mingling with her own, and it seemed to take an eternity to scroll down through the pages of comments before finally reaching the end.

"Nothing," she said with a relieved sigh.

"And there might never be."

"Maybe not. But maybe there will. Frankly, if I've got a serial killer interested in me, I'd rather stick with you and your people."

A low growl of frustration was his only response.

"I know I'm only a civilian. . . ."

A piercing stare burned the rest of her words out of her mouth. His eyes gleamed in the dim light as he visually devoured her hair, her eyes, her face, her mouth. His voice shaking with emotion, he snapped, "Damn it, Sam, don't you get it? I don't want to think about this bastard even knowing you exist."

He might have intended to sound like an FBI agent. But the look in his eyes and the barely restrained anger said he was talking as a man.

The look made it clear her interest was fully reciprocated.

The anger told her the rest: He was afraid for her.

Sam said nothing, letting the reality of the situation wash over her, filling in the answers to the questions she'd been asking herself since they'd left D.C.

Yes, he'd noticed more about her than just that she was female. Yes, he'd realized something was happening between them. Yes, the attraction was mutual.

No, he wasn't thrilled about it. No, he didn't know what to do about it.

No, neither did she.

She lifted a gloved hand, not even knowing why. To

reach for the door handle? Or to cup his cheek and lean close enough to kiss the mouth she'd been wondering about since the minute he'd shown up at her door? One hint, one movement from him would tell her which.

He stared at her, not leaning closer, but not pulling away, either. Equally as drawn. Equally as unsure.

Tension flooded the car. *Shake his hand? Or dive onto his lap?*

Suddenly a horn blew. They both flinched. Sam's hand dropped instinctively, and Alec jerked back, clearing his throat and shaking his head as if he wanted to clear it of crazy thoughts.

She should be grateful. She had been about to do something that could have left her feeling very foolish had he rejected her. Still, she couldn't muster up much gratitude. Only a sad sort of what-if.

A minute went by. Then another. Until Alec finally broke the silence, his voice throaty and low. "It's been less than three days."

She didn't feign misunderstanding. He was talking about how long they had known each other. "I know."

"You should stay as far away from me—from this ugliness—as possible."

"That's not going to happen," she replied matter-of-factly. "Like I said, I'm in this."

"Not if I can help it."

"Are we still talking about the case?"

"Yes. No." He thrust a frustrated hand through his hair, already tousled from their long day, looking as completely unsure as she felt. "Hell."

Seeing his frustration, Sam regretted pushing him. Heaven knew he had a lot more on his plate than worrying about the feelings of a wound-licking divorcée he'd just met.

The timing was bad and she knew it, but she still wanted Alec Lambert. Wanted him to be the one to awaken her from her year of icy exile. Nothing serious, nothing permanent, just one incredibly sexy man around for a little while. And frankly, he was worth waiting for. Holding off until the ugliness surrounding them was taken care of didn't seem like too much of a sacrifice if she got what she wanted.

She had decided the destination—she had to give him some room, let him set the pace.

"You should go," she said. "It's a long drive back."

Not entirely sure whether or not she wanted him to refuse, she held her breath. The ball was in his court. Not about the case—no way was he going to shake her off that, if there was any chance she could help. But as far as what happened between them personally, his had to be the next move.

He made it. With a sigh that said he had no idea whether he was doing the right thing, he finally ended the suspense.

"You're right. I need to go. Good night, Sam."

Chapter 9

As Samantha and the stranger sat in the car outside her building, Darwin struggled to get his anger under control. A difficult feat, considering how furious he had been to see her arrive home in the company of that man.

That man.

He had made such an effort to hurry to her tonight. Racing to put away his telescope, he had left the hotel and driven as fast as he safely could. His blood had been hot and thick in his veins after he'd watched the operator in flight. The excitement had filled him until he'd been able to think of nothing else but sharing the moment with someone. With Samantha.

Even knowing he shouldn't visit her two nights in a row, for fear he would be noticed, he couldn't help it. He wanted to watch her move around inside and had been denied that pleasure last night. More, he needed to be there for the moment when, sitting at her desk, she would receive his delayed response, never suspecting its sender was less than fifty yards away.

So, arriving on her street and seeing her car parked outside, but her apartment completely dark again, had been disappointing. Watching her pull up a few minutes ago in an unfamiliar vehicle, driven by an unknown man, pushed him from disappointed to fucking outraged.

Bitch. He had been out doing the world a service, proving the point he had been trying to make to her. And she had been whoring herself to another man.

It took all his willpower to remain in his SUV, two spaces back, and observe through the windows of the truck that separated their vehicles. Especially when what he most wanted was to wait for the interloper to open his door and step outside so he could run him down right in the middle of the goddamn street.

Restraint. Impulsivity was an excuse for the weak minded.

He managed to remain in place, taking no action. Hunched down in his seat, he watched their silhouettes inside the dark sedan. The car's engine was running and they remained inside where it was warm, the low lighting making them easy to watch.

He idly considered shooting them both in the backs of their heads.

The man for his interference. Samantha for her betrayal. *City violence. Drive-by shooting.*

He refrained. He had never killed a person in his life. Watched them kill themselves, yes. But he had never pulled a trigger. And there had been a way out for the sheep every single time. Even the boys could have made it if they had kept their heads and worked together to move to the frozen shore. But ending a life with his own hand had never occurred to him.

Funny, then, how much he suddenly wanted to pull the trigger. It said something about how deeply Samantha had invaded him, mind and soul.

No. He was not ready to give up on her yet. "It isn't a betrayal if she doesn't know she's yours." He kept his voice low. Though no one was close enough to hear, he believed Samantha must be able to sense him. How could she not feel the magnetic pull as strongly as he did? Especially now, when he was so close he could almost reach out and take her?

"I can forgive you," he told her.

He meant it. It wasn't entirely her fault. He had been remiss, not acting sooner. A woman as beautiful as Samantha would, of course, draw male attention. He'd assumed her unhappiness over her divorce would keep her locked up at home, licking her wounds, until he was ready to come for her. That was a mistake Darwin intended to rectify very soon.

Not yet. Do nothing for now. Just observe. Wise idea, and he followed his own instincts, wondering, as the minutes ticked by, why the pair had not gone up to Samantha's apartment.

He began to feel hopeful. Perhaps this was not a romantic date. The driver could be a casual acquaintance giving her a lift home.

Then the two of them turned and looked at each other. The exchange was thick with expectation; they stared at each other with raw intensity. He knew the moment to be a critical one when Samantha lifted her hand, appearing poised to reach for the stranger, to draw him close enough to kiss her lush mouth.

Darwin nearly vomited. Unwilling to witness such a thing, he furiously pounded his hand on the steering wheel, hitting, by accident, the horn.

Her hand dropped. The moment had ended.

Good thing for them. His remarkable self-control might not have lasted if he was actually forced to witness the only woman he had ever wanted in the arms of another man. He could possibly withstand knowing it was happening, but he could not be expected to watch.

So drive away.

He reached into the glove compartment instead. Retrieving his silencer-equipped Beretta nine-millimeter handgun, he dropped it on his lap. Just in case.

Leaning forward, over the steering wheel, he craned

to see more of the stranger's car, desperately wanting a glimpse of the license tag. But from here, blocked by the truck, he couldn't see any lower than the lid of the trunk.

Suddenly, the passenger door ahead of him opened. He sank farther, watching as Samantha stepped out, her beautiful profile washed with illumination from the streetlight.

The driver's door remained closed. *Tsk*ing, he whispered, "Not a gentleman, are you? Not seeing a lady to the door. Who knows what dangers might be lurking in the night?"

A good thing he was here to see to Samantha's well-being.

Darwin's spirits—lifted by the thought that his Sam had not invited the driver in—were dashed when the other door opened as well. Watching in dismay, he saw the tall stranger exit and join her on the sidewalk. The man was young, good-looking.

Darwin lifted the gun. Flicked off the safety.

Instead of curling an arm around her slim waist, leading her up the stairs to a night of carnal pleasure, however, the driver bent into the backseat of the car. When he stood, he held a large cardboard box. It appeared hefty; he had to shift it around to ensure a good grip before turning to follow Samantha to her apartment.

"What are you up to?"

There were any number of possibilities. Perhaps this was merely a friend, helping Samantha with a heavy purchase.

At midnight? Doubtful.

A lover, then, bringing sexual devices, toys with which to play, pornographic images to share in her soft bed?

His bile rose again. Holding his breath, Darwin watched as the two of them reached her floor, releasing it with an angry hiss when she beckoned her visitor inside her home, closing the door behind him. Shutting him, and the rest of the world, out.

"One. Two. Three," he whispered.

In one minute, he would drive away. Staying here, knowing another would be spending the night in Samantha's arms, was too much for even him.

"Four. Five. Six."

He fingered the trigger of his Beretta. *Maybe* he would drive away. Maybe he wouldn't.

"Seven. Eight. Nine."

The tension dragged out with every second. By the time he reached forty, one hand was clenched around the grip of the gun. The other clung to the steering wheel. Which way he would go when he said the word *sixty*, he honestly couldn't say. It was as undetermined as the random flip of a coin.

At fifty-five, the apartment door opened. His rival stepped out, no longer holding the box. Samantha remained within. They exchanged a few words. No kiss good night. No warm smile. No intimacy. Then the man walked toward the stairs, and Samantha shut the door.

Good girl.

The tension that had pushed him nearly to his breaking point began to ease; his breath returned; his heart took up its regular beat.

Calm, yes. Relieved, too. But he didn't relax. Nor did his anger dissipate.

Nothing sexual could have happened in the brief time they were inside, and they had not kissed good night. But there had been that moment, that expectant moment in the car when they had almost instinctively leaned toward each other before the sound of his car horn had pushed them apart.

Not lovers . . . but not long until they will be.

Revolted by the thought, he put the gun down long enough to turn the key in the ignition, then immediately picked it up again. The Beretta heavy and warm in one hand, he flicked a button with the other, sending the passenger-side window on a quick, soundless descent.

The stranger had reached the well-lit stairs, which faced the street, and began to walk down them. He didn't look back, or even ahead, instead focused on something in his own hand.

Fool not to watch where you're going.

Slowly pulling out, he let the vehicle drift forward noiselessly, watching every move the stranger made. By the time Darwin pulled his SUV even with the long cement walkway leading to the stairs, his rival was halfway down. One pull of the trigger away. One tiny little pull.

A flip of the coin.

Yes?

No. Samantha might react badly to having someone she knew murdered on her doorstep. She could retreat out of sight, making it impossible to find her again.

He could do nothing.

Frustrated, thwarted, Darwin pushed the button to lift the window, keeping only the lightest pressure on the gas pedal. His headlights off, he was nearly invisible as he rolled quietly through the night, out of range, leaving his prey unaware of how close to death he had come.

"Damn it! Who is he?"

The speculation would drive him mad. He wasn't accustomed to Samantha varying her routine like this. First last night, her apartment showing no sign of life at two a.m. Now this.

Maybe she wasn't home at all last night. Perhaps, like tonight, she had been with him, the rival.

Darwin mulled over the idea, suddenly realizing what else about last night had bothered him: her night-light. It hadn't been on. Not when he had arrived, not when he'd left shortly after two. Every other time he had visited, it had cast soft illumination through her bedroom window.

So. She hadn't been home at all. She *was* seeing someone.

He forced himself not to be disappointed in her. It wasn't her fault. She was vulnerable, lonely. She had been ripe for the picking, and that bastard in the dark sedan had obviously picked.

There was only one thing to do: Find out who the other man was and eliminate him.

How careless he had been to let his impulsive anger drive him away in such a hurry. He might have been able to see the tag as he pulled up to the car. Though he considered going back, he quickly discounted the idea. Not only was it risky to enter the neighborhood again; he was also several blocks away. The interloper was long gone by now.

All was not lost, though. There was another option. He had other resources to find out what Samantha was up to, another way to peer into the darkest recesses of her private life.

And he intended to use it.

As soon as Alec had said he was leaving, Sam had gotten out of the car. His decision was made; no way would she make things uncomfortable by getting pissy or whiny about it. But, as he'd gruffly informed her, he wasn't going to let her carry her CPU up by herself. So she'd been forced to wait there while he hoisted the large box and lugged it up the outside steps, trying not to feel embarrassed at having been shot down.

Leading the way, she'd tugged off one of his gloves so she could retrieve her keys from the bowels of her purse and unlock the door. "Just leave it on the desk," she said once they were inside. "I know you're ready to go. I can take it from here."

With a curt nod, he did as she asked, then turned to go. The man obviously intended to ignore what had happened between them. He seemed anxious to get out before the pathetic, horny, cheated-on ex-wife leaped on him or something.

Don't be stupid. He was playing this smart. A lot smarter than her.

She had somehow managed a cordial tone as she handed him his gloves. "Don't forget these. Thanks for letting me borrow them."

As he took the bunched leather, his fingers touched hers ever so lightly. She managed to maintain an impassive expression, despite the way her fingertips sizzled in reaction to that brief, innocent brush of skin on skin.

"You're welcome," he said in a low growl, waiting for her to let go.

She forced herself to. And then, with a simple good night, he was gone.

The moment she closed the door behind him, Sam heaved a disappointed sigh. She stood there for a long moment, trying to go back three days in her mind, to before her world had turned so upside down. Wondering how things could feel so off-kilter in such a brief amount of time. She felt like a different person, as if the real Samantha Dalton was finally showing her face again after her long, self-imposed period of penance and isolation.

Penance for being stupid enough to get involved with someone who she knew would inevitably hurt her. Isolation to try to prevent it from happening again.

So why on earth was she getting hung up on a man who had been shot by a woman less than six months ago and now refused to talk about it?

"You're crazy," she told herself. "And you're lucky he left."

The words might have emerged from her mouth, but they didn't sink into her mind or her heart. Because when a knock sounded on the front door a few seconds later, she yanked it open without a single hesitation, not knowing why he had come back, just glad of it.

The first thing she noticed: Alec wasn't frowning. In fact, if she had to name it, she'd call his expression rueful.

"Is something wrong?"

He stepped inside, closing the door against the cold. Looking down at his own hand, Alec made a small sound that could have been either groan or laugh—or both; then a smile widened the sexy mouth. "Uh, Sam?"

"Yes?"

He lifted the bundle of leather she'd given him a couple of minutes before, holding the glove by a finger. Glove. Singular. "Black hole of death strikes again, huh?"

"Oh, God, I'm so sorry." A quick, frantic glance confirmed the mate was lying on the floor nearby.

Grabbing it and handing it to him, she noted a glint of wicked amusement in his eyes. The brooding, angry man from the car was gone, as was the frustrated FBI agent, at least for the moment. Here was the flirtatious charmer she'd glimpsed a time or two since they'd met. The one who took her breath away.

"No wonder you have a dozen odd gloves. You steal 'em one at a time, huh?"

The change of mood had been so quick and unexpected, Sam could do nothing but laugh in response. Alec hadn't exactly returned for a passionate kiss or a promise that they were going to do something about this thing they were both feeling. But he was smiling. Which, in her book, was a pretty good second choice. "It wasn't intentional, I promise."

"It's okay. I never wear them and could have lived without them."

She tilted her head, eyeing him curiously. "So why did you come back?"

He didn't reply at first, merely staring at her. A battle seemed to wage behind his eyes, as if he honestly didn't know what to do—something she doubted was a frequent occurrence for this competent man. Finally, when she had half decided he was just going to turn around and walk back out without another word, he admitted,

"Because I didn't want to leave you here to build this up in your head even more than you already have."

"Oh, you're a mind reader now?"

He leaned a shoulder against the doorjamb. "It wasn't too hard."

"Are you profiling me?"

"Any guy who's ever wanted a woman would know what you're thinking, Sam."

She tried to stay huffy, but melted a little instead at his admission that he wanted her.

"You wear a shield that says, 'Back off.' When you finally dropped it in the car, you didn't deserve to think I hadn't even noticed."

"I knew you noticed," she shot back. "I just figured you were too chickenshit to do anything about it."

His quick bark of laughter told her the insult had rolled right off. Lifting a hand to her face, he smoothed back a strand of her hair, rubbing it lightly between his fingers. "So you knew exactly what I was thinking, huh?"

She swallowed hard, fighting not to curl her cheek into his palm. "Yep."

"Okay." He dropped his hand again. "But in case there's any last doubt, let me clear it up. The answer is yes. I did want to haul you onto my lap and kiss the taste out of your mouth."

The strength drained from her legs, and she leaned against the back of a chair. She'd been wanting some physical connection; now she wondered if she had bitten off more than she could chew. Then again, choking on someone who excited her as much as Alec didn't seem like such a bad way to go.

Someone else's weak, breathy vocal cords asked, "Why didn't you?"

"Because this whole thing has been a little crazy. Fast. Unexpected." He shrugged in resignation. "What can I say? I was trying to be a nice guy."

She waited, wondering if there was more to that sentence.

Now do you not *want to be a nice guy?*

The words didn't come. Instead, he cleared his throat and straightened again. "I just thought you should know that. It's not lack of interest; it's lack of ability to focus on much of anything except the job right now."

"I get that," she murmured, meaning it. "Thank you for coming back and telling me."

"You're welcome."

He didn't say anything else, didn't offer promises or make plans for what might happen later, when things were a little less crazy. Instead, he just stood there by the door, his hands shoved into his pockets, visibly torn about how to proceed.

Sam took the decision out of his hands. "I don't have any scotch. And I don't own a video game system."

His eyes narrowed in confusion.

"But if you can stand tequila, I do play a pretty good hand of Texas Hold 'Em. No strings. No making things any more crazy. I just thought, if you want to blow off some steam, and extend our less-than-three-day relationship by an hour, you're more than welcome."

Relationship. A strange word to describe what was going on between the two of them. But she couldn't take it back, and she couldn't regret saying it.

He didn't step forward. Nor did he turn away. Instead, he did something much more unexpected. "It wasn't what you were thinking."

"What?"

"The shooting. I didn't have an affair with a witness, or do anything inappropriate with her."

Embarrassed that he had so correctly guessed where her suspicious mind had gone, she put a hand up, palm out. "You don't have to tell me this."

He ignored her. "We were chasing a man suspected of

kidnapping and multiple homicides. I'd gotten friendly with his mother, felt sorry for her, you know?"

Feeling like the world's biggest witch for what she'd thought of him, she mumbled, "Alec, really . . ."

"I let my guard down. When we got too close and she knew we were going to nail him, she pulled out a semiautomatic and started firing. I took two in the chest, one in the shoulder. Another agent took one straight through the heart. I came home afterward. He never did."

Oh, God.

He continued, not hesitating to allow her to express any sympathy she knew he didn't want. "I'm not telling you this for the tequila, because one shot would put me out for the night and I have a long drive home. I just wanted you to know." A hint of promise darkened his eyes. "For next time."

Next time. Meaning he believed there would be a next time. Or, in their case, a first time.

Someday.

"I understand," she replied softly. "Thank you for confiding in me."

The trust he had expressed in her, and the knowledge that they had taken a step forward, moving closer to what she thought could be something special, made her want to return the favor. Her fingers curled tightly into fists by her side, she admitted something very few people knew. "I was the one holding the golf club."

His brow furrowed in confusion.

"I beat up my own laptop."

"Oh." Alec didn't make some flip comment like, *Should I be scared?* as if knowing what it had cost her to make the admission. And realizing how far she must have been driven.

"My husband's wasn't working right. . . ."

"You don't have to get into this," he said, echoing what she'd told him.

He hadn't taken the easy way out. Neither would she. "So he borrowed mine to take on a business trip."

He shook his head in disgust, obviously knowing where the story was headed. It wasn't an uncommon one. "Internet porn?"

"Not exactly."

"Online sex?"

"Yeah. But only as a substitution for the real sex they were having at home."

"Bastard."

"His girlfriend didn't want him to feel too lonely, so she sent lots of pictures. Some of her, some of him, some of them together. All of which I found when I got the laptop back."

"Jesus," he muttered, looking as though he wanted to tug her close, but not doing it. As if he knew she needed to get it all out now, if only so they would never have to talk about it again.

"Can't say I wasn't a little shocked." She managed a dry chuckle, surprised she didn't have to force the laugh. Maybe she really had healed if she could actually find amusement in this for the first time since the night it had happened. "I guess he was lucky not to be there. The computer took the brunt of my seven-iron wrath."

He wasn't fooled by the attempt at humor. Shaking his head in disbelief, he said, "What a fucking moron. First for doing it, then . . ."

"For not deleting the evidence?" she asked, certain he had thought of it as a law officer, but hadn't wanted to say so for fear of sounding insensitive.

"Yeah."

"Oh, he deleted it. He just forgot to empty the recycle bin."

"Repeat: fucking moron."

Yes, he had been. Because while she hadn't been perfect, she had tried hard to be a good wife and to make her marriage work. Right up until the moment she got slapped in the face with the kind of close-up pictures of another woman no heterosexual female would ever want to see.

"He was rich and spoiled and used to getting whatever he wanted, whenever he wanted it. One day he wanted me. The next he wanted her. It was pretty open-and-shut in his mind."

"Too bad the son of a bitch did it on your computer. Whacking the hell out of his would have been much more satisfying."

"Probably. But the claims he made during the divorce were bad enough. Painting me as a vindictive, low-class psycho who destroyed his belongings would have made things worse."

This time, he didn't hold back. Alec stepped closer, put his hands on her shoulders, and drew her to him. Sam resisted for half a second, by habit now, rather than mistrust. Then she relaxed into him, amazed at the feel of physical connection she'd told herself she didn't miss.

He was hard and strong, the rugged planes of his body such a contrast to the soft curves of hers. Yet they fit together perfectly. With her cheek pressed into the angle between his shoulder and neck, and every inch of her pressed against the rest of him, a sigh couldn't have fit between them.

Alec didn't take things any further, and she didn't ask him to. His hands remained above the waist; their mouths did not connect. She simply took what he was offering, enjoyed it while it lasted. Then, with a nod of silent gratitude, she stepped away, giving them both the space she suspected they needed to keep their heads on straight.

"I appreciate your telling me," he said as they eyed each other.

"I appreciate your listening."

"I guess we're both carrying a lot of baggage."

"I guess." Wanting to make things clear before they

went any further—if they were going any further—she said, "I might be ready to put that baggage down finally. But that doesn't mean I want to pick a new set up right away."

He got it immediately. "I'm not exactly ready to go on a long trip anytime soon myself." He probably had as much reason as she did to avoid romantic entanglements, because of both his physical scars and the breakup he'd mentioned earlier tonight.

"No long trips," she murmured, "meaning an overnight one here or there might be okay?"

He didn't laugh, because she hadn't been flirting. Though couched in innuendo, her meaning had been straightforward, and they both knew what she was saying. "Yeah, Sam. I think it might."

She let out a slow, easy breath, wondering why she wasn't dizzy with nervousness. She had just blatantly propositioned the sexiest man she'd ever met, asked him to have a short-term fling with her, and he had accepted. But her emotions were in control, her mood relaxed. They could have been talking about getting a bite to eat rather than having the one-night stand they had both just admitted they wanted.

Maybe the lack of tension was because she had known this was coming from soon after she'd met him. And because desperately wanting someone as emotionally unavailable as she was seemed safe. They would have no entanglements, no expectations, no emotions that could leave her crushed and devoid of any feeling at all, the way she'd been just one year ago.

An affair with Alec would be a perfect way to finish the healing process and begin to move on. To become whole and complete again, a fully realized woman, in an intensely pleasurable way.

"But not now. We've got to get through this case first," he said, though he didn't sound happy about it. Crossing his arms as if to prevent himself from reaching for her, he added, "You're a potential witness, and that has to be my focus until we catch this guy."

"I get it."

She did. Just the knowledge that they were going to share something intimate and sexual was enough for now.

That didn't mean she was ready for him to leave. Though she saw the fatigue in his face, she wanted him to stay. She wasn't desperate and physically hungry like she'd been in the car. This was softer, gentler. She just wanted to spend some time with the man.

About to ask him if he still wanted a hand of poker, with coffee instead of alcohol, she remained quiet when a ringing sound came from his pocket. Alec flinched, equally as surprised someone would be calling on his cell at this time of night.

He quickly grabbed it, checking the caller ID. Opening it, he snapped, "Wyatt? Has something happened?" He immediately fell quiet, listening. Seeing his body tense, she knew something had, indeed, happened. "When, tonight? Do we know which cell tower? Any way to pinpoint it further?"

More silence, except for the low, muted rumble of his boss's voice through the receiver. She could make out no words. Whatever Agent Blackstone was saying, however, had Alec alert and on edge. Finally, he nodded. "Okay. I'll be there early. If you need me before that, just call." Then he cut the connection.

"Everything okay?"

"I don't know yet," he admitted. He said nothing more, obviously not able to talk about it. She had been part of things today, personally drawn into the situation by the very suspect they were chasing. She had no further claim in it, however. So she had no right questioning him.

"I really need to go. I've got a long drive and an early morning."

"I understand." She opened the door, stepping out of

his way to let him go. "Thanks again for coming back up to clear the air."

"You're welcome. Good night, Sam."

She fully expected him to walk right out, since he'd set the boundaries between them until the case was over. Instead, he did something far more surprising. Without warning, he slid his hands into her hair, tugging her close. With a low groan of surrender, as if he simply couldn't help himself, he covered her mouth with his, kissing her hard, fast, and deep. His mouth was hot and demanding, his hunger for her so obvious her whole body went weak.

He let her go abruptly. Sam sagged back against the doorframe, stunned, excited, anticipatory.

All of those feelings doubled when he spoke again, his voice almost shaking. "As *soon* as this case is over."

The man wanted her desperately. How amazing.

He left without another word. Though it was freezing cold, Sam walked outside onto the landing, watching him go again, feeling much different than she had the first time. His pace quick, he jogged down the steps. He looked up only once, after he was behind the wheel. With a quick flash of that sexy smile, he started the car and took off.

Once he was gone, she quickly went back inside. She had been standing out there under the bright security lights, fully visible from the dark street below. It had been a disconcerting feeling: almost like being exposed, as if anyone could have been watching her from the shadows.

She laughed at her own vivid imagination and shrugged off the odd thought. After all, it was late; every window around here was darkened, not a soul out in this bitter weather. And she wasn't exactly the most exciting personality in Baltimore.

Who would possibly want to watch her?

Chapter 10

After the murders of Ryan Smith and Jason Todd, when investigators realized the boys' cell phones had not been in their submerged car with their clothing, the families had been instructed not to cancel the accounts. Nobody had believed the Professor would be careless enough to use one of his victims' phones, but you never knew.

So when word had come in that Ryan's phone had been used last night, Alec had been anxious for the details. Wyatt hadn't known much, certainly not enough for any members of the team to head back in at one in the morning. Going home, Alec had grabbed a little sleep, then returned to headquarters.

Taggert and Fletcher were already there, as, of course, was Wyatt. They all looked up and greeted him, Wyatt with cordiality, Dean with a noncommittal nod, and Lily with a friendly smile. No glares. No turning away, like what he might have gotten at the BAU. *Progress*.

"Conference room at seven thirty, all right?" Wyatt said as he departed.

Alec knew Wyatt wouldn't want to go over the new evidence more than once. Waiting a half hour for everyone else made sense, even if he was impatient for the details.

Intending to go to his office, he hesitated when he heard Stokes's voice. "Man, somebody needs to call the weatherman and tell him to send this cold shit away. I have had enough."

"Sorry, it's only January. The shit's staying for at least two more months," said Taggert, sounding almost as if he were joking around. This must be a good mood for him. Then again, his partner, Kyle, wasn't in yet to light his short fuse.

When Stokes finally saw Alec standing in his doorway, her eyes widened. She looked almost surprised that the new guy had shown up for work a full hour early like the merely mortal agents.

Alec lifted a brow to tell her he knew what she was thinking. "Problem?"

"Nah," she muttered, sounding reluctantly amused. "I guess you might cut it after all."

"No more 'hotshot' remarks?"

"Deal."

He managed to keep a straight face when he asked, "And I get to drive?"

"Don't push it."

"Yeah, don't push it, Lambert," said Dean. The other agent confirmed his good mood with a real smile, which made the usually serious face look a whole lot more approachable. "You think she's bad behind the wheel, wait'll you experience her talents as a backseat driver."

Alec grinned. "At least I won't get killed in a wreck."

"You might wish you had."

"Hey! I didn't hear you complaining when I drove your butt home last week." She turned to Alec. "Our boy has a new live-in lady friend who needed to borrow the car."

"How does your husband put up with you?" Dean asked.

She ignored him. "How is Stacey, anyway? She settling in to city life okay?"

"Yeah. She starts her new job with the Montgomery County Sheriff's Office next week."

"Gonna be a lot different from Hope Valley. But she'll be running the place in no time."

The serious man actually chuckled. So the guy obviously had a soft side, if only for his cop girlfriend. Suddenly recognizing the name of the town Jackie mentioned, Alec asked, "Hope Valley? The Reaper case?"

"Yes," Dean replied.

"Wait—are you talking about the sheriff who helped you bring him down?"

"Stacey Rhodes," he said, obviously proud. "She was sheriff at the time, but didn't run for reelection. She was ready for a change and wanted to—"

"Move in with your grouchy self," Jackie said.

"Leave him be," said Lily, who had been quietly listening to the exchange from just inside the small, cramped break room: a glorified closet with a coffeemaker and a sink.

Though a member of the team, Lily seemed to hover on the periphery, and not merely because she wasn't in the hall with the rest of them. The woman appeared comfortable being slightly on the outside, not in the middle of things, as if she hadn't totally let down her guard. Alec didn't take it personally, having noted the separation was from everyone, not just him.

"Don't pay attention to either of them, Alec. We really aren't that nosy around here."

"Yeah, we are," another voice said. Kyle Mulrooney had arrived. The barrel-chested man, his slicked-down black hair unmoved by the windy weather, removed his coat and tossed it on a rack. "So nosy we've got a few questions for you, Lambert."

Alec stiffened. He had been waiting for this, wondering when they'd work their way up to asking him about the rumors. Anybody who bothered to look into the case would know he had been shot by the sixty-year-old mother of the suspect. Not a girlfriend, not a wife, not a young suspect he'd gotten tangled up with against all policies and agency rules. But few people were interested in looking into it.

An agent had died. Alec was to blame. That was all they needed to know.

"There's something Dean's been dying to ask you," Mulrooney said, his jowly face pulled into a frown. "Uh, who's your tailor?"

"Bite me, buddy," Dean said.

Stokes snorted, and Alec felt the tension leave his body. His coworkers were going out of their way to welcome him today, while they hadn't the previous few. It was as if they'd waited for him to prove himself and, somehow, yesterday he'd done so.

Now they were intentionally bringing him into their world, letting him know that, even though he hadn't been a Black CAT for long, he was one of them. And whatever they'd heard about him before he'd arrived, they were giving him a chance, as their boss had.

At least, that was how he interpreted it.

"Ignore them. We're glad to have you," Lily said, confirming he was right.

He couldn't name a moment in his career when he'd been more appreciative. "Thanks," he murmured, saying more than just that simple word.

Lily got the message. "There's no outside garbage here; we drop it at the door."

"Yeah, 'cause everybody treats us like garbage, anyway," Kyle said with a wide grin, as if not bothered by the idea whatsoever.

Alec thought he understood. There was a certain freedom in being ignored due to Wyatt's infamy. The ability to operate under the radar, investigating an unsub who appeared to be a serial killer the BAU had been hunting for years, for instance.

Kyle continued. "I guess you might be good enough to become a gen-u-ine Black CAT."

Smiling as he realized the team didn't seem to mind the nickname, which he'd already gotten used to himself, Alec said, "Thanks. I'll do my best."

Lily stepped out of the break room, closer to the group, though still maintaining a few feet of distance. Not fully joining in, but trying. "And I hope you're not second-guessing yourself about yesterday. Trying to engage the unsub through Mrs. Dalton's Web site was an excellent idea, and we all wanted it to succeed."

Stokes jumped in. "There's still a chance. I checked the site this morning; comments are still coming in. Not from Darwin, but he could be watching."

"If Darwin is the Professor, he's definitely watching," Alec murmured, feeling sure of it.

He didn't mention that he had also checked the Web site every hour throughout the night. And every time he checked, he found himself wishing he could have kept Sam out of this nightmare.

"He's the Professor," Jackie said, sounding certain. The other three agents nodded, the conclusion a unanimous one among the team. "We all know it."

"I agree," Alec said, wondering if they heard his lack of happiness about that.

He hated to admit it, knowing they needed the lead, but he wouldn't be completely disappointed if the man who had reached out to Sam was not who they were after. She'd been through so much already. Hearing what her bastard ex had put her through had broken his heart a little. That she had been drawn out only because a psychopath had zoned in on her as some kind of ally seemed not only unfortunate but damned unfair.

She could *already be out of it.*

If only he could believe that. Though as of an hour ago their unsub had not returned to Sam's Web site, Alec knew it could still happen. The Professor was out there, an angry, murderous bull, and Sam was holding the red cape that could enrage him.

He would worry about any civilian in this situation; it was his job. But last night, Alec had realized he no longer had the impartiality of his job to hide behind when it came to Sam. Already, this was deeper. This was personal.

He let himself repeat it, if only in his head: His feelings toward Sam Dalton were personal. It had taken a lot to say good night and leave her in the doorway last night, when neither of them wanted him to go. He'd been tempted by a lot more than the friendly poker game she'd suggested. Losing himself in the softness of her mouth, which he suspected hadn't been offered to any man since her prick of a husband had tossed her away, it had taken serious willpower to walk away after just one kiss. But a second helping would have led to only one place: bed.

Maybe when this is over . . .

Yeah. Maybe then. What might happen, he couldn't say. Maybe it was only attraction, as he'd told himself at first, and his liking and admiration for her wouldn't come into play.

But he doubted it.

"You think he's just waiting it out, wanting to get more of her blog visitors riled up, screaming for his blood, before he comes back and 'instructs' everyone?" Lily asked, making the very point Alec had been considering.

"Yes, I do. I think he's intentionally letting the debate rage on, liking the attention and the drama he started. When it dies down . . ."

"He'll stir the pot again," Kyle said. "Like a sous chef straight outta hell's kitchen."

Right. And when and if Darwin stirred the pot, they'd be watching. Alec had only one fear—that Sam would stir it first.

He couldn't think about that. He needed to focus on the case, stop the Professor before he hurt anybody else. Before he dragged Sam deeper into his nightmare.

That included finding some other way to talk to Jimmy Flynt.

"There is one other possibility about why Darwin didn't come back last night." Lily's shoulders were slumped, looking as though they carried the weight of the world. She didn't have to continue. They all knew what the other possibility was.

The Professor might have been out killing someone.

"What's going on? Did I miss a staff meeting?" Brandon Cole entered the office. Pink shirt today, loud tie. Alec felt pretty sure he'd seen the look on a billboard or on the cover of *GQ*.

"Perfect timing; we're about to go in," said Jackie.

Alec glanced at his watch. Seven twenty-five. Tossing his briefcase onto his desk, he joined the others in the conference room. Wyatt was waiting for them, poring over some paperwork strewn out on the table. Glancing at one file, Alec realized these were copies of the evidence report from Ryan's and Jason's murders.

"Anything of use?" he asked.

"The forensics came back as expected. Not a single usable fingerprint on the car, other than those belonging to the boys or Jason's family members. The same can be said for the duct tape, the most popular brand on the market. There was a black fiber trapped in the weave of it, however. It might have come from a knit glove."

And how many of *those* could there be in the northern hemisphere?

"The metal folding chair was a brand distributed through a couple of big-box retailers all over the country."

The hits just kept coming.

"So what's the deal with the phone?" Taggert asked.

Wyatt pushed the forensic report back into the folder. "Someone used it for more than three minutes last night. Ryan Smith's father has been checking his son's account every night, and he noticed a call took place around nine p.m. The phone company has the account flagged, and they would have noticed it this morning. . . . Thanks to Mr. Smith, we knew twelve hours in advance."

Smart man. Or simply a grieving father who felt powerless and wanted to do something to help solve his son's murder.

"The cell phone provider should be calling at any time with the information on the tower, and the approximate location of the caller."

Meaning, if the Professor had used the phone himself, they would know where he had been less than half a day ago. Where he had really been, not just what Internet sites he had cruised. Alec forced himself not to even think of that issue, not wanting his head clouded today by his concern for Sam.

As if Wyatt had willed it to happen, the office phone rang. The dour receptionist, whose name Alec couldn't even remember, hadn't arrived yet, so the boss answered the call himself from the phone in here. They all quieted when he started speaking, but every person actually fell silent as soon as they realized he was not talking to the cellular provider.

"Yes, Detective, we are assisting the Wilmington police."

Something about the boys.

It was impossible to glean anything from merely the words Wyatt uttered on his side of the conversation. It was not, however, difficult to spot the way their boss shook his head and covered his eyes at some bit of particularly bad news. "Yes, of course." He reached for a pen and paper, jotting something down, then continued. "Morning traffic will tangle us up a bit, but we should be able to get there by nine or shortly thereafter. You will still be working the scene?"

Oh, damn. Another crime scene?

Every other person in the room realized the same thing. Jackie groaned in disgust. Lily's pale face lost what little color it had. Kyle and Dean both muttered expletives, and Brandon flipped open his laptop, ready to dive in with whatever information Wyatt gave them.

Their leader hung up, rising and stuffing the forensics pages back into their files. "It appears we don't have to wait for the phone company. Ryan Smith's cell phone was discovered at a crime scene. Lily and Brandon, please remain here to provide us with off-site support, as well as monitoring Mrs. Dalton's Web site."

"And the rest of us?" Jackie asked.

"We're going to Baltimore. A woman's body was found this morning."

Alec jerked to his feet. "Not Sam . . ."

Wyatt immediately shook his head. "No, no. Of course not."

Thank you, God. His conscience was already heavy over what had happened to Ferguson. One death—another agent's—was all the guilt he could carry. A civilian's could break him.

Samantha's? Well, that could crush him for good.

No one commented on Alec's response, probably because they'd all seen him sit in this room with her for nine or ten hours yesterday. They knew he felt responsible for his plan not working, and would feel even more responsible if Sam was hurt because of it. They couldn't know he had gotten personally interested in the woman, though Jackie did eye him speculatively.

He didn't care. Those few brief seconds thinking something had happened to Sam had thrust the reality of his feelings toward her home with the power of a blade. There was no *maybe* about it. When this case was over, he would be knocking on her door for that shot of tequila, that poker game. That kiss. And whatever came after it.

"Let's go," Wyatt said.

Everyone rose quickly. Grabbing coats and keys, they hurried out, Blackstone shooting details over his shoulder. "Baltimore police were called by a construction foreman before dawn. A woman's naked body was spotted on the grounds of a waterfront site. She was a thirty-eight-year-old operator, unmarried, living with a female roommate in the city. Judging by the body temperature, it appears she's been there all night."

Alec didn't have to think long before he caught the vision. "Blindfolded too, right? Then left alone to stagger around helpless and fall to her death."

The others simply stared. They hadn't been after the Professor as long as Alec had. God willing, they would never know him as intimately as he did.

"Very likely," Blackstone said. Inside the elevator, he added, "They found her clothes and ID on the top level of the building, along with a cell phone that they quickly discovered had belonged to a murder victim. The Wilmington police directed them to us."

"Ryan Smith's," Alec confirmed.

Wyatt nodded.

"So I guess we know why Darwin wasn't hanging around online last night," Jackie said, shaking her head in disgust.

"Yeah," Kyle said, ever the blunt one. "He was busy tossing an operator off a building."

But he probably wasn't busy now. In fact, the unsub was likely relaxed, sated for the time being. Perhaps he had some time on his hands. Maybe even enough to do a little Web surfing.

Wyatt seemed to read his mind, not the first time his boss had exhibited some pretty amazing intuition. "Brandon and Lily will notify us the moment he shows up on her site."

Alec eyed the other man warily, wondering if his reaction in the conference room had revealed more than he'd intended to about his relationship with their witness. "I know," he said, wanting to place a quick call to Sam to give her a heads-up that Darwin might be back online this morning.

But it would have to be from the road. They were all anxious to get to the crime scene before too many people had gone through it. Alec needed to look at every inch if he wanted to try to imagine what the Professor had been thinking and feeling.

Thinking, yes. Feeling? The Professor? Probably not so much. He suspected the unsub didn't have feelings, that he was completely detached from what he was doing. One step removed from the human race, as if they were his subjects, or his guinea pigs, free to be played with and disposed of at will.

He only wished they had stopped him before he'd had a chance to play his deadly game with the poor woman lying cold and dead on the ground in Baltimore.

Considering Sam had spent the last couple of days wrapped up in a murder investigation, mourning the loss of a nice kid, and wondering whether she had attracted the attention of a serial killer, she probably shouldn't have been so surprised to forget an important date. In most cases, such a lapse in memory could probably be expected.

Except, of course, if the date was her own birthday.

It wasn't today. The official anniversary would occur tomorrow. However, this was the day her mother had decided to celebrate. Why? Because the older woman had a Saturday-night date and needed all of tomorrow to prepare. Who said mothers weren't sentimental?

If it's with someone she met online, I'm going to lock her up and throw away the key.

"So you will be there for lunch?" the older woman asked. "Eleven forty-five a.m. at Raphael's, that lovely café I like on Charles Street?"

She shouldn't have answered the phone this morning when it startled her awake a few minutes ago. Actually, she wished she hadn't turned the ringer back on last night. She had thought, however implausibly, that Alec might decide to call her and fill her in on what that mysterious phone call from his boss had been about. But no, the only call had been this reminder from her mother. Which effectively removed any chance of Sam using the legitimate excuse that she had forgotten about today's lunch.

"Samantha?"

"I'll be there."

"You won't forget? I know how you are when you get busy doing that computer thing."

That computer thing. Oh, her livelihood?

"I said I'll be there," she insisted. Then, knowing the reaction she would get, added, "I asked Tricia to join us."

Tricia hadn't committed to the invitation, mainly because she and Sam's mother had their own mutual non-admiration society. But considering how contrite Tricia had sounded when e-mailing and calling to apologize for the answering machine snafu, she'd probably show up.

Not that Sam had responded to her pleas for information about who had been there to hear the amplified conversation. Tricia had naturally assumed it was a man, but Sam wasn't ready to go there yet, not even with her best friend.

"She's such a wild girl, Samantha." Her mother's disapproval came through the phone loud and clear.

"That wild girl has been my best friend for two decades."

"Well, it is your birthday. I suppose you should decide who you want to spend it with."

Magnanimous. "She is so looking forward to seeing you, too."

Her mother harrumphed. "There's no need for sarcasm."

Sarcasm had been her go-to defense for a year now, but she usually didn't target it at her normally easy-to-get-along-with mother, who was only a pain in the ass in the way that all mothers were a pain in the ass. And because she was a little lacking in the commonsense department. "Sorry."

"It's all right, and I'm sorry, too. I know how close you two are. I'm sure Tricia can be on her best behavior for one lunch. She does know better than to do anything inappropriate, doesn't she? Nathan cannot afford to be seen in the midst of a scandal."

"Uncle Nate is a big boy," Sam replied. Big and tough, with a reputation as one of the strictest judges in town. Scrupulously honest, but open to no bullshit, as criminals like Jimmy Flynt had learned. Nate had presided over Flynt's state trial and had tried to dissuade Sam from talking to the man, being very protective of her. He might be a hanging judge on the bench, but she knew him as a quiet, loving pseudo-uncle.

"I told him to meet us at eleven forty and no later. I know it's early, but it's such a popular spot, that was the only lunch reservation available. Tell Tricia the same thing, will you?"

Sam had wondered more than once why Nate still put up with being bossed around by his late partner's widow. There was only one explanation: She suspected he had feelings for her mother. The hope that she'd someday see him in that light and return the sentiment had to have been what kept the man coming around all these years, through other men, other marriages.

He must truly love her. But her mother was too flighty to see him as anything more than the stodgy, reliable big-brother figure who'd hovered in the background for so very long.

"I must run. Can't wait to see you, honey!"

"Me, too, Mom."

On most occasions, she didn't mind seeing her family. Hers had always been a small one. Her grandmother's death had made it even smaller, as had Sam's divorce. So Nate's and Tricia's presence had become even more important, and she usually wanted nothing more than to share holidays and special events with them.

Frankly, though, she'd rather skip today. Tomorrow, too. What was so great about turning thirty-one? Last year's birthday—thirty, and two weeks divorced—had been bad enough. Now a whole year had gone by and she was no closer to being "back to normal" than she had been when hitting the big three-oh. She had begun to wonder if "back to normal" was overrated.

It's not.

Hearing that voice in her head, she paused, gave it some thought, and suddenly realized her attitude had begun to change. Maybe because of Alec, who was certainly not overrated. Thinking about him, and about those unexpected moments they'd shared last night, she knew he was anything but.

The nearly imperceptible quake in his voice when he'd told her about the shooting, the tenderness in his eyes when she'd told him about her marriage—they had done something to her, made something begin to thaw. So had their single kiss, which had left her more aware of herself as a woman than she'd been in a long time.

It wasn't just sex. She'd almost felt as if she could start coming to life again, begin the process of moving on.

Sam smiled, letting the truth of it flood her. A return to warmth and vibrancy and sensuality was not overrated. In fact, for the first time in what seemed like forever, she was starting to look forward to rejoining the land of the living. Not fully yet, not with this awful investigation looming and a psycho talking to her. But beyond that, into the future. The long-term one that meant a return to the world she'd shut out.

Moving on. What a simple concept. And what an exciting one.

Throwing back the covers with a laugh, she greeted the day a lot more pleasantly than she had in a long time. After a quick shower, she picked out something to wear that would meet her mother's conservative standards and Tricia's outrageous ones.

Venturing to the kitchen, she made some coffee, then sat at the table to jot some notes for the new book. By hand. It wasn't until she had filled a page that she acknowledged what she had been doing: avoiding the living room, avoiding her desk. All so she could avoid the computer on her desk. Contrary to her daily routine, she had never even flipped the thing on, even though she'd hooked it back up last night.

Within a half hour, she had the shakes, Internet withdrawal setting in so badly she was almost sweating. But she remained torn, wanting to check in, wanting just as much to stay checked out of the awful situation in which she had found herself.

Coward. Just get it over with.

Alec had called and left her a message while she was in the shower, saying Darwin had not posted to her message board overnight. But there was still that twinge of concern. Not to mention the awful possibility the psychopath would decide to try educating her by personal e-mail, rather than posting publicly.

Yet she couldn't steer clear of the cyber world forever. Bad enough the need to check her site, her regular blogs, and her e-mails; she also needed to look up the damn address of the restaurant. She hadn't seen an actual hard copy of a phone book in a couple of years.

So, with her heart somewhere in the vicinity of her larynx, she sat at her desk and flipped on her connection to the rest of the world, hoping one particularly vile part of it had not once again reached out and connected to her first.

The team had caravanned up to Baltimore in three cars. Unfortunately, sometime during morning rush hour a tractor trailer had devoured a MINI Cooper on the beltway. Two northbound lanes and the shoulder were blocked, and a ride that had taken about an hour yesterday took almost three this morning.

When they arrived at the scene, Alec noted the chaos. Uniformed officers from the city's police department guarded the entrance. Somebody had gone through a whole lot of crime scene tape circling the fenced lot. On-lookers ranging from suit-wearing businessmen to dock-workers milled around on the street. Guys in hard hats clustered in small circles, wondering when they could re-turn to work. Also wondering what she had *looked* like, you know, afterward.

He could almost hear them.

Stokes swung their car directly behind Wyatt's, get-ting out quickly, her badge already in her hand. Alec fol-lowed suit, but moved more slowly.

"Well?" she asked, impatience evident in her inflection.

"Go ahead," he said, waving her forward. He wasn't really paying attention, already completely focused on following the path the victim—and possibly her killer—must have taken.

He hadn't circumnavigated the site, but judging by the severed chain on the ground and the residual fin-gerprint powder on the post, this was where the de-tectives believed the suspect and/or the victim had entered. He walked through, his gait slow. His foot-steps crunched on the frozen dirt as he stepped past shards of woods and masonry nails. With every step, he pictured the scene, thinking the victim's thoughts, thinking the unsub's.

He doubted the Professor had incapacitated the woman and brought her here against her will. Even late at night, anybody could have driven by; a late worker could have left one of the nearby businesses. This wasn't like the woods or an enclosed warehouse, where he could knock out his victims and then position them.

Lured her here, somehow. Fraudulent investment?

No, she wasn't the type. Nor would she have come here late at night for a job interview, like the warehouse victim.

Personal, then.

Come, it'll be special. Wait until you see the view.

He walked on, his head down, careful to avoid the marked evidence. Usable footprints would probably be doubtful, given the amount of activity on an average construction site. But he wasn't about to make the forensics guys' job any harder.

The bits of information continued to churn in his brain, coming together like puzzle pieces that didn't quite fit and had to be repositioned. At some point, the entire puzzle would take shape, but for now, he simply played with the pieces.

A thirty-eight-year-old operator. Lived with a roommate. Unmarried.

A spinster? Maybe a dating-service scam?

Reaching the exterior walls of the building, he heard Wyatt and the others talking to the local detectives. Again, he barely listened, continuing to move toward the core of the facility, to the construction elevator in which the victim must have risen to meet her doom. Mulrooney and Taggert watched him in visible curiosity, but Wyatt merely nodded as he passed.

She's anxious. Nervous. It's night, off the beaten track. The top of the building? Are you sure it's safe? I'm afraid.

He reached the elevator. Inside, a tech continued to swab the grating, yawning widely as he went through the motions by rote. "You need to go up?"

"When you're through."

"I've cleared a zone to haul people up and down," the other man said.

"Find anything?"

"Got some prints; ten to one says any that aren't from the crew are from the victim."

He wouldn't take that bet.

"Stay in that area, okay?" the man said, pointing to a corner.

Alec entered as directed, turning to stare out at the water through the side grates as they slowly ascended to the top of the building.

Slow. It's so high. Choppy water. Cold and black like a night sky without stars, falling away from my feet. Lights across the harbor? Far away. No one can see. All alone. Private.

Perfect.

The victim's impression? Or the killer's?

The higher they went, the easier it was to see. Not just the panorama—the water, the shoreline, the ships—but the past. The crime.

Come with me; I'll show you the city as you've never seen it.

She trusted him enough to trespass on a closed construction site.

She's willing but she's nervous, excited. He keeps her calm. Earns her trust. How?

He slowly turned in a complete circle, trying to imagine what she'd felt, what she'd thought as she had been drawn inexorably closer to that date with death.

Did you ride up with her, calm her fears, then strike her into unconsciousness?

That didn't sound like their man. The Professor's past crimes had an element of detachment. His letters claimed his hands—and conscience—were clear. He'd never killed anyone, never hurt them, just put them in situations to kill or hurt themselves. Like incapacitating the boys in a car accident before putting them out on that ice to fight for their lives. Impersonal.

She rode up alone. He told her to come up to meet him and she did it.

Why, he couldn't say.

Deep in thought, he stared down, removing the distraction of the water, wanting to imprint the scene in his head. Make it come to life.

Before it could, though, he saw a tiny red spot near his shoe. He crouched down close, not touching it. No more than the size of a pen's tip, it must have been overlooked by the tech in his hurry to clear an area to take detectives to the roof.

Not blood; too light. Too waxy.

On his hands and knees, he bent closer, until his face nearly brushed the metal. He suddenly realized the tiny drop was actually the tip of a larger blob that had slipped through the grate. The material had solidified into a tiny icicle hanging from the floor beneath the elevator.

And it wasn't merely waxy. It *was* wax. "Candles," he murmured.

"What?"

He pointed to the spot. "Make sure you get this. I suspect it's candle wax."

Red candles. You romanced her, didn't you, you son of a bitch?

That was the opening. The one detail that allowed him to build the entire scenario in his head from that starting point.

He had romanced her.

They reached the top floor and the tech, visibly embarrassed, immediately descended on the spot of wax. He couldn't risk grabbing it here; it could fall, and he was probably eager to go back down. "It's all right," he said, waving the man away as he stepped out.

A few feet away, another crime scene investigator was carefully bagging clothing. Yet another was on his hands and knees, outlining footprints left in the faint layer of construction dust. Even from here he saw they had been made from bare feet.

"Here's where she took the dive," one of them said, looking up at Alec and obviously recognizing him as a fed.

He nodded, but didn't walk over. Instead, he stood his ground, still visualizing.

Taped hands. Blindfolded. Did she even try to fight you?

He doubted it. "Any signs of physical attack? Blood splatter?" he asked.

"Nothing so far inside the building," one of the techs said. "There's a splash zone outside, where she landed, like something you'd see at a water park."

Grim visual.

"But in the elevator and up here? Not yet."

Which just reinforced his belief that the Professor hadn't physically tangled with her at all, either before he'd stripped her, or after she'd regained consciousness. The tox screen would be important on this one, especially because the unsub had used ketamine, a fast-acting drug, on the help-wanted victim.

He added that piece to the story puzzle in his mind, letting the scene roll out like a snippet of a movie. The operator came to meet some wonderful man in response to an e-mail. Maybe even a phone call, if the Professor was the one who had used Ryan Smith's cell the previous night. Alec wouldn't put it past the man to intentionally taunt authorities in that way.

She got into the elevator; the scene had been set. Candles. So romantic. Her guard down, she had consumed something. She lost consciousness. The Professor waited until she was down, stepped into the elevator, took her out, and got her ready.

You never even laid eyes on the man you came to meet, did you?

"How did he leave her clothing?" he asked the tech who had just bagged them. "Neatly piled, folded?"

"Yeah, very carefully," the guy said, further cementing Alec's image of what had happened. "Hose tucked into the shoes, underwear inside the dress. All neat and tidy. Which is pretty funny, since they had been cut off her."

Check for cuts. He wasn't sure it would be possible, given the condition the body must be in, but he wanted to know. Had the Professor wounded her while cutting off her clothes? If she was conscious, she would have struggled; there would be signs, nicks.

But there had been no blood. *She wasn't conscious.* She didn't struggle. Any wounds would have been inflicted out of carelessness or for the unsub's own pleasure.

The Professor was never careless.

Besides, the way he'd folded her things hinted at such restraint, such calmness.

You don't hurt your victims, right? Your hands are totally clean.

Alec would lay money the woman didn't have a mark on her from the knife. What the construction debris she'd hit on the ground had done to her, however, was another story.

"Think I'll walk around a little," he said, already looking past the technician.

"Sure. You know the drill."

Of course he did. He remained on the periphery, stepping only into already cleared areas. He studied the cut edges of the security netting, the patterns of bare footprints in the dust, running in circles until a straight pair disappeared off the side of the building.

For the next hour, he lost himself in thought, staring at the clothes, the elevator, the footprints, the water, the shoreline. Not seeking evidence, but understanding. Reconstructing the crime in his head, he saw it so well. Yes, there were holes, gaps, but for the most part the picture was clear. The woman, the lure, the romantic touches, the drug, the trap, the terror, the fall.

The only thing unclear was the killer. Where had he been? Had he set this awful scene in motion, then blithely walked away, not even knowing whether his victim plummeted as he expected her to, or somehow survived by keeping calm and waiting for rescue?

He didn't know. They had no way of knowing whether the Professor had watched his other victims die. Couldn't be sure if he had stayed on that cold, snowy night, listening to the cries of those boys, until the earsplitting crack of breaking ice predicated their final plunge.

One thing he suspected: The Professor would not have remained on this roof until the very end. Someone could have seen the victim fall, cutting off his own escape from the building. That didn't mean he hadn't stayed close by to watch his morbid fantasy play out, waiting with bated breath for a pale form to tumble from the sky and a sharp scream to rend the night.

Alec needed to know. Needed to get inside the man's head, figure out how he thought of his victims—as worthy of his attention to their final moments?

No, it didn't sound like him.

But as vehicles of sheer entertainment? That seemed much more plausible.

Or as validation for his own theories—wanting to see the inevitable moment when his victims "failed" their tests? Another valid reason for him to watch.

So where would he go? How long would he stay? What vantage point would provide him with an adequate viewing area without exposing him to capture?

Not for the first time, he thought about what Sam had said the previous night. About that con man, Jimmy Flynt. The one who seemed to think like this unsub, viewed his victims the same way, even used the Internet to reach out to them and destroy their lives.

Also not for the first time, he realized talking to Flynt was a good idea. Which he was sure would please Sam. She wouldn't be pleased, though, when she found out he was going without her.

Grabbing his phone, he speed-dialed back to the office and asked for Lily Fletcher.

"What's up? Anything useful on the scene? Does it look like the Professor?"

Alec covered one ear with his hand, straining to hear her despite the whoosh of the wind flying through the open building. Stepping closer to the solid face of it, he found a little bit of a buffer zone and answered, "Yeah, I'm pretty sure. Listen, Lily, I need information on an inmate. James T. Flynt. He did time in a federal pen; now he's in a Maryland lockup."

"Hold on." He heard a faint clicking—her keyboard. Within seconds, she said, "Got him."

"Can you contact the prison or his attorney? Try to arrange a meeting? I want to talk to him."

"About this case? Do you have a new lead?"

"Possibly. I think he might be of some help."

"Sure thing."

He hated to even concede the possibility, but time was of the essence. "Look, try not to use her name if you don't have to, but if you get resistance from Flynt, see if Sam Dalton's presence would make a difference in his attitude."

"Ahh," she said. "One of those types? Sleazy criminals who will spill their guts to a pretty face?"

"Something like that. The sooner, the better, okay?"

"You got it. I'll let you know as soon as I get it set up."

"Thanks."

He cut the connection and was about to drop the phone back in his pocket when he noticed the message symbol on the screen. Frowning, since he hadn't even heard the thing ring, he dialed his voice mail, learning a call had come in about ten minutes ago.

"Alec, it's Samantha Dalton."

He muttered a curse, wishing he'd thought to set the phone on vibrate. Then he stepped even closer to the wall, listening intently.

"I . . . Oh, hell, I feel stupid for calling. It's, uh . . . Something weird happened. At least, I thought it was just weird at first. Now I'm beginning to wonder if it's scary, instead."

She went silent, amid background noise. Voices, the clank of dishes. Someone saying, "Samantha, get off the phone; we'll lose our table!"

Then another voice. "Welcome to Raphael's. Is your entire party here?"

"Sorry, I should go. I'm having lunch with my mom." She hesitated, as if debating whether to continue, then mumbled, "Do me a favor, okay? Check my blog. There's a new post, but I didn't put it there. I thought it had been hijacked by spammers; they've targeted me before. It wasn't even until after I left my place that I thought of another possibility." Her voice shaking, a hint of fear so obvious it clutched at his insides, she added, "Can't deny it has me a little rattled, considering last night."

The call ended abruptly, with no good-bye.

His heart pounding, he punched a button to call her back and cursed when he got her voice mail, too. "It's Alec; I just got your message," he said. "Call me back as soon as you can."

Disconnecting, he set the phone to both vibrate and ring. *Don't panic. She sounded okay.*

He wasn't panicked. He was just concerned. He wouldn't relax until he knew what had put that note of fear in Sam's voice.

Alec suddenly felt completely cut off. The elevator hadn't returned—the crime scene technician, still smarting from missing the candle wax, was probably going over every millimeter of it. He was stuck hundreds of feet in the air when what he wanted was to drive straight to that restaurant, wherever it was, and see what had frightened Sam.

He dialed Lily again.

"Hey, I'm good, but I'm not a miracle worker. I called about setting up the meeting with Flynt, but I need more than ten minutes to get a response."

"It's not that. Are you at your desk?"

"Of course."

"Do something for me, would you? Pull up Samantha Dalton's Web page."

"I checked it forty minutes ago. He hadn't posted."

"Humor me."

This time, the clicking was more audible, since he was more sheltered from the wind. And he easily heard her when Fletcher murmured, "That's new."

"What?" he snapped. "Is it Darwin?"

"No, no. I guess Ms. Dalton has some kind of inside joke with her regulars or something. She put a new blog post up. Kind of unusual, too."

Alec's heart pounded. Sam had not done any such thing. "What does it say?"

"Just five words, in big, bold print. They take up the whole screen."

"Read them to me," he ordered.

"It's not threatening or anything."

He gritted his teeth. "Lily?"

Apologizing, she did as he asked. "It says, 'What was in the box?' "

Chapter 11

Trying to maintain a smile and a normal conversation, despite the nervousness rising higher with each passing minute, wasn't the easiest thing Sam had ever done. Somehow, though, she pulled it off. With her shaking hands clasped together on the table, a steady supply of water in her dry mouth, and constant chatter from her mother and Tricia to cover up her silence, she honestly thought she conveyed an I'm-perfectly-fine attitude.

Not an I'm-freaking-out one.

She hadn't freaked out at first. In fact, when she'd first logged on this morning, she'd been so relieved to find Darwin still had not responded to her blog post, she'd been almost complacent. A quick check of e-mail and of her site right before she walked out the door an hour later had been simply a matter of habit. So it hadn't sunk in at first.

Oh, she'd noticed the fake blog post immediately, but, as she'd said in her message to Alec, it wasn't the first time. It hadn't happened often; usually the content management software she used for blogging was good enough to prevent such attacks. But spammers loved to target sites like hers, if only to show they could "get" the Spaminator.

Today's annoyance, therefore, hadn't been unusual enough to inspire panic. Already running late, she had figured she'd handle it when she got home from lunch.

The panic had come a few minutes later. Not wanting to deal with parking, she'd grabbed a cab, and while sitting in the backseat, idly staring at passing cars, she'd finally allowed herself to really think about the words that had filled the screen.

What was in the box?

Her heart had nearly stopped, though she'd called herself a fool. It was pure coincidence that someone would post such a thing less than twelve hours after Alec carried the boxed computer up to her place.

But what if it wasn't?

Jesus. What if it wasn't?

"Hello, Earth to Sam!"

She jerked when Tricia waved a heavily ringed, spangle-braceleted hand in front of her face. Tricia Scott wasn't a typical real estate agent. No conservative blazers or Lincoln Continentals for her. The attractive redhead wore silky pantsuits in jungle patterns and drove a monster SUV when showing her clients around the city. She'd managed to survive the downturn in the market through sheer personality and verve. Sam had stayed with Tricia for a short time after she'd walked out on her marriage and credited her friend with keeping her sane.

"Sorry. Just deep in thought."

"Well, stop it," her mother scolded. "You look so serious. You'll get frown lines."

"You don't have any, Mrs. H." Tricia's smile was far too ingratiating. Her next words showed why. "Who's your plastic surgeon?"

Beside her, Uncle Nate, who had hovered in the background, quiet and content to be surrounded by chatty women, coughed into his napkin to hide a laugh. Love Sam's mother he might, but he also saw Christine Harrington for what she was: a somewhat vain, overly romantic woman who longed to be taken care of and kept herself in tip-top shape as she watched for the next prospect to do exactly that. That she had never even considered him as a prospect had to have hurt him, though he'd never said a word.

Her mother had sparred with Tricia for too many years to be surprised by the jab. She smirked. "I'll get you his number; I can see you already need it."

Tricia snorted a good-humored laugh. The two women had a lot in common. Though they would never admit it, they also liked each other.

"Do you have any special plans for your birthday tomorrow, Samantha?" Nate asked.

Staying alive would be good. Avoiding a certain psycho who might have been watching her last night? Good also.

"Not really," she murmured. "Maybe I'll take you up on your standing offer to come up to the sportsmen's club and learn how to shoot."

He appeared pleased. "You know I'll teach you anytime you want." He leaned over and patted her shoulder, studying her closely. "A girl can't be too careful nowadays."

"Neither can a judge," she said with a pointed stare.

"Touché," he replied, his slight smile acknowledging that he had a gun somewhere on his person at all times.

Tricia had overheard. "I should learn, too. You wouldn't believe some of the sleazeballs in my business. A few weeks ago, I did an open house for one of my listings, and this couple came in, but then disappeared. I went looking and found them in the master bedroom closet, going at it right on a pile of the owner's dirty clothes."

Sam's mother wrinkled her nose. "Imagine that. I'd have to throw everything away and buy a new wardrobe."

"Disgusting, yeah. But as disgusting as being the one to lie naked on somebody *else's* dirty underwear to have sex? Talk about doing the nasty," Tricia said.

Sam honestly didn't know which was worse: coming home to find your dirty clothes all sexed on, or going at it with someone on a pile of dirty clothes belonging to a stranger. Either way: ick. Yet somehow, she found herself smiling at the conversation, rather than cringing. Because after the week she'd had, it was nice to watch her best friend try to scandalize her mother, and the older woman take it in good grace, their typical song and dance.

Falling silent, Sam sat back and listened to the others converse. It was more than nice; in fact, being here was pretty wonderful. Watching the verbal sparring, seeing the reactions. It was all so normal. Which felt better to her right now than any wild, dangerous adventure ever could.

She wanted to let them know that, to thank them for coming and admit she might actually have reached a personal milestone and would hopefully be returning to some kind of normal life.

Before she could say a word, though, a male voice intruded. "Sorry I'm late." Sitting in the empty chair beside her, he smiled pleasantly at everyone, particularly Sam. "Happy birthday."

She gawked. "Rick? What on earth are you doing here?"

His brow went up in confusion. Sam cast a quick glance across the table and saw the excitement sparkling in her mother's eyes.

Matchmaking. I'll kill her.

How could her mother do this? Jeez, so much for starting her bright new life. A vivid reminder of her dark old one had just plunked down right beside her.

"Uh, wait." Rick stared back and forth between Sam and her mother, obviously embarrassed. She couldn't imagine what he must have thought when her mother had invited him to meet them, probably saying Sam had been all for the idea, despite her rejection of a dinner date two days ago.

He immediately confirmed as much. "Please don't tell me you didn't know I was coming."

Her mother glared, silently warning her not to be rude. Sam was about to do the nice thing and lie her face off, but before she had to, the most welcome words she had ever heard interrupted. "Sam, I need to talk to you."

She was rising from her seat before she'd even looked up to confirm who had spoken. Something inside her simply responded to Alec Lambert's voice, excitement picking up her pulse, her breath tripping to rush in and out of her body.

Mixed with the excitement was relief. He had come. He'd heard her message and responded to it, and was here to tell her everything was okay. That she had simply made a mountain out of a box.

"Hello, Alec," she said, wondering if something about her expression or the warm tone of her voice would reveal how she felt about this man to the people who knew her better than anyone else in the world.

Those people had gone utterly silent, watching wide-eyed. All four of them. Not only because Alec's arrival was so unexpected, but, at least for Mom and Tricia, because they had to have been struck a little dumb by his good looks. He was that kind of man, the type women couldn't help staring at. Wondering about. Maybe not as classically perfect as Samuel Dalton Jr., but more masculine, more rugged. Way more sexy.

Tricia obviously noticed. *Sex on a stick!* she mouthed.

Sam thought quickly. "Alec is a friend. He's, uh, helping me with some research."

Seeing the grin Tricia didn't try to hide, Sam knew what kind of research she was imagining. Her mother was smiling, too. Nate watched curiously, and poor Rick Young looked as if he wanted to climb under the table.

She took pity, bending over to grab her purse from the back of the chair, taking the opportunity to whisper,

"Sorry; my mom's a terrible matchmaker, but give Tricia a chance anyway. She's fabulous."

He mumbled, "Thank you," which told her he might not realize she'd said that so he could save face.

Straightening again, she looped her purse over her arm and addressed the others. "Will you all excuse me for a minute?"

"Aren't you even going to introduce us?" her mother asked, sounding highly excited.

Knowing she wouldn't get away without doing it, she quickly made the introductions. Uncle Nate, always polite, asked Alec to join them.

"I appreciate the invitation," he said. "And I hate to be a killjoy, but the truth is, we have a bit of a situation, and I'm going to have to ask Sam to come with me."

Sam froze, her hand on the back of her chair, reading between the lines. Noting the tense way he held himself, she realized he definitely hadn't come here to tell her everything was okay. That had been a ridiculous, wishful hope. His presence indicated the exact opposite. She'd just been so relieved to see him she hadn't wanted to admit it.

This was bad.

"Darling, you can't just run out!"

Walking around the table to her mother, she put her hand on the woman's shoulders, bent down, and kissed her cheek. Her voice low, she gave the older woman the only excuse that would allow her to escape without a battle. "Mom, he's someone special."

Her mother's mouth rounded. "Oh. You were going to tell us about him a few minutes ago, weren't you? I'm so sorry."

"Next time," Sam muttered, avoiding the question, "forget about the matchmaking, would you? I'm doing all right on my own." Heck, maybe it wasn't even too big a lie. She wouldn't say she was having a wild, passionate affair with the handsome man waiting impatiently to take her out of here. But stranger things had happened. Even to her.

Lately? Especially to her.

Noting the thumbs-up from Tricia, she let Alec lead her to the door and help her with her coat. The moment they were outside, he pulled her out of view of the restaurant window. "I'm sorry I interrupted. I tried to call."

She shook her head in silent apology. "I was accused of being incredibly rude for using the phone before we'd even been seated, and was glared into turning it off. Believe me, I would have called you again the minute we were finished."

Staying close beside her, his strong hand warm on the small of her back, Alec led her to his car, which was parked up the block. He didn't look at her, his gaze continually scanning the sidewalk, the side streets, even glancing back to the pedestrians behind them.

He looked like someone who expected trouble. "Let's get out of here, go somewhere private where we can talk."

Forcing herself to remain calm, she asked, "How'd you get here so fast, anyway?"

He paused. Not even realizing it, she kept walking, going two steps forward before having to turn around. "Alec?"

"I was in town," he admitted. "Down by the harbor."

"Has there been a break in the case?" A possible explanation suddenly arose. "Oh, my God, you haven't been in Baltimore all night, since your boss called you, have you?"

"No." He started walking again. "Come on."

"Where are we going?"

They had reached his car. Alec unlocked it and opened the door for her, not replying until she'd climbed into the passenger seat. Then, with a firmness that didn't disguise the hint of worry in his voice, he finally answered her question.

"Somewhere as far away from your apartment as I can take you."

Figuring out Samantha Dalton was working with the authorities to try to capture him had been the most disappointing moment of Darwin's entire life.

Worse than the death of his parents in that stupid, completely avoidable accident when he was a child. Worse than finding out he was an orphan, wanted by no one. Worse than being thrown into the foster-care system. Even worse than the first time his foster father had slipped into his room at night for a *special* lesson that was to be their secret.

He had not been crushed by any of those moments. Expecting nothing more than bad things made receiving them less bitter.

But her . . . He had expected more from her.

You betrayed me.

She had destroyed something inside him. Not only her actions, but the realization that he had misjudged her.

Betrayed me.

He would never allow himself to be vulnerable again. Never let anyone build his expectations, only to be crushed by their inevitable failures.

Betrayed.

Thank God he had been there to see that man leaving her apartment last night. If he hadn't, his suspicions might never have been aroused. He mightn't have gone snooping into Samantha's e-mails, into her private files, using the passwords and account information he had obtained during his extensive visit to her apartment on Christmas Eve.

In the dark hours of last night, he had read her correspondence, all nicely archived on Gmail. Noting the absence of any mention of a man, he had grown more confused. Until, finally, he found one clue. A message from her whorish friend Tricia, apologizing for having left a rude voice mail the previous day when a mystery man had been there to hear it.

There had been nothing else. The trail had gone cold, and he'd almost given up. Then he'd thought of something. He had already figured out Samantha hadn't been home a few hours after posting her article. Was it possible she had actually been gone much longer? A full twenty-four, perhaps, until the following night, when she'd come home with that man? Had she posted her entry and her follow-up comments from somewhere else?

And, if so, would knowing where help him learn whom she had been with?

Not as easy to find out, but not impossible. His notes from that night at her place were thorough, so he knew which blogging package she used. He'd been able to in-filtrate her blog as if he owned it. Becoming an instant administrator, he saw what she saw, the history laid out in front of him like a well-traveled road.

One of the detours on that road had been a glimpse at the hidden server logs, specifically, information on her own posts for the week.

Samantha's comments Thursday had come from a new IP address. Not merely a new ISP, which would be expected. But a completely different Internet provider than she had *ever* used before. One from Washington, D.C.

His suspicions at a fever pitch, he'd dug further. It had taken two more hours of research, visits to government Web sites, law enforcement databases, and conspiracy-theory blogs, but he had finally put it all together.

The IP she'd used to post her responses to him ser-viced the federal government. More specifically, the Federal Bureau of Investigation.

Damn her. Damn them.

He had no idea how the authorities had seized upon his Darwin comments as being of any importance, but they had. And Samantha had helped them.

The man who had escorted her home had been an FBI agent.

Part of him was relieved that the stranger's relationship with Sam was not a personal one.

Definitely not a sexual one.

Another part truly didn't give a fuck; he just wanted to kill them both.

Funny, really, given all the efforts he had gone through during the night to identify his rival. For today, the truth—including the identity of the FBI agent who was working with her—had been simply handed over to him. And Alec Lambert had gone on his personal list of people whose presence in this world needed to come to an end.

Samantha's name was there as well.

Patience. He had to be careful, had to use his intellect.

Darwin had always known the day would come when he would have to deal with the deadweight dragging Samantha down. Those closest to her had no redeeming qualities, as far as he could tell, and he was already positioned to begin eliminating them.

Now, however, he no longer wanted to free her from them in order to help her live up to her fullest potential. He wanted to hurt her. Crush her completely. Emotionally first, then physically.

He had given the matter careful consideration before deciding his next move, knowing he had to cut her down in stages, like a charging animal being broken by a hunter. Finally, he'd come up with a way to torment her, as well as let the FBI know he was onto them. Hijacking her own blog, he had posted a very personal message this morning.

He had known it might not hit her at first, might merely confuse her. But once she did begin to suspect, Samantha's shock and nervousness would bring her to the very edge of terror.

Then he would push her over it.

*   *   *

Alec took her to headquarters. He didn't give her a chance to argue; he didn't go by her place for clothes or supplies. Anything she needed, they could get her. No way was he taking her back to the apartment where, he firmly believed, she was being stalked by a serial killer.

Fortunately, Wyatt was in agreement. He had been every bit as worried about this morning's Web attack, seeing it as Alec did—as a taunt to Sam, a way to say he could get to her if he wanted to. His boss had begun arranging for Sam's protection right after Alec called him from the top of that high-rise.

He'd also sent the damned elevator back up.

The very second his feet hit ground level, Alec had taken off across the city to find Sam. Thank God for GPS. And thank God he'd heard the name of the restaurant where she was dining.

"Maybe we're all overreacting," Sam said as Alec parked the car once they reached D.C. It wasn't the first time she'd voiced the theory since he'd grabbed her from the restaurant.

"No, Sam. We're not. I told you what Lily said when she called just now. It's not only the blog post; he left a taunting comment on the message board less than fifteen minutes ago."

An ugly one. He hadn't even told her exactly what it said, though Lily's voice kept echoing in his brain. *You're worse than the brainless sheep. How can you be smart and yet such a whore?*

No. He did not want her hearing that. She was already frightened enough without realizing this psychopath had made this extremely personal.

"Now let's go."

His thoughts, his focus, were strictly on getting her protected, then going back and finding the son of a bitch who had been watching her. They knew the Professor had been in two places in Baltimore last night: the harbor area where the operator was killed, and in the vicinity of Sam's apartment building. Finding evidence of any vehicle or person who had been spotted at both could be exactly the lead they needed. In addition to watching Sam's message board, Lily was also working on satellite imagery of the two locations. Wyatt and Jackie had remained on the scene of last night's murder, but Dean and Kyle had taken the third car over to Sam's neighborhood, looking for anyone who might have seen a strange car. Brandon, armed with Sam's passwords and IDs, was trying to trace whoever had hacked her Web site.

Something would break. It had to.

He walked around to open her door but she didn't get out. Nor did she even look up at him as she mumbled, "I told you I've been hacked before. How can we know for certain this is any different?"

The beautiful woman wasn't being difficult or sulky or stubborn. She was simply afraid, like any normal person would be in her situation.

Alec crouched beside the car, putting a hand over hers, which were clenched together on her lap. "I know you want to believe that, and honestly? Part of me does, too."

Surprise softened her expression.

"Thinking that monster knows where you live and has taken a personal interest in you scares me to death," he admitted. "The very idea that he was out there last night, watching us . . ." He swallowed as anger rose high enough to choke him. "What if he saw us through the window? Watched me kiss you? It makes me sick."

Lord, how stupid had that been? Everything he'd told himself, everything he'd told her about needing to keep things strictly business, at least until the case was over, and he hadn't been able to keep his mouth off hers for one night.

He should regret it deeply. But until this morning, when he'd realized they were being watched, he hadn't.

How could he regret feeling the softness of her hair tangled around his fingers, the warmth of her breath, the sweetness of her mouth?

It won't happen again, though. Not until this case is over.

"But—"

"Look, I'm a believer in coincidence as much as the next guy, but we have to be realistic," he said, cutting off her arguments. "It goes way beyond me carrying a damn box up the stairs and somebody mentioning a box twelve hours later. Even beyond him making a crude comment on the message board."

Though Sam eyed him curiously, he did not elaborate, instead pushing on. "Darwin was in Baltimore last night, less than ten miles from your home."

She blanched. He'd told her there had been another murder, nothing more.

"So look at the big picture here." He ticked off the truth, one point after another, needing her to believe it, if only so she kept her guard up so high nobody could climb over it. "We know a highly intelligent, highly organized serial killer reached out to communicate with you. We knew he would be cautious about responding once you directly addressed him. That he would check you out, make sure he could trust you before taking that next step of actual interaction, especially if there was something in your responses that aroused his suspicions."

There might have been. He just didn't know.

"You've already admitted you wouldn't be that hard to find if somebody really looked. And he is somebody who would look."

"So he looked and he didn't like what he saw."

"Exactly."

She sat with her head down, letting the truth of it fill all the doubting corners of her mind.

He wished he didn't have to remove that doubt. Would give anything if Sam could go on thinking ugliness like she'd seen in the past few days really wasn't so close to her, so intricately entwined with her normal life.

Neither of them had the luxury of denying the truth.

"You're right," she finally whispered.

She wrapped her fingers in his and let him help her from the car. Once outside, she didn't release his hand, as if needing to keep him close. Only when they walked into the building and approached security did she let go and step away.

A few minutes later, inside the elevator, Alec jabbed the button, watching the doors close. When they were alone, he turned to her. Pure adrenaline and worry had been driving him since the minute he'd heard her message. Now, inside a safe zone, he finally allowed himself to let it go. He also resisted the urge to put his hands on her shoulders, not sure whether he most needed to hold her close or shake her like a kid who had run out in front of a car for scaring him the way she had with that message and by then turning her phone off.

"When am I going to be able to go home?" she asked.

"When he's in custody."

She shook her head. "I can't believe this is happening. Why me? How in the name of God did I attract the notice of this psycho?"

"I don't know what drew his eye to you." He rubbed his temple to try to ease the pounding. "It could have been anything. Ryan Smith could even have said something about you warning him before the Professor left him to die."

Grief visibly plunged into her, making her body quiver. *Jackass.*

"Or he could just have been researching scams to lure his victims and found your book," he quickly added. "Who knows why or how he first became aware of you. Once he did, though, I think I know why he stayed around."

"Why? What possible interest could he have in me?"

"Didn't you say that Flynt guy was interested in you because of the way you were trying to help the very people he liked to victimize?"

Nodding, she murmured, "Yes, he was. I think I amused him, in a sick way. Are you saying this Darwin is the same? That he enjoys seeing my sad little efforts to help people?"

"It's possible. And he's angry that you're working with us to try to stop him."

Alec had another, darker thought, though he didn't share it with her. Sam was a beautiful, intelligent woman whose personality sparkled on the pages of her book and her Web site. For all they knew, the Professor might see her as someone like himself, educated and informed, not readily deceived. But someone who'd gone to work for the "wrong" side, wanting to save the very people he wanted to kill.

A man with an ego the size of the killer's might relish the challenge of trying to change Sam's mind. To educate her, perhaps, win her over to his way of thinking. His posts of Wednesday night, when he seemed to be trying to make rational arguments that contradicted her rant column, certainly leaned that way.

Now, though, he no longer wanted to educate her. Alec greatly feared he wanted to punish her.

"How could he know I'm working with the authorities?"

"Because he saw you with me last night."

"You weren't exactly in uniform."

Far from it. But the license plate on the car he had been driving would have provided a big clue. Damn, he couldn't believe he hadn't noticed anything suspicious. His focus had been in the wrong direction. He'd been tunnel-visioned, seeing Sam's involvement in this only as a personality, a Web site owner, not as a person who might interest their unsub.

"He has survived and gotten away with what he does by being very cautious and very thorough. He would have worked on it until he figured out who I was."

"And me working with the FBI, you think that was what made him go from wanting to be my teacher to wanting to scare the crap out of me?"

"Yes. It angered him."

"So he was trying to get me back for being untrustworthy. To let me know he's out there, watching."

He shifted his gaze. Darwin hadn't called her untrustworthy; he'd called her a whore. "Right."

She simply nodded, as if she'd been seeking only to understand rather than reacting emotionally. Smart woman. Smart to have been afraid. Smart now to have calmed down and assessed the situation logically.

Everything about her was so put-together. Maybe it hadn't been when he'd first met her. There had been no missing Sam's self-imposed isolation, the lack of confidence and the uncertainty about herself. But in the past few days, she'd thrown off those restraints. Sam had revealed herself to be exactly the kind of woman he most admired: reasonable, rational, with a lot of common sense and a quick wit.

That she was sexy enough to stop his heart and one simple kiss had sent every ounce of his blood straight to his groin just made her even harder to resist.

Alec managed to keep those thoughts off his face as they reached their floor and he led her to the office. Once inside, they headed straight for the team's two IT specialists. "Lily and Brandon have been working on figuring out how the blog attack could have happened," he said. "Knowing how he got in could help us find him."

"How?"

"Let's let them fill us in on that," he said, feeling suddenly uncomfortable. He didn't want to discuss some of the possibilities Lily had mentioned on the phone. Like the idea that this bastard knew so much about Sam—

about her personal life—that he had been able to guess her passwords.

"Everything okay?" Lily asked when they entered. "Are you all right, Sam?"

"For somebody being watched by a serial killer, I guess so."

"It'll be okay." The blonde briefly touched Sam's shoulder. "We're not going to let anything happen to you—you have an entire team watching your back."

"Thanks."

"Can I get you something to drink?"

"Got any Jack Daniel's?" she said, with a humorless laugh.

"Sorry. But I made the coffee, not Brandon," Lily said. "So I can promise you it won't put your heart into arrhythmia and keep you awake for ninety-six hours straight."

Brandon smirked. "Yeah, yeah, you just wish you had my energy."

"Wishing for your energy would be like wishing to live inside a tornado."

Beside him, Sam's body relaxed as she listened to the pair go back and forth like siblings. The very normalness of their sniping seemed to bring the tension down a notch. Which was, he assumed, exactly what they had intended. Not for the first time, he realized how glad he was to have ended up here, with this particular group.

"Coffee would be great," Sam murmured. "Thanks."

"Not a problem."

Though Alec wanted to get right back to Baltimore, something about Sam's expression made him stay. She might like Lily and Brandon, but she'd fixed on him as a personal ally. Someone more than a law enforcement professional trying to help her.

Maybe because he'd kissed her breathless about twelve hours ago.

"Okay, Cole, show us what you've got. And make it good," he said.

The younger man nodded. "You live in an apartment in Baltimore, right?"

She nodded.

"Security? Alarms?"

Sam's face paled, and she cleared her throat before answering. "It's a good neighborhood, though not an upscale one. As secure as an older apartment building can be, I guess." She wrapped her arms around herself as if to ward off a chill. "Certainly not the kind of place where I'd expect someone to sit outside with a pair of binoculars, trying to watch me through my windows."

"Is there any chance he's been closer than that?" Brandon asked.

Sam went very still. "What do you mean?"

Alec had a feeling he knew where this was going, and he did not like it.

"This wasn't a random hack attack, and it wasn't a dummy front page." Brandon clicked a few keys on his keyboard and brought up a blog hosting site. "This post was made directly on your account. Whoever this was, he knew exactly which content-manager software you were using, Sam. He was logged in as an administrator."

Hell.

To his surprise, Sam took the statement with utter calm. "Figuring out the CMS wouldn't be that difficult."

"No, it wouldn't." Brandon leaned forward, dropping his elbows onto his knees to stare intently at her. "But your ID and password—they weren't exactly common. It's not like you were using your dog's name; they were random letters and numbers."

She looked away. "Well, not exactly random."

Brandon tilted his head, waiting.

"I know, the expert who says to never use relevant dates or initials, right?" She blinked, as if her eyes had suddenly grown hot. "The initials are my late grand-mother's name. The numbers are the date she died."

"Ahh." Brandon sat up straight, nodding. For some reason, he looked almost relieved, though Alec didn't know why this was good news. As if realizing that, he looked over and explained. "Anybody who Googled Sam here . . ."

"Would find my name in my grandmother's obituary," she said. "Along with her initials and date of death."

"You were close?"

She nodded. "I have mentioned her on my blog on a few occasions. She, uh, was my inspiration, the reason I became Sam the Spaminator."

The eyes blinked again, moisture definitely in evidence. Alec somehow suspected he was finally on the verge of learning why Sam did what she did, beyond the need to take some time out of life to heal from what her ex had done to her. This crusade she was on . . . it suddenly sounded as though it had started for very personal reasons.

"Even better," Brandon said.

"Why better?" Alec asked.

"Because we already know he reads her site. If he knew she was close to her grandmother, and he was trying to figure out her passwords, it would be a logical thing to try. Especially if you've mentioned her as an inspiration, Sam." Brandon nodded, as if convincing himself of what he said. "This really is good news."

He didn't have to explain further. Alec got the alternative. If Sam's relationship with her grandmother had been a closely held secret, that would imply the unsub had dug deeper into her life. Something none of them really wanted to contemplate.

"Okay." Brandon tapped his fingers on his desk. In the brief time they'd worked together, Alec had noticed the guy couldn't remain still, a picture of frenetic energy. As if his body had to stay in motion to keep up with his constantly moving mind. "So forget my concern that he might have actually gotten into your apartment."

Sam flinched as if struck. *"What?"*

"No, seriously, forget it. It was a passing concern, when I thought your password was totally random."

"Jesus, Cole," Alec muttered, seeing the way Sam's face had completely lost its color.

"Master of tact," Lily added. She had just returned, holding a steaming cup of coffee, which she placed on the desk close to Sam. "Ignore him."

"Sorry," Brandon said. "Gimme a sec to check something." He swung back around, attacking his keyboard with a vengeance, muttering something under his breath.

Lily took a seat at her own desk. "I've got satellite images from last night. Too many vehicles on Sam's street at the time you took her home," she said, sounding disappointed. "And nothing within two blocks of the construction site. He probably intentionally parked in another area, since a vehicle would have stood out there."

"Red-light cams between the crime scene and Sam's?"

"Already working on them." As if suddenly remembering, she added, "Oh, and I heard back from Flynt through his attorney."

He glanced over at Sam, who didn't appear to be paying attention to anything except the images flying across Brandon Cole's monitor.

"And?"

"His client would be happy to talk to you. *If* Ms. Dalton accompanies you."

"Damn."

"Told you." The softly spoken comment came from an obviously listening Sam.

Lily wasn't finished. "He also has a time restriction. This weekend or never."

"Arrogant bastard."

"You've no idea." Another interjection from Sam.

Alec gave her his full attention. "Do you honestly think it's worth talking to this guy?"

She thought about it, not snapping off a casual reply. Sam was in this up to her neck now; she knew they had no time to waste. Every minute they didn't catch the unsub was another one she had to spend in fear and in hiding.

Finally, she nodded. "I do. I'm no expert, but I really think he is just a less violent version of your Professor. If you want to think like your suspect thinks, Flynt's is a good mind to explore." She offered him a weak smile. "Besides, it's not like you can just dump me at home now, anyway. If you have to keep an eye on me for my own protection, what could be safer than doing it at a prison filled with armed guards and security?"

"She has a point," Lily said. "In case you're wondering, when Wyatt called to see if you were back yet, he said to tell you to go with your instincts if you think it is worth pursuing."

Great. All obstacles cleared. There really was no legitimate reason for him not to bring Sam with him to interview Flynt. Nothing except his own reluctance.

"Do you need to go today?" Brandon asked, looking over his shoulder. "I'm trying to track any failed password tries on the account, figure out where he posted from. I might need some input from Sam."

"I need to get back up to Baltimore this afternoon, anyway," he said. "Maybe talk to Flynt tomorrow."

Sam sipped her coffee, then said, "My day's pretty wide-open."

"Why do you want to do this?" He had no idea what she was up to—why she wanted to remain involved with something she'd admitted scared her spitless.

Alec had at first assumed she needed to feel as if she had some control over what happened in her life, like anyone who'd had a brush with a violent crime would. Since this morning's developments, though, she hadn't just brushed up against the world of a psychopath; it had turned and aimed directly at her. He'd figure any smart person would be lying low until the threat was eliminated.

"What else am I supposed to do?" she asked with a simple shrug. "Sit at home and worry some more? That hasn't gotten me very far."

They were talking about more than a visit to the prison; he knew that much.

"I need to start taking an active role in my life again, instead of merely reacting to what goes on around me," she added. "Not just with this case, but with everything."

Meaning *them*. She'd certainly been active last night, laying out what she'd wanted. Though the sexual invitation had been wrapped in innuendo, it had also been pretty damned clear.

"Can you understand that? The need to act, to move on, get past the fear and insecurity?"

Oh, hell, yeah, he could understand that. It was exactly what he'd been trying to do since the minute he'd come back to work: Regain his footing, his confidence in his own intuition. He needed to stop seeing the mental pictures of Ferguson taking a bullet to his heart, to stop feeling the slow, steady pump of his own heart pushing the blood out of his body, to stop hearing the blasts—*pop-pop-pop-pop*—and to stop wondering if he was ever going to be able to trust his instincts again.

"I understand."

He meant it. But he still didn't like it.

The woman who had started out as a one-shot interview had practically become his pseudo-partner. Not to mention the target of a serial killer. Could things possibly have gotten any more fucked-up from the day he'd walked through the Black CATs' doors?

"You should know, Jimmy will say he's cooperating, but he'll talk in circles," Sam said.

"It's okay. Alec has a built-in bullshit detector, from what I hear." Lily printed off the directions to the prison, which was situated between D.C. and Baltimore, and handed it to him.

"Guess it's that profiler thing," Sam murmured.

He wondered if Lily heard the same undeniable note of warmth in their witness's voice, or if it was audible only to Alec, like the knowing, confident whisper of a lover. Which they both knew they were going to be, sooner or later.

Alec abruptly stood. Sam was in good hands; she was relaxed and calm. And most of all, safe. She didn't need him here. "I want to get going. Sam, would you allow us to search your apartment, on the off chance this son of a bitch is watching you even closer than we suspect?"

"Are we talking hidden-camera stuff?"

His jaw tight, he nodded once.

She reached into her purse and dug out a key ring. "Do you think ... Could you maybe ask Agent Stokes to grab me something to wear?"

"Want me to tell her to pack your all-men-suck nightshirt?"

She chuckled. "Nah. I'm beginning to think maybe they don't. Not all of them, anyway."

There went that soft, intimate tone again. And this time, judging by the quick look of surprise on her face, Lily had noticed.

If she read anything into their light banter, Lily had the discretion not to mention it. "We'll take good care of her." She glanced at Sam. "I've already booked a suite at a local hotel. Jackie will take you over this evening, and I'll come and relieve her at ten or eleven, so she can kiss her kids good night."

"Oh, okay." Sam nibbled her bottom lip, as if not exactly thrilled with the arrangement. As if she thought someone else would be her babysitter.

Huh. If she thought Alec was going to stay with her, she needed to rethink, and fast. He was good at his job and knew how to do it, but talk about putting the fox in charge of the henhouse. No way would he be able to spend a night alone in a hotel room with her without letting things get a whole lot more personal than either one of them could afford right now.

Next week? Maybe.

After this case was over? Definitely.

But not now. Not while the Professor was still out there.

Not while he had Sam Dalton in his sights.

Chapter 12

Under normal circumstances, Lily would never have minded stepping in to help Jackie out because one of her kids was sick. She hadn't met them yet, but her co-worker's son and daughter looked adorable in the pictures on her desk, and she obviously loved them deeply.

Unfortunately, tonight wasn't normal. As Lily escorted their witness, Samantha Dalton, to the downtown hotel where they intended to keep her under protection, she mentally scrambled to figure out what to do.

She'd told Anspaugh she would be available this evening to continue posing as Tiger Lily. She had started the charade last night, in a chat room on the site their suspected pedophile had frequented before. Having no luck, she had left a chatty post on a message board. And this morning, Peter Pan responded to it.

God, he responded. This could really work.

Anspaugh and his team were salivating, smelling the end of the chase. They wanted her online again tonight to lure their prey farther into the trap, and they had to be so cautious. No way could she chat from a hotel with an easily identifiable Web connection; she had to use the proxy server that had been set up for this undercover operation.

That would have been just fine had Jackie been able to take the first shift with their witness. But she hadn't. Now Lily was stuck needing to do two things at once.

It's your own fault for not just going to Wyatt about this.

If she'd been more forthcoming with her boss, they could have dealt with the conflict. Of course, if she'd been more forthcoming with her boss, he might have asked her what she thought she was doing getting caught up in somebody else's case when she had her own to work on.

Okay. So get out. Tell Anspaugh you can't do it.

Maybe it was time to let go of the need to catch Lovesprettyboys. Time to let the crimes-against-children specialists do what they did and focus strictly on the job she'd been so grateful to get with Wyatt and his team.

More, maybe it was time to let go, period. Her sanity, not to mention her dreams, would probably be better off if she did what everyone from Wyatt to her therapist and grief counselors said she should do—got on with her life. Catching Lovesprettyboys wouldn't change what had happened. He was just the substitute, another monster to take down, since the one who'd destroyed her family was already safely locked up. There would always be another one out there; she couldn't catch them all.

But God, how she wanted to catch this one.

"Is everything all right, Agent Fletcher?"

Lily realized her concern must have been showing on her face, because Samantha Dalton was watching her closely, concern visible in the line between her eyes.

"Oh, yeah, fine. Nothing to worry about. And please call me Lily."

Pulling her lips up at the corners in what would hopefully pass for a smile, Lily led the woman to their room, swept it, then beckoned her inside. As far as safe houses went, it wasn't bad. Not five-star, not on Uncle Sam's dime, but it was clean and modern. Two rooms, one with

a bed, the other with a sleeper sofa, plus a small kitchenette. A decent home away from home until they could
get their witness out of the danger they had so unwittingly put her into.

Now Lily just needed to get herself out of the mess
she'd unwittingly put herself into.

Brandon would come and stay with Sam Dalton if she
asked him; she knew that. But she hated to drag him
deeper into her situation. Dean, Kyle, and Alec were all
still in Baltimore. Jackie was unavailable, and there was
no way she could ask her boss.

She couldn't bring in an outside agent because she
didn't think one would come. Sometimes, it didn't pay
to be part of a team so on the outs with the rest of the
bureau. At other times, it was great, incredibly freeing.

Tonight was not one of the great times.

She needed to talk to Wyatt. No more of this off-hour
maneuvering between jobs. Lily wasn't doing anything
wrong; in fact, some would say she was going above and
beyond. She doubted, however, that Wyatt would see it
that way. Especially not since he'd warned her not to let
herself get caught up in something because of her own
history.

"I guess there are worse places to be imprisoned,"
Sam mused.

"Would you like me to order some dinner?" They had
stayed in the office all day and hadn't stopped for a bite
en route to the hotel. "I can order in."

"I'm fine, thanks." The other woman walked to the
window and peered out at the city, spread far below
them. The dome of the Capitol was visible in the distance, and she stared at it for several moments. "Since
Agent Stokes can't come tonight, will someone else be
bringing some clothes for me?"

"Yes," Lily said, her hopes quickly rising. She'd almost
forgotten that. This might work out after all. If one of
the other agents showed up with clothes and toiletries,

Lily could ask him to cover and slip away for an hour or two.

As long as they show up on time. For all she knew, they could be pulling an all-nighter.

"Did she have to leave before Alec—um, Agent Lambert—got back there with my keys? I mean, was she there to gather my things?"

Hearing a hint of embarrassment, Lily reassured her. "They're all good guys, Sam. I can promise you none of them went through your underwear drawer."

The other woman looked away, not meeting her eye. Her hands fisted on the windowsill. "You don't know that about Agent Lambert yet, do you? Isn't he pretty new to your team?"

Lily nodded slowly, hearing the frank curiosity. She had the strange suspicion, as she had earlier at the office, that their witness was personally interested in the newest member of the Black CATs. "He just started this week."

"But he's doing a good job."

"A very good job," Lily admitted. "Nobody was quite sure how it would work out, but I think it's going to be great. We're lucky to have him."

She didn't know Alec very well yet, though she suspected she was going to like him. Still, there were a lot of stories about the agent. Stories about him getting too close to a female witness, and another agent getting killed because of it.

She had no business warning Sam off—though she wouldn't hesitate to say something to Alec if she thought it needed to be said. Still, something made her murmur, "Agent Lambert's a very handsome man."

Sam's head jerked.

Lily hid a sigh, knowing her intuition had been right. "Look, Sam . . ."

The other woman put her hand up to stop her. "You don't have to say it. I am well aware that I'm a witness and he's an agent, and there's no way he's going to let down his guard around me and get himself shot again."

Lily gawked. It sounded as though Sam knew a lot more about Alec than even his coworkers.

Sam's eyes were wide, as if she feared she'd revealed a secret. "You ... Everyone knew he had been shot, right?"

"Well, yes. I'm just surprised you do."

"We talked."

That was obvious. "So, he told you about the shooting? That, uh ..."

"That a woman shot him? Yes, he did. And I felt about two inches tall for being so judgmental about it at first, until I found out she was the elderly mother of a suspect and he felt sorry for her."

Lily remained very still. This was more than even she knew. Not that she couldn't have found out, if she had chosen to dig around in her new colleague's past. She hadn't, not wanting to be nosy. But she couldn't deny an interest.

"This transfer to your team, it was kind of a new start for him, right? A chance to rebuild his career?"

Lily rolled her eyes. "More like a chance to bury it."

Sam left the window and sat on the couch, eyeing her quizzically. "What do you mean?"

Taking the seat opposite her, Lily admitted, "They call us the Black CATs. But what they really mean is the black sheep."

"You're kidding. You guys are all so good."

"We all have baggage."

"Baggage," Sam snapped. "I hate that word. What does it mean, anyway?"

"Okay, then, let's say we all have reputations."

"Even your boss?"

Lily curled one leg under her and made herself more comfortable in the chair. "Him more than anyone. Wyatt has a lot of integrity, and he sees things very black or white, right or wrong."

Which made it even harder to tell him how far she'd gone into shades of gray regarding her job.

"He took a stand against a few things," she said, not going into detail. "That earned him the enmity of some of our colleagues."

Not pressing for more information, as if knowing Lily couldn't provide it, Sam moved on. "And the rest of you?"

"Dean Taggert's a badass former street cop with a temper."

"That doesn't surprise me."

"Jackie has an attitude."

Sam grinned. "Also not a surprise."

"Mulrooney is a bit of a blowhard. Brandon's a wild card."

"And Alec?"

"The circumstances surrounding his shooting were . . . less than ideal."

Sam rolled her eyes. "Especially for him. Getting shot and all."

The woman was absolutely right, and Lily agreed with her. There was simply no way to explain bureau politics, that Alec's survival might have been viewed with skepticism because the other agent had not survived. It wasn't fair, especially now that she knew more about what had really happened. No more than what had happened to Wyatt was fair. It was just the way things went in an agency made powerful by J. Edgar Hoover, the king of intrigue himself.

"What about you? What's your story?"

Lily wrapped her arms around one upraised leg, staring down at her own knee. "I'm a little too emotional."

"Considering I've felt like screaming, crying, or punching someone since just about the minute you guys showed up in my life, I can see where that would be a problem."

Unable to resist Sam's sarcasm, Lily had to smile. She seldom spent time with anyone outside of the office these days, and had forgotten, since Laura's death, how much she enjoyed simply hanging out and talking with another woman. As much as she liked Jackie Stokes, the other agent was older, and in a different place. Lily honestly couldn't remember the last time she'd gone for a girls' night out, or indulged in a man-griping session with a single woman her own age.

It had been at least two years ago; that was certain. Before Zach's life had intersected with a monster's.

The dark thoughts immediately pulled the smile from her lips and the good humor from her heart. Sam eyed her curiously, but before she could ask anything, Lily's cell phone rang. Seeing Anspaugh's name, she took a deep breath and answered.

"Where are you? What the hell's this message you left, that you might have a problem?"

"Sorry, Anspaugh. Something came up. I'm at a hotel in the city. I have to stay with a witness all night."

"Damn it, Lil, we need you!"

She bit back an annoyed *don't call me that* response and said, "You guys know what you're doing. It's not like the suspect is going to realize a man is typing rather than a woman. None of us are children."

"Yeah, but you can make it sound more legit; I know you can. Just that shit about knowing whether a real boy would call himself Peter Pan. I wouldn'ta thought of that, and you did."

She didn't know that Anspaugh had the sense to know a boy wouldn't call himself Cinderella.

"And if the son of a bitch suddenly asks for a voice chat, you've got a whole lot better chance of pulling that off."

Lily blew out an impatient breath. "I in no way sound like an eleven-year-old girl."

"Well, you sure as hell sound more like one than me or my guys do."

Closing her eyes, she rubbed at the inside corners of them with her fingers, trying to figure out a way to give everyone what they needed. "Look, if I can work something out, I'll let you know, all right? Otherwise, you're just going to have to proceed without me. I'm sorry."

When she opened them, she saw Sam waving and mouthing something from the other side of the room. Lily covered the mouthpiece with her hand and raised a brow.

"I can stay here by myself," the other woman insisted in a loud whisper. "You don't have to babysit me; it's not like anybody in the known universe knows where I am."

Lily was shaking her head before the other woman finished speaking. "If I leave my assigned position, I would not only lose my job; I would deserve to."

Sam opened her mouth to persist, then closed it again, realizing Lily was right and not arguing it. A woman of common sense, this one, which made Lily like her even more.

"Look, if you're sitting on a witness," Anspaugh was saying, "why don't we swap? I'll send one of my guys over to keep watch; you come do this, and you'll be back there in two or three hours, tops."

She waffled. It made sense. She wouldn't be leaving Sam with anyone other than another FBI agent.

"Come on, I know you want this guy as bad as we do."

"Yeah, I do."

"He's been on this site for weeks. No telling how many kids he's already been in contact with. Christ, for all we know, he's already molested some of them."

Lily felt the blood drain from her face. Anspaugh definitely knew which buttons to push.

"Let me think about it. . . ."

"We don't have time for you to think about it," he said, his belligerence showing.

She kept cool. "Then the answer is no."

Anspaugh breathed heavily through the phone, his anger a living thing. Men like him didn't like being told no. One more reason Lily wanted to finish this double life and stop working with the man. Because sooner or later, she knew, he was going to ask her a more personal question, and would like hearing *no* even less.

"Would you just think about it?" he asked, every word bitten out from what sounded like a rigidly clenched jaw. "If you're in the city, I can have a car pick you up within a half hour. It's only seven twenty. If you can swing it anytime before nine, call me, okay?"

"Fine."

He disconnected without another word.

"Problem?"

"Another case," she admitted, shaking her head and wondering how on earth she'd gotten herself into this situation.

"Why would you need to talk like a little girl?"

Reaching into her purse and pulling out a bottle of aspirin, Lily popped a couple of them to ward off the headache building in her temples. Then she admitted, "I've been helping another team try to capture a sexual predator."

"Sick bastards."

"Yeah. This one is especially bad." At least, if they were indeed on the trail of Lovesprettyboys, he was. Whatever else he had or hadn't done, the degenerate had definitely tried to set up the pay-per-view murder of a little kid.

She looked at the door, wondering if she dared take Anspaugh up on his offer to have someone replace her. He was a supervisor, requesting her assistance, providing another agent to cover her. It was a legitimate solution.

Somehow, though, she sensed Wyatt wouldn't see it that way.

Besides, she didn't totally trust Anspaugh. He had such a big chip on his shoulder about her boss, she couldn't count on him to send over somebody really good to protect Sam.

No. She couldn't do it. If Anspaugh called back, she'd just have to make it clear she was not abandoning her post. Hopefully they could string Peter Pan along, get him on the line, and tomorrow she would be there to help reel him in.

It wasn't an ideal solution for her, personally, but it was the professional one. She owed Wyatt her loyalty. And she owed Samantha Dalton the best protection she could give her, not a pass-off to someone she didn't even know, who had no idea of the kind of crazy man who was after her.

"It'll work out," she mumbled, talking more to herself.

"If you say so."

When a knock suddenly sounded on the door to the suite, Lily leaped up, gesturing for Sam to remain quiet. She skirted the wall, not approaching the entrance head-on. They had not ordered any food; no one was supposed to know they were here. Sam hadn't even contacted her family members, who, she said, were used to her being out of touch and wouldn't miss her.

Her hand on her service weapon, Lily moved to the peephole, looked out, and saw a familiar face. "It's okay," she said, reaching for the handle.

Definitely okay. As she opened the door, she nodded in decision. Because a solution to her problem had just landed in her lap.

She was going.

Alec didn't seem too happy about playing babysitter. He'd agreed, when Lily had asked him to step in for a couple of hours, but he sure wasn't smiling about it. Sam had the feeling he wished one of his fellow agents had been the one to swing by the hotel with a suitcase of clothes and toiletries from her apartment.

She knew why. It wasn't that he didn't want to be around her. She suspected the problem was that he did, a little too much. And he didn't entirely trust himself to be alone with her in an anonymous hotel room.

Which was why, since Agent Fletcher had departed a half hour ago, Alec had been sitting on a chair by the window, far from the couch where she sat. His very posture discouraging conversation, he'd spent his time looking out at the cityscape. He'd answered a few questions—mainly confirming that they found nothing suspicious in her apartment—but beyond that had managed only a few comments asking whether she was hungry and if the room was too cold.

Finally, she'd had enough of it. "Would you please stop acting like you're afraid I'm going to jump on you?"

He jerked his head to stare at her over his shoulder. "Excuse me?"

"For heaven's sake, Alec, you're sitting over there with an invisible chastity belt wrapped around yourself, as if you're in need of protection. Like you have to be stern and pissy to keep the horny divorcée from tempting you into letting down your guard while on duty."

He half coughed, or might have laughed. "Horny divorcée?"

Sam stood and crossed to the window, staring down at him. The lamplight didn't extend far into this corner of the room. His face was bathed in shadow, so she couldn't tell if those sensual lips were smiling or those amazing green eyes glinted with humor.

"I get it, okay?" she said. She wrapped her arms around herself, surprised by how much cooler the room was over here. "Despite what happened last night, this thing between us isn't going anywhere else until the case is over. I'm not Eve. I know I can't seduce you, and I'm not going to try."

He slowly rose to stand before her, so close she felt the warmth of his body and the brush of his clothes against her own. The chill permeating the glass windows was suddenly banished, pure heat washing over her. His voice thick, he admitted, "It's because you could that I've been staying put over here."

She managed a weak whisper. "Could?"

"Seduce me," he admitted. He lifted a hand, brushing the tips of his fingers across her cheek, sliding them into her hair. The touch was simple, restrained, nonsexual, but also loaded with possibility. She could tilt her face into his palm, kiss the pulse point at his wrist, whisper a plea for an even more intimate touch.

"You could make me forget what I'm doing here tonight and what the stakes are."

"Really?" she asked. Part of her reacted with pure excitement, knowing she could make something happen between them tonight if she pushed it. Another with pure feminine pleasure that this amazing man genuinely wanted her.

"Yeah. Really."

"I'm not much into the seduction game," she whispered, "and I know I should retreat to my separate corner and let you keep this barrier in place. But I can't deny a big part of me just doesn't want to."

"Ditto."

A helpless moan emerged from the back of her throat when he touched her neck, sliding the side of his thumb against the vulnerable flesh beneath her earlobe. Sam closed her eyes, remembering what it felt like to have a man's hands on her body. Acknowledging how much she'd missed it.

It had been so long. A year since her divorce, months before that since she'd realized how thoroughly her husband had betrayed her and had cut him out of her life. She'd grown cold and hard. Her nerve endings had dulled, her skin desensitized during all that time without any type of human connection.

All those sensations came roaring back with a vengeance, warmth turning into fire, want becoming desperate need.

"This has never happened to me before," she said, unable to resist lifting one hand to his chest, running her fingers as lightly there as he was on her neck. "I mean, something this physical, this soon."

She wondered if he could say the same. Alec's innate charm and the glimpses of flirtatiousness she'd witnessed said he had a lot of experience with women. But his tension and aloofness also said that part of his life might have changed when he'd nearly died.

"It's not just physical," he admitted, not sounding exactly happy about it. "I want you, but I also like you, Sam. I think I could like you a lot. I don't want anything to happen to you, especially not on my watch."

She understood. He wasn't stopping her, wasn't pushing her away. With a few more whispers, the soft press of her mouth on his throat, perhaps, she could probably have what she wanted. What they both wanted.

Tempting. Oh, God, so tempting.

"So would you do me a favor?" he asked, even as he leaned down, his face so close to hers they exchanged breaths that further dispersed the chill. "Would you walk back over there and sit down?" He didn't give her a chance to answer. Instead, he leaned even closer, until that last sliver of space between them disappeared and their lips touched.

No frenzied, frantic kiss like last night, this was a soft caress, a gentle plea. Even a promise that there would be more to come, later. When the time was right.

He lifted his mouth from hers far enough to whisper, "Please?"

Breathless and every bit as aroused by his tenderness

as she'd been by his hunger the night before, she still somehow managed to nod. "Okay."

"Thank you."

On shaky legs, she retreated. Part of her should have resented that he'd done the unimaginable and kissed her before shooing her away. Another recognized that he'd been unable to stop himself, any more than she'd been able to refuse.

Resuming their previous positions, they descended into silence for a few minutes. She could think only how lucky it was that they were in a two-room suite. If there had been a big, king-size bed between them, she didn't know that she could have come down off of red alert back to just orange.

Finally, when she felt like she could speak without sounding as though she hadn't drawn breath in twenty minutes, she said, "I could probably use something to eat now, if that's okay."

He nodded, glad for the distraction. "Yeah, sure. Check out the room service menu." Glancing at his watch, he added, "Maybe we should order something for Lily, too."

"Do you think she'll be back so soon? What if this creep shows up and wants to talk?"

Alec, who had walked to the desk to retrieve a leather-encased room service menu, tilted his head in confusion. "What creep?"

"This pedophile she's after."

He still appeared puzzled.

"I guess it's another case you guys are working on? She said she was going into a chat room posing as a little girl to try to lure a pedophile."

With a frown, he admitted, "Doesn't sound like something Blackstone's team is supposed to be dealing with."

"Don't you mean your team?"

Sheepish, he nodded. "Right. I guess I'm just not used to that yet."

Again, she wondered about the reason for his transfer. He had never come out and said exactly why he had taken it, but from the few things he had let drop, and Lily's brief comments earlier tonight, she sensed the topic was a sticky one.

Things had been sticky enough tonight. So she avoided even going there.

"Why wouldn't your group work on a pedophile case? Isn't that exactly what the Cyber Action Teams do?"

"Not this one. Their—*our* focus is a little narrower. We look at murders with an Internet connection."

"Oh." She blew out a soft breath. "Then this pedophile, he must be someone who ..."

"Yeah, he must."

Though the idea that a sick degenerate was out there trying to find a child to molest and kill filled her with revulsion, Sam didn't ask any more questions. She was in an odd position: a civilian, yet so wrapped up in an investigation she'd started feeling right at home with the investigators. She wasn't one of them, however, and had no business being inquisitive.

Nor was she sure she really wanted to know any additional details. The one ugly corner of the world she had been sucked into was enough. She didn't want to visit any more of them if she could help it.

Taking the menu, she glanced over it, told Alec what she wanted, and watched him call in an order. The tension eased, the simple act of deciding on dinner cutting through some of the physical awareness. It wasn't gone, merely banked for now, set aside to deal with at a more appropriate time.

And that turned out to be a good thing. Because their evening together stretched out a lot longer than either of them had anticipated. A whole lot longer.

"It's eleven o'clock; where the hell is she?" Alec asked later that night. They had expected to see Agent

Fletcher back by nine and had easily filled the first couple of hours with dinner and some casual conversation, back-and-forth chitchat more appropriate to a first date than a night at a safe house.

Of course, given the tension simmering between them, they had moved far beyond first-date territory. At least, *her* first-date territory, though it had been so long since she'd had any kind of date, she couldn't be sure.

"Isn't this good news? I mean, doesn't it mean she was successful in trying to get the guy she's after to talk to her?"

"I suppose," he said, not sounding convinced. The tension that had slipped away over the last couple of hours had eased back, evidenced by the tense set of his jaw and the stiffness of his shoulders.

"Still no answer on her cell phone?" she asked as she watched him try to call again, then slam the phone shut.

"No." He ran a frustrated hand through his hair. "I don't like this."

"I'm okay staying by myself, really."

He looked at her as if she'd said something utterly ridiculous. "I mean, I'm worried about Fletcher."

"Oh." Noting the lines on his brow as his frown deepened, she knew he meant it. He wasn't frustrated about having to sit here with her and pretend they hadn't kissed a couple of hours ago. He was genuinely concerned about his colleague. Which increased her concern about the other woman, too.

"This pedophile investigation, what else did she say about it?"

"Nothing more than I already told you." She racked her brain, trying to recall every word. "She got a call, said she couldn't help out with it because she had to babysit me; then you showed up and she realized she could go after all."

"Who called?"

Sam closed her eyes to concentrate.

"Taggert and Mulrooney were with me all day; Jackie went home to her kids. Was it Brandon? Wyatt?"

She shook her head. "No. I would have remembered if she had said one of their names. It was something else—Anderson? Wait, I think she said Anspaugh."

"There's nobody named Anspaugh on our team."

"Well, she certainly didn't sound like she was making it up," Sam said, truly confused.

About to go on asking why another agent would conceal her investigation from her own coworkers, she was interrupted by a brief knock on the door. As Lily had before him, Alec approached it carefully, flinging it open only after he peered out and obviously recognized whoever was on the other side of it.

"I'm so sorry," Lily Fletcher said as she pushed past him into the room.

"Where the hell have you been?"

The blonde's eyebrows shot up. "I didn't mean to inconvenience you...."

"It's not the inconvenience. It's you dropping off the face of the earth, not answering your phone. And a pedophile investigation? Why haven't I heard about it? What is going on?"

Lily looked back and forth between Sam and Alec. The other woman certainly hadn't asked Sam not to say anything about the mysterious errand she had to run, yet Sam still felt a little embarrassed, as if she'd betrayed a trust.

"I'm helping another CAT, trying to track a pedophile who operated at Satan's Playground. He slipped through the cracks then; we think we have a line on him now."

Alec crossed his arms and leaned against the small kitchen counter. "Why did you say you could cover Jackie's assignment here, then? Wyatt could have called one of us back sooner."

Seeing a slight flush in Lily's cheeks, Sam suddenly rose. "I'll leave you two alone," she said, heading into the bedroom. The aura of secrecy surrounding Agent Fletcher was undeniable. The other woman's color was high, her eyes bright. Excitement and nervousness had wafted off her from the minute she'd returned, and, though they were close to the elevator, she had been out of breath, as if her heart were racing after a run.

Oh, yes. The agent was hiding something.

Sam shut the door behind her and stayed in the bedroom, trying not to hear the voices. It wasn't difficult; there was just a low, dull hum, indistinguishable as anything more than brief conversation.

Then Alec's voice grew a lot louder. "You mean Wyatt doesn't know? He didn't approve this? Damn it, Lily!"

More mumbling. Sam winced, feeling sorry for Lily. Because as intimidating as Alec probably was right now at having been kept out of the loop, their boss, Wyatt Blackstone, would be much worse. Sam found his very presence intimidating. Strong and intense, serious and intuitive, he didn't look like someone who even knew how to crack a joke. She suspected a mind like his was always going, always working. As if he could read the thoughts of everyone around him, anticipate their actions.

Well, one thing was sure: He hadn't known what Lily Fletcher was thinking, and he apparently hadn't anticipated her actions.

Which, she suspected, meant some very serious trouble was heading straight at the pretty young agent.

Though there were three state penitentiaries in Maryland, James T. Flynt was incarcerated in the closest, in a town just south of Baltimore. Since they didn't have to leave too early for their one p.m. meeting, or allow much time for the drive, Alec spent much of the morning planning his interview with the convicted felon.

Well, that, thinking about Sam, worrying about how deep she was getting in this, angsting over how little they had discovered about their unsub, and wondering what

the hell he was supposed to tell Wyatt Blackstone if he
was asked about Lily's unexpected departure from the
hotel last night.

To say he had a lot on his mind this morning would
be an understatement. Which would probably be pretty
obvious to Sam. Not to mention to Lily, who opened the
hotel room door to him, looking as tense and nervous as
she had the previous night.

"Morning," she said, her tone subdued.

"Good morning." Alec didn't pull any punches.
"You're still planning to talk to Wyatt while Sam and I
are gone, right?"

That had been their deal last night. Alec wouldn't
make an issue of Lily leaving her post for so many hours
as long as she brought their boss in on what she was
doing.

Not that Wyatt should mind. Cooperation between
CATs was a cornerstone of the division. Another group
reaching out to Wyatt's was a sign that maybe they were
on the road to being accepted. At least, that was one way
to interpret it.

Lily, however, was nervous as hell. Which meant she
did not think Wyatt was going to approve of her extra
duties.

Obviously there was more going on here than he
knew; something was at work beneath the surface.
Maybe even between Lily and their boss, though, from
what he'd seen of Wyatt so far, the man would never
allow anything personal to develop between him and
one of his employees.

"I'll talk to him; I swear." She ran a weary hand over
her eyes, drawing attention to the dark smudges beneath. Her face pale, her eyes bloodshot, she looked as
if she hadn't slept at all.

"Are you all right?"

"It's this case. I've been working on it for so long, I
just didn't expect it to come together so quickly. Despite

his responding on the message board yesterday, I half expected him not to show up in the chat room last night and still can't quite believe he did. Boggles the mind that I actually talked to this bastard."

Lily had told him a little about what she was doing last night, though nothing in depth. "And you really think this is the same guy you were after last summer, from the Reaper case?"

"I do. I've gone over all the transcripts from this site, checking it against everything we saw Lovesprettyboys say. And I believe we're dealing with the same man who tried to hire Seth Covey to rape and murder a young boy for his own viewing pleasure."

He shook his head in disgust. "So hopefully this will be over soon."

She nodded. "God, I hope so. Once Wyatt finds out . . . Once I tell him I truly believe we're getting close to that sick degenerate, I'm sure he'll understand."

Alec didn't respond, knowing she was trying to talk herself into it.

"Why wouldn't he?" she mumbled.

"I don't know. Why wouldn't he?"

She sucked her lip into her mouth and shook her head, hinting that there was a lot he didn't know. Frankly, he didn't want to. He had no time to deal with any other conflicts right now; he just wanted to stop the Professor before he hurt anyone else. As much as he wanted Lily to help in that effort, he knew her quest was just as important to her.

"Tell Wyatt," he ordered, quickly turning away to watch as Sam emerged from the bedroom.

Since Jackie hadn't stuck around all day yesterday, Kyle Mulrooney had grabbed clothes from Sam's apartment. Dean had been busy taking off every AC vent and outlet cover, looking for hidden cameras. And Alec hadn't trusted himself near her lingerie drawer.

In Alec's opinion, Mulrooney had done a damn fine

job. The black skirt Sam wore wasn't exactly an obscene length, but it definitely didn't do much to hide those long, silk-covered legs, emphasized by spiked black heels. It was also tight, hugging her round hips, emphasizing every curve. For his own sanity, if it clung just as nicely to her backside as it did her front, she was going to have to walk by his side, definitely not ahead.

Of course, looking at the front of her wasn't much easier. Her blouse was every bit as dangerous. Silky and slinky, it was cut low, revealing enough cleavage to make him breathe hard, though not quite enough to stop his heart.

Then he thought about who else was going to see it. "Go change."

She gawked. "Well, good morning to you, too."

"You're not walking into a prison looking like that."

Sam frowned, stalked over, and stuck her index finger into his chest. "Well, you should have thought of that before you grabbed a bunch of one-size-too-small dress clothes and a pair of do-me shoes from the back corner of my closet, rather than just pulling some jeans and sweaters out of my drawer. This is about the best thing I've got. Do you not know the difference between a pair of cords and a little black cocktail dress, for God's sake?"

Beside her, Lily grinned. "She's got a point. She showed me what you brought, Alec, and this is the best of the bunch."

"I didn't pack your stuff," he admitted, deciding then and there to strangle Mulrooney the next time he saw the man. "Kyle did. Damn it."

"I think he's been watching too much late-night Cinemax," Sam said as she shifted and plucked the black fabric away from her hips. "Women don't consider this professional day wear unless they're starring in soft-porn movies as secretaries about to get ravaged by the boss."

He ignored the ravaged-by-the-boss part. "But jeans and a sweater would be?"

"For me? Are you kidding? That's dressing up." She

grumbled, again tugging at the skirt. "And despite what you might see on the average Barbie doll, most women don't like wearing their clothes this tight."

He didn't ask her why she had the tight clothes in her closet. It was a chick thing, the need to have entire wardrobes in various sizes. His sisters were the same way. Who knew why?

All he knew was that if Jimmy Flynt had a thing for Sam, he was going to love watching her walk into that jail today. Which already filled Alec with enough anger to make him want to yank a coat over the woman and keep it there.

"What about the clothes you had on yesterday?"

"You mean the pizza-stained ones?"

Crap.

"Look, let's just go, okay?" She slipped into her coat, murmuring her thanks to Lily for the overnight babysitting.

Alec did the same, adding, "Call Wyatt," before stepping out into the hall. He checked both directions, then beckoned Sam out. As they walked to the elevator, he murmured, "Maybe we could swing by a mall or something. . . ."

"Oh, for heaven's sake, I don't look like a hooker." She almost sounded amused by his he-man protectiveness.

Since Alec had never reacted that way toward another woman, he didn't find it particularly funny. "You're not going to lay yourself out like some kind of appetizer for a felon who's already got a thing for you."

"Not even if it makes him more talkative?"

"Especially not then. I don't want him thinking you did this for his benefit."

They reached the elevator and he punched the call button, wondering why the sight of her, so beautiful and feminine in the formfitting clothes, with her thick hair pulled back and a hint of makeup on her face, made him want to shove her back into her room and lock the door. To protect her. Since nobody knew where she was, he couldn't say whom from.

Maybe himself?

Damn.

Alec's annoyance and his worry, combined with Sam's defensiveness, made the bulk of their car ride out of the city a silent one. Beyond asking if the hotel room had been okay overnight, he kept his mouth shut and his thoughts to himself.

Finally, though, as he began seeing signs for the exit, he bit out, "Try not to interact with him, if you can help it. In fact, the best thing that could happen is for you to come in with me, let him know you're around, then step out while I talk to him."

"Yeah, right. You're going to think somebody put a muzzle on him the second I walk out the door."

"What is it with you and this guy?" he asked, frustrated and, even more, confused by Sam's relationship with the man.

Sam glanced at him from the passenger seat, her mouth opening, then closing quickly. He let her be, knowing she had to work up to whatever it was she wanted to say.

It took a full minute; then, finally, she admitted, "He thinks he did me a big favor."

"By helping you with the book?"

"Not exactly. The reason I stopped reading his letters a few months ago was because one of them really bothered me. He wrote that he'd run into an old friend of mine."

"A friend. In prison?" He made no effort to hide his skepticism.

"He said he had learned one of the men who helped ruin my grandmother was doing time in the same facility."

He thought about the *ruined my grandmother* part, remembering what she had revealed yesterday about her passwords. Obviously there was a lot more to the story. But they were within a few miles of their destination and time was running out for storytelling, so he didn't ask for more details.

"Jimmy told me he'd 'put a hurting' on the guy. I took

it to mean prison-yard justice. Anyway, I didn't really believe him, but I guess he thinks I did. So in his mind, I could be feeling appreciative and maybe I'm coming to 'thank' him in person."

"Fuck," Alec muttered, tempted to turn around. "The last thing you need is somebody like James Flynt deciding you're in his debt."

"No kidding. But you can see why I was pretty sure he'd talk to you if I came along."

Of course he did. Good old slimeball Jimmy was thinking he could make something happen with this beautiful woman.

Fat chance, pal. You're not getting one second alone with her.

"You really believe he was lying?" he asked.

"Yes, I do. It's the kind of manipulative person he is. I don't know if the con men who ruined my grandmother and caused her death were ever even caught, much less imprisoned. Jimmy said he—"

"*Caused* her death?"

She swallowed, nodding once. "She was taken in gradually, over several months. First with standard pyramid schemes, fake stock purchases." Her tone growing bitter, she added, "I tried to get help after they wiped out her checking account. Went to the FBI. Cyber Division, in fact. They did nothing."

It was a wonder she hadn't slammed the door in his face the other day when he had identified himself.

"I thought she had learned her lesson the first time, so it didn't even occur to me that she would get sucked in again. This time it was a charity. Feed starving children in Africa."

God, there were some sick people in the world to prey on the helpless and elderly. "I'm sorry. Sorrier than I can say."

"Me, too. When she realized she'd given the thieves enough information to wipe her out completely, down to emptying every penny from her retirement account, she just couldn't take the strain. They say it was natural causes, but I'm pretty sure the stress contributed to, if not outright caused, her heart attack."

Something made him reach across and take her hand. Their fingers twined together. "I can't imagine how tough that must have been."

Sounding bitter, she said, "I gave her the damn computer to begin with, saying, 'Come on, Grandma, join the cyber age!' Oh, yeah, I'd call it tough."

The whole story of Samantha Dalton suddenly came together. The picture of her life, why she'd made the choices she had, why she lived the way she did—all of it became clear. The pieces of the puzzle had started coming together the other night when she'd told him about her marriage. Now the rest filled in, explaining why she had started her Web site, why she had written her book. Why she took Internet fraud so personally.

Only one question remained in regard to Sam—was she ready to let go of the past, climb out of her self-imposed isolation, and start living again?

"This was how long ago?"

"It started right after I got married. But she died about three years ago."

Of course, right around the time her site had gone up. Hard to believe how difficult it must have been, going from that nightmare into the pain of a cheating husband and a bitter divorce.

He could only repeat what he'd already said. "So sorry."

She nodded her thanks, then hurried on, as if afraid to let herself dwell further on the past. "The bastards who robbed her were never caught."

"How did this Flynt even know about your grandmother?"

She rubbed a hand over her eyes. "Honestly, I'm not

sure. I certainly didn't tell him anything personal about myself when I interviewed him."

"Smart."

"He claimed he has connections on the inside, found out who one of them was and 'took care of him,' whatever that means."

"That's a stretch. If it's like most other Internet crimes, the men who did it were probably from far away, likely even in another country."

"Actually, we know at least one of them was local. My grandmother apparently met with him a day or two before she died, and he somehow convinced her to give him access to her accounts. He cashed one out in person at a bank in western Maryland."

Surprised, Alec couldn't help thinking how much harder that must have made things for Sam. Not just knowing her grandmother had been ripped off online, but knowing she had actually been face-to-face with someone who wanted only to steal from her.

The possibilities of what could have happened at such a meeting must have kept her up for many nights afterward. And that somehow made it worse.

But it also made it at least possible the two inmates could end up doing time at the same facility. "It's still a long shot. A very long shot."

"Don't I know it." She shivered lightly. "But Jimmy doesn't know I think he's full of shit."

Which could, indeed, work to their advantage. As long as Flynt kept a respectful tongue in his mouth. He'd better not make one single suggestion to Sam that was out of line.

If he did . . . well, honestly, Alec wasn't sure it would matter how much the man could help them. No way would he allow Sam to be any more abused than she'd already been. No way in hell.

Chapter 13

This was going to be okay. Alec was right beside her. She kept telling herself that.

It'll be okay.

When Sam had come to interview James Flynt for her book nearly two years ago, she'd been alone. Not inside, of course, and certainly not with the inmates. She'd received thorough safety instructions from the warden, and a guard had escorted her at all times. But she had pulled into the facility by herself, and had sat in her car, wondering why she had ever decided to arrange a meeting with a scumbag cyber thief.

Fortunately, she had come after the original maximum-security facility—more than a century old and renowned for its violence—had been shut down. The buildings still in operation were modern, nondescript, looking as if they could have housed any other government agency.

If not for the razor wire. And the guard towers.

As she'd learned the last time, the medium-security site where Flynt was incarcerated was only one of several lockups in the complex, which sprawled for many acres. It was perfectly safe and not too intimidating. Not as nonthreatening as the women's building, the minimum-security one, or especially the boot camp, but it still beat having to walk into the maximum-security facility.

"You okay?" Alec asked, as if sensing her trepidation once they parked in a guest lot.

"Yeah. It's just not my favorite place."

"You don't have to do this."

"Do you really want to talk to Flynt?" she countered. He nodded once.

"Then I do have to do this."

Not arguing, Alec got out of the car and came around to open her door. She walked close beside him, aware of the watchful eyes scanning the security monitors, the guards high in their towers, the workers in the office windows, and even inmates getting some fresh air in the yard.

Once inside, Alec headed not toward a general visitors' area, but toward a special law enforcement one. They were met by two armed guards who photocopied their identification and asked a few questions.

"Oh, you're coming to see old J.T., huh?" one of the guards said when he read the sign-in log. "He's been bragging that his girlfriend was gonna be here today."

Alec could have cracked a walnut against his stiff jaw. "We're here on official business."

"Tell that to Jimmy."

"I intend to."

Sam shook off her unease and forced a reassuring smile. "It'll be fine."

"Ma'am, you'll have to leave your coat here," one of the guards said. "Your bag, too. We'll secure them for you."

She knew that, from the last time. Slipping out of the long wool overcoat, she passed it over to the man, seeing his quick, not-very-discreet glance over her attire.

Damn. Maybe she should have let Alec stop at a mall. She thought so even more when she heard a crisp, hard-edged voice say, "Your dress is inappropriate."

Sucking in an embarrassed breath, she glanced over
to see the prison warden, Connolly. The gruff, stern-
looking man, who had been at least polite on the phone,
now stared at her with flinty-eyed disapproval.

"Warden Connolly," she said. "I'm Samantha Dalton.
We spoke on the phone?"

"You do know we have a dress code for a reason,"
he said, not acknowledging her greeting. He frowned
as he stared at the length of her skirt. Though what
she wore was perfectly acceptable for a party, it wasn't
for a prison, where women's skirts, if she recalled correctly, had to reach the knee. "Many of these men are
unused to the presence of females. We prefer to keep
them docile, and having a young woman in the area is
difficult enough without adding provocative attire to
the mixture."

Her face flushed hot. Sam hadn't been called out on her
clothes since she was a teenager and her mom wouldn't
let her wear a pair of jeans with one of the ass pockets
torn down at the corner. She kept her cool, though, saying, "I apologize. I forgot about the dress code."

"We won't be seen by any of the general population,"
Alec said, stepping close, lending silent support, as if he
read her embarrassment. "Maybe she could leave her
coat on?"

The older man didn't unbend. "Coats are against regu-
lations, too. I don't make the rules—the state does—but
in this case, I agree with them. It is an issue of safety—of
the inmates, my men, and you, ma'am."

Alec pulled out his badge, which he'd just tucked
away after showing it to the checkpoint guards. "Mrs.
Dalton is assisting me with an investigation, Warden,
and I really need her help. Can you not make some type
of accommodation here? Search the coat thoroughly,
perhaps, and let her keep it on? I assume the prohibi-
tion is because of the fear of weapons?"

Warden Connolly held Alec's gaze, and for a second,

she thought he would refuse. How embarrassing would that be, sent out to wait in the car like a recalcitrant child because her damn skirt was two inches too short?

Finally, the man let out an annoyed sign. "Very well. If it truly is urgent." He gave a quick nod to one of his men. The guard patted down Sam's coat, put his hands in the pockets, felt the lining, then handed it back to her.

"Please do keep buttoned up. It is difficult enough to keep these animals in check," the warden said. "I do not want any trouble because one of them loses his head over a nicely turned leg. They've preyed on society enough on the outside; I won't allow them to cause any disruptions in here."

Harsh. Obviously the guy took his job seriously. "I understand," Sam said, feeling as small as she ever had. She vowed to go through her closet and get rid of all her too-tight clothing just as soon as she got to return home.

"Good." The man spun away with a few crisply issued orders and a nod at his guards.

Once he was gone, Alec leaned close to murmur, "I'm sorry about the clothes."

She buttoned the coat from neck to thigh, knowing she'd be a sweaty mess within minutes, but not about to get tossed on her ear for not obeying the rules. "It's okay."

Once she was suitably concealed, they were led to a private interview room. Her previous meeting with Flynt had taken place in a regular visitors' area, thick Plexiglas separating her from the man. This was different, a private room used for law enforcement, obviously meant for interrogation rather than personal inmate visits.

It hadn't occurred to her that there would be no barrier between her and the criminal they'd come to see. She didn't worry for her own physical safety. First because Jimmy hadn't been incarcerated for doing violence; he was here for being a damned thief. And second, because even if an armed guard hadn't walked inside and stayed with them, she knew Alec would never let Flynt lay a hand on her.

But the situation promised to be an uncomfortable one. As Alec had said, she was setting herself out as bait for someone she detested. She suddenly found herself glad for the strict dress code, knowing how unpleasant it would have been to sit here in her tight clothes and be ogled by the creep. Not to mention counterproductive, since Alec would never have stood for it.

She was especially glad when Jimmy entered the room, led by another guard, accompanied by his attorney. In his orange jumpsuit, with his hands chained together, he still managed to smile like a host greeting a guest at an exclusive party. "Samantha," he exclaimed, stepping closer, as if he fully intended to greet her with a warm hug. "Happy birthday!"

Her birthday. God, she'd totally forgotten.

The guard put a stop to Jimmy's attempted contact, even as Alec stepped in front of her, giving her a quick it's-your-birthday-and-you-didn't-tell-me? look. Sam offered him an apologetic shrug, then got back to the reason for their visit.

"Hello, Jimmy," she said, trying to sound pleasant, and also trying to hide her shock at his appearance.

The last time she had come here, Flynt had looked like a healthy, middle-aged man, with thick dark hair, robust features, and an inmate's weight-lifting physique.

This Flynt was much different. So visibly unhealthy, she felt a stab of sorrow for him.

He had lost at least fifty pounds. His loose, baggy skin hung from protruding bones. Dark circles surrounded his milky eyes, and his cheeks held red blotches and tiny scabs, as if he were too easily cut while shaving. His hair had thinned and was now salted with gray, and he moved slowly, like an old man.

She noticed the slight yellow tinge of his skin right

before he said, "I got the hep C. Trashed my liver. Didn't want to worry you, so I didn't put anything about it in my letters."

"I'm sorry," she murmured.

He shrugged. "Not like livin' in here is so great I'm gonna miss it."

"There's nothing—"

"I guess convicted felons don't shoot right up to the top of the transplant list."

She disliked this man, hated everything he had done and all he represented, but Sam almost wished she could reach out and touch his hand, offer a moment of human warmth. Dying in this place was a harsh punishment, even for all his crimes.

"Hello, Mrs. Dalton, nice to see you again," said the attorney, extending his hand.

"Mr. Carter," she said with a smile. The fiftyish lawyer, who was well-known and highly successful in Baltimore, had been very helpful when she'd been working on her book. He had even made himself available to answer her questions long after the prison interview, insisting on the privilege of taking her to lunch to do so. Recently widowed, he had seemed rather lonely.

"Have you been getting my letters?" Jimmy asked.

"Yes." She hadn't opened those letters, not in a long time. Not since the one when Jimmy had claimed he'd taken vengeance on her behalf.

"Thank you for seeing us, Mr. Flynt." Alec stepped into the line of sight between Sam and the convict. "I'm Special Agent Lambert. Why don't we sit down?"

Jimmy shuffled to the side to peer around Alec. "You doing all right?"

Sam nodded briefly, then gestured toward the table and chairs. Once they were all seated, Alec tried again to engage Flynt in conversation. "As you might have been told, I'm interested in talking to you about your past. We're not trying, in any way, to implicate you further.

We're just hoping some of your knowledge could assist us in future investigations."

Flynt didn't even glance at him. "Aren't you hot in that coat, Samantha?"

Sam shifted on the hard chair. Yes, she was hot; she could feel a line of fine sweat on her upper lip and along her hairline. The room was already warm, and the bright overhead lights didn't help. Despite that, she managed a smile. "I'm fine, thanks."

Alec leaned over the table. "Mr. Flynt—"

"You don't look fine. You should take it off."

"Jimmy, look," Sam said, feeling Alec's impatience, "I really would appreciate it if you'd talk to Agent Lambert. He came here today specifically on my recommendation."

The convict's rheumy eyes widened in pleasure. Knowing how his mind worked, she imagined he was building up quite a scenario about how impressed she must be by him. Flynt might have stolen millions, but at heart he was still a petty crook. He just used computers as his weapons, rather than standard burglary tools.

"I would consider it another personal favor if you'd help him out." Swallowing her own revulsion, she added, "You know, because of my family background."

Jimmy's quick, indrawn breath said he'd taken that exactly the way she'd intended him to—as an acknowledgment that she believed he had already done her a favor. A big one.

"You're welcome." He cast a questioning glance at his attorney. "This is all off the record, right? Nothing I say can be used against me?"

Carter confirmed as much with Alec, then nodded once. "You're free to speak."

"Good." His thin, bony hands twisted together on the table and he said, "Course, it probably wouldn't matter, even if you could use it against me. I'll be dead long before anybody can convict me of shivving another inmate." His eyes gleamed as he added, "It was worth it,

Samantha, for what him and the others did to you and your poor grandma. I never preyed on old folks, never stole a dime from somebody who couldn't afford it."

She doubted that. What she didn't doubt, however, was the passion in Jimmy's voice. This didn't seem like the BS line she had expected from the man. It sounded, in fact, as if he almost believed every word he was saying.

Sam's breaths quickened, coming from a shallow place in her lungs, and her head suddenly seemed a little light. The heat, probably.

But maybe more. For the first time, she wondered if there was a kernel of truth in Jimmy Flynt's story. If he really had found one of the nameless, faceless men she'd hated for so long, and done something to him.

Was it possible?

"He was a bad man," Jimmy said, as if knowing what she was thinking. "Tried to deny it, but I knew the truth about what he did to your grandma, wiping out her retirement and all."

The room spun, and she clutched the edge of the table to keep herself grounded. Yes, Sam had given interviews when the book came out, and had touched on a personal, family reason for her actions. But the details Flynt provided weren't something that would be easy for him to find out, especially not while incarcerated, legally prohibited from going near a computer.

"He won't be stealin' some other old lady blind, driving her to a heart attack, ever again."

Sam rose to her feet, unsteady though they were. How could he know that? Unless it was true. Unless this other thief had realized one of the victims he'd scammed had died during the height of the torment. She swayed a little.

"Sam!" Alec leaped up beside her, and, across the table, Flynt and his lawyer rose as well.

Alec slid a steadying arm around her waist. "Are you okay?"

"I'm fine," she whispered. Closing her eyes, she wiped the back of her hand across her brow, feeling the moisture there, using it as an excuse to cover her shock. "I'm just hot. I need to step outside and cool off."

"Take her coat off her," Jimmy snapped.

Alec ignored him and led her to the door. The guard immediately opened it. But before she stepped out, Sam knew she had to do something or the interview would be over before it began. The minute she left, Jimmy would lose his reason for cooperating.

Yet she couldn't stay. She just couldn't.

Swallowing, she forced a small smile and looked over her shoulder at the man. "I'm fine, really. It's my own fault; I can't take my coat off because I forgot about the dress code."

His mouth rounded into an O, as if he imagined she was wearing nothing but a bikini under the coat.

Swallowing a grimace, she continued. "Jimmy, I need to get outside, but please, can you just try to help Agent Lambert here, as a personal favor to me? It's very important to me, and I'd be *forever* in your debt."

The inmate's sallow face split into a broad smile, and his sunken eyes almost sparkled. All because he was going to get to do her another favor. Something personal. Something he thought would make her like him?

God, if she didn't feel ready to faint, she'd probably burst into tears. Confused by her conflicting feelings of revulsion and sorrow, horror and gratitude toward the man, she didn't know how she was going to get past them.

So she did the only thing she could. Even without a confirmation that the inmate would do as she asked, or that Alec would get his interview, Sam pushed out of the room, leaving Jimmy Flynt and his pathetic existence behind her.

Wyatt Blackstone was not a prideful man. Yet if he ever did think about his one personality trait of which he could be proud, it was his ability to remain fully in charge of his emotions.

He'd seen as a young child the horror that ensued when someone reacted from a place of anger, jealousy, or resentment. Having firsthand knowledge of the dangers of being a slave to feelings, he never allowed emotion to do a job meant for intellect. Even when he'd been targeted by people he had once admired, he'd somehow managed to restrain himself and face his colossal career crisis impassively. At least in the daylight hours, when anyone else could bear witness.

None of that, however, could prevent the hard kernel of pure anger deep inside him from taking root and growing with every word Special Agent Tom Anspaugh spoke.

"What do you mean, you're taking Agent Fletcher to Williamsburg for a sting operation tonight?" he asked, managing somehow to keep his voice calm and evenly modulated. Though, if the agent had any brain at all, he would almost certainly see the tic in Wyatt's temple and the narrow set of his mouth.

"Like I said, last night went so great, him chatting for hours, we think this crazy Lovesprettyboys SOB is really hooked."

Wyatt stiffened in surprise at the name, schooling his features to reveal absolutely nothing. Lily's involvement began to make sense.

"Last night?" As in, when Lily was supposed to be guarding their witness?

"Yeah, the chat went on forever, her still acting like she thought he was a twelve-year-old boy. Lil made out like her parents were going to be out for the night and she's babysitting her kid brother, and this guy was practically panting trying to find out where she lived."

Wyatt said nothing for a moment, putting the pieces together. Anspaugh had blown into his office five minutes ago, without a knock, much less an appointment.

He'd launched into a conversation that he obviously expected Wyatt to follow.

Unfortunately, Wyatt hadn't had any idea what the hell the other man was talking about. Not that he was going to reveal that, not yet, anyway. He knew Anspaugh. More important, he knew other men like Anspaugh. Admitting a disadvantage to someone so ambitious and cutthroat was a mistake only a fool would make, and Wyatt was no fool.

Even though he was beginning to feel fairly certain one of his own people, Lily Fletcher, had taken him for one.

Because, judging by what Anspaugh had revealed, Lily had been clandestinely working with another team on a pedophile investigation. Which bothered him for two reasons. First, he could not have untrustworthy people on his staff. Lily's secrecy about the whole thing had obviously been to one purpose: to keep Wyatt from finding out what she was doing.

That was probably because of his second reservation—Lily's history.

He understood the need to stop other children from being abused and taken the way her nephew had been. But he hadn't fooled himself; Fletcher was still fragile. Still a little broken inside. It was obvious in the haunted emptiness in her eyes and the hollow sound of her infrequent laughter. Which was why, when she had begun to get so wrapped up in the activities of the sick pedophile from Satan's Playground, he had cautioned her against letting her emotions mix with her job.

But you didn't forbid it.

No. He hadn't. He had counseled against it, but he hadn't told her she could not help a CAT working child protection during the Satan's Playground investigation. Her decision to hide her involvement, however, meant she knew he would be against it going on this long.

She'd walked a fine line, not disobeying a direct order

because there had never been one. But for only one reason—because she had never asked him to change the boundaries of their original agreement.

His first impulse was to ask for her transfer, and he still might. Absolutely the only thing preventing that was his own culpability in the whole thing. He had known Lily's weaknesses when he'd brought her on board. He'd seen her reaction to the child abuse at the cyber playground. And he had not refused her request outright.

"Why does Lily have to actually be there for the take-down?" he asked, wanting to know just how deep his agent had gotten.

Anspaugh shrugged. "Well, for one thing, with the way I suspect she feels about this Lovesprettyboys dude, I think she'll want to be."

"So you truly believe this suspect will visit the house tonight. Why? If he's passing himself off as another child, why would he expect this young girl to allow him to enter?"

"We already know that psycho's not just into assault-ing little kids; he wants to see them hurt, killed."

That was exactly what the man had wanted when he'd tried to pay a small fortune to have the Reaper do it for him.

"So we're not thinking he's a regular perv, trying to se-duce a young girl into meeting with somebody she knows is a man. This creep could just be looking to act quickly on opportunity—a house with two young kids alone. One of them is his favorite victim type, an eight-year-old male, the other a weak little girl who could be easily subdued while he does what he wants to with the boy."

Wyatt nodded in acknowledgment. It was possible. He didn't know that the unsub was desperate enough to go after the first unsupervised boy he could find. Then again, he had seemed pretty desperate when he'd of-fered to transfer a fortune to a stranger just so he could get to watch a video of an attack.

A knock sounded on his partially closed office door, and Lily Fletcher herself stuck her head in. "Sir, can I have a minute?" She obviously couldn't see who was sitting across from him.

Wyatt waved an expansive hand, beckoning her in. "By all means; what perfect timing."

She stepped inside, then stumbled over her own feet when she saw Anspaugh. Her face drained of color and her mouth fell open on an audible, shocked inhalation.

"Special Agent Anspaugh and I were just discussing tonight's operation," Wyatt murmured, not revealing by expression or tone what he thought of the whole situation. "Not to mention your assistance in the investigation."

Lily stared at him in silence, obviously knowing he didn't want to get into the discussion they needed to have in front of an outsider.

"Hey, Lil, figured I'd try to work things out boss-to-boss, so you don't have any more conflicts like last night," the other agent said.

Seeing the way her eyes narrowed almost imperceptibly and her cheeks flushed, he knew what Lily thought of several things, including the nickname, the interference, the idea of Anspaugh as her boss, and the other agent himself. Lily Fletcher was nothing if not easy to read, her emotions always visible just beneath the pretty surface.

"Last night I didn't abandon my post, sir. Mrs. Dalton was alone. . . ." As usual, when flustered, as she often seemed to be around him for some reason, Lily stammered and stumbled over her words. "I mean, she *wasn't* alone, not for a minute. Alec Lambert was there the entire time; I'm sure he'll verify that."

Wyatt said nothing, merely tenting his fingers on his desk.

"Look, Blackstone, she wasn't irresponsible. She did tell me she couldn't do it if she didn't get coverage,"

Anspaugh said, though his tone said he begrudged having to explain—to Wyatt, of all people.

Wyatt ignored the man. "Is Agent Stokes available to be on duty all night?" he asked, wanting to make sure the logistics were covered before he made any decisions.

Lily nodded. "I just talked to her and her daughter's fine, so she's good to go." Her hands fisting and unfisting by her sides, she quickly continued. "Alec and Mrs. Dalton are on their way back from the prison. He's staying with her at the hotel until this evening; then Jackie will come at around ten to relieve him and spend the rest of the night."

"So we're good?" Anspaugh asked. Fortunately, the man was tunnel-visioned and didn't ask any questions about the case they were discussing. A normal agent would at least express a passing interest, given the need for witness protection and prison visits. Anspaugh, however, saw only his own investigations, his own ambitions.

Which made Wyatt even more uncomfortable about tonight's operation.

"There are conditions to Agent Fletcher's involvement."

"What conditions?" The other man's eyes narrowed in suspicion.

"Lily is not a field agent. She has no experience, and I will not have her put in jeopardy during this mission."

"Sir, I'm fine, really—"

He cut her off with an abrupt wave of his hand. "She remains off-site, an observer only, nowhere near the takedown location."

Anspaugh rolled his eyes. "Oh, for Chrissakes, we're talking about a pervert here, not Jack the Ripper."

Wyatt merely lifted a brow. "Is that a no?"

The other man hesitated.

"Very well, then. I'm afraid I will not grant Agent Fletcher permission to assist."

"Wait a minute, Blackstone," the other man said, his

neck growing distinctly red above his tight collar. "It's not a problem. She can hang back in the surveillance van; she won't be alone for one minute."

Lily opened her mouth again, but Wyatt met her eye, silently telling her it was this way or no way. He already half regretted letting it go this far.

She snapped it closed again.

"Very well. Agent Fletcher, you are free to assist Agent Anspaugh tonight."

Anspaugh beamed, apparently not even noticing Lily's tension, the way her hands twisted in front of her and she kept her head down. He was so pleased with himself, he got up and said, "See? All good. Toldja I'd take care of ya. I've got a few guys wiring up the empty house down in Williamsburg right now, but we need to get there soon. Be ready to go in about thirty minutes," before swaggering out of the room.

He hadn't offered a handshake on his departure any more than he had on his arrival. Which only meant Wyatt wouldn't have to reach for the hand sanitizer. His office felt grimy enough just from the agent's used oxygen.

"Shut the door."

Lily did so, keeping her back toward him until the latch clicked. Then for a few seconds longer. Her whole body straightened visibly before she turned around. "I was on my way in here to tell you."

He made no effort to hide his skepticism. "Of course you were."

"I mean it. This all got out of hand so quickly; I was just doing some computer stuff for them, a little brainstorming." A bitter laugh escaped her. "Honestly, at first, I thought Anspaugh was just trying to hit on me and I was about to tell him to go away."

"Which was when he dangled an actual suspect in your face."

Appearing stricken, Lily asked, "Do you think he's lying?" She immediately shook her head and answered for him. "No. I don't think he is. The area fits geographically. Plus, I read the transcripts. Lovesprettyboys used the word 'delightful' all the time in Satan's Playground. This supposedly young boy is using it, when no real kid ever would."

"Even if he's not lying, you have been."

Lily sank into the chair. "I'm so sorry."

At least she hadn't tried to deny it, or downplay it as only a lie by omission. That garbage didn't fly here, not with the stakes in their job.

"I'm serious, though, about planning to tell you. You can ask Alec. I promised him last night that I would let you know today."

He leaned back in his chair and crossed his arms. "I don't need to go back and forth between my people confirming their stories. That's not the kind of office I run. Either trust is there, or it's not."

Her eyes closed briefly, her throat bobbing as she swallowed hard.

Not letting up on her, he pressed on. "Right now, it's not. I'm questioning your loyalties, wondering if I can trust you."

"You can. . . ."

"But you obviously don't have much trust in me if you kept this secret."

"That's not true," she snapped, her chin jerking up as she reacted angrily for the first time since she'd walked into the room. "I trust you. I trust every member of this team."

"Then why? Why did I have to find out what one of my own team members was up to by hearing it from a fool like Anspaugh?"

The steam left her as quickly as it had come on. "It's this guy, Lovesprettyboys. That's all; it's this one perp. I want to stop him, Wyatt."

She had managed to call him by his first name without prompting. Progress.

"But it's not just wanting him stopped, is it?" he asked.

"No. It's about *me* stopping him."

Exactly as he'd expected. "Because you've let this become personal."

She jerked to her feet, thrusting a frustrated hand into her blond hair, sending it spilling from its loose bun. "It's not personal. I'm not confusing this guy with the demon from my own past. I just . . ."

Wyatt dropped his arms onto his desk and straightened in his chair. When Lily didn't explain, he did it for her. "You just want to stop feeling helpless. To do something instead of having it done to you."

Lily turned to glance at him, her lips trembling as she whispered, "Yeah."

Glancing down, Wyatt rubbed the back of his neck, trying to ease away the tension and the stiffness. Also trying to put himself in the young agent's shoes.

No, he didn't like that she'd hidden this from him. But he couldn't positively say he wouldn't have acted the same way. Even someone with the power to segregate his emotions from nearly every aspect of his life probably couldn't stand feeling so powerless, so victimized, without any chance at changing it.

For someone like Lily, who he sometimes thought was too soft to be in the bureau at all, it was utterly impossible.

"All right," he finally said with a heavy sigh. "Go do what you have to tonight."

"Thank you," she whispered.

"Don't thank me. Just do some thinking, would you? About what you really want, where you really see yourself. Because if you can't move past this and focus on the here and now rather than what happened to your family, then I can't have you here working these kinds of violent crimes."

She caught her bottom lip between her teeth.

"Think about it. And decide, soon, if you want to put in for a transfer. Once you are absolutely certain, I'll support you either way." He closed his eyes and rubbed his aching neck again. "Now go. Before I change my mind."

She said nothing. Within a few seconds, the clicking of the door signaled she had gone, hopefully not slinking out in humiliation, but rather ready to do what he'd asked her to do: Think about her life and decide whether to start living it again.

Fortunately for Alec, after they left the prison, Sam had asked him to stop at a mall so she could pick up a few things, including the jeans and thick sweater she now had on. They were much better for his sanity, as he again sat with her in a hotel room, than if she'd still been dressed as she had been earlier.

He'd also insisted on buying her a birthday ice-cream cone, though she seemed anything but interested in celebrating. One hell of a way to spend a birthday.

"What do they call this, déjà vu all over again?" she asked with a soft sigh.

Considering he was again parked by the window, and she again across the room, he could only echo the sound.

"So are you ever going to finish telling me what Jimmy had to say this afternoon?"

He had begun filling her in about his odd conversation with the convict right after they'd left the prison a couple of hours ago. Then Lily had called to arrange tonight's safe-house schedule, and he'd been able to think about nothing else but playing another round of try-to-avoid-sleeping-with-the-witness.

"He's a strange guy. Plays the 'I'm just a poor, dumb convict' role pretty convincingly, but there's real cunning there."

"No kidding. But was he of any help?"

"Yes, actually, I think he was."

"In what way?"

Leaving his window seat, Alec moved to a chair in the small kitchenette, pulling it close to the dining table. He reached for his laptop case and pulled out a notebook on which he'd jotted his thoughts during today's interview. "I think I was the most surprised at the way he talked about his victims—at least, once you were out of earshot."

Sam left the sofa and took the chair opposite him. "I'm not. When I talked to him the first time, I got the impression that he really looked down on the people he stole from, had no sympathy for them." She shook her head and added, "Elderly grandmothers notwithstanding."

Unable to resist the impulse, Alec reached out and covered one of her hands with his, squeezing lightly. "I hate like hell that you went through that nightmare today. What he said . . . Did it change your opinion about his claims?"

"Regarding the supposed other inmate? Maybe. It's hard to see how he could know as much as he did."

"Look, Sam, you said yourself this guy was good enough to bilk hundreds of people through the Internet. You really think he couldn't find out everything he wanted to know about you and your family history? He certainly knew today was your birthday."

"I don't know how he found that out. His sentence forbids Internet access."

"Sentences usually also forbid drugs, pornography, and weapons in prison. You honestly think there aren't any? I have no doubt Flynt has at the very least found himself in the vicinity of someone who has online access and can find out anything he wants to know."

She conceded his point with a nod.

"He really knocked you for a loop, didn't he?" he murmured.

"I guess."

"You feeling better now?"

"I'm fine. I was fine almost right away, once I got out of that hot room. But I didn't want to interfere, so I didn't even think about coming back."

"I'm glad you didn't. I don't think I'd have kept Jimmy's attention if you were there."

"It wasn't a hardship. Despite being a prick about women's skirts, the warden was pretty nice to let me wait in the privacy of his assistant's office, rather than sending me to the car. I guess he felt bad for making me keep the coat on."

He tried to lighten the mood with a teasing smile. "And no dress code?"

"No dress code. Now, back to Jimmy?"

His smile faded immediately. "I don't think it was just that he had no sympathy for his victims, although that was certainly true." Alec thought about it, trying to put his impressions in words. "He seemed almost . . . disgusted with them, I guess, for being stupid enough to fall for his line."

"Like they had it coming?"

"Exactly. Had a very Nietzschean philosophy that some people were predators and some were prey and that's just the way things are. That it was no more wrong for him to steal from them than it was for a hungry wolf to cull the weakest sheep from the flock to fulfill its needs."

"Sociopathic," she murmured.

"Probably. He honestly saw himself as doing the world a favor by teaching these fools a lesson, even though he doubted most of them learned from it."

"Kind of like your unsub."

Alec nodded. "Most definitely. He has referred to his victims as fools, called them stupid."

They both thought about it. Alec kept playing Jimmy's words in his head, knowing there was something he had overlooked. Some natural conclusion he should be able to reach; yet it remained elusive, hiding in the corners of his mind.

"Lucky him to have found a way to lure gullible people," Sam mused. "I bet it's not hard for him to find people he considers stupid online."

And just like that, something clicked. He sat very still, closing his eyes, thinking about her words. "Lucky," he whispered. "Yes, he just sends out a blanket lure and waits for the right type of victim to respond."

Sam seemed to realize he was talking more to himself than to her and remained silent.

"But maybe he doesn't see it as luck. Maybe it isn't random."

"What?"

Alec rose from his chair and paced the room, trying to verbalize the idea he couldn't quite nail down. "I mean, maybe he's not just trying to find miscellaneous victims to satisfy his need to kill. He intentionally sets his lures up to be easily avoided. The scams are simple to check, the backgrounds so obviously faked. Even the crime scenes, which seem like such senseless deaths, usually have a way out."

"So the objective . . ."

"Isn't just to kill." He placed his hands on the back of the chair he had just vacated, and gripped it. "The victims aren't random. The means he uses to pull them in ensures that he's getting *exactly* the kind of people he wants to kill, and the farther they venture into his path, the more they confirm their status as sheep to be culled. The ones he considers unworthy, stupid."

"Like the world would be better off without them?"

"Yes!" He dropped back onto the chair, mumbling, "Darwin. He wasn't just referring to the survival of the fittest. He is trying to help evolution along by thinning out the gene pool."

Sam shook her head in disgust. "Unbelievable."

"But true," he said, nearly certain of it. He just needed

a little more information to firm up his theories. "His first several victims, the ones he killed without the e-mail scams . . . There must have been something that attracted him to them."

The victims hadn't had any surface connections. They'd been from widely different backgrounds, different ages, sexes, socioeconomic groups. Yet there must have been something to swing Darwin's big, evil eye in their direction.

Alec flipped open his laptop and opened his documents on the case. The details of each murder were here, and he refamiliarized himself with them, again acknowledging that there were no surface similarities.

Acting on a hunch, he went a step further and established an Internet connection. "We checked the backgrounds on every one of these people and found absolutely nothing that linked them. Now, I wonder if Darwin himself does," he muttered.

Sam eyed him curiously, but he didn't explain. Instead, he typed the name of one of the victims and the word *Darwin* into a search engine, and pressed enter.

The returns were almost instantaneous, and they were numerous. He scanned down the first page, glancing at each snippet, not entirely sure what he was looking for.

And then, he quite simply found it.

"Here it is," he murmured, his heart thudding in his chest.

"What?" she asked, scooting her chair around so she could see.

Alec clicked on the link, though he didn't need to read the entire newspaper article that came up to know what it contained.

"Oh, my God," Sam whispered after she read the first few paragraphs.

"The Darwin Awards," he said. "They're not only real; the expression is commonly used to describe people who survive after doing something stupid that should have killed them."

"Thereby cleaning up the gene pool."

Exactly. Before their unsub had begun bringing the stupid masses right to his door via the Internet, he'd had to go out and hunt for them. He'd found them by watching news feeds from up and down the East Coast, keying on that one expression, on the word *Darwin*. And had, over a period of a few years, found six people to slaughter.

Alec reached into his pocket to retrieve his phone. Wyatt needed to know about this. If Alec's hunch was right, and the other victims all had a similar Darwin Awards–type incident in their past—which a little more digging should confirm—they had another tool with which to view the psyche of the man they sought. But before he could even retrieve it, the thing rang.

"Speak of the devil," he said as he answered the phone.

"Alec, are you near a computer?"

He tensed, hearing the concerned tone of Wyatt's voice. "Yes."

"Is Samantha Dalton with you?"

Wary, he replied, "Yes. She is."

Sam looked up in curiosity, but Alec shrugged to tell her he did not yet know what the call was about.

"You need to go to her blog."

Fuck. "Did he do it again?"

"It appears so."

They hadn't changed Sam's passwords, actually hoping Darwin would hack in again, because every effort he made was another clue in finding him.

"Keep her calm, question her thoroughly, and get back in touch with me. I've already got Taggert and Mulrooney heading in and will put them on the road to Baltimore as soon as they arrive. You need to get some information and get back to me with names and addresses."

"Why?" he asked, not asking specifics because he honestly didn't want Sam to read anything into the one-sided conversation. What he really wanted to ask was, *Why Baltimore? Whose names and addresses?*

"You'll understand when you read it. Just remember, keep her calm; tell her we are on our way and we already have the Baltimore police on notice."

This was not good. "I'll call you back in a couple of minutes."

"No more than that," Wyatt cautioned.

Cutting the call, Alec reached for the laptop and began typing. Sam's gaze followed his fingers and she immediately realized what words he was typing.

"Don't tell me he hacked me again."

Alec didn't respond; he simply waited, his fingers resting on the keys. As the page loaded, he realized he was holding his breath. He also realized Sam's hand had moved over and dropped onto his leg, just above his knee. She was squeezing him, as if needing to physically grab something and hold on tight. He covered her hand with his. And the screen filled in.

"What?" Sam mumbled, obviously not understanding the words, so stark and bold, just like the last hacked-in message from Darwin.

It took Alec a split second less to figure it out. Something inside him died a little as he thought of what this meant for Sam, who seemed to have so few people in her life.

Because it appeared one of those people might soon be *out* of her life.

" 'You're too late to save her'?" Sam murmured. "What does he mean? I'm right here."

Alec scrolled the screen down with a flick of his finger on the touch pad, already knowing there was more. And he was right.

So sorry, Samantha, dear, but it has to be done. Too bad she didn't listen to you and learn a bit of caution—you did

*warn her about men like me, didn't you? Do remember to
avoid wearing mascara to the funeral ... it won't hold up
under your tears, and you're far too lovely to have dark
smears beneath your eyes.*

Sam read the words and finally grasped them. "Oh,
my God."

Alec nodded once.

"He's gone after someone I love."

She leaped to her feet, already racing toward the door
before he even had time to stop her.

"Sam, wait. I need to know who it could be. Wyatt
and the others are ready to charge to the rescue; we just
need to know who the target would most likely be."

Her expression terrified, her breaths merely short
gasps, she said, "She had a date tonight with someone
she met on the Internet. I did warn her, but she didn't
listen."

"Who are you talking about?"

"Alec, that psychopath has my *mother*."

Chapter 14

Even though he'd needed to make some adjustments this evening after a highly unexpected development, the ambush had gone exactly as he had expected it to. As usual, his plan had been flawlessly designed and easy to carry out. Glancing at his watch, Darwin realized he was right on schedule. A few hours, at least, until he'd need to dump her, leaving him with sufficient time to get her ready for her night on the town, as it was.

Once he'd had her in his hands and knew he'd gotten away clean, he had posted his message on Samantha's Web site. She had probably already read it; the FBI almost certainly had. All of them were, right now, in a blind panic, racing to save the stupid cow behind him.

That cow had been so stupid, she'd never even been the least bit suspicious. She hadn't checked him out, had never questioned him. She had not even second-guessed the location for their get-together when he'd called her a couple of hours ago. She'd walked blindly into her fate, as so many had before her.

But she wasn't like all those who had gone before her. This one was special, if only because of how much losing her would hurt Samantha Dalton.

"Silly, impulsive, reckless woman," he murmured,

though, of course, she was unconscious and couldn't hear him. "You really don't value yourself very highly, do you, my dear?"

Fortunately, he had known this moment would come, so he'd been paving the way for weeks. Reaching out to her through e-mail, he'd let her get to know him, or think she did. He'd called himself Randolph Gertz, a wealthy widower dabbling in various investments. And her greedy little soul had been unable to resist him.

His companion had entered their arranged meeting place right on schedule and had never even seen him come at her with the chloroform. Not being sure he would be able to get her to drink something right away, he'd had to resort to the slightly riskier means of taking her down.

He'd *kept* her down with a few sharp blows to her face and head.

Regrettable, his losing his temper like that; he so seldom did. But something about seeing her lying there, helpless and vulnerable, when she should have been Samantha, had enraged him.

"A few hits won't kill you," he said, speaking casually over his shoulder to the woman sprawled in the back of the van. A trickle of blood from her nose smeared one cheek, her lip was swollen, and a bruise was forming beneath one eye. He imagined she would have a terrible headache if she ever woke up. Still, she didn't look too much the worse for wear.

In fact, she should fit right in where he intended to take her.

"You're lucky, you know. There's a very good chance tonight's ordeal won't kill you, either. You could be lucky, or you could be unlucky. You could play it smart, or you could panic and get yourself killed." He smiled, thinking about the way he most wanted it to turn out. "I rather hope you live through it."

Live through it enough to talk about it. To tell Samantha about it. To reveal her pain and her agony and ask *why* something so awful had happened.

Because it would be awful. Of that he had no doubt.

In fact, he might be able to assure it. Because as he'd beaten her, he'd been quite surprised to find himself growing erect. No, her prone body was not the one he wanted ... but violating it was almost as good. Something to keep in mind, if he had the time.

Reaching the storage facility where he'd rented a garage, he quickly got out and pulled the van inside, needing privacy. The stupid bitch probably wouldn't wake up, but just in case she did, and made a fuss, he did not want to have to answer any questions. The facility would more than likely remain deserted at this time of the evening, but it didn't pay to be careless.

Once within, he quickly closed the rolling door and flipped on the portable lights he always left here. He positioned them toward the sliding panel door of the van, wanting plenty of illumination while he got her ready, then opened it.

"In the spotlight," he said. "Believe me—you're soon going to look like someone who likes it that way."

Eyeing her—bloody and bruised, unconscious—without pity, he reached for his knife. And began to remove her clothes.

Sam vacillated between terror and utter rage as she and Alec tore through the night, heading for Baltimore. At first, he'd told her he wouldn't take her to her mother's place. He'd wanted to stay in D.C., to let the others handle it.

Yeah. Right.

She'd told him she was going, and the only way he would stop her was if he threw her out the window, and then he'd better hope she broke both her legs.

"Try her cell phone again," Alec snapped, as if knowing she was on the verge of letting out a high, keening wail.

She did as he asked, even though she'd been calling every minute since reading that awful message on her site. Just like with every other call, she got her mom's voice mail on the second ring. "It's still turned off." She dialed the house number, got the answering machine again, and left what was probably her tenth message.

"Do you have any idea where she was going, or who she was with?"

Leaning forward in her seat, as if urging the car to go even faster, Sam shook her head. "She played it so close to the vest. I had really given her hell about even considering online dating, so she obviously wasn't going to talk to me about it."

"But you're certain she was planning to go out tonight with someone she had met online?"

"Like I said, she wasn't confiding in me, but I knew she had a date, and was being incredibly secretive about it."

"Because she knew you were against it."

"Exactly." Tension making her quiver, she added, "Plus, if she is meeting with Darwin, do you think he might have told her to keep the details hush-hush?"

"Yes, he probably would have."

She hadn't really wanted the confirmation. "Damn it, Alec, why is this happening? Is it really possible one blog post brought the wrath of this monster down on my mother's head?"

"I don't know," he said, sounding frustrated and weary. "It seems so out of character for the Professor. He's always been methodical and organized, cautious, taking weeks, months, once even a year between his crimes. For him to spin as wildly out of control as he seems to be this week—not only how frequently he's attacking, but also taunting you the way he has—it seems like something else is at play here."

"Like what?"

Alec didn't say anything at first, merely staring out

into the headlight-broken darkness, weaving the car in and out of traffic without ever slowing. She didn't know if he was thinking about her question, or already knew the answer and didn't want to say it out loud.

"Sam," he finally said, "have you met anyone who's made you uncomfortable or shown you particular attention in the past few weeks or months?"

She understood him immediately. "You think there's more to this than Wednesday night's rant. That he actually knows me."

His slight nod acknowledged her suspicion.

Sam's blood gushing hard in her veins, she still managed to keep her cool and think about his question, rather than come out with a quick, instinctive reply. "I've been a hermit," she said, "as I think you already know. Honestly, Alec, I've met almost no new people since my divorce."

He didn't give up. "Okay, what about before that? It's possible the Professor has been watching you for a long time, since before he came out to you on your site."

That question was a whole lot easier to answer, though it certainly wouldn't help them narrow things down. "My ex-husband and his family are socialites, running with the horse-breeding set up in Hunt Valley. I met hundreds of people in their circle, though I probably couldn't recall the names of more than a dozen of them."

Not even thinking about it, Sam flipped her phone open. Dialed. Heard her mother's chipper message. Hung up.

"Rich, huh?"

"Filthy," she replied, knowing he was asking about Samuel. "And as spoiled and selfish as you'd expect someone raised that way to be."

He shrugged.

"What?"

"My family's rich."

She stared at him from across the car. Somehow, she'd

already known the man came from money; he carried himself like it, and wore clothes that one wouldn't expect on a federal employee's salary. But he was about as different from her ex as any man could be, and she knew better than to judge him based on that one bad experience. "Point taken."

Getting back to their conversation, he said, "So nobody stands out. Nobody condescending, for the most part, but a little too friendly toward you?"

"Not that I can remember," she said, shaking her head. "Okay, so let's say he knows me, and has known me for a while; why would he suddenly become so murderous toward me and people I care about? Why this . . . what did you call it? Acceleration?"

Even in the dimly lit car, she saw the way his hands tightened on the wheel. "We already assumed he was trying to scare you because he figured out you were working with us."

"Going from scaring to slaughtering is a pretty big leap."

"Not for someone like the Professor."

Sam let out a slow, shaky breath, leaning back in her seat. It seemed too crazy to be believed, that one person's very normal reaction—trying to help the authorities solve a murder—could be construed as some sort of betrayal of someone she didn't even know.

But maybe you do know him. Alec's idea wouldn't leave her mind. As upsetting as it was to think she might have already had personal contact with a psychopath, it almost seemed better than thinking all of this had been caused by such a random thing, just some bastard cruising the Net, seeing her site, and getting angry about her blog.

"Okay, tell me which way to go," Alec said, which was when she realized they had already reached Baltimore and were close to her mother's place.

Sam gave him the directions, craning to see through

the windshield. As they rounded the corner, her mother's house became easy to spot. It was the one with all the cars parked outside. Including police vehicles with emergency lights spinning.

"Oh, no."

He grabbed her hand. "Don't. They're here because Wyatt asked them to come check on her; it doesn't mean anything."

She kept reminding herself of that as they reached the house. She jumped out of the car before Alec had even cut the engine. When a uniformed officer stepped in front of her, she snapped, "This is my mother's house."

Alec, who had hurried after her, asked, "Anything?"

The officer shook his head. "No signs of life. Place is locked up tight as a drum, no lights on. Everything looks pretty normal. Do you have a key, miss?"

Sam nodded, waving her key ring at the man.

"Let the officers check it out first, Sam," Alec said. She saw by the firm set of his mouth that this was non-negotiable.

Handing him the keys, she stood outside with Alec for what seemed to be the longest several minutes of her life. Finally, the cops who had gone in stepped back onto the front porch of the house Sam had grown up in, and beckoned to her.

"Nobody here, miss. Nothing appears out of place," one of them said.

Good on one hand—her mother wasn't lying murdered in her own living room.

Bad on the other—they had no idea where she was.

"Thank you," she mumbled, telling herself no news was good news.

Alec stepped in. "The rest of my team should be showing up any minute; in the meantime, I'm going to have Ms. Dalton check her mother's computer records to see if we can find out where she might be."

Inside, Sam went straight to her old bedroom, now

used as a small office. The desktop computer was turned off, and as she flipped the switch, she said, "Mom uses the same password, my dad's middle name, for everything. She might have added a number on the beginning or the end, but it shouldn't be hard to get into whatever dating program she's gotten hooked up with."

Alec nodded and waved her on, then grabbed his phone and called his boss again. Sam barely listened to his side of the conversation, focused only on finding out anything she could that would help them find out whom her mother had been going out with tonight, and where they were headed.

Pulling up the browser, she checked the cache and had no problem locating the dating Web site. And she didn't even have to play a guessing game, varying her dad's middle name with his birth date, because the ID and password were saved right on the screen.

"I'm in," she said, not five minutes after she'd sat down.

Alec finished his call and stepped behind her, watching over her shoulder.

Quickly figuring out how the site operated, Sam found all the private communications, the profile requests, the personal Q&As her mother had received and had sent. A few of the men sounded skeevy—and judging by her lack of response, Mom had thought so, too. A few others, though, seemed to have caught Christine Harrington— aka Missy Chrissy's—interest.

"Damn it," she muttered, flipping through screen after screen to see if she'd missed anything.

"What's wrong?"

"Nothing about a date. No mention of an in-person meeting."

Feeling hot moisture begin to flood her eyes, Sam willed herself to remain strong and not give in to her rising panic. Just because her mother hadn't left an easy trail to follow didn't mean there wasn't one. It was entirely possible the communication had gone to private e-mail.

Five minutes later, though, after she'd gone through every Outlook message for the past several weeks, she'd still found absolutely nothing.

"I don't know whether this is good news or not," she said, hearing her own voice shake. "Maybe they moved on to phone communication. Maybe they did it all with IMs."

"We can trace those."

"Not fast enough," she snapped.

Desperate to do something, she quickly surfed over to her own site, wondering if the psychopath had left another taunting message. But there was nothing beyond those ugly words that informed her he had robbed her of someone she loved.

"Does she have other e-mail addresses? Most people would create a new one to deal with Internet-dating correspondence. Would she really give out her personal one, the one you use?"

Sam snapped her fingers and went back to work. And judging by how close to the top of the cache the mailbox site was, her mother did, indeed, have a backup address.

But it wasn't saved to the computer. Neither was the password.

She ran through a number of variations, anything she could see her mother using, to no avail. Within ten minutes, she was ready to scream in frustration.

Alec realized it. He put his hands on her shoulders, squeezing. "It's okay. Let's think of other options. Who else might know what she's up to? Any close friends?"

"She has lots of casual friends, but probably the only one she talks to every day is Uncle Nate." Would her mother really have confided in him, though, considering he was every bit as disapproving as Sam?

"He's her brother?"

She shook her head, already digging her cell phone

out of her purse. "He's not really my uncle. He was my father's partner many years ago."

Alec's head tilted in confusion.

"Dad was a Maryland state trooper. After he died, Nate quit, went to law school, ended up a judge about seven or eight years ago."

"And he's still close to your mom?"

"Very." She found the home number and dialed it. Getting no answer, she immediately dialed his cell.

"Hello? Samantha?" he asked, answering on the second ring. He sounded distracted, a little out of breath.

"Yeah, it's me. Listen," she said, trying to keep her voice calm, not wanting to upset the older man, "I'm at Mom's. I'm trying to find her."

"Why?"

Not sure how much to say, she kept it simple. "There's some trouble, and I really need to talk to her, to make sure she's okay."

"Well, of course she is, dear."

Her heart leaping, she asked, "You mean you know where she is?"

He hesitated, then finally murmured, "Yes, I do. She's right here with me."

Something was wrong; Lily felt it. He hadn't showed. It was nine thirty; Lovesprettyboys should have been here by now, and he hadn't made an appearance.

"Damn it, why isn't he here yet?" Lily muttered.

The agent handling the electronic surveillance of the scene, a guy named Vince Kowalski, whom Lily had met for the first time a few hours ago, shrugged, obviously not concerned. "These things are always a gamble. You think for sure the creep's gonna show; then he gets spooked or he gets sidetracked or he even gets a conscience."

"Not this guy," she whispered, talking more to herself than to the other agent.

The two of them sat in an unmarked, nondescript van,

parked about ten houses up from the Williamsburg home where Tiger Lily was supposedly babysitting her bratty-but-cute little brother. They'd been sitting in here for hours, having arrived well before dark in case their suspect decided to scope out the neighborhood in advance.

Yet nothing had happened.

Lily honestly didn't know what she would do if he didn't show. Having thought about this night, pictured it, almost willed it to happen since that August day when she'd first seen that awful cartoon avatar doing unimaginable things to a cartoon boy, she needed this to happen. For him to be caught, justice to be served.

For him not to come, to have built this up until she wanted to scream with the pressure . . . She just wasn't sure she could stand for it to come to absolutely nothing.

Maybe it's for the best.

She tried to ignore that little voice in her mind, which often sounded remarkably like her mother's, who had, along with Lily's father, died in an accident when she was a child. Then, thinking about it, she realized that just as her mother had always seemed so wise in life, she still sounded that way in Lily's mind.

Maybe it *was* for the best. Not that they didn't catch the man from Satan's Playground. He had to be stopped, had to be locked away where he could never destroy the innocence of any child he happened to get his hands on. But maybe, just maybe, Lily wouldn't be the one to stop him. Because if she didn't let it go, get her mind back where it needed to be, she was going to lose a job she'd come to love. Leave a team she worked so well with and thoroughly admired, and a boss who not only had the most integrity of any man she'd ever known, but was also one of the most exciting ones.

Don't even think that way. Having any kind of crush on Wyatt Blackstone was not only immature and stupid; it was probably career suicide.

Just like sticking to this case would be.

But could she let it go? Could she really?

"Wait! I see something."

Lily leaped from the seat, crouching beside Kowalski.

He pointed to the computer screen, which displayed views from the three discreet cameras a crew disguised as phone repairmen had set up in the neighborhood early this afternoon. "See him?"

Lily did. A man had moved into the top frame, rounding the closest corner, slowly shuffling up the sidewalk. Walking with his head down, he was further disguised by the raised hood of his jacket. His hands were shoved in the pockets, his shoulders hunched.

Both his appearance and his movements seemed out of place in this residential neighborhood. The hooded jacket such an obvious attempt to conceal his face, the trepidation of his walk—he was most definitely up to something.

She held her breath, watching him draw closer, step by step. When he got within two fenced yards of the target, he paused, glancing behind him, then in front, then back again. Their van was parked several houses away, and the windows were tinted to conceal the inside from the out, but Lily still almost held her breath, as though afraid he could see them.

Apparently feeling the same way, Kowalski released a low breath of his own once the man turned and began walking again. He spoke into his headset, his voice a whisper: "Tommy, we've got a live one out here."

Anspaugh immediately came on the line, loud, sounding excited. "I see him. Don't move; don't do a thing."

"Wouldn't dream of it."

"Lil's okay?"

She gritted her back teeth. Kowalski appeared to notice the grimace and chuckled. "She's fine." When he cut the connection, he cocked a brow. "Aren't ya, Lil?"

"Don't even go there."

He chuckled again; then they both got back to business, focusing on the screen. The man in the jacket had finally reached the front walkway of the target house. Lily knew what he was seeing—the outside lights on, every window illuminated. She had made the suggestion, though Anspaugh hadn't liked it, thinking the guy would be scared off by the possibility of being spotted. Lily had argued it. An eleven-year-old babysitting for the first time would do exactly that, have the place blazing with light.

Her gut told her the choice had been the correct one.

"Go; what are you waiting for?" Kowalski said as the man lingered, his gaze scurrying constantly, like a rat trying to decide whether to go for the cheese in a trap.

God, did she hope this rat went for it.

Finally, his suspicions apparently assuaged, the suspect took a single step toward the house.

"He's on the move again!"

The man continued walking, now appearing in the second camera, which was positioned directly above the front door. He reached the porch and walked right up onto it.

"Ballsy," Vince said.

"Very." Lily hadn't expected this. She'd figured the guy would skulk around to the side, slip into the backyard, where he could find some privacy to break a window.

Not that he'd rung the bell; he wasn't that brave. Again, he just stood there, glancing back at the street, then edging closer to the front window. Close enough to peer in, cupping one hand around his face.

"He's trying to see if there really are kids inside."

Anspaugh's voice crackled. "What the hell's he doing? Why hasn't he made his move?"

"He's still checking things out," Vince said.

"Ask him if he put the toys all over the living room, in full view from the windows, and has cartoons jacked up loud on the TV," Lily murmured. Another of her suggestions: Mom and Dad were out; kids would go a little wild.

Anspaugh confirmed as much.

"Keep holding tight," Vince advised. "The worm's trying to grow a big enough set of balls to go through with it."

That wasn't difficult to believe. If this guy was Lovesprettyboys, he had already shown himself as someone ready to pay others to do his nasty work for him. Not that she truly believed that meant he hadn't molested any children yet; something deep inside her already knew better. But his innate cowardice—the cowardice of anyone who raped small children—would leave him suspicious of any new situation, always on the lookout for a setup.

The man moved. Staying low, beneath the bottom ledge of the window, he scurried across the porch to the side of the garage. Where there was a door.

"He's going for it," she whispered.

Their suspect opened the door and stepped inside. They lost him from view. Then, suddenly, voices shouting, Anspaugh barking orders, screaming at someone to "Get the fuck down!"

More shouts. "No, dude, you got it all wrong!"

"Tell it to the judge, slimeball," Vince said with a wide grin. He gave Lily a not-very-surreptitious thumbs-up.

She smiled back, liking the man a lot more than she liked his supervisor. "It's over," she said. "We got him."

At least, they got someone. Lily truly hoped the man they had caught in that house was Lovesprettyboys. But something inside her had begun to suspect she wouldn't fall apart if he turned out not to be. Because, no matter what, she'd been part of bringing down some sick bastard who'd had very dark intentions toward two young children.

She'd acted instead of reacted. Had done something strong and powerful instead of just being a victim.

"It's enough," she whispered. It didn't bring Zach or Laura back, but she'd actually made a difference. She could return to Washington and tell Wyatt she was ready to get back to her real job. Back to her real life. Maybe even get back to actually enjoying living it. Though it had been so long, she wasn't sure she remembered how.

"Let's go enjoy the show," Vince said, reaching for the handle on the back door.

"Let me get my jacket."

Grabbing it from the passenger seat, she turned around to see Kowalski hop down onto the street. He appeared to be waiting for her; then suddenly his attention was drawn somewhere out of her range of vision. "Who the hell are you?" he asked.

Lily didn't know whom the other agent was talking to. She didn't even know if he was concerned or merely curious in the final seconds of his life.

She didn't hear the gun, didn't anticipate any danger. She just knew, as she watched Vince Kowalski's brains and half his head erupt against the inside of the open door, that he'd been shot in the face.

Lily grabbed for her weapon. Her fingers brushed the grip. But before she had even pulled it from its holster, she felt the first bullet strike. The force flung her back.

Then another shot. *Such pain.*

And her world went dark.

Chapter 15

Christine Harrington's life had been saved because of a determined man who had apparently been in love with her for a long time.

At least, that was the gist of what they had gotten during Sam's brief phone conversation with her mother. So far, they hadn't had a chance to confirm it. When the woman arrived home, safe and sound, in the company of the man Sam called Uncle Nate, mother and daughter had fallen into each other's arms and cried together, not saying more than a few loving words.

Alec's heart twisted, hearing her, watching Sam's terror give way to relief. But she was with the right people to deal with it. Family. Friends.

He stayed in the background, hovering with Wyatt and the other members of the team, who had shown up within minutes of Sam's conversation with Judge Nathan Price. All of them stood outside in the cold, because Sam had flown out the front door and down the steps the very moment Price's car had pulled up.

Finally, Sam pulled away, rubbing her tears onto her own sleeves. Her gaze shifted, quickly scanning the faces of those nearby, until it lit upon his face, as if, now that she knew her mother was okay, she needed to see him. And only him.

Her smile took his breath away. The softness in her eyes stopped his heart midbeat.

She had feelings for him. It was crazy, given the brief time they'd known each other, but it was also true.

More bizarre? He felt the same way. That liking he'd been feeling for her had somehow built to the point where he'd do bodily harm to anyone who tried to hurt her. He wanted to commit violence on their unsub just for putting those tears in that woman's eyes.

Love? He had no idea, never having experienced it before.

But it was more than liking, and damn sure more than lust.

"Mrs. Harrington, do you mind answering a few questions now?" Wyatt asked.

"Of course not, and I hope somebody else will, too," the woman said. "I'd like to know why on earth my daughter believed I had been murdered."

"Oh, God, Mom, you have no idea. I thought you were going out on a date with somebody you met online tonight."

"I was supposed to. It was all set up, and I backed out at the very last minute."

Which was probably why Darwin had jumped the gun, posting his vicious message on Sam's blog. How infuriated he must have been when she'd canceled.

Then again, knowing how he liked to torment his victims, he could very well have done it intentionally, just to hurt Sam and laugh at the FBI.

"Nate showed up here and, well, talked me out of it. So I canceled my other plans."

She was obviously trying to be tactful, but the way she and this Uncle Nate looked at each other, it was pretty clear they were involved.

Sam was a little less tactful. A fist on her hip, she said, "Well, it's about time."

The older gentleman, who had hovered in the background, not intruding on the reunion, smiled sheepishly. "You don't mind?"

"Are you kidding? I've been waiting for you to make your move."

"I'd given up on him ever making it," said Mrs. Harrington.

"Hence the desperate online-dating idea?" the man asked, one brow quirked.

"I wasn't desperate. Just curious."

Sam squeezed her mother's hand. "Don't forget what curiosity did to the cat, okay? Now, we need to go inside so you can talk to these people and tell them everything you know about the man you were supposed to go out with."

"Randolph?"

"That's his name, ma'am?" Alec asked.

She nodded. "Yes. Randolph Gertz. He's a widower and seems very lonely. I felt bad about breaking our date tonight." Nate Price's hand landed on her shoulder and she smiled up at him. "Though not too bad."

"Is there any particular reason you weren't answering your cell phone?" Sam asked.

"Why, yes, dear. Because I turned it off. This date was a long time coming, and I didn't want to be disturbed." Her smile said a lot about that date, and Sam looked either ready to hug her fondly or strangle her.

Gathered inside, Wyatt related what was going on. He didn't tell them everything, just enough to let them know how serious the situation was. When Sam's mother realized she might have broken a date with a psychopath, she paled, but seemed much more concerned that said psychopath had any interest in her daughter.

Though the local PD left, the rest of them remained in the house for a few hours, going through the computer history, getting every bit of information they could on this Gertz character. By the time they'd covered every base, Sam looked ready to drop, and so did the older couple.

"Mrs. Harrington, I think it best that you stay somewhere else for a little while, rather than remaining here at home," Wyatt said as they all decided to call it a night.

The judge laid a hand on her shoulder. "She'll stay with me. So can Samantha."

"No way," said Alec.

"Believe me, son, I am quite used to needing protection and have an alarm system as well as a permit to carry a weapon at all times. You needn't fear for either of these women." His tone vulnerable, he murmured, "They're my family."

"You're in a very good position to help keep Mrs. Harrington safe and out of sight, sir, but I'm afraid the obstacle Sam is up against is a little more serious."

The judge met his stare evenly, and Alec made no attempt to lighten his grim expression. He asked no questions; he didn't need to. He got the message loud and clear. "Very well."

"Thank you."

"I'll be fine, Uncle Nate," Sam said. "They've taken great care of me so far, and I know they won't let anything happen to me. Mom, I'll keep in constant contact, okay?"

"Please be sure you do. We need to talk so we can reschedule your birthday lunch as soon as possible."

"Deal."

Her mother managed a tremulous smile. "Promise?"

"Absolutely." She lowered her voice to add, "But no more setups. You got it?"

Alec pretended he hadn't heard, remembering the man who had been at the table the day before. The one who'd looked disappointed when Sam got up and walked out of the restaurant. Of course, the moment her mother stepped out of earshot, the suspicious part of him had to ask, "The setup? Not somebody she met online, right?"

"My divorce attorney."

"Ouch."

"Tell me about it."

With a few more assurances, the exchange of contact information, and another half dozen hugs, they all finally made their way outside to their vehicles. Alec didn't even think about it; he just opened the car door for Sam, assuming he was the one who would drive her back.

"Alec? Do you want to call Jackie and ask her to meet you at the hotel?" Wyatt asked.

"It's almost midnight. By the time we get there, it'll be one. I hate to drag her out, away from her kids, in the middle of the night."

"Are you all right staying with Mrs. Dalton until daybreak, then?"

Frankly, he wasn't sure he could let her out of his sight if ordered to. "Sure."

"Very well. Let's touch base in the morning. I'll leave a message for Lily, asking her to come in to help Brandon with the communications between Mrs. Harrington and this stranger."

"She, uh, tell you what she's up to tonight?"

Wyatt nodded once, only the tightness of his mouth indicating what he thought of it.

Alec didn't ask. It wasn't on him to get between his boss and one of his teammates. As long as Lily had come clean, he was out of the equation.

"Ready?" he asked Sam, who had already gotten in the car.

"More than."

Alec didn't even consider the ramifications of his overnight assignment until after they were in the car, driving back to D.C. He had offered to spend the night with Samantha Dalton. In a hotel room. Not more than a few hours after he'd realized he had feelings for the woman.

Shit. He was in for a long night.

Sam didn't seem to share his concern. She was too busy being grateful her mother was okay and, apparently, safely in the arms of someone who had loved her for a long time. "My God, imagine if Nate hadn't gone over there?" she said, not for the first time. She stared out the passenger window, shaking her head. "What if she'd gone to meet a murderer?"

"We don't know that this Randolph Gertz guy is Darwin."

"You said yourself that his e-mails were way over the top. Like the ones he used on other victims."

Yes, they were. He and Wyatt had read every one while Taggert and Mulrooney had gotten on the phone with Brandon to get tech advice on how to proceed. They were worded strangely, with some outrageous claims. Then again, this was online dating they were talking about, where fifty-year-old salesmen claimed to be twenty-nine-year-old bodybuilders.

"Okay, they were fishy. But I bet so are a lot of the other subscribers to that site."

They fell silent for a while, and he knew she was sitting there playing the what-if game.

Finally, she whispered, "After tonight, I have never been so glad for life."

Odd choice of words. "Glad for life?"

"Glad for hers." She turned in the seat, tucking one bent leg beneath her. "And mine."

"Ahh."

"I haven't been. Letting myself get so down and miserable for the past year—longer, really—was like turning my back on life." Yawning, she added, "That's over now." She leaned her head to the side, resting it on the back of the seat. Within moments, her lids closed.

Alec kept his eyes on the road. That didn't mean,

however, that he didn't glance over at her a few times, watching her sleep. Watching her dream. Hoping those dreams were good ones for a change. He hoped she had an entire night full of them.

In the next room. Far away from him.

Sam was being chased. An evil, malevolent force kept up with her as she ran through shadowy streets. Every terrified gasp she made brought a low laugh. Each step seemed half the length of the monster's following her.

The neighborhood was familiar—her mother's. But all the houses were shuttered and unwelcoming, no friendly faces from her childhood in sight. Suddenly she reached a cliff, where there had never been a cliff, and her terror propelled her off it until she flew. Swimming through the air, which was so much heavier than water, she couldn't go far. Not nearly far enough.

A scrape of claws across her ankle; she began to fall.

"No!"

Sam awoke from the nightmare, shooting straight up in the bed. She choked in a few deep, gasping breaths as her heart sprinted. The room was dark, the only light the glow of red from the bedside clock.

The color confused her. Red, not green?

Then she remembered. The hotel.

And she remembered something else. Her nightmare was merely a reflection of what her life had become. A monster really was out there in the night, stalking her.

"Sam?" The door pushed open a few inches. "Are you okay?"

"Not as okay as I'd like to be."

"Bad dream?"

"Yeah."

"You weren't supposed to have those tonight."

"Tell my subconscious that." Sam threw the covers back and got out of the bed, wanting one of the bottles of water in the small fridge. "I need a drink."

Her eyes hadn't yet adjusted to the darkness of the room, and she put a hand out, reaching for the edge of the door but connecting with firm male skin instead.

She froze, realizing her hand had landed on his broad chest. His broad, *bare* chest, judging by the ripples of muscle and the crisp hair brushing her fingers.

"Why don't you let me turn on a light?" he said, sounding as though he was pulling the words out of a constricted throat.

"Please don't." She stepped closer, until they stood only inches apart. Warmth emanated from the man, such a contrast to her coldness. She had on a flimsy, silky negligee that she'd worn perhaps twice in her life—his friend Mulrooney's idea of appropriate nightwear for a woman in a safe house—and had been freezing for the past two nights.

Suddenly, though, she found herself not minding her attire as much. Her eyes had begun to adjust, and there was no way she could miss the outright hunger in Alec's as he visually consumed her, his attention locked on the lacy edge of the gown that barely covered her breasts.

He made a sound like a low growl and muttered, "You should go back to bed."

Staring up at him, she replied, "I intend to." Then she further stated her intentions by pressing the entire length of her body against his. Heat and silk, his glittering eyes, and the strength of the man, all combined to bring shivers of delight and full-on desire. Lifting her other hand, she made a thorough study of his broad chest, tangling her fingers in that spiky hair, tracing them across thick ropes of muscle.

His body was every inch hard. Utterly male.

Yet, still vulnerable. When her hand brushed over a small, rigid lump just below his left clavicle, Sam immediately knew what it was. She leaned close, covering the scar with her lips, kissing it and mentally cursing the woman who had caused it.

"Sam . . ."

"Shh."

In the darkness, she kissed along his chest and up to his shoulder, finding another of those damned scars and treating it tenderly. Moving on, she tasted and nibbled her way up the side of his strong neck until she felt the rasp of his rough cheek against her own. "I'm so sorry you went through such pain, Alec," she whispered as she flicked her tongue across his earlobe.

He said nothing, keeping still, his jaw flexing, his neck muscles strained. He seemed to be holding on to his control with both fists.

That was admirable. But frankly, she'd had enough of it. Something had happened to her tonight. She had already realized she was ready to stop hibernating, to begin forward motion again. Now she didn't just want to step forward; she wanted to race into her future. Thinking she had lost someone she loved hammered home the need to go full throttle, to grasp happiness with greed and abandon. What an utter waste, throwing away a year on sadness, anger, and regret. She had completely cut herself off from human contact, emotional and physical.

Right now, she craved both.

"Alec, I know the timing's not right. And if you really want me to back off, I will. But to tell you the truth, after what happened tonight, I've decided it's time to start reaching out and taking life instead of letting it pass me by. To grab each minute and make it as spectacular as I can." She pressed a warm, openmouthed kiss on the pulse point just below his ear. "I think we could be pretty spectacular."

With a groan of surrender, he put his hands on her hips and tugged her harder against him until she felt the powerful erection pressing into her belly. Her mouth fell open on a soft, helpless sigh as her hips arched forward; she needed that heat, that strength.

Burying his face in her hair, breathing her in, he admitted, "I know we could be."

There was no triumph at having seduced him, or having appealed to his innate sexual nature. They were both winners in this, both doing what they'd wanted to do since they'd met, and Sam could muster up no regret about it.

Especially not when his hands moved, those strong fingers caressing her hips before sliding around to curve over her backside. He kissed her earlobe, as she had his, pressed that warm mouth on her own neck, bending her back so he could sample the hollow of her throat.

"Alec," she groaned, "I need—"

He cut her off by taking her mouth. His lips opened on hers, his tongue hot and demanding. Sam met the warm thrusts, glad for his strong grip on her as all her strength seemed to depart. She became one quivering mass of desire, existing for nothing more than this man's hands and his mouth. And, oh, God, the rest of him.

He didn't even stop kissing her as he lifted her by the hips. Her legs parted instinctively.

She wrapped them around his lean hips, grinding against him as he carried her to the bed and tossed her onto it, immediately following her down.

Deep kiss followed deep kiss, his touch inflaming her wherever it went. He slid her gown up and off, tossing it away, then tasted his way down the entire front of her body. At the rasp of his tongue against her nipple, she arched up for more.

Twining her fingers in his hair, she cried, "Yes," as he gave her what she wanted, sucking fast and hard. But only for a few seconds. Then he tortured her, moved away. Built the tension all over again before finally giving in to her demands and suckling again.

"You taste so good, Sam," he murmured as he continued a downward journey, devouring her body, savoring her as if she were a banquet laid out before him.

She hissed when his lips reached the hollow just above her pelvic bone, and cried out when they moved even lower. He held her hips, keeping her in place when she wanted to roll and thrash and demand the chance to taste him as he was tasting her. Not that she really minded. God, no. When he found her pulsing center and began caressing it with his tongue, her cries were definitely not ones of complaint.

She shook and thrust as an orgasm washed over her, the first she'd had with another person in a very long time. Alec pulled back to watch her, his eyes glittering with satisfaction as he beheld her helpless cries of pleasure.

Sam savored it, but not for long. She wanted more. So much more. Sitting up, she pushed Alec onto his back and reached for his pants. "You're a little overdressed, don't you think?"

Easily remedied. He let her tug off his pants, then his boxer briefs. She sat back on her heels, sighing and staring in avarice at his thick arousal. "I've wanted you so much," she mumbled as she reached out to encircle him, amazed by his heat and his silky smoothness. "Since the minute you knocked on my door."

"Ditto."

She could drag this out, could taste him and suck him into madness, the way he had to her. But she was too impatient. It had been too long; she needed to be filled. She slid up his body, straddling his thighs, quivering at the delicious scrape of his rougher skin against her own.

"Sam, are you . . ."

She knew what he was asking and nodded, thankful as hell that she hadn't gone to the doctor and had her IUD removed. "Covered. I want to do lots of things with you, Alec, but right now? I just have to take you."

His lazy smile and the brush of his hand against her hip said, *So take*.

She did. Staring down at him, she moved over his

erection, sighing a little in anticipation. Fully aroused and wet, she slid down an inch at a time, savoring the penetration after such a long period of going without. Down and down, until she'd taken all of him and he was touching the very core of her body.

He groaned. "God, you're gorgeous," he muttered, reaching up and burying his hands in her hair. Tangling his fingers in it, he pulled her down for a hungry kiss. Each thrust of his tongue was matched by one from his hips, and Sam could only whimper with pleasure.

Despite the position, she didn't take control as their bodies began to dance in the most intimate sort of give and take. They shared it, matching each other's rhythms, anticipating each stroke. At one point, Alec flipped her over, plunging into her hard, both of them driven beyond thinking, beyond anything but sensation as he imprinted himself on her mind, body, and soul.

Finally, he groaned and she knew he was about to go over the edge. She let herself go, too, and cried out her own climax seconds after his. But she didn't release him, keeping her arms around his shoulders and her legs around his waist for several long minutes as they both let themselves float back down to earth.

He eventually left her, rolled onto his side, but stayed close, one arm draped across her waist. Pressing gentle kisses on her face, he murmured sweet, nearly unintelligible words about how beautiful she was and how much he wanted her.

She had never felt more cherished. Not once.

"Thank you," she murmured, feeling happier than she had in forever, despite everything that had brought them to this moment.

He smiled, a picture of male confidence. "Hey, it was totally my pleasure."

"I meant, thanks for knocking on my door," she said with a low, husky laugh. "Though, thanks for the sex, too."

"You're doubly welcome."

He nuzzled her neck, then ran a possessive hand all over the front of her, roaming and exploring, until he reached the juncture of her thighs and began to lazily stroke her back up to a fever pitch. "Be sure to tell your friend that your girl parts most definitely have not dried up and fallen off."

Laughing as she remembered that first phone call, she began to utter a sultry reply about becoming wetter by the minute. But those words died in her throat.

"Oh, my God."

A thought burst through her mind, sudden and completely unexpected. She hadn't given her best friend a thought after she'd read that awful message on her blog post tonight. Her thoughts had gone in only one direction, toward her mother. For the second time in as many hours, she lunged straight up in the bed, gasping and terrified.

"What is it?"

"Tricia." She stumbled out of the bed, wanting to get to her phone. "God, Alec, what if the target was Tricia?"

Quick impressions . . . Voices. Pain. And cold.

Tricia tried to open her eyes. Couldn't. They were disconnected from her brain somehow.

Where am I? God, what happened to me?

She didn't know, could barely think. Something about a meeting. Showing a property, an old warehouse. Buyer had been on the hook for weeks. Was coming through town, wanted to meet. She'd unlocked the lockbox, stepped inside.

Then blackness.

"Hey, baby, looks like you don't need no more of that bottle. How 'bout sharin'?"

Strange voice, echoing. Every word repeated twice in her head.

"Mm-mm, girl, I think you had enough." Another voice. Deeper. Laughing.

"Yeah, she looks wasted."

How many were there?

"What's that on her chest?"

Someone moved closer. "Help me," she whispered, though her voice was so weak, she barely heard it herself.

A loud bark of laughter split her skull. "Check this out. Bitch wants to get it on!"

Movement. More voices. Hands reaching for her. Groping. Sliding up her bare leg. *Where are my clothes?*

"No need to beg. I'll give it to you."

"Hey, motherfucker, back off. I saw her first."

"She got enough to share. Gonna slice me off a piece of that."

Fingers digging into her thighs, pulling them apart. She struggled, managed to get her eyes open. Blinked to bring her vision into focus, saw she was outside, on the ground, men around her, beside her, above her.

"Wha . . . ?"

"Shh," the closest one said, leaning close so she could smell the reeking breath. "We're gonna give you what you wanted."

He reached for his pants. She tried to scream.

"What the fuck is going on out here?"

Another man. Loud, strong—massive.

"Please . . . help me," she whispered, staring up at him as he tossed the others out of the way. She stared into his dark brown eyes, kind eyes, despite the huge, beefy body, the gangsta clothes, the gold jewelry.

"Please."

She felt hands on her. Moving her. Lifting her.

The light faded as she slipped into unconsciousness once more.

Chapter 16

They located Tricia at a city hospital a little before dawn, after making frantic phone calls throughout the rest of the night. A woman of her description had been brought in a couple of hours earlier. Though nearly incoherent, she'd come around enough to say her first name.

For what seemed the dozenth time in a week, Alec found himself driving between the nation's capital and Baltimore, a panicked Sam sitting beside him. Only now, she wasn't just a witness, not just an attractive stranger. She was his lover, in every sense of the word. And she was on the verge of shattering into a million pieces.

His fault. Jesus, it was all his fault. If he had never shown up at her place, never knocked on her door, never gotten her involved, perhaps she wouldn't have drawn the attention of a madman. A madman who now wanted to punish her by hurting those she loved.

Of course, if he'd never shown up at her door, they wouldn't have shared the amazing hour in that hotel bed. But he'd trade it in a second to make her happy, safe, and whole again.

He had tried calling Wyatt, but had received no answer. Even after working for him for only a week, Alec already knew that was very unusual for the man. Leaving him a message, he'd then called the others, reaching everyone except Lily. They all sounded as exhausted as he felt, but every one of them said they'd be in Baltimore as soon as possible.

"What exactly did the police say?" Sam asked.

He'd told her twice but knew she needed to fill the time until they got there. "That she was found in an alley in a bad part of town, wearing next to nothing, holding a half-empty bottle of booze, with an obscene note pinned to her bra strap."

It was a miracle the woman hadn't been raped. Apparently Tricia had been at the center of a gang of young hoods when a bar owner had spotted them and put a stop to it. The bystander had brought her to the hospital.

"I guess Good Samaritans really do exist," he murmured, feeling a quick stab of satisfaction that at least part of the Professor's hateful plan hadn't worked.

When they arrived at the hospital, they were escorted to Tricia's room, finding a city police officer standing guard, as Alec had requested. He flashed his badge as Sam peered in, her bottom lip between her teeth. When she let out a cry of relief and flew through the door, he knew Tricia wasn't quite as bad off as they'd feared.

He glanced in, watching their reunion for a moment, realizing Tricia, while weak, was conscious and able to talk. He'd need to question her, but wanted to give the women a few minutes alone. In the meantime, he had other things to do.

"Can you direct me toward the man who brought her here?" he asked.

The officer pointed toward a nearby waiting area. "You can't miss him."

Something about the officer's tone warned him, so when he walked into the room and saw Tricia Scott's rescuer, he wasn't entirely taken by surprise. Because the Good Samaritan, who immediately rose as he entered, was one of the most intimidating-looking people he'd ever seen. Truly huge, he dwarfed Alec in height, and had enormous shoulders, thick hands, and a shiny, boulder-size bald head. He was the kind of man who made nervous women cross the street on sight. But right now, he looked genuinely concerned, worried about the one he'd rescued last night.

This guy broke every stereotype the Professor had relied on.

Alec extended his hand to the man. "I'm Special Agent Lambert, and I want to thank you for doing what you did."

"She gonna be all right?"

"I think so. But I hear it was a close call. You really saved the day."

"Those asswipes were too drunk to realize she'd been attacked and was drugged out of her head. Like any woman would really write something like that on herself."

"The note?"

"I gave it to the detective who was here earlier."

"What did it say?"

The other man growled in disgust. " 'My boyfriend dumped me. I need to be fucked bad.' "

Every muscle in his body flexed. Alec wanted to hurt the Professor. Wanted to take the bastard's neck between his hands and squeeze the life right out of him.

But arresting him and throwing his ass in jail was the best he could do. So he'd damn well better get to work doing it.

Thanking the other man again, and asking him to wait a little longer until his colleagues could show up for a more thorough questioning, Alec went in search of the detective. The guy was in a nurses' station, sipping coffee from a foam cup, yawning between each sip.

"You the FBI?" he asked.

"Yes. Can I see the note?"

The man reached for a satchel, retrieving a plastic

sheath in which a single sheet of paper had been placed. Despite Alec's first impressions, the guy seemed to be at least somewhat professional. He'd had the common sense to treat the evidence carefully.

Holding the plastic by a corner, Alec lifted it in the air and read the hand-scrawled words. But they were hard to read because light shining through the cream-colored paper made writing on the other side bleed through.

He turned the page around. Realized what he was looking at. And his heart stopped.

"Looks like a page torn out of a book," the detective said, not noticing Alec's shock. "Autographed. Maybe we should talk to the person who signed it, the Sam Dalton guy."

"That's a good idea," Alec whispered. "A very good idea."

Though Alec let her spend a half hour alone with Tricia, Sam knew he needed to question her. She had been loath to leave her poor, bruised, battered friend, but at least knew she'd be in good hands. Still, before she could leave, she'd needed to apologize, to explain as well as she could why she was partially to blame for what had happened.

"Bullshit, girl." Tricia showed a hint of her usual spirit and her no-nonsense attitude. "Nobody's to blame for this except the prick who did it."

"I provoked him."

"If you hadn't provoked him, maybe he'd have stayed underground a little longer, slaughtering a few more people along the way before he popped his slimy head up out of his hole." Tricia's voice was weak, but her grip pretty strong as she clenched Sam's hand. "Don't you regret this. I'm fine. A little banged up, but"—Tricia released her hand and glanced at her own lap—"the doctor says I wasn't, uh, violated in any way."

Thank you, God.

"I know that's all my parents will care about," Tricia added. "They'll be here in a couple of hours—they're driving up from North Carolina."

Sam bent to kiss her cheek, whispering, "I know you're all tough and bad, but I also know that your mind was raped even if your body wasn't."

Thick tears fell from her friend's pretty eyes, confirming what Sam had suspected: Tricia wasn't as okay about this as she was trying to pretend.

"I'll be there for you," Sam added. "I promise. As soon as you get out of here, I'm coming over to take care of you, nurse you back to health."

Tricia's bruised mouth quirked. "You? Leave your cocoon?"

"No more cocoon for me. This caterpillar has become a butterfly at last."

"It's about time. I gotta meet this guy."

"You've met him," Sam said, not surprised at how well her friend knew her, either.

"Sex on a stick?"

"Uh-huh."

Tricia's wan smile and murmured, "You go, girl," revealed how tired she was.

Regretting keeping her from sleep, Sam stood, kissed her forehead, and left the room. Tricia would be okay; she was a survivor. But oh, God, had it been another close call.

Hearing Alec's voice, she wandered toward the waiting room. Most of his coworkers were there: Jackie Stokes, Mulrooney, and Taggert. They were huddled together, talking in whispers.

"What is it?" Sam asked.

As if they were being jerked by the same string, all four immediately focused their attention on her. "Sam, I need you to look at something." Alec lifted a clear plastic Baggie that contained a single sheet of paper.

Seeing a few scrawled words, she swallowed hard and crossed her arms over her chest. "Is that the note?"

"Yes, it is." He flipped it over, showing her the other side.

She had to look twice before she grasped it. Then she realized what it was. Somehow, she felt no surprise. Nothing this psychotic madman did could surprise her anymore.

"He's met me," she said flatly.

"Apparently so."

The sheet was the inside title page from one of her books. It had been torn out; the top area, where she usually personalized inscriptions, was missing. All that remained was the title, and her cheerily scrawled, *Stay safe in cyber land!* Below it was her signature.

"I know it will be next to impossible for you to remember whom you signed it to, but if you could give us information on any of your book signings . . ."

She shook her head. "No."

"You can't?"

"I mean, no, it's not impossible." A bitter pleasure rose up within her. "That bastard may have made the mistake that will lead you right to him."

All the other team members listened closely.

"I have a special brand of pen I use for my signings. Very specific, smooth, just the right texture and consistency." She nodded toward the page. "And it's not red. Not *ever*."

"This is a forgery?" Jackie Stokes asked.

She shook her head. "It's mine. I did a signing after giving a guest lecture right after my book came out, almost a year ago. My trusty favorite pen sprang a leak and got black ink all over my skirt. Someone stuck a replacement in my hand so I could finish the autographing."

Alec muttered a triumphant, "Yes! A red pen."

"It gets better. The event was part of an attendees-only legal symposium at a local college, for the police, lawyers, judges, and the like. Uncle Nate was involved; he brought me in to talk about cyber crime."

"Excellent." Mulrooney chortled. "We'll get hold of the list of attendees."

"And your unsub's name should be on it," Sam said.

"What's your uncle Nate's number?" Alec asked. "He can tell us who the organizers were."

She gave it to him, feeling so confident they'd finally made a breakthrough, she wanted to throw her arms around Alec's neck and kiss him. She didn't, of course. His boss might not be here, but it was still inappropriate.

Curious about that, she asked, "Where is Agent Blackstone, anyway?"

"I have no idea," Alec said, sounding thoughtful. "Strange that he's been out of touch for this long. Brandon said he was going to keep trying to reach him. Maybe that's why he's not here yet."

The others echoed him, Jackie adding, "I've left three or four messages. I couldn't get in touch with Lily, either."

Alec frowned. "I hope nothing happened with that other case she was working on."

The rest of the group appeared curious, but didn't ask questions. They all had other things to do. Alec got on the phone with Uncle Nate. Jackie interviewed Sam about Tricia's life and habits. The others talked to the detective.

When they were finished, Sam asked, "Where is the man who brought her in? I want to thank him."

"He went for coffee," Jackie said. "He's a good guy, doesn't want to leave until he knows she's okay."

Remembering what Alec had muttered in the car about the Good Samaritan, she felt the same rush of pleasure, not only because Tricia was okay, but that the Professor had failed. He hadn't anticipated a good guy, only rapists and killers who might easily have attacked Tricia, or left her for dead.

And while they hadn't confirmed that the man her mother had intended to meet was the same one who'd attacked Tricia, Sam would lay money it was true. Meaning the bastard had been foiled twice in one night. That made her doubly grateful. Somewhere, someone was watching out for those Sam loved. She only hoped the guardian angel stuck around long enough to ensure she survived, too.

A short time later, as Sam stood in Tricia's room, watching her repeatedly thank her rescuer, Alec entered. "We're going to take off now."

"We?"

"I want you here, safe and sound, with the detective and the officer watching you. Jackie, Kyle, Dean, and I will go to the college." He frowned. "I hate for all of us to go, but without Wyatt, Brandon, and Lily, we're a little shorthanded. The professor who organized the symposium sounds very disorganized. There are apparently a bunch of boxes to sort through, and I want to get through them as quickly as possible."

"You're sure you don't need my help?"

"I'm sure. I just want you protected, Sam. Right here, with lots of people—and police officers—around you. I'll come back here with any lists we can get, copies of credit card slips, whatever, and together we'll go over the information, okay? You stay here with your friend."

Her friend was still softly chatting with the big, dangerous-looking man who'd saved her, eyeing him as if he were a cuddly teddy bear. "She's going to be okay," Sam whispered, as much to herself as to Alec.

"Yeah, she is. And we're going to find the man who did this to her and stop him from hurting anyone again."

Alec reached for her hand and squeezed it. His colleagues were right outside, her friend and a witness just a few feet away, so there was no way he could kiss her the way his glittering eyes told her he wanted to. God, in all the insanity, it had actually slipped her mind that she'd made incredible love with this man a few hours ago.

She smiled and shivered in satisfaction at the very thought of it.

"Stop it."

"Stop what?"

He leaned close. "Stop looking at me the way you did when I was inside you."

"Get used to it."

He pulled an inch away, met her gaze, asked a dozen questions without ever opening his mouth, then turned and walked out of the room.

After he was gone, she wondered where that sassy, sultry comeback had come from. Because when he'd commented about being inside her, she'd turned to mush.

"I could probably use a little sleep now," Tricia told her rescuer. "Thank you again. Call me soon, okay? I want to take you out to dinner to thank you when I don't look like somebody ran over me with a truck."

"That's a deal. You concentrate on getting better," the big man said.

Once he was gone, Sam stepped to her friend's bedside. "I'll let you sleep. I want to call Mom and tell her what happened."

"Tell her I really need that plastic surgeon's number now, 'kay?" Tricia cracked, her voice weak but her wit still sharp.

"You got it. But not too soon. You're so damned gorgeous, the rest of us finally have a shot at getting some attention."

Tricia's eyes were closed, but she said, "I'd say you're getting more than that."

Even woozy and injured, the woman had damned good perception.

Sam slipped out, realizing her friend was already drifting off. Smiling pleasantly at the police officer stationed at the door, she said, "I'll be in the waiting room."

"I'll be right here, ma'am."

Before she had even stepped away, though, her cell phone rang. She cast a quick, guilty look around. She was not supposed to use it inside the hospital, and had intended to use the complimentary landline in the waiting area. When she saw the name on the caller ID, though—MD HOUSE OF CORRECTIONS—she answered in spite of herself.

The reception wasn't great, with static on the line, but she finally heard, "Mrs. Dalton? This is Dale Carter, Jimmy Flynt's attorney."

"Yes, of course. What can I do for you, Mr. Carter?"

"Ma'am, sorry to bother you so early on a Sunday. . . ."

As if she hadn't been up almost all night, anyway. "It's all right."

"I have some bad news. I'm at the prison, got called down here first thing this morning. Jimmy passed away during the night."

"He's *dead*?"

The officer tensed, and Sam waved to let him know all was well.

"He's been very sick, as I'm sure you noticed. I'm told he took ill last evening; he was brought to the infirmary and he expired at around two o'clock this morning."

Sam didn't know what to say, what to think, what to feel. She had never liked Jimmy, and had always known he liked her too much. But her visit yesterday had thrown her, made her wonder if he had been less full of crap than she'd assumed him to be.

"It was nice of you to call, Mr. Carter," she said, "though I'm not family or anything. In fact, I barely knew him."

"That's not why I'm calling. They contacted me about Jimmy's belongings, since he has no known family. He left a thick envelope with your name on it."

She froze. Love letters from a dead inmate did not appeal in the least.

As if reading her mind, the attorney said, "I glanced

through them to make sure there was nothing objectionable or criminal. There doesn't appear to be, just some odd ramblings that don't make much sense to me, but might to you."

"Ramblings?"

Papers shuffled. "Something about your being careful, danger heading your way."

She had been only half paying attention to what the attorney said, still trying to believe Jimmy had died, but his words made her straighten up and take notice. "Danger?"

"Yes. He mentioned e-mail scams, that some people might use them to hurt people rather than just robbing them."

Good God. "What else?"

He cleared his throat. "This part says, 'There's rumors. Somebody's watching you and I'm worried for you.' "

Was it really possible? Could Jimmy have known something about this case? It seemed crazy. Then again, so had the idea of him finding the man who'd ruined her grandmother and taking vengeance on him. Yet she had begun to believe it had happened.

"Can you come down to the prison to retrieve this?" he asked. "Since it is addressed to you, the prison wants to release it to you directly."

"I don't know. . . ."

"I will understand if you can't. Jimmy was a rather unlikable person. Just because he fixated on you as an ally doesn't mean you have any obligation to him now that he's gone."

Rather than making her feel better, the attorney's words made her feel worse. As if she owed Jimmy something. Hell, maybe she did. She just didn't know. "I'll try. Maybe later today?"

"Very well," he said. "You should call and let the prison know you're coming, since it's a Sunday and there aren't a lot of administrative people here."

"All right. Thank you, Mr. Carter," she said, hanging up.

The officer, who had been watching her closely, asked, "Everything okay, miss?"

She rubbed her temple. "I'm not sure."

Not at all sure. One thing she did know: She wanted Alec's opinion. She quickly dialed his number, but got only his voice mail. She left him a detailed message about what had happened, asking him to call back.

"Damn it," she muttered as soon as she'd hung up, heading to the waiting room to think things over. Sam wanted to read Jimmy's letters. More so with every passing minute. The wording had been too precise to be completely coincidental. Whoever Jimmy's contacts were on the inside of that prison, they seemed to actually be aware of what was happening out here.

Maybe because one of them had contact with the Professor? Was it possible?

It could be.

Alec and the others could be another couple of hours. She was doing nothing but worrying in a hospital waiting room. Rather than wasting time with the trip when they returned, she should go and be back here with the documents before their arrival.

But she couldn't. She certainly wasn't stupid enough to leave by herself, and didn't have a car to do so, anyway.

"Hey, ma'am, just wanted to let you know I'm heading out of here," a voice said. "Officer Gilbert will stay in position at your friend's door until the FBI agents return."

Seeing the detective, to whom she had been briefly introduced earlier, Sam had a sudden thought. "Are you still on duty, or are you going home?"

"Gonna be working all day. Never-ending paperwork."

She hesitated, not wanting to put him out. Then, knowing it could be important, she bit the bullet and asked, "Is there any chance you could give me a ride somewhere?"

Chapter 17

To everyone's surprise, just as they reached the college, Wyatt called Jackie Stokes and told them he was on his way. No explanation about where he'd been, no questions about the case, just a few terse words. He was in town and would come straight to the campus to meet them. And he wanted the team all together when he did so.

He obviously had been very close. They had barely opened the boxes of file folders, where the elderly professor in charge said the archived registration forms and book sale receipts should be, when Wyatt showed up.

He had also obviously not been kidding about everyone being together, because he was not alone. As their boss walked into the empty lecture hall they were using, Brandon Cole walked beside him. Their somber expressions said this was bad. Very bad.

Brandon's hair was disheveled, and he wore faded jeans and an MIT sweatshirt, as though he'd yanked on the first thing he could find. His eyes were suspiciously bright, his shoulders slumped.

Wyatt was in even worse shape. The man's white dress shirt was wrinkled, untucked, and smeared with dirt. His usually crisp pants actually had a tear, and his shoes were caked with mud.

Worst of all was his demeanor. His boss seemed to have aged a decade since last night. Dark circles ringed his eyes, and his stubbled face was gouged with both anger and grief.

This isn't just bad.

Rising to ask what had happened, Alec heard his cell phone ring. He glanced at it, saw Sam's name, but, knowing she was safe at the hospital, didn't answer. He quickly punched the power button, cutting the noise midring. Because the tension on Wyatt Blackstone's face said he had something to say and that he wanted to say it only once.

"Oh, no," he whispered under his breath, suddenly having an awful suspicion.

Wyatt confirmed that suspicion with four baldly spoken words.

"Lily Fletcher is dead."

Jackie let out a shocked cry; Mulrooney lowered himself onto the seat he'd just vacated. Taggert snapped an obscenity, stalked to a corner of the room, and slammed his palm against the wall.

Alec just stood there. This was painful for him, even after knowing Lily for only a week. For the rest of the team, who had worked with her day in and day out for months? With what he'd gone through in Atlanta, he knew they were in for an awful time.

Wyatt gave everyone a minute to regain focus; then he explained. Since Alec had known about the mission with the other CAT, he didn't need as much backstory as the others. But when it came to what, exactly, had happened last night, he was all ears.

"Why the fuck wasn't she protected?" Taggert asked after Wyatt told them about the sting.

"She was supposed to be. The agent in charge assured me she would stay in the surveillance van. Unfortunately, they were all tricked."

"By?" Alec asked.

"The unsub hired a vagrant to scope out the house while he watched from a few streets away. When he realized it was a trap, he tried to flee the scene. Apparently his accomplice was too smart for him, anticipated a setup of his own, and stole the car keys so he couldn't be left behind."

"So the real target panicked," Brandon said, his voice barely more than a whisper. Having shared an office with Lily, he had probably been the closest to her. "He had no other means of escape."

And then he spotted the FBI van nearby.

"Apparently Lily and the surveillance specialist assumed everything was under control, the suspect in custody," Wyatt said. "The other agent stepped out of the van and was shot down immediately."

"And Lily?" Jackie asked, her voice tremulous and her eyes full of tears. The first time he'd ever seen any sign of weakness in the strong woman. Considering the sheer awfulness of it, he couldn't blame her.

Wyatt didn't answer directly. "The agent in charge called me at one o'clock this morning, just as I got back to D.C." His eyes gleamed with suppressed rage. "Why he waited three hours to call me, I don't know. I caught a chopper ride down to Williamsburg. They had put out an APB on the van."

"*And Lily?*" Jackie repeated, sounding agonized at having to wait for the rest of it.

Wyatt's head dropped forward. His voice low, he told them the rest. "The van was spotted on Route 17, between Newport News and Yorktown a couple of hours after the ambush, driving erratically, weaving in and out of traffic. Police pursued, but the vehicle crashed off the Route 17 bridge into the York River, right at the mouth of the bay."

Good God. Alec had driven that bridge when stationed in Richmond. It was pretty damn high.

"They were pulling the van up when I hit town," Wyatt explained.

"Was she . . . Had she drowned?" Jackie asked.

"They still hadn't found either body by the time I left. The back door was open; both of them must have washed out. They're still looking in the river, but they might have been swept into the Chesapeake." His shoulders slumped and he shook his head, as if processing this whole thing for himself for the first time. "I thought I should fly up here and let you all know what happened before you heard it from someone else."

Stokes rose shakily to her feet. "If there's no body, maybe she's all right. What are we doing here? We should be down there helping with the search!"

Wyatt put a hand on the woman's shoulder, steadying her, maybe even steadying himself. "Jackie, the interior was soaked with blood."

"The other agent . . ."

"No," he insisted, killing her hopes. All their hopes. "He was shot outside the vehicle, but there was a large blood-stain soaked into the carpet inside, as if someone had been lying there for a long time. It was Lily's blood type."

"God," Taggert whispered. "I can't believe this."

"He shot her, carjacked her." Wyatt's voice filled with audible, barely controlled rage. "And then he let her bleed to death in the back while he tried to evade the police."

"Fucking bastard," Brandon said as he covered his eyes with one hand.

"Even if there were some slim chance she was still alive despite the blood loss, she would never have survived the crash and couldn't possibly have swum to safety."

Everyone fell silent, thinking about it. Remembering Lily's shyness, her sweet smile. The way she always seemed just a little sad.

Emitting a strangled sob, Jackie stalked out of the room, followed by Brandon.

Wyatt watched them go, then blew out a heavy, shaken breath. "I need to go home, shower, and change. Update me by phone if you find anything." He leveled an even stare on the three of them, Alec, Kyle, and Dean, adding, "We still have a job to do. The Professor isn't going to take a day off to grieve, and neither can we."

Message received. After one more moment of silence, all three of them returned to their places around the table and began removing files from the box, one by one.

Without another word, Wyatt Blackstone slipped from the room, leaving them to it.

Sam liked Detective Myers, who had been on the Baltimore PD for two decades. He talked only a little, asked no obtrusive questions, and showed no sign that he resented driving her to the prison. A perfect escort.

She still hadn't talked to Alec. She had tried him again, leaving a message about her field trip, stressing that she had an armed escort. Hopefully by the time she heard from him, this brief errand would be finished and she would be on her way back to the hospital.

As they neared the prison, Sam remembered she had promised to let them know what she was doing, and dialed the number from which Mr. Carter had called her. A male employee answered. When she asked if the attorney was there, he put her on hold for several long moments.

Finally, the guard came back on the line. "He's waiting for you," he said. "We'll leave word at the gate. When you get here, follow the signs to the administrative parking lot. There's an entrance directly into the main offices; park there and he'll meet you at the door."

Thanking the man, she relayed the directions to Myers.

"You must be a big shot," he said with a wry grin. "I've never been invited to the superspecial parking lot."

"I'd gladly forgo the privilege if it means I never have to come to this place again."

They reached the complex probably no more than an hour after Carter's initial call, the light Sunday-morning traffic helping to shorten the trip. As promised, the guard at the gate had been expecting them and directed them onto a private drive leading to the reserved lot. In it, two cars stood close to a door marked RESTRICTED ACCESS: AUTHORIZED ADMINISTRATIVE PERSONNEL ONLY.

"Guess that's us," Myers said as he parked.

Having been here yesterday, in the visitors' lot, where there was much more activity, Sam found the emptiness strange. Myers apparently felt the same, because he stuck close as he walked her to the thick metal door marked STAFF ENTRANCE.

Though they'd been told Carter would be waiting for them, no one was in sight. Myers tested the handle, to no avail, then glanced at her. "What do we do now?"

She cupped her hands around her eyes, peering through the small, barred window, and saw movement. "There he is."

The door opened. But to her surprise, they were greeted by the warden, rather than Dale Carter. "Yes?"

"Sorry to disturb you," she said, still flustered around the man after yesterday. "We're supposed to be meeting Mr. Carter."

The unsmiling warden stared at her, then at Myers. His frown deepening, he mumbled, "Who are you?"

He flashed his badge. "Detective Myers, Baltimore PD. I'm escorting Mrs. Dalton."

"This door is for authorized personnel only."

Jeez, the guy was a stickler for rules.

"We were told to come this way," Myers said. He crossed his arms over his chest and raised a brow, as if challenging the warden to make them go around to the public entrance.

"Fine, fine," Connolly said, not sounding happy about

it. He stepped back and ushered them in, quickly shutting the door.

They stood in a small, private alcove just outside the warden's office. Obviously the man's job came with perks like an excellent parking place.

Unlike yesterday, when there had been at least some activity, despite the weekend hours, today this part of the building was practically deserted. Their footsteps were the only sounds, and they seemed to echo down the empty corridor, underscoring the feeling of abandonment. Certainly, in other parts of the huge building, there were hundreds of people—guards and inmates. But it appeared the admin staff got Sundays off. At least, everyone except the warden.

"Now, what is this all about?" he asked.

"Dale Carter called me this morning and asked me to come down here to pick up something left for me by Jimmy Flynt."

The man's head jerked. "Flynt?"

"Yes. An envelope with my name on it."

The man's eyes narrowed; he appeared puzzled. "I'm confused. I thought you no longer wanted to receive mail from Flynt."

"This isn't typical mail," she explained. "Mr. Carter said it was a packet."

"I knew nothing about it." Turning abruptly, he said over his shoulder, "We'll get to the bottom of this. Come with me, please."

Sam exchanged a look with Myers, realizing he, too, felt like a schoolkid with the principal. But they both followed the man, who led them through a door to his secretary's office, where Sam had waited out the interview yesterday.

"I apologize for the mess," he said with an expansive wave of his hand. Furniture had been pushed to the side, plastic covering most of it, and a large drop cloth had been spread across the floor. He gestured toward a brown stain on the ceiling. "We had a leak. I have a man working on it. I'm overseeing, which is why I'm here on a Sunday morning rather than at church."

"It's fine," Sam said. "I'm sorry to disturb you. I just need to sign for the package and we'll be on our way."

Again came that frown. "As I said, I am completely unaware of this situation. You say Dale Carter told you to meet him here."

"Yes. He called me not two hours ago. Said Jimmy Flynt had died, that he'd left me a package, and I should come get it."

At that, the warden's jaw dropped in shock. "*What?* James Flynt is dead?"

Sam froze. How could the warden not know one of his own prisoners had died? Sure, the place was big, but the death of an inmate seemed like something the head guy should know about.

"How dare they not inform me?" The angry man strode through the receptionist's area into his own office, heading for his phone. He yanked the receiver and began barking at someone, leaving Sam and Myers standing in the reception area, utterly confused.

"This seem normal to you?" the detective asked.

Sam shook her head slowly.

"This lawyer. How well do you know him?"

"Not well," she murmured.

Not well at all.

Sam gripped the edge of the closest bookcase, shocked by a sudden, awful possibility.

"And he called you directly, this Carter guy. Told you to come here." Myers unbuttoned his coat, revealing the service pistol strapped to his hip. "I don't like this."

"I don't either," she whispered, eyeing the door, still open to that long, deserted corridor, where anyone could be lurking. "I need to call Alec."

She reached for her phone. But she hadn't even touched it when a muffled *pffft* sound split the morning.

She didn't even realize it had been a gunshot until Myers dropped like a stone.

After Wyatt left, Taggert and Mulrooney had buried themselves in the work, each lost in his own thoughts. They'd managed to shove aside their emotional reaction to Lily's death for a little while, but something like that couldn't be held at bay for long. Soon they were both muttering worried questions about Lily as well as Jackie and Brandon, needing to know more, needing more than a few minutes to grieve, despite the case.

Assuring them he was fine to continue going through the stack of files—damn this stuffy institution that archived actual paper rather than just keeping a computerized version—Alec waved them off. "Why don't you take a break? I'll dig through this last box."

Taggert nodded; then both men departed to find the others.

It figured that the box they needed would be the last one they looked in. Almost immediately after opening it, Alec spotted the right file and tugged it out. It was thick, stuffed with registration forms filled out by each attendee of the event, and there were at least two hundred.

"Damn it," he muttered as he thumbed a few pages. This was a waste of time. He needed to bring the folder to the hospital and ask Sam if she remembered any of these guys, anyone who acted strangely, asked a lot of questions, paid her personal attention.

Sam. She had called as Wyatt was walking in and he'd totally forgotten. Turning his phone on, he dialed his voice mail, doodling idly on a yellow legal pad as the call connected. Two messages. *Shit.*

When he heard the first one, he froze in disbelief. Jimmy Flynt dead? Talk about timing. The guy had looked pretty bad yesterday, but they certainly hadn't left that hospital thinking he was breathing his final breaths.

"So call me when you get this, would you? I'd like to try to get down there; obviously I can't go alone."

Damn right.

He waited for the second message, surprised to hear Sam's voice again. "It's me. Look, I'm going to go ahead down to the prison."

He almost dropped the pen.

"Before you panic, Detective Myers is escorting me."

So she wasn't taking chances. He had hoped she'd stay put until he returned, but he did see where she was coming from, especially when she said, "I saw no point in wasting a couple of hours after you return. This way, I'll be back with the letters close to when you are and we save some time."

She was right, not that he liked it. Cutting the connection, he quickly dialed her back to find out where she was. And to make sure Myers knew how serious this situation was.

He got no answer. It was possible they hadn't even left the hospital yet and were in Tricia's room. Or the phone might not have reception inside the iron fortress of the prison. Both plausible—but he couldn't deny that a hint of concern crawled through him.

He wanted to hear Sam's voice.

She's fine. She's protected.

Knowing she wouldn't be there even if he took the file back to the hospital right away, he paused, unable to get Flynt off his mind. The man had known so much, especially if his note was to be believed. But how? How could he have realized Sam was in danger, that someone was using e-mails to "hurt" people? Was it possible the Professor had an accomplice, somebody who was now imprisoned and might have talked? He questioned whether the unsub would trust anyone, but how else could Jimmy know?

Though he thought about it, no answers came to him. He didn't get that buzz he usually experienced when he was on the right track. And he didn't have any time to waste.

"All right, enough," he told himself. Alec shook his head and put his attention back on the task at hand. Glancing at his pad of paper, he realized just how deep in thought he had been. He'd been doodling all over the page and hadn't even realized it. He'd written Sam's name, Jimmy's, the Professor's, Darwin's.

Darwin. He'd scratched the letters boldly, in all caps. For some reason, Alec couldn't stop staring at it.

And just like that, the buzz started. Thoughts clicked in his head, as they often did when he sensed he was on the edge of something important.

He'd called their unsub the Professor for so long, it had been hard adjusting to the name he'd chosen for himself. The killer had never referred to himself that way until Wednesday night, when he'd posted those responses to Sam's blog. Right there, in black and white, spelling out his motives, his philosophies.

Darwin.

Only . . . in one of those three posts, he had spelled it differently, hadn't he?

Darwen. He wrote it down.

A typo? But the Professor didn't make mistakes. At least, not often. The page from the book was the first, and it was pure luck the man hadn't realized how that red ink would stand out. So why would he misspell what he considered his own name?

Alec stared at the letters, tracing them again with his pen, digging even harder until the paper tore beneath the pressure.

"Son of a bitch!" he snapped, suddenly seeing a possibility.

His hand moved, almost of its own volition, rearranging the unsub's chosen name—not the correctly spelled version of it, the other one. And those six letters transformed into another word entirely.

The answer had been right in front of their eyes all along. "Dar*wen*. You bastard."

Frantic, he leaped to his feet, grabbing the files, knowing he'd need proof but desperate to get on the road. Because Sam was headed to the prison.

Shoving everything into his briefcase, he cursed as one of the slick, glossy brochures for the legal symposium slid out. He grabbed it, spared it a glance. Then glanced again.

Right on the front of it was a paragraph describing the backgrounds of some of the speakers, though not naming them. One stood out. And when he flipped the brochure open to read the name that went with the title, he knew he had just identified the killer for certain.

The Professor had been toying with them.

No, not the Professor; Darwin. Or rather, Darwen.

Warden.

"My God, what have you done?"

Sam stared in horror at Warden Connolly. He stood in the doorway to his office, a gun in his hand, calm and cool, despite having just cold-bloodedly shot a police officer.

A police officer she truly liked. Sam started to bend down, to check Myers's pulse, to stanch the blood flowing freely from his chest.

Connolly *tsk*ed and shook his head, reading her intent.

"Why?" she asked, unable to form another word.

He made a motion with the gun. "Turn to your right. About five inches."

She did, until she was nose to nose with the book-laden shelf she had grabbed onto for support a few moments ago. Nose to nose with a copy of her own book. Reaching for it, she was not surprised to see the title page had been torn out.

No, not at all surprised. Sam had realized a few minutes ago that she had been lured here by the very man she had been trying to evade, the killer known as the Professor. She'd just been wrong in thinking he was Dale Carter.

"You were at the law enforcement symposium last winter," she murmured.

He smiled, delighted. "Ah, you remember! How wonderful."

She didn't respond, didn't let on that he had made a mistake when using that red-inked page. "Is Mr. Carter all right or did you shoot him, too?"

"He's fine. I sent him away right after he'd played his part with his phone call. I told him you'd called and said you couldn't come today after all."

So she could look for no help there.

"Where is your FBI friend? I expected to see him with you and had arranged this whole scenario just to catch his blood on that drop cloth." Connolly waved his gun toward Myers's limp form. "I was disappointed to see this fellow instead."

Sam kept her mouth shut, knowing she had to tread carefully. Saying the wrong thing could set him off.

She did want one question answered. "Is Jimmy really dead?"

"Oh, yes. I'm afraid Jimmy was a bad boy. Writing that note about how someone was using e-mail scams to hurt people. That was supposed to be our little secret."

Understanding washed through her. "He helped you."

"Just a bit. And in exchange, I made sure he got the medication he needed."

Sam's heart twisted in pity for Jimmy Flynt. A thief he might have been, but his last days couldn't have been pleasant with this psychopath holding the strings to his failing liver.

"I went to see him last night, to ask him about his interview with the FBI, and saw what he'd been writing. Poor Jimmy ingested a deadly dose of medication shortly thereafter."

God. This man talked about murder as he would talk about flicking off an ant.

"Too bad, really. Jimmy had a good mind, despite his coarse methods. He took care of another inmate who was giving me trouble, all because I whispered in his ear that the man had done something to hurt *you*, Samantha."

She understood immediately. "So the man he attacked had nothing to do with what happened to my grandmother?"

"Of course not. As I said, Jimmy was very helpful."

"I would think criminals like him would be part of the gene pool you'd want to clean up."

His eyes widened and his mouth opened in delight. "Oh, my dear, you've gotten it, haven't you? I knew you would understand."

She wished she had kept quiet. She did not want to be considered his ally.

"Yes, the filthy inmates inside this prison are indeed the ticks on society's scalp. But they're sucking from a worthless bloodstream. Their victims are worse—stupid sheep, not merely uneducated, but unwilling to educate themselves. Like the fools who respond to my messages, despite all the warnings not to. The flock must be culled for the good of the future."

Sam wrapped her arms around herself, wondering how he could sound so normal when spouting such hateful rhetoric. "Tricia is not stupid, and she didn't deserve what you did to her."

"She was greedy, thought I was a rich investor looking to buy some expensive property. Plus she was convenient, especially since your mother broke our date," he said with a smile.

A shiver rolled through her at the confirmation of something she'd already, deep down, known. Her mother had been this monster's first target last night. Wanting to wipe that smile off, she said, "By the way, your ugly plan didn't work. Tricia's fine."

The lips remained curved up, though his gray eyes hardened. "I don't believe you."

"Call St. Joe's. She's a little out of it, but otherwise okay. Not even *assaulted* the way you obviously wanted her to be."

Staring at her, he thought about it, as if to gauge her honesty. Then he chuckled. "She's lucky I had no condoms. I thought about breaking her in before I dumped her but didn't want to leave any evidence. Not to mention risking any diseases from the little whore."

Sam didn't think, didn't plan; she merely reacted with fury, lunging toward the bastard.

He jerked back, but she didn't surprise him enough to overtake the man. The hand holding the gun came up, and she stopped when the muzzle actually touched her forehead.

"I thought you were a smart woman."

Sam closed her eyes, shivering at the feel of the cold metal against her skin. Her heart pounded wildly, her breaths rushing as she tried to control her fear. The acrid smell of the recently fired weapon made her sick, as did the scent of blood rising off of the man on the floor behind her.

It was the smell of life slipping away that finally brought her back under control, knowing she was as close to death at this moment as she had ever been.

"Nice and calm now?"

She swallowed, then managed to whisper, "Yes."

The gun lowered to waist level. "Good. Now come inside my office, over by my desk; that's a girl."

Shuffling sideways, never turning her back to him, she did as he ordered. Desperate to find something, a weapon, a second exit she could dash through, she frantically looked around the room. But the office was immaculately kept, no loose, heavy items in sight. The massive executive desk held nothing of use—certainly not a paperweight, or something sharp.

Connolly retrieved a pair of handcuffs from his pocket. "Get on your hands and knees."

She hesitated.

"I know; it's not very dignified," he said with a mournful shake of the head. "But I promise it's only for a few minutes, my love. I have to move our detective friend to the car, and I can't have you roaming about while I do."

Sam reluctantly dropped to her knees, so disgusted by his endearment she had to look down lest he see the revulsion in her eyes.

"Lower, now, lean on your elbows. Hands out."

Again, she obeyed, knowing he would shoot her if she didn't. Seeing the way he looked at her, the flash of lust as he studied her in the provocative position, Sam forced herself to stay calm. She filed away his sexual interest in her, knowing she might be able to use it to distract him if she had the chance.

Sam wasn't some old-movie heroine who would rather die than use any means possible to escape. The very thought of having this sick monster's hands on her was revolting, but if it took letting him think she was compliant to get him to put the gun down, she'd do it in a heartbeat.

"Attach this to one of your wrists," he said, dropping the cuffs to the floor.

"Please, you don't have to do this; I won't do anything stupid."

"Do it." Connolly lifted the gun an inch, and lifted one impatient brow as well.

Sam did as he'd ordered, snapping one metal ring in place, not pushing it any farther than she had to in order to engage the clasp.

"Now, loop the cuffs around the foot of the desk and attach the other one."

Sam slid forward, doing as he asked.

He bent and felt the cuffs, tightening each one until they bit into her skin. Seeing her wince, he patted her hand. "It won't be for too long, dear, I promise."

Her hope that she might somehow shift the desk died when she saw him test its weight with his much bigger back and shoulder. It didn't budge an inch.

"You see? No point in even trying. I promise it will only be for a few minutes."

He reached out to touch her hair. Sam jerked back, not wanting contact with those brutal hands. Hands that had killed Ryan and his friend, that had brutalized and beaten Tricia.

"You're upset," he said, shaking his head sadly. "I understand. But don't worry. You'll get used to your new circumstances very soon."

Circumstances?

She couldn't believe this was happening in a building where hundreds of other people, many of them armed guards, went about their business.

"I had planned to kill you immediately, but seeing you here, like this"—his eyes roamed over her again, that dark desire easily visible—"well, I've changed my mind. I think I'll keep you around for a while."

"Won't your receptionist notice me chained to your desk?"

He chuckled. "Calm and witty even on your knees. I was right about you: You're one of a kind." He produced a roll of duct tape from a nearby shelf. "Come on, now. I can't have you making any noise."

"No," she whispered, knowing he intended to tape her mouth shut. "Nobody's around to hear me, anyway."

"I know that. But there's no point in risking it."

Swallowing her revulsion, knowing she had very few chances and her voice would be one hell of an asset, she murmured, "I understand the handcuffs, but I'd be very grateful if you didn't tape my mouth closed." She forced a note of humility and added, "I'm nauseous. I'm afraid I'll get sick and choke. Please?"

He studied her face, gauging her sincerity. Sam kept her eyes down, not wanting him to see the hatred there, and finally he murmured, "Very well. But be warned, I specifically scheduled certain events today to ensure nobody would be in this wing. Just as I'm going to ensure the guard shack is unattended when you and I drive out of here in our policeman friend's vehicle. I control this entire facility. Every guard, every angle of every surveillance camera. I have ensured our privacy. So don't waste your breath screaming."

Sam nodded, quickly processing what he'd just said. He planned to drive her out of here, to take her God knew where. Afterward, he could make up any story. He'd make sure he had surveillance footage from one of the towers showing the car departing—though not showing the driver. Connolly could disavow any knowledge of what had happened to her and Myers once they left the property.

Meanwhile, he would have her stashed someplace. Doing whatever he wanted to her. For however long he chose to keep her.

Keep it together.

This wasn't hopeless. Even now, Alec and the others could be discovering Connolly's name on the symposium records. She stayed calm. Forcing slow, deep breaths, she watched through the doorway as Connolly rolled Myers's body in the waterproof tarp, bound it, then dragged it out the door. She had a minute or two and thought frantically, needing an advantage. Suddenly, under the desk, she spotted something shiny. She craned lower, peering into the depths, and realized it was a pen. Not a disposable plastic one, but a finely crafted executive one, hard and sharp.

Twisting around, she pushed her arms forward, but was short by a few inches. "Damn it," she cried, feeling tears of frustration well.

Sam shifted, pulled her upper body as far from the desk as she could, until her wrists and shoulders screamed with the effort. Scissoring her legs, she managed to get one underneath. After a few tries, she was able to nudge the pen several inches. Enough so that, when she quickly turned back around, she could grasp it in one cuffed hand.

A door slammed. He was coming back.

Jesus, was she insane, thinking she could go up against a vicious killer with a damn pen?

It's better than nothing.

She slid the thing up under her sweater sleeve, hoping the elastic at the wrist would hold it there. Hoping even more that she had a chance to use it.

Then he was back, sticking his head in the office with a cheery, "Hello, again."

He didn't enter, instead busying himself putting the reception area back together, including the furniture. He tore down the plastic, then peered closely at the walls and the baseboards, occasionally spritzing a spot with industrial-strength cleaner and wiping it down.

Myers's blood.

She didn't have to pretend she needed to retch.

Finally, when he was satisfied, he returned to the office. Tossing her the keys, he said, "Unlock one cuff, stand up, then reattach it. It's time to go. And don't try anything silly, not now that I've decided I'd like to keep you alive for a little while."

A little while. An hour? A day? A week?

Just long enough to rape her?

Sam swallowed, doing as the madman ordered, all the while keeping her sleeve tight against her wrist. Within minutes, they were back in the unmarked police car, Connolly in the driver's seat, his gloved hand on the wheel.

His other was draped across his lap, the gun pointed at her. "Off we go. I've got the perfect spot to keep you until I decide whether you're worth keeping."

He started the car and backed out of the space. But before he'd even turned it around, he said, "Why did you ask about the symposium?"

Sam didn't dare tell him the truth about the red ink. No way was she giving him any warning. "When I saw the book on the shelf, I remembered talking with you at the signing. It was several months after we met here when I came to interview Jimmy." That was a lie; she honestly didn't recall Connolly being among the hundreds at the signing that day. But he couldn't know that.

"Yes, it was. How lovely that you remembered me."

She managed to keep her lips from curling in a tight, grim smile. *Got you, bastard.*

Alec would come. He'd figure this out, and he'd find her.

And if he didn't show up in time, Sam would wait for the perfect opportunity, then drive Connolly's own pen right through his vicious throat.

Chapter 18

Not willing to waste one second looking for the others, Alec called Dean Taggert as he ran from the classroom toward his car. Telling them what he knew, he asked them to follow, seeing them in his rearview mirror, running to their own cars, as he tore off down the street. They were probably less than a half mile behind him now, all racing toward the state prison, though he doubted any of them felt the frenzy that surged through every inch of Alec's body.

"Let her be okay," he muttered for the hundredth time, not knowing if it was a prayer or an order. He couldn't say it to Sam directly because her phone was turned off.

Everything that had happened since last night—Tricia's attack, Sam's mother's near miss, and, of course, the news of Lily Fletcher's death—had strung Alec to his tautest point. He felt on the verge of snapping, careening wildly out of control, knowing something happening to Sam Dalton would send him over the edge.

"My fault," he whispered. "Should never have brought her into this."

He hadn't. Logically, he knew that. The Professor had known Samantha long before Alec had shown up at her door a week ago. Still, he couldn't shake off the feeling of responsibility.

She might be okay. Her second call, as she'd left the hospital, had been one hour ago. So she had been at the prison for no more than twenty minutes. Myers's presence might keep Connolly from doing anything crazy.

But this whole thing smelled like a setup to him, the call about Flynt a way to get Sam into his clutches. Deep down, he feared the Professor would not be forestalled by the presence of any city cop. Alec leaned forward, hunching over the steering wheel, as if he could make the remaining few miles to the prison disappear faster beneath the tires.

Finally, he reached the exit. Flying off it, he followed the same route he'd taken less than twenty-four hours ago.

Jerking to a stop at the prison guard shack, he flashed his badge. "Special Agent Alec Lambert."

The guard ambled out, glancing at his clipboard.

Alec debated pushing him. But he had no warrant; he had no real proof that this guy's own boss was a psychotic murderer. Coming off like a raging lunatic wouldn't get him inside any sooner and could delay things.

"Don't see your name here."

"I'm working an active investigation and have a hot lead."

The man shrugged in boredom, law enforcement visits not unusual. "Okay."

"Did an Officer Myers come through here with a young woman this morning?"

"'Bout a half hour ago," the man said. He jerked a thumb over his shoulder. "Went up the private drive to the admin office. Warden's orders."

Good God.

The guard handed the ID back and Alec took it. "Several other members of my team are on their way here; they're minutes behind me," he said.

"Well, you can go, but your friends are gonna have to wait. Warden called me a few minutes ago and asked me to go down to the basement at eleven a.m. and check the electrical box. I guess they had some problems with the gate last night, right at eleven."

Alec frowned; the story sounded incredibly suspicious. This guy couldn't be too bright not to question it. "You're leaving your post?"

"The entry gate will be locked down." The guard pointed to the towers high above. "Nobody'll get by, and anybody wanting to come in will have to wait."

"My colleagues can't wait," he bit out, his nerves screaming.

The guy scratched his head. "I guess I could call up to the warden. . . ."

"No!" Alec snapped, not wanting Connolly to have any warning. He glanced frantically at his dashboard clock. Ten fifty-seven. "Just give them another minute, two tops. I'm sure the other agents will be here by then. Now, I really need to get in."

The warden wanted the gate unattended precisely at eleven a.m. Which meant something or someone would be going through it and he wanted no witnesses.

Like a car with a woman stuffed into the trunk?

The guard finally nodded, pressing a button to open the enclosure. Alec gunned it, but rather than heading to the public area, he immediately swung onto the private drive Sam and Myers had used. The guard yelled from behind, jogging after him and waving his arms.

Alec ignored the man. Racing up the drive, he was conscious of every second that passed. *Ten fifty-eight.* Was he getting in the car even now? Tying Sam up? Hurting her?

Suddenly, Alec spotted a dark vehicle coming toward him from the direction of the administrative wing. He swerved, straddling the center lane, blocking the route. "You're not getting past me, you son of a bitch."

His darkest suspicions were confirmed when the vehicle suddenly veered off onto a gravel access road. *Connolly*.

Swerving to follow, Alec felt the car fishtail. He steered out of the spin, flooring the gas pedal. As he roared away, he saw the guard, still jogging toward him, screaming and waving for him to stop.

"No fucking way, buddy," he snapped, hunkering down and taking off.

The prison grounds were expansive, covering a few hundred acres, and this narrow, on-site road was obviously intended for maintenance vehicles only. The warden had the advantage of knowing where it led, if it eventually came to any kind of gate that would allow him to escape.

Alec, however, had the advantage of being desperate to save the woman he was falling in love with.

Dust hung a foot off the gravel, kicked up by the dark sedan he was following, now no more than ten yards ahead. Close enough for him to make out the license plate and realize Connolly was driving the detective's Baltimore PD vehicle. He didn't want to think about what had probably happened to Myers, who would never have given the vehicle over freely. Right now, he could focus only on Sam.

Brake lights suddenly flashed. A few yards ahead of the police vehicle was a small building, probably a storage shack for road salt and lawn equipment.

The road ran out directly in front of it.

The Professor was cornered. Which would make him very angry, and even more dangerous. His brake lights flashed again, gravel spewing up and spitting on Alec's windshield a few yards behind.

Alec quickly ran down the possibilities. He could ram the car, hope to incapacitate the suspect before he could retaliate against Sam. An accident could hurt her just as badly, however. Maybe even more so if she was already injured.

He didn't want a hostage situation, especially not here,

on the warden's own turf, where his own men might be slow to react against him. But he wasn't about to let the bastard get away.

Out of time, Alec jammed the brakes, spun the wheel, and slid his vehicle's passenger side to within inches of the other car's bumper. He blocked the entire width of the road, eliminating any turnaround room. If Connolly wanted to drive around him, he'd have to plow through a couple of trees.

Leaping out, his weapon in hand, he remained crouched down for cover, yelling, "Give it up, Connolly. There's no way out of here!"

He counted to five, praying the man would have enough self-preservation instinct to give himself up, not go down in a blaze of glory. But since Connolly had to know how he, a former warden, would be treated in prison, Alec didn't figure it would be that easy.

Movement in the car ahead; then the passenger side door opened.

"Nice and easy," he called, the gun trained on the kill zone.

But Connolly didn't step out. Sam did. Her eyes were wide, frightened, her hands cuffed together in front of her, but she appeared unharmed.

"You okay?"

She nodded once but didn't run to safety. He realized why when he saw the tip of a handgun pointed at her spine. Then the warden stepped out, grabbing her by the back of her neck, the weapon never dipping below its deadly target.

"Step away, Agent Lambert, or I'll kill her," he yelled. The man's voice shook with rage. His hand, however, was remarkably steady.

"You have no escape," Alec said. "There are other agents pouring through the gate right now, and armed guards everywhere."

"Guards who are loyal to me," the man said with a sneer. "They'll do what I tell them to."

"Aid and abet in a murder? I don't think so."

Connolly's eyes blazed with hatred. "I said the sheep will do what I want them to!"

Alec didn't respond, merely kept his weapon pointed at the man's head, able to do nothing else. He would not lower it. This wasn't some average, scared thug who could be reasoned with. The man would blow her head off the very second he thought he could.

Alec's finger tightened on the trigger. His stare found Sam's, silently pleading with her to trust him, to understand that he would find a way to get her out of this.

Something in her expression, though, made him hesitate before again focusing on Connolly. She lifted her cuffed hands an inch or two, looking down at them pointedly, though keeping her head very still. As he watched, she reached into one sleeve with her other fingers, extracting something long and slender, something silver and sharp-looking.

She had a weapon. A knife? Letter opener?

Alec wanted to tell her not to do a damned thing, to let him handle it. But he wasn't that stupid. If they were both going to get out of this alive, he needed her help. If she could distract Connolly for a second or two, escape from his line of fire, Alec could take him out.

"I'm afraid you're blocking me in," said the warden, icily polite. But the words didn't disguise the insanity of his twisted smile. "Put the gun down and get over there into the trees. Leave your keys in the ignition. The lady and I are going to drive away."

He shook his head. "I can't let you do that."

"Then I'll shoot her."

That cold, matter-of-fact tone said he meant it. He was growing tired of the standoff, ready to act.

They had no time. Alec's eyes shifted toward Sam's

face. She mouthed the words, *On three*, and he nodded almost imperceptibly.

"I hadn't wanted it to end this way."

One.

"But you're leaving me no choice."

Two.

"Good-bye, my dear."

Three.

Sam's hands jerked so quickly, Connolly was caught completely off guard. She punched her fists up, hard, aiming directly at the suspect's face and making contact.

He screamed, letting go of her neck as blood gushed from his wound. Sam dropped to the ground, the gun swinging wildly just above her.

"You're dead, bitch!" the Professor raged.

But he didn't make good on his threat. Because Alec pulled the trigger and put the man down.

"A pen? Jesus, you stabbed him in the eye with a pen?"

Sam didn't know why Alec kept saying that—had been saying it for several hours, since right after he'd shot Connolly to the ground and raced to her side. He'd been there; he'd seen it; he knew exactly what had happened.

"It worked, didn't it?" she said.

And nobody had been more shocked by that than Sam.

She had hoped to, at most, jab the bastard with the sharp tip of his own engraved writing utensil so he'd let her go and she could run. She'd never imagined actually hitting a serious target, plunging the thin rod directly into Warden Connolly's eyeball.

He'd be blind on one side. At least, he would be if he recovered from the shot Alec had centered right in the man's chest.

She still couldn't believe it had all happened. Her

head hadn't stopped spinning all day, not during those insane minutes when she'd seen her own death seconds away. Not afterward, when Alec had wrapped his arms around her and held her close. Or when the two of them had dragged a somehow still-breathing Myers from the trunk. When they'd wondered if they should seek refuge in the maintenance shack, waiting for backup against what could be an army of angry prison guards whose boss lay bleeding on the ground.

Thank God that stubborn guard from the front gate had followed Alec all the way out onto the maintenance road. He'd witnessed everything and had helped defuse the situation when more responders started showing up.

It had all seemed crazy, the kind of nightmare scenario that happened to other people. Not to Sam the Spaminator, who didn't even leave her house unless there was an ice-cream emergency.

"It feels like I've been gone for a month," she said as she entered her apartment that evening. Alec had brought her here after a long day of interviews, police reports, and questioning.

And sadness—when she'd learned about the death of Lily Fletcher, she had cried long and hard, though she'd known the woman only a few days. It was just so damned senseless. All of it, everything that had happened in the past few weeks, from the minute Ryan had IM'd her ... insane and senseless.

"I know. I'm sure you're ready to get back to your normal life."

Alec didn't look at her as he said the words, and his face was set in stern, serious lines. It had been all day, since the moment he'd come charging to her rescue, against all odds getting there before Connolly had made her disappear off the face of the earth.

"What's wrong?" she asked him as she tossed her coat on the back of a chair and kicked off her shoes, wanting to feel normal, safe, and at home.

He shook his head briefly. "Nothing. Just glad it's over."

"Me, too."

She stared at him, finally realizing he hadn't taken off his coat as well. And certainly not his shoes. In fact, he looked stiff, poised to turn and walk out of here again. That was crazy, of course. After everything they'd been through, surely he wouldn't . . .

"I should go."

Her jaw dropped.

"It's been a hell of a day."

"Hell of a week," she said slowly, trying to figure out what was going on here. She and Alec had just shared the most intense day of her life, after what had been one of the craziest nights of her life. From frightening to sensual to terrifying, all in a matter of hours, and all with this man right by her side. And now he thought he was going to just walk away?

Uh-uh. No way. Not happening. "Where do you think you're going?"

One brow shot up in surprise at her aggressive tone. "I, uh, figured I'd head home."

"And then what?"

He knew she wasn't asking something mundane, like whether he was going to go right to bed or stop for a shower first. She didn't have to put it into words; they both knew what she really meant.

"And then I'm staying there," he finally admitted.

Alone. Never to come back.

Sam swallowed away a stab of hurt, knowing there was more to this. Alec wasn't the type to walk away having gotten what he wanted. He wasn't that guy; she knew it down to her very soul.

More, he felt something for her. She knew that, too, just as she knew she had developed feelings for him as well.

"No, you're not," she finally said, remaining calm and resolute.

He finally met her stare directly, and she saw the genuine emotion in that handsome, weary face. "Sam, you told me last night how glad you were for life."

"I am."

"So I want you to go start living it."

That was exactly what she wanted to do. "I intend to. No more locking myself away here; there's a lot going on in the world and I plan to be a part of it."

A faint smile widened his mouth. "I'm glad."

She wasn't finished. "I plan to be a part of yours, too."

Though a spark appeared in his eyes, the smile faded. "I don't expect that."

She pounced on his words. "You don't expect it? Or you don't want it?"

"Semantics."

"No, it's not," she snapped. "One implies that you're about to walk out of here for some noble, it's-for-your-own-good reason. The other says you got what you wanted last night and don't care to repeat the experience now that I'm not in any danger and you're not stuck babysitting me."

Anger tightened his features as he stalked over, grabbing her shoulders. "Don't you say that. Don't even think it."

"Then take off your coat, stay here, and prove me wrong, damn it."

His hands dropped. The coat remained on. An invisible veil of determination separated him from her as finitely as one of the fences from that hellish prison.

She stared up at him, searching for the truth, needing to understand why he was trying so hard to walk away when he sounded as though he wanted to do anything but.

God knew Sam had a lot of reasons not to trust men after what her loving husband had done. But she trusted him. She trusted them—what they could have together, if only he'd let them. Lifting a hand to his face, she cupped his cheek. "I'm falling for you, Alec."

His eyes closed.

"I'm not some inexperienced kid who confuses lust with love. I've had relationships; I've been in love. I've been married; I've been divorced. And I've never felt for anyone—even after years—what I feel for you now, after less than a week."

He finally looked at her again, but that emptiness remained. "In that time you've seen someone you love brutalized, your own mother targeted. You've been kidnapped. You've had to stand by and watch an injured man bleeding at your feet. And you've learned about the death of a woman you were coming to like. All in less than one week. So where's this newfound gladness for life gotten you so far?"

The truth dawned. She finally began to see. Alec wasn't intending to walk out on her because he didn't care, but because he did. He'd decided she should be happy and had the crazy idea that his job, his life—the way he lived it—meant she wouldn't be.

"Alec . . ."

"You've lost a lot of people you loved, Sam. Your father. Your grandmother. Hell, even your slimeball of a husband. Those losses nearly crushed you. So why on earth would you want to keep going down this dark road with me when you've seen over the past several days just how easily it could happen again?"

Sam licked her lips and tried to make him understand. "I know you're aware of how I've lived for the past year, hiding out here, licking my wounds. But I'm not a weakling, Alec."

"I didn't mean—"

She cut him off. "I know you didn't. Let me finish. Honestly, it wasn't fear that kept me here, safe inside these four walls." She shrugged helplessly, knowing she had to admit everything if she wanted any kind of future with this man. "It was humiliation. Sadness. The desire not to get hurt again, not the *fear* of it." Stepping closer, she slid her hands around his neck, and pressed her body against his. "And you wouldn't hurt me."

He remained stiff. "You can't know that."

"You wouldn't hurt me on purpose," she clarified.

"Christ, Sam, you could be hurt just by association."

She leaned up on tiptoe and brushed her lips against his, feeling his hands move to her hips as if unable to help himself. He didn't push her away, though his body remained stiff and unyielding. "Do you really think my mother regretted being with my father? That she would change anything, lose the years she had with him, so she could avoid the lonely ones that came afterward?"

He slowly shook his head.

"And you think Detective Myers's wife is right now sitting by his bedside wishing she'd never married him so she wouldn't have to go through the pain of wondering if he's going to make it?"

"Of course not. But—"

She kissed him again, stopping him from saying more.

"I know you were shot a few months ago. I know there are risks. And I know the shooting made you question everything about yourself, your job, your future. It made you wonder if you are even worthy of having any of those things."

He eyed her in shock, as if wondering how she could know him so well when he hadn't confided so much in her.

He hadn't needed to. She already knew this man well enough to know how his mind worked. The conversations they'd had about the incident had made it very clear that a part of him thought he had deserved to feel those bullets tear through his body.

"People die. Lily died. And that other agent down in Atlanta. It's very sad, but it wasn't your fault."

"You don't know—"

She put her fingers over his mouth. "I do know. And

so do you. Deep down, you know he could just as easily have checked that woman for weapons. Could have asked you to, could have been more suspicious."

His reluctant nod confirmed her words.

"It comes down to this: You didn't pull the trigger. Just like you didn't put Ryan and Jason on that ice or trick that poor woman onto that rooftop. None of it was your fault."

It seemed to take forever but was probably only half a minute before his tense shoulder muscles eased. His body relaxed against hers, the stiffness in his jaw disappearing. The flint disappeared from his eyes, replaced by tenderness. And gratitude.

He might not have accepted it entirely, but Alec knew she was right.

"I'm not proposing here. I'm not saying we're going to be together forever. But I think I'm falling in love with you."

He sucked in a surprised breath that she'd so baldly put the words out there. Heck, she'd almost surprised herself, but she didn't regret saying them.

Nor did she regret adding, "I think you're falling in love with me, too. If I'm wrong, and you're not, then yes, you should keep that coat on, turn around, and walk out of here." She leaned up again, stealing another soft kiss, exchanging another tender breath. "If I'm right, though, please tell me you'll stay so we can figure out what happens next."

She didn't kiss him again. The ball was in his court, their future in his hands. Whether that future included a passionate affair or a lifelong commitment, she didn't yet know. She knew only that she wanted the chance to find out.

Alec didn't reply, not with words, anyway. Instead, he stepped away from her, with a smile on his lips and emotion in his eyes.

And then he took off his coat.

Don't miss the thrilling conclusion to the Black CATs trilogy. Turn the page for an exclusive sneak peek of

Black at Heart

Available now from Signet Eclipse.

Supervisory Special Agent Wyatt Blackstone, the enigmatic leader of the group, has a reputation for being strong, brilliant, and utterly without fear. Nothing can stop him—not the killers he chases or the bureau officials who want to keep him in his place.

But something has reached out from Wyatt's past, shocking this dark and tortured man to his very soul. And it will take his entire team to keep him—and the woman he loves—from falling into a diabolical trap set by a pair of vengeful killers.

Supervisory Special Agent Wyatt Blackstone had never had to attend the memorial service of one of his own team members before. After today, he hoped to God he never attended another one.

Especially since it was his fault Lily Fletcher was dead.

Against his better judgment, he had allowed a woman he knew shouldn't be in the field to participate in a sting operation with another Cyber Action Team. She'd had no business being there. Lily had been an IT specialist, a computer nerd, young, untried, sweetly enthusiastic. But also haunted by her own demons. Those demons had driven her to secretly work a case she should never have been involved in, had pushed her to be in on the takedown of a suspected pedophile whose twisted cyber fantasies had haunted her dreams.

And then, everything had gone straight to hell.

One agent dead on the ground. Lily wounded, trapped, and bleeding to death in a vehicle driven by a desperate madman.

The thoughts of those awful, desperate hours he knew she had endured still tormented him.

The service had been small and quiet. The FBI had

not made the event a media circus, as they could have. Wyatt hadn't wanted it that way; none of the group had. Because of the fuckups that had led to her death, and his team's recent successful capture of a serial killer known as the Professor, the bureau acceded to his demands.

She'd had no surviving family, few nonwork friends. And though many agents and FBI supervisors had attended the service in the nondenominational chapel, few had continued on to the cemetery. Rather than at Arlington, Lily's grave was at a small, private cemetery, beside her sister's and her nephew's, as she would have wanted.

He hadn't even realized her parents had died on the same day during Lily's childhood until he read their headstones, too.

An entire family. Gone. Plucked off one tragedy at a time.

The graveside service had been simple and brief. Only Wyatt and the other members of his team, who had formed a pseudo-family of their own, had remained after the chaplain's final prayer. And then they'd all drifted away, lost in their own sadness, wondering how things might have turned out differently.

He didn't think he would ever stop wondering.

Even now, hours later, as he sat in the dark in his own house, nursing a tumbler full of whiskey, Wyatt found it hard to believe. Sweet, quiet Lily, so eager to please despite being so visibly wounded by the horrors that had befallen her, was gone. Senselessly killed by someone who hadn't been fit to touch a single strand of her golden hair.

"I'm sorry," he murmured, lifting his glass to his mouth. "I should have protected you."

He sipped once. Then again. He needed the fire to spread through his body, burning out the anger, the helpless frustration. The sadness.

Wyatt never allowed himself to grieve. He'd learned

as a child how futile it was to wish someone back from the dead, to ask why horrible things happened, to give in to sorrow.

But Lily? He could grieve for Lily.

Realizing it was almost midnight, he finally rose, needing to go to bed. The past several nights had been sleepless ones. Tomorrow was another workday, another chance to keep moving forward, stopping whatever ugliness he possibly could.

Moving through the familiar darkness of the house, he headed for the stairs. Before he even reached the first one, though, his cell phone rang. Wyatt pulled it from his pocket, wearily flipped it open, and lifted it to his ear.

"Blackstone."

No response at first, but a hollowness told him the line wasn't dead.

"Hello?"

Another long pause. Then a soft voice emerged from the silence like a specter appearing out of his own memories.

"Wyatt?"

He froze, haunted by the pain in that one whispered word. "Who is this?"

"Help me, Wyatt. Please help me."

Also Available
in the all-new series filled with
"HOLD YOUR BREATH ROMANTIC SUSPENSE"
(*New York Times* bestselling author JoAnn Ross)

LESLIE PARRISH

Available Now

FADE TO BLACK
A Black CATs Novel

After transferring out of violent crimes and onto the
FBI's Cyber Action Team, Special Agent Dean Taggert is
shocked to encounter a case far more vicious than any
he's ever seen. A cold and calculating predator dubbed
"The Reaper" is auctioning off murder in the cyber
world and is about to kill again—unless Dean and
beautiful sheriff Stacey Rhodes can stop him.

September 2009

BLACK AT HEART
A Black CATs Novel

After the loss of a vulnerable young agent for whom he
cared deeply, Wyatt Blackstone is starting to crack. For
not only does he have a vigilante murderer to track
down, but the clues to the crimes lead to an impossible
suspect: the very woman he thought he'd lost.

Available wherever books are sold or at penguin.com

Penguin Group (USA) Online

What will you be reading tomorrow?

Tom Clancy, Patricia Cornwell, W.E.B. Griffin,
Nora Roberts, William Gibson, Robin Cook,
Brian Jacques, Catherine Coulter, Stephen King,
Dean Koontz, Ken Follett, Clive Cussler,
Eric Jerome Dickey, John Sandford,
Terry McMillan, Sue Monk Kidd, Amy Tan,
J. R. Ward, Laurell K. Hamilton…

You'll find them all at
penguin.com

Read excerpts and newsletters,
find tour schedules and reading group guides,
and enter contests.

Subscribe to Penguin Group (USA) newsletters
and get an exclusive inside look
at exciting new titles and the authors you love
long before everyone else does.

PENGUIN GROUP (USA)
us.penguingroup.com